A MODEL MIND

A Novel By

BRAD KASH

Published By
SENIOR
RICHARDSON

Acknowledgments

I was born into a family of writers. My great-grandmother, Nellie Richardson was a farmer turned poet who had four poetry books published during her lifetime. My grandmother, Faith Senior, was a secretary for the OSS/CIA and later created and published her own pet magazine – *Granny's Pet Gazette*. And my mother, Joanne Kash, was a photojournalist whose photographs and positive human interest stories have been published by newspapers and magazines across the globe. I've always believed that writing, or creativity in general, is buried in one's DNA, and if so, I'm very fortunate to have inherited those genes. Thank you, ladies.

Writing is definitely a labor of love. *A Model Mind* took well over a year to complete, the story coming to life usually during daily early morning sessions before work or late at night after everyone else had long gone to bed. Coffee was always a necessary close companion as was my sidekick angel of a pug, Sophie.

The story you will read in these pages was inspired by my father who we lost in early 2015. He was without a doubt the greatest man I have ever known and I will never stop missing him. However, his passing and long struggle with Alzheimer's disease also lit a fire in me to no longer put off doing today what I think I might do tomorrow. So thanks, Dad … I never would have been able to finish this story without the work ethic and strength you instilled in me. I know you've been sitting next to me all throughout this journey.

Some people unfortunately never find their true soul mate. My wife, Stephanie, literally danced into my world when I was only twenty-one years old; although we often joke that we likely first crossed paths several years earlier at the 1982 World's Fair since we were both there on the same day. She is my muse and my best critic, and I value her presence in my life more than she will ever know. Nothing I've ever accomplished, including this book, could have happened without her. Thank you, Stephanie. You are truly my best friend. All my love.

CHAPTER ONE

"AND THE WINNER OF THE 1989 *ENTERTAINER OF THE YEAR* is ... for the fourth straight year in a row, the incredible, Mr. Tommy Model!"

The celebrity-packed venue erupted in a roar of applause as peers and fans leapt to their feet in enthusiasm for Tommy's latest accomplishment. Its recipient, however, did not share in their elation.

Over the past five years, Tommy Model had sold over one hundred million albums worldwide, earning him twenty-one gold and multi-platinum album certification plaques. He had been bestowed with so many accolades and trophies, that an entire room in his fifteen thousand square foot Beverly Hills mansion was dedicated to display his successes. Receiving another award for the top-selling, fan-adored rock star had become such a frequent occurrence, he initially turned down the invitation to attend the night's festivities. As a result, the award show producers had been forced to bribe Tommy to make an appearance, and his boredom throughout the broadcast had been obvious.

Tommy toured relentlessly and consistently sold out stadiums and arenas across the globe, usually as soon as tickets would go on sale. Because of his meteoric rise and sustained success, he had become one of the wealthiest entertainers on the planet. He not only recorded great music that his fans continued to relate to and clamor to buy, but he also wrote nearly every song he released. As a result, his royalty earnings as both a recording artist and a songwriter seemed secure for years to come. Touring income and merchandise sales were icing on the cake, generating over one hundred million dollars annually. But while his fame and wealth grew, unfortunately so did his ego and arrogance.

When he stood from his seat in the audience to make his way to the stage, there was no denying that he looked the part of the superstar he had become. His pale-skinned, chiseled good looks and elegantly-styled, thick, spiked, blond hair was perfectly paired with his tailored black suit. The lapels of his jacket framed a white dress-shirt unbuttoned halfway down his chest exposing a large silver cross hanging from a chain around his neck. Dark sunglasses covered his eyes. The look was classy, but still very rock & roll and would further confirm his growing influence on the fashion world as well.

With his first step toward the stage, Tommy lost his balance and fell back into the arms of a well-known pop singer. He immediately pushed Tommy forward, and choice words were exchanged that somehow made it past the bleeper. Television viewers sat up in peaked interest as it seemed a train was about to wreck before their very eyes. Tommy laughed off the incident along with the audience, but something was definitely amiss.

Unbeknownst to anyone in the theater or watching at home, Tommy had downed a fifth of vodka in the limo before walking the red carpet only two hours earlier. Now with little else in his system, the full effects were taking their toll on his equilibrium, as well as his state of mind.

Regaining his composure, Tommy quickly scaled the stairs to the stage, took the trophy from the presenter's hand, and walked off without even saying a word. He raised the award high over his head as he disappeared from view. Again, the audience exploded with cheers and whistles. Many held their mouths wide open and turned in amazement to those standing next to them as if to say, *what in the world just happened*? The television production team struggled to fill dead air.

As on so many other occasions throughout his short career, Tommy crossed lines no one else had even dreamed of stepping beyond. In this particular case, he looked like a brilliant bad-boy artist to the world, but in reality, he was just being an ungrateful jerk. Tommy was tired of giving acceptance speeches, so he didn't even pretend to care. Instead, he simply walked off stage and out the back door of the theater. There, Tommy lit a cigarette, took a long drag, then exhaled while looking down at his shiny, gold award. He shook his head, partially in disbelief, partially in frustration.

Although now a successful millionaire many times over, Thomas Maddock, who would eventually be transformed into the persona and brand, Tommy Model, had grown up in an extremely poor, rough section of Edinburgh, Scotland. His future seemed uncertain until as a teenager he discovered a natural gift for singing and writing songs. At sixteen, he joined his first band, Velour. After some local success, they were soon selected as an opening act for several headlining bands and artists while they toured throughout Europe.

Tommy's mother desperately wanted him to become the family's first university graduate. Although Tommy initially tried to balance music with his educational studies to avoid disappointing her, eventually the pace of the touring schedule forced him to drop out of secondary school altogether. He was soon earning more performing live with his band than his father was bringing home from his welding job at the shipyards. The oldest of four children,

Tommy began helping his parents financially to provide a better life for his brother and two sisters still living at home.

As Velour's lead vocalist and primary songwriter, Tommy was soon approached by the head of A&R for Honeycutt Records, a well-respected label in the UK. Tommy tried to convince the executives at Honeycutt to sign Velour as a band, but they ultimately only wanted him as a solo artist. The name change to Tommy Model soon ensued, and with his first single released in 1984, it was immediately obvious a new star had been born. It started off relatively effortless for Tommy, and it only seemed to get easier from there.

Now five years later, he stood alone on the back loading dock of an awards show venue. As cigarette smoke burned his eyes while staring at his latest achievement, there was still a small part of him that never expected all of his many successes. However, an even bigger part wanted the ongoing winning streak to be more of a challenge.

As his career progressed, most of the artists who were considered his direct competition were typically putting out only one decent single per record. But Tommy had continued to deliver multiple hits from each album. Doing so provided more exposure and opportunities because of longer runs on the album, radio single, and video charts.

Unable to keep up with the impatient, money-hungry desires of the music industry, most of the artists he had greatly respected and competed with during the mid 80's had now faded or were struggling to avoid getting dropped from their record labels. In contrast, Tommy had recently renegotiated with Honeycutt for a previously unheard of twenty million dollar, non-recoupable re-signing bonus. He only had two more albums to deliver, and the money would be all his. The problem was, he had all but lost any inspiration. As a result, his songwriting was in a desperate funk.

Tommy flicked his still smoldering cigarette through the air as he walked down the loading dock ramp and around the side of the building. He searched the long lineup of limos awaiting their star clients. Eventually, he found his driver who quickly opened the back door providing Tommy with a stealthy, photo-free exit from the paparazzi amassed across from the limo staging area. Like birds on a high-line, they all stared in the opposite direction anxiously awaiting the flood of celebrities soon to be exiting the awards show. In doing so they missed Tommy's impromptu appearance altogether.

As his limo sped away, Tommy used the in-car cell phone to call his assistant who he instructed to place an all-night order for his two favorite escorts. Rather than attending any of the various after-parties where he would surely be celebrated as a guest of honor, he preferred to spend the evening with two supermodel caliber women, but still high-class hookers nonetheless.

Tommy had learned the hard way to avoid large parties where numerous Tinseltown wannabes bribed or otherwise leveraged their way in to proposition him for favors, drugs, sex, or money. All could come at a very high price if attached to an agenda for a much more significant prize.

He had already suffered through three civil lawsuits that tied him to allegedly fathering children with women he had supposedly met at parties and raves. These were claims that ultimately proved to be false but were a mess to deal with just the same. After those experiences, Tommy felt it was more enjoyable and much less expensive in the long run to hire and party at home with escorts. They understood the rules of the transaction and the confidentiality that accompanied it.

Tommy lived a carefree yet socially limiting lifestyle, making it virtually impossible to establish a meaningful relationship with anyone. It was a situation he regretted and occasionally attempted to resolve when he was able to expand his courage wide enough to make an effort. Unfortunately, all personal involvements with women who could prove to be *the one*, and whom his mother regularly begged him to find, rarely lasted longer than a month. Beyond that, the trappings of his abnormal existence eventually created a rift in the relationship, damning him back to bachelorhood.

AROUND 3:00 A.M., TOMMY AWOKE entwined in the naked bodies of the women he had shared the evening with. He slid out of bed and quietly made his way downstairs to his home studio where he eased onto the bench of his beautiful, black grand piano. Tommy flinched at the coolness of the wood seat against his bare skin. He gathered his thoughts and spontaneously began to play a beautiful melody. After repeating the same bars several times, he eventually started layering in vocal pairings. The lyrics were only incoherent combinations of sounds and words at first, but soon matured into a meaningful, unique turn at what seemed to be developing into a love song.

Unfortunately, as on so many recent occasions, just when it seemed he was breaking through to greatness, suddenly it all fell apart. As quickly as it had come, Tommy lost his momentum, failing to develop a climb and chorus that felt right enough to satisfy his inner perfectionist. He pounded his fingers on the keys in sheer frustration, creating an uncomfortable explosion of sound.

Seeking an escape, he ran back upstairs. Against the smooth surface of the bathroom vanity, he buried his face into several lines of cocaine then returned for another round with the escorts. He hoped they would briefly help him forget about his persistent inability to recapture the songwriting prowess that had made him a mega-star. But the worrisome thought of failure hung over the bed like an ominous, looming storm cloud. He was quickly falling into a deep, dark hole with seemingly no way out, and he had absolutely no clue how to fix it.

CHAPTER TWO

THREE WEEKS LATER TOMMY WAS STILL STRUGGLING to write songs for his next album. In between bouts of extreme depression, along with the sex, drugs, and alcohol coping binges it brought on, he had somehow managed to cobble together a dozen or so mediocre compositions. Now the day had finally arrived to start the recording process, and he was panicking, desperately looking for a way out.

After postponing the recording sessions two weeks beyond their original scheduled start date, Tommy arrived two hours late to Los Angeles' famed Junebug Studios. He carried with him the monkey of another alcohol-induced hangover.

Tommy's long-time producer, Bizzy-B Jonson sat patiently waiting at the studio's massive recording console. He sipped a cup of black coffee as Tommy made his subdued entrance.

"Good morning, Tommy, my man! You ready to lay down some tracks?" Bizzy excitedly asked.

Tommy's dark sunglasses veiled his bloodshot eyes. He slowly waved his hand back and forth in front of his face, silently scolding Bizzy for his loud and all-too-peppy inquiry.

"I'm feeling pretty rough, mate. I don't know if I'm up to this today," replied Tommy in his deep-voiced, Scottish accent, making one last ditch effort to stall for more time.

The problem with a continued delay was that Honeycutt Records was required to pay Tommy a five hundred thousand dollar advance once he started recording, with an additional one hundred thousand going to Bizzy. Unfortunately, the label's CEO, Paul Watkins had already threatened to hold both advances until a later date if Tommy failed to meet one more recording session deadline.

Since studio time was blocked out specifically for their project, Junebug was charging thousands of dollars in room and equipment rental fees every day, regardless of whether Tommy was recording or not. With costs being incurred without results, the label was now in corporate pushback mode and prepared to take drastic measures to get their star back on track. The intimidation had worked, but forcing him into submission only further fouled Tommy's mood.

"We've got to get started today," pleaded Bizzy. "The label execs are getting ticked off, and we don't get our advances until we start rolling some tape."

"Don't lecture me. I'm well aware of the situation. We'll start recording when I'm good and ready," responded Tommy."

"Look ... I know you're a mega-rich rock star who doesn't need the dough, but both my bookie and my dealer are breathing down my neck. So I've got to get them some cash pronto or this could be the shortest album project I've ever worked on."

"Are you kidding me?" retorted Tommy.

"Make light of it if you want. I'd prefer not to be buried in a shallow desert grave for some mangy pack of coyotes to dig up and leave my bones to be picked clean by vultures. Have you seen what those birds do to road kill? It's not pretty, man. And you gotta admit ... that would be a horrible way to go."

"Always the drama-queen, Bizzy. That is such an insane bunch of pot-fueled paranoia."

"It's not paranoia. These are some really bad dudes I'm talkin' about."

"Well, you were stupid to put yourself in that position. To be honest, I'm not completely buying it. It sounds to me like you need the money to keep yourself buried in nose candy while you're rolling dice on the ponies. And if that's all you care about, then maybe I should find another producer who's willing to put the music first above all of his vices!" barked Tommy.

"Whoa, whoa, whoa! Hang on a minute, buddy. Chill out. You should know by working with me for the past five years how passionate I am about the music we record together. So don't lay that on me. And you're a fine one to talk about vices. I've been sitting here like Rip Van Winkle under a tree for two weeks, waiting for you to show yourself!"

Feeling himself starting to lose control, Bizzy paused his diatribe. He briefly closed his eyes, pressed his index fingers to his thumbs and took a deep breath to calm himself, then continued.

"I'm simply saying that if we can please record a little bit of instrumentation, that should be enough to show the label we got started, and hopefully we can both get paid. If you want to go all Johnny Cash and crawl back into your cave for a while longer after that, then that's your business."

"Look at you pinching your fingers and taking deep breaths. What are you a yogi or something? A monk? You're nuts, Bizzy! I'm out of here."

Tommy stormed out of the studio. Bizzy desperately ran after his meal ticket, but his quarry was faster than expected. By the time Bizzy stepped outside, Tommy was already revving the engine on his sleek, black, European sports car. He flipped off his producer and smoked the tires out of the parking lot, leaving Bizzy standing shell-shocked in a burnt-rubber haze.

Tommy's overreaction to their argument wasn't as serious as he made it seem, but he had been searching for any way out of the recording session. Bizzy unknowingly served it up hot and fresh, and Tommy seized upon the opportunity when he saw it, caring little about the consequences.

BACK HOME AT *MODEL MANSION*, Tommy poured himself a Scotch whisky, neat. He grabbed the bottle, kicked off his shoes and headed out to the pool deck. Laying in one of the many chaise lounges surrounding his aquatic oasis, he closed his eyes, took another sip of scotch, and began whispering to himself.

"What in the world are you going to do, Tommy? If you can't get your act together and write some hits, this is all going to be over as quickly as it started. You're better than this. God, please help me," Tommy pleaded, looking above into the vast emptiness of the pale blue sky.

Although Tommy undoubtedly loved the high life, he had been raised with his parent's even higher conservative, religious values. He tried to remain faithful to those core beliefs, even though doing so seemed to be a major contradiction most of the time. Unfortunately, he wasn't living in a normal existence, and the indulgence and excess that constantly swarmed around him usually proved much stronger than what he believed God could offer in the moment. The process of succumbing to temptations, followed by the onset of deep guilt afterward, was the hamster wheel of life that Tommy ran on.

What he perceived to be writer's block was an agonizing experience, but he just couldn't determine how to break out of the death-grip it held on him. He prayed relentlessly, but seemingly to no avail. This led him to assume that God must be punishing him for all of his many sinful deeds, a belief that only led to more excess. To make matters worse, he had been much too proud to share his challenges with anyone, so mentally, he had been all alone on his island of despair.

The fact that so many people depended on his success didn't help the situation. There was his record label, distribution company, manager, business manager, and talent agent for starters. Then, his music publisher, band members, publicist, tour support personnel, and various sponsors and business partners all added to the mix. Collectively, everyone involved employed hundreds, if not thousands of people who believed and trusted in Tommy to deliver. When he closed his eyes at night to try to get a few hours sleep, he often saw many of their faces in his thoughts, frozen in time like poorly lit, red-eyed snapshots. They stood transfixed, looking his way with desperately anxious expressions, waiting for him to drop the greatest album of his career. But it wasn't happening.

He poured another scotch, sipped it slowly, and sat in silence staring at the smooth surface of the pool. The only interruption was the slight boil from the underwater circulation jets. Like the water, his mind seemed completely blank, and he had no idea what to do to resolve his predicament.

Tommy was extremely close to his father, Frank, but had rarely asked for his advice during Tommy's short twenty-two years of living. It was an avoidance partially based on ego and partly on the fact that Tommy didn't want either of his parents to worry about him. But if ever he needed some honesty and life guidance, it was now. After a few more generous pours of whisky he worked up the bravery to call his father for the first time in several months. Tommy finished off what was left in his glass, ran into the house to get his wireless phone, and began dialing before he lost his nerve.

It was nearly 10:00 PM in Edinburgh, Scotland when Frank Maddock's telephone rang. It startled him awake from where he had fallen asleep reading a book in his recliner.

"Hello?" answered Frank in a low raspy, half-asleep voice.

"Hi, Dad. It's Thomas. How are you?"

"Thomas, my boy! It's great to hear from you. It's been a while. I'm doing good, Son. How are you? Is something wrong?"

"No, not really, Dad. Is Mum okay?"

"Your mother is doing well when I'm not aggravating her about something. She's already gone to bed, but I can wake her if you like."

"No, no. I was hoping you and I could talk for a little bit. I know I said there was nothing wrong, but I could really use your advice."

"Sure, you know I'm here for you anytime."

Frank tried not to reveal that Tommy's request made him extremely nervous. He wasn't quite sure what was coming next, and he felt intimidated as to whether he could provide the level of guidance his son's famous existence might require.

Tommy took a deep breath and began explaining the state of the songwriting funk he was fighting. He detailed the pressures he felt were contributing to his inability to break free of the chains that were binding his mind. For Frank, it was rare that Tommy called, much less asked for his input on something. It was obviously a serious matter, and he wanted to understand the situation fully, so he listened intently without saying a word.

After nearly ten minutes of spilling his guts, Tommy abruptly stopped.

"Dad, you're being awfully quiet. Did you fall asleep?"

Ever the jokester, seizing an opportunity in his state of nervousness, Frank faked as if he had dozed off. He snorted his nose, pretending to come to, and replied, "Huh? Me, fall asleep ... no, I was listening."

"Dad, you totally zoned out on me. Never mind, I'm gonna go now," Tommy responded in frustrated disappointment.

"Thomas, I'm kidding. I heard every word you said ... seriously," confirmed Frank, wishing he could take a mulligan against his poor comedic timing.

"Okay, then ... so what do you think I should do?"

It was obvious that Tommy was desperate and lost. Frank paused briefly searching his mind for the right words. He knew a well thought out response was not going to be genuine or what Tommy needed to hear right now. He stood from the comforts of his well-worn chair and paced, carrying a serious look of determination and focus, as if preparing to address a losing Scottish football club at halftime.

"Thomas ... I think all you can do is write the best songs you can, and take the pressure off yourself to be perfect all the time. I know you want to take care of everyone. Heck, you've been taking care of me and your mum, and your brother and sisters ever since you were seventeen years old. But it's time to remove that burden and focus on you for a while. Everyone else will survive just fine."

"That's it?" sarcastically asked Tommy. "You think simply focusing on myself will solve my writer's block?"

Sensing that he was oversimplifying his point Frank continued, "I know you were hoping I would tell you exactly how to fix the problem, but you can only do what you can do, right? Worrying about it only makes things worse."

"Yes, but not worrying about it doesn't really seem like an option."

"Well, God blessed you with a wonderful talent, and what that gift brings you at any given point in time has to be part of the bigger plan for your life. Doubting yourself and lacking faith is probably why you are so conflicted right now."

"So if the songs I'm writing are obviously not at the same level of quality they have been in the past, it's what's meant to be?"

"Yes, maybe. Or perhaps your new songs are as good as others you've written, but in their own unique, special way. It's just that what you define as good or bad has become based on beliefs that other people have built up in your mind over time."

"That's for sure. Plus everyone pushing me to sell millions of records, dominate the charts, and sell out concerts creates a tremendous amount of pressure. Through all of that, I'm somehow supposed to write incredible songs that will allow all of those things to continue."

"Right. But as long as you are true to yourself and giving it your all, then how can you honestly say that anything you create isn't as good as it can possibly be."

"That's heavy, Dad. I don't know. I was looking for a solution, not so much a psychological theory."

"I realize it's a bit deep, Son. This is something I'm not that good at, but I'm really trying to help."

"I know. And I appreciate it."

Frank looked down at the book laying on his chair, then continued. "Hey, I just thought of something. Let me try to give you an example that may come as a bit of a surprise from your old man."

"Okay."

"As you know, I like reading biographies and history books. So last week I found this interesting biography on Van Gogh ... you know, the painter. I was reading this one section and looking at the pictures of his artwork earlier tonight, and I thought to myself ... some people might look at that famous 'Starry Night' painting and think a child may have created it. It's that basic in appearance. But others see a masterpiece, perhaps partially because they know it is a Van Gogh and it's supposed to be great. After reading more about him, I see and understand the spark of genius and courage it took to create that particular work. Are you still with me, Thomas?"

"I'm here Dad. I'm just shocked you're studying Van Gogh, but go ahead."

"I know ... it's a bit odd, but anyway ... what I learned about him was that his art was birthed by his emotions, not through some paint-by-numbers formula guaranteed to make him famous. Actually, his popularity came much later after he was dead. And now that I think about it, this may not be the best example because he supposedly committed suicide."

"Oh no," replied Tommy.

"Yeah, but the point is ... the book said something like, *every piece of great art is unique and unlimited by definitions.* So in your case, I think we could take that to mean that if you only focus on the commercial aspects and not what is coming from your heart and soul, then some of your best work may never see the light of day."

The left-field example his father shared resonated with Tommy in a way he didn't expect, and he felt an immediate return to calm confidence.

"Believe it or not, I get what you're saying, Dad. And I think you're right."

"That's a relief. I was starting to overwhelm my brain with all that. I'm a pretty simple fella, you know."

"Come on, Dad. You're much smarter than you've ever given yourself credit for."

"I hope I helped."

"You did. I can see a tidal wave of opposition coming my way if I do stick to my guns with the songs I've written. The various decision makers I have to contend with all want a sure thing over a pre-fame Van Gogh. But I'm going to give it my best shot. Thank you for helping me get my mind back on track. It's so easy to lose myself in this crazy business."

"You're very welcome, Thomas. Call me anytime. That's what I'm here for. You're gonna be fine no matter what happens. I love you, my boy."

"Love you too, Dad. Give my best to Mum. We'll talk soon."

Frank closed his eyes tightly, praying he had not led his son astray. He was worried, but he also knew that if anyone could follow his own course and be the trendsetter instead of a lemming, it was his son, Thomas Maddock.

After Tommy pushed the *off* button on the phone, he screwed down the cap tightly and returned the bottle of scotch to the bar. There would be no more drinking for now. It was time to sober up and get his voice back in shape so he could record twelve of the greatest songs of his career.

CHAPTER THREE

∞

TWO DAYS LATER, Tommy and Bizzy-B had buried the hatchet and were back at Junebug Studios with plans of beginning the recording process. Tommy had previously recorded rough demos of each song to give them a guide to work with, but until now, Bizzy had not heard any of the new music.

Unfortunately, as Tommy had feared, Bizzy shot off several negative comments during the initial listening session. Dismayed by the lack of quality and maturity of the compositions, Bizzy didn't hold back on expressing his opinions. But Tommy was determined to stay true to his father's advice. Not being swayed by his producer, he held his convictions close and pushed back, demanding that they forge ahead to build upon and record the songs he had already written.

The problem was, Bizzy had placed all of his chips on Tommy, and was now highly concerned that the project would not bring the same massive success as the four previous albums. He had put off several other artists who had requested to work with him in hopes they too could capture the same lightning in a bottle he had repeatedly delivered with Tommy.

As a producer, the quality of any artist's songs is no light consideration since personal success directly ties to their hit-potential. But with no apparent chart-toppers, Bizzy would not likely earn more than his recoupable royalty advance. And being attached as the producer of such a lackluster record, could carry career-damaging impacts for years to come.

Reluctantly for Bizzy, the recording session commenced. With no musicians in the studio due to the uncertainty of whether Tommy would even show, the plan for the day was to overlay new vocals on top of the demos in hopes of tightening the melodies and phrasings. But on take-one of the very first song, and halfway through Tommy's singing of the second chorus, Bizzy stopped the instrumentation playback. He waved his hands to get Tommy's attention through the glass partition separating the control room and the vocal booth. Angered by the abrupt interruption, Tommy ripped off his headphones and slammed them to the ground, yelling into the microphone.

"What are you doing, Bizzy? That was a great take, mate!"

Tommy picked up his headphones and placed them back over his ears to hear Bizzy's response through the control room microphone.

"Yeah ... well ... uh ... I think we need to talk some more about all of this, Tommy. I'm telling you, man ... this song, and every other one you played for me, really sucks. I'm struggling to see where this is heading, buddy. I mean ... if it was something I could doctor up with effects and production that would be one thing. But from the lyrics to the melodies, to the phrasings, these are not Tommy Model caliber compositions."

"Oh really?"

"Yes. And it's my job to tell you when you're off and to help you find your way. So I honestly think we should scrap all of these and start over. I'll help you write new material if you're having a hard time. Writer's block happens to a lot of artists, especially with the kind of pressure you're under."

"Are you through?" Tommy snapped back.

Bizzy threw his hands in the air as if surrendering in advance to the verbal attack he knew was coming. Tommy stormed out of the vocal booth and charged into the control room.

"Let's get one thing straight, Bizzy ... I'm the artist and songwriter here, not you! Your job is to push some buttons and twist a few dials to capture my music so I can share it for the world to hear."

"Is that all you think I do?" asked a dejected sounding Bizzy.

"Pretty much. And if you think I'm going to let you claim a fifty percent co-writer's share of my publishing royalties by you inserting yourself into the songwriting process, you are even more out of your mind then I thought you were."

"Oh, come on! I'm just trying to help."

"Well, I've already told you that I believe in these songs and they are what I am going to deliver to the label. So right now, I'm going to try to calm myself and get back to what I was doing before you rudely interrupted. Let's take it from before the second chorus."

Tommy turned to go back to the vocal booth, but Bizzy once again halted his progress.

"I don't think so, Tommy."

Tommy pivoted and glared at Bizzy, his face red with anger and a spaghetti western cowboy squint hijacking his left eye. Bizzy swallowed hard and continued.

"You need to understand that I've been waiting to start recording your next album for nearly a year now. During that time, I've turned down numerous offers to work with some of the top recording artists in the world because I believe in you. We've accomplished some great things together, and I've been honored to know and work with you for as long as I have. But you seem determined to stay on a course that I am sure will end in failure. I think you know that it will too. But for some reason that I can't begin to fathom, you are committed to using songs that will obviously have no commercial appeal."

"Says you, Bizzy! You're not the rest of the world."

"No, but I think anyone with common sense would agree. Just know that your decisions will not only adversely impact both you and me, but everyone else who has a vested interest in working with you. The end result is, we will all suffer financially and professionally. Career-wise, I can't afford a failure because I need to maintain a certain level of income to support my lifestyle. I'm sorry, but if you're not going to change your mind, then I guess I'm done, and you'll have to find another producer this time around."

Tommy looked at Bizzy in disgust. The anger, clearly showing on his face, intensified even further as he volleyed his return.

"You're a real piece of work ... you know that, mate? How soon you forget where you came from."

"Oh, here we go."

"Yeah, that's right. You were a nobody, a garage band producer who came to one of my first U.S. shows in New York City right after I got signed. Remember how you bribed a bouncer to get backstage? Then you barged in on an interview I was having with a radio station DJ."

"Yeah, I remember."

"You were so desperate to give me your production demo tape ... and you spouted off that big spiel about how you really believed in what I was doing, and that you wanted to produce my first album. I had been approached by several highly successful producers at that point, so I definitely didn't need you. But you had an enthusiasm beyond anyone else I had met with, so I was intrigued."

Bizzy squirmed uneasily in his chair while he listened to the account of their early history together. Tommy's intensity subsided as he continued.

"So I listened to your stupid tape, and to be honest ... I thought it was horrible. But I called you anyway because I felt a connection I couldn't quite explain. I'm sure you'll also recall that we had dinner a couple of days later. And through that second encounter, we found that we actually had a lot in common."

"Yes, we did, Tommy."

"Right. And it was at the end of that dinner that I promised I'd give you a shot to produce at least one song on the record. What I never told you was, Honeycutt had planned for me to record the entire album with Autry Redstone. As you know, he has a major track record of success and is one of your idols. But I told them I had already committed to this young, eager guy with a dumb, fake name, and I wanted to see what we could come up with together before I began working with Autry. They pushed back hard, but I eventually prevailed. When we began recording that very first song, it was obvious that I had made the right decision. Soon Autry was out altogether, and now history speaks for itself."

The last thing Tommy needed was to lose Bizzy on top of his writer's block issues, but at the same time, he couldn't believe the sheer ungratefulness he was receiving from his long-time musical partner. For a brief second, he thought about giving in to his insecurities and agreeing to start over with new songs. Then, recalling his father's inspiring words, coupled with the uncertainty as to whether he could write better songs even if he tried, Tommy held firm to his beliefs. He took a deep breath to regain his composure.

"Bizzy, all I'm asking from you is a little trust that these songs are as good as any others I've written. Are they a little different?

Sure. But as an artist, I have to strive to break new ground and stay fresh. I could use your help bringing them to life."

"You're like a brother to me, Tommy, and I do appreciate everything you've done. But if you're not willing to write some stronger songs, this is going to be a complete waste of my time. As I mentioned before, I owe lots of money to some really bad dudes, and I can't afford to attach myself to a dead-end project. I could start the recording process with you so we can get our advances, but I'd only have to give the money back if I bailed afterward. And one hundred-G's by itself isn't going to solve my problems."

"If you need money that bad, I'll loan it to you," offered Tommy.

"I appreciate that, but I need to produce a hit album that will earn millions of dollars in royalties as the last four have. You also haven't been the easiest guy to work with lately. It's as if you have no respect for me whatsoever, and that person is no fun to be around. Besides, Jackie James and his band Silverback are ready to start recording their new album right now, and they are projected to be the next big thing. I've been asked to produce them and I want to do it. They've got some big hits in the hopper, with an amazing new sound that I really believe in. I'm sorry man, but under the circumstances, I gotta do what I gotta do."

"You're leaving me for Jackie James and his three-chord posse? Are you kidding me? Silverback didn't even crack the top forty with the singles from their last LP. I had three number ones on my last album alone, you idiot!"

"See, that's what I'm saying, man. Why the name-calling? I'm sorry, Tommy. I had better go before this gets any worse. I hope it all works out for you."

Bizzy gathered his notebook and coffee mug and slung his backpack over his shoulder as he walked towards the door. He turned back to give Tommy one last forlorn look before exiting the control room. Tommy stood alone in the near-silence of the studio, the low hum of an amplifier bleeding through a microphone, the only audible sound.

CHAPTER FOUR

TOMMY AND HIS MANAGER, BOB WALKER, sat across from Milt Hamstein, Tommy's long-time time attorney. Milt hunched forward over his desk intently scanning Bizzy-B's signed producer agreement. Leaning back in his leather chair, he pushed his Buddy Holly style, black-framed glasses off the tip of his nose and smiled.

"So, here's the thing Tommy ... the producer agreement is between you and Bizzy. Sure, we could sue him for breach of contract. But legally we can't force him to produce your record, which is what you really want. We could try to go after him for damages related to the additional time and costs that his abrupt exit may eventually cause you. But even that's a long shot since he hasn't been paid his advance, and that's essentially what binds him to the terms of the contract. I'm guessing he may have been advised of that fact by someone, and if so, that could be why he stepped away when he did."

"Well, Milt ... I don't even know why we have contracts if they can't be enforced. That's crazy. He's putting me in a difficult position."

"Listen, Tommy ... your recording agreement requires a long-term, well-defined commitment to the record label. A producer agreement, on the other hand, is basically just an understanding of what a producer will do for you during a recording project and how they will ultimately get paid. Since you're a mega-star, I'm sure you can have your pick of any producer out there. Why not save yourself some grief, find a replacement, and move on?"

"Because Milt ... Bizzy and I have a thing. It's a chemistry and a camaraderie, and my music depends on it. It can't be replaced. Unfortunately, it's become all about the money with him because he's an addict. I heard he's getting six points for producing Jackie James. That's two better than the norm. I bet that little weasel locked in that deal with his attorney before he even heard my new music. If so, he had no intention of recording with me when I came back in yesterday, and all of that crap about my songs being below standard was just for show. He gave up on our argument way too easily. We've had far worse disagreements than that, and my new songs aren't that bad."

Tommy paused, stared out the window, and sighed, giving in to the conclusion that he was his only solution. He looked at Bob for confirmation, but all he received in return was a non-committed shoulder shrug.

"Well, I guess I don't have a choice, but to produce the album myself. Prince did it, so why can't I? I have a great engineer, mixer, and mastering team, so I think we'll make it through just fine."

"It's your call, Tommy," replied Milt.

"Thanks, Milt. Send my business manager the bill. I'm sure I've already put your kids and grandkids through college with what I've paid you over the past five years, haven't I?"

"Yes you have, my friend. I'm here for you anytime though."

"I'm sure you are," Tommy replied, standing and shaking Milt's hand across the desk.

AN HOUR LATER TOMMY WAS BACK AT JUNEBUG STUDIOS
determined to find a way to get motivated. He not only needed to
inspire himself but also the other musicians who would eventually
join him in the recording process.

Bizzy's contributions had been highly unique and creative, and
although subtle in many cases, they were the little things that went
a long way. It was the way he asked Tommy to breathe after a certain
lyric to reinforce the emotion beyond the message. Or the unusual
instrument sounds and note progressions Bizzy would develop.
Many of his creations would ultimately become the catchy musical
hook of a recording that listeners would find themselves unable to
purge from their minds.

Bizzy's ideas were addictive and had been critical to the Tommy
Model musical experience. But now, all of the creative decisions
would fall on Tommy alone. The weight of that dual role, coupled
with what he knew were lackluster songs to begin with, terrified
Tommy even more than writer's block.

In complete shutdown mode to the outside world, over the past
few days, he had purposefully ignored numerous phone calls from
Honeycutt Records CEO, Paul Watkins. After reaching a mental
breaking point regarding his biggest star's disrespectful attitude,
Paul decided to pay a surprise visit to the studio. He needed to find
out exactly what was going on and how his company's money was
being spent.

Before entering from the lobby, Paul stopped to watch Tommy
through a small square window in the control room door as he sat
alone at the mixing board. With no one else in the studio, Tommy
held a scotch in one hand and a smoke in the other. He remained in
a motionless daze for several minutes, never lifting his glass or
cigarette to his mouth. When an inch-long, hanging ash finally fell
on Tommy's leg, the fear of a burn hole in his designer jeans snapped

him back to reality. He leapt to his feet and feverishly brushed off the white powdery remnants.

Paul barged into the room, surprising Tommy who jumped back with both fists raised as if ready to fight off a mugger.

"Paul! Oh man, you scared me! What are you doing sneaking up on me like that?"

"Well, since you won't return my calls I had to come here in person to see how things are progressing. You see, I had this incredibly discouraging conversation with Bizzy-B's attorney this morning telling me his client was no longer involved in your project, and to not send his advance payment."

"I knew it!" barked Tommy.

"You knew that he had called me?" replied Paul.

"No, no ... I had a hunch his attorney got in his head, and Bizzy signed on to produce Silverback even before he walked away from working with me. That pretty much confirms that it was a predetermined deal or his lawyer wouldn't have called you so quickly. But yes, he quit the project because he's a disloyal, no-good loser who can't handle his drugs and gambling."

"Well now that we're being straight with each other, what are your plans for the album, Tommy? We're depending on you to deliver your best one yet. Sales have been down with the rest of the roster lately, so we need another winner."

"It's under control, Paul. I've decided to produce the album myself."

"Really? That's interesting."

Tommy was surprised at Paul's submissive response, and added, "I figured why not cut out the dead weight. It's pretty much all me anyway."

Paul paused as if contemplating his next move before continuing. "I tell you what ... it doesn't look like you're that busy today and I was going to take my fishing boat out for a spin. Why don't you come with me? It'll be good for you to get a little sun on that vampire skin of yours."

"Thanks for the invite, but I really don't have time. I have to ..."

"I insist, Tommy. It will only be a few hours. Come on."

Tommy reluctantly followed Paul out to his car. Together they made the short ride to a yacht club in Long Beach where Paul's ninety-foot, custom-built sport-fishing yacht was docked. On board, Tommy continued to try to search for a way out as Paul started the engines and untied the mooring lines. But the effort was in vain.

"Seriously, Paul ... I get easily seasick on boats. I don't know why, but I do."

"Are you afraid of the water?"

"Not at all. I recently started surfing, so I love the ocean. But something about not being able to see land from a boat does something to my equilibrium. I'd prefer you not to see me like that. Besides, if I puke, the acid could mess up my voice for days."

Prepared for any excuse Paul countered, "Nonsense, you'll be fine. It's like a lake out there today."

As they cleared the long jetty-way into the open Pacific, Paul throttled the engines to three-quarter speed as he captained the boat from the flybridge, high above the water. Tommy stood next to Paul wearing sunglasses and slathered in white sunblock just a shade lighter than his lily-white complexion. He held tightly to the aluminum rail on the side of the helm console. There was only a slight swell across the ocean, but from the tension on Tommy's face, they were preparing to face the brunt of a full force gale.

"See, Tommy ... it's gorgeous out here today. Let's head over to Catalina. We can be there in a little over an hour. I'm a member of the world-famous *Fisherman's Club* where we can have a late lunch, and then head back this evening."

"Do I have a choice?"

"Not a big fan of the unexpected adventure, are you? Since I'm the Captain of this ship, no you don't have a choice. You need to relax a little. Being so uptight is why you have writer's block."

"Who told you I had writer's block?" nervously asked Tommy.

"Do you really think there's anything that goes on with my artists that I don't know about?"

"I've written twelve great songs," Tommy protested. "We've just got to get them recorded and the album will be ready to go."

"So Bizzy quit the project after producing four multi-platinum albums with you simply because he's got a few bad personal habits? Is that what you're telling me? It wouldn't have anything to do with the songs you've written not being up to snuff?"

"I don't know who's told you what, but I feel good about the songs I have to work with. And I don't appreciate you or anyone questioning me about it. I've delivered hundreds of millions of dollars to the label, and I'd venture to say that even this boat was paid for by my efforts. If you're going to hold me captive on this little voyage, can we at least drop the criticisms and innuendos?"

"Relax," Paul replied with a scant smile on his face, seemingly pleased he was getting under Tommy's skin.

AN HOUR LATER AND STILL WOBBLY from the gentle rhythm of the ride over, Tommy braced himself against the table as they sat. At Paul's request, they were seated on the open-air deck at the back of The Fisherman's Club, a members-only club for fishing enthusiasts whose prestigious members have included past presidents and well-known celebrities, stretching back to the late 1800's.

"See, you made it without getting seasick. Let's get some lunch and have a few drinks. A round of Cuba Libres for me and my friend," Paul ordered from the server. "And I think we'll start with the grilled octopus. Isn't it beautiful, Tommy? I love sitting out here overlooking the harbor cradled in the arms of those towering green hills in the background. Stunning!"

"Yeah, it's okay," grumbled Tommy.

"I'm still surprised you don't like being on the water since you grew up near the sea in Scotland, and with your father working on ships and all."

"As I said, earlier ... I love the ocean. I'd just like to know what we're really doing here. You haven't spent any time with me other than dinner the night we signed my record deal. Maybe there has been a few award show after-parties since then, but nothing ever this elaborate. So forgive me, but I'm waiting for the shoe to drop."

"Always the pessimist. That's why you're having the problems you are now, my friend. I want to help you clear your mind so you can get back in the studio and record a great album for us. Is that so sinister of an agenda? If you can do that, I promise to spend more time with you if that would make you happy. Ah, here are our drinks. Perfect! Let's toast to the future. Cheers!"

Tommy and Paul touched glasses. Tommy hesitantly sipped his Cuba Libre, which his taste buds discovered was merely a fancy name for a rum and cola with some lime juice added in for extra flavor. He was still suspicious of Paul but decided to try to make the best of the afternoon, as they downed several more libations, along with the octopus appetizer, and a lunch of steak and crab cakes. With the help of rum, the discussion eventually loosened up, and it wasn't long before Tommy seemed to be enjoying himself. The two men barely noticed as the sun began to set behind the high hills above the town of Avalon.

"Paul, I hate to be the overly obvious one here, but should we be thinking about heading back? It's going to be dark soon."

Paul snapped his left wrist upward, his watch revealing the late hour.

"Oh gosh! You're right, Tommy. The time got away from me. And you know what ... I am really hammered, so I'm going to go call a couple of friends and see if they will skipper the boat back to L.A. for us. I'll be right back, okay?"

Paul stood and walked inside the back door of The Fisherman's Club to make his call, while Tommy continued to sip the watery remnants of his drink, sucking the last drop of rum from the half-melted ice cubes.

CHAPTER FIVE

PAUL AND TOMMY SAT ON THE EDGE OF THE DOCK next to the boat, their feet dangling over the side. The sun's distant glow had long since disappeared from the sky as they waited for Paul's friends to arrive. Below them, a school of baitfish casually floated in the circular beam of a dock light. Without warning, a barracuda slashed the surface. Its aggressive action dispersed the school in a frenzy before it disappeared back to the shadowy depths, taking at least one victim with it.

Tommy pulled his feet up in a reflex move before asking, "Did you see that, Paul?

"Yeah. That's just the way it goes sometimes. One can never be too confident that they won't be eaten by a bigger fish."

Tommy anxiously looked at his wristwatch before asking the burning thoughts on his brain, "So where are these guys? Should we maybe get a hotel room? It's pitch black out there."

"A hotel?" casually slurred Paul and obviously in no condition to navigate a ninety-foot yacht. "No, I actually own a home here, so we don't need to pay for a room. But I really need to get back for a meeting in the morning. Hey, here they come now!"

In and out of the shadows of the sporadically placed dock lights Tommy saw two massive figures moving towards them. Their silhouettes were those of bodybuilders who had likely stopped lifting a couple of years ago. Subsequently, their muscles had since blended like a protein shake into the fat of one too many steak and potato dinners.

Paul introduced Ricardo and Joe Joe. Their thick puffy palms and fingers swallowed Tommy's, as they shook hands. All business and no-nonsense, the duo quickly boarded the yacht. Ricardo climbed to the flybridge and started the engines while Joe Joe untied the lines.

"So, have you guys driven this ship before?" Tommy asked while Joe Joe pulled the last rope into the boat.

"Sure, it's no problem," replied Joe Joe in a heavy accent as the boat began to move forward, idling out of the slip.

"Are you from Hungary, Joe?" inquired Tommy.

"Yes, how did you know?

"I toured through Hungary years ago and for some reason the accent of the people I met there stuck in my head.

"I see," Joe Joe casually responded, as he walked over to a built-in storage cabinet abutted against the cabin. He flipped the latch and opened one of the doors. From inside he slid out two white, five-gallon buckets. They appeared to be quite heavy, even for someone with Joe Joe's apparent strength.

"What's that, Joe?" asked Tommy, a little surprised that Joe Joe knew the buckets were where he had found them.

"It's Joe Joe! Not Joe," he sternly retorted.

Joe Joe removed the well-secured lids from the buckets before continuing, "What we have here is a potent mixture of a lot of rich, gooey blood and guts, straight from the Butcher of Avalon."

"The Butcher of Avalon? He sounds like an axe-murderer," nervously joked Tommy before inquiring further. "Please forgive me for asking so many questions, but exactly why do we have two five gallon buckets full of animal entrails with us this evening?"

The ship was now up to cruising speed and cutting through the warm night air with little resistance from the ocean below.

Joe Joe looked at Tommy and smiled from ear to ear. "I guess Paul didn't tell you? I'm not surprised. We're going to do a little shark fishing on the way back to L.A. It was our deal with him for agreeing to navigate the boat. Ricardo and I make shark's tooth jewelry, as well as sharkskin bags and purses. We also sell shark meat to local restaurants."

"Uh ... no, he didn't tell me that!" Tommy snapped as he stormed towards the ladder leading to the helm-station above where Paul was sitting with Ricardo.

As Tommy passed Joe Joe, the musclebound hulk grabbed his arm and squeezed it tightly.

"Calm down, little man. There is nothing you can say to Paul that will change what's going to happen tonight. I suggest you just chill out. Okay?"

Tommy jerked his arm away from Joe Joe's grip. "What do you mean, 'There is nothing I can say that will change what's going to happen tonight?' Do you know who I am? If not, you better figure it out real quick, and never touch me again! Got it?"

Joe Joe smiled at Tommy as if giving him a pass for the moment. Still fuming, but unsure exactly how far he could push it, Tommy sat in the fighting chair affixed to the center deck. The boat continued for another twenty minutes before coming off plane and slowing to a stop.

Tommy looked up to the flybridge, threw his hands in the air, and yelled, "What now?"

Ricardo turned on the underwater, stern light, illuminating a few feet beneath the surface and beyond the rear of the yacht. He looked down and gave the thumbs up to his partner. Joe Joe began methodically drizzling the bloody concoction from the buckets over the back of the boat. In a matter of seconds, the under-lit blue shimmer turned to dark red. A few minutes later, the first fin slowly sliced through the surface. It was followed by the quick slash of a tail before the large shark disappeared back into the mire of the chum slick.

"You have got to be kidding me?" raged Tommy as he looked to where Paul was shielding himself from sight. "Paul, what in the world is going on? I didn't sign up for this!"

Ricardo climbed down the ladder. Back on the deck, he began readying a stocky fishing rod affixed with an enormous reel. The bail was filled to nearly overflowing with thick monofilament line. Carefully he weaved the gigantic, three-inch hook in and out of a chunk of meat. He then cast the bait a few feet behind the boat, free spooling the line. The bloody bait slowly drifted beyond the range of the glow.

Tommy was beside himself and went to climb the ladder to where Paul was hiding. As quickly as his foot met the first rung, Joe Joe was on him again like a lion, grabbing him by both arms and pulling him back. Tommy tried to wrench free from his grasp, but Joe Joe's hands seemed locked onto his skin.

"I told you before you muscle-bound freak, get your mitts off me!" Tommy continued to struggle, but there was no breaking free. Joe Joe, now roaring with ominous laughter, dragged Tommy to the back of the boat. "Get off me!" anxiously shouted Tommy.

Joe Joe turned Tommy to face the stern. In the light, he saw two sharks pass each other, their massive bodies churning the crimson water.

"You want me to let you go, Mr. Rock Star? Huh? Okay, I'll let you go!"

With little effort, Joe Joe picked up Tommy like a rag doll and threw him over the rail. He awkwardly splashed in the center of the blood pool, and all became eerily silent as the boil, and foamy head of his plunge faded away.

Ricardo nervously asked Joe Joe, "What's going on, man? Do you think they got him already? It's not supposed to go like this. Dude, you gotta go in and get him!"

"I'm not going in there. This was your idea ... you go!" protested, Joe Joe.

"My idea? It wasn't mine, it was his!" Ricardo rejected as he turned to point at Paul who was now watching intently from the upper deck."

"All right ... one of you knuckleheads need to get him out of there!" instructed, Paul. "That's enough! You were only supposed to scare him, not actually throw him in!"

Tommy's head broke the surface as he gasped for air, flailing about wildly in the blood and guts all around him.

"Give me your hand!" demanded Joe Joe.

"I'm not touching you!" surprisingly protested Tommy.

Ricardo leaned over the gunwale and grabbed Tommy by his shirt, pulling him closer as a fin pierced the surface nearby. With reality and fear finally kicking in, Tommy frantically locked wrists with Ricardo. The thug pulled him on board as an enormous Mako shark careened towards Tommy's leg. Its mouth was wide open, baring multiple rows of razor-sharp daggers. Just missing, the beast's massive head rammed into the boat hull below, impacting with a deep thud.

Tommy leaned against the arm of the fighting chair where he stood dripping wet, with small chunks of animal bits clinging to his clothes and face. Desperately, he tried to catch his breath. Paul dismounted the ladder onto the main deck and walked over to Tommy handing him a towel.

Tommy now realized he was staring into the eyes of the mastermind of the events that had just unfolded. His brain struggled for how it was remotely possible that the entire day was designed to lead to this moment. Did Paul actually intend for him to be eaten alive by sharks? Or had he grown a conscious in the last moment as the events transpired? Ricardo and Joe Joe flanked their victim and Tommy began shaking at the thought of what might happen next.

Paul smiled and calmly spoke in a low, intense tone.

"That's the kind of thing that happens to people who mess with me. You see, I don't much care if you live or die if you aren't going to deliver hits for me. If those sharks had taken you down, they would have done me a big favor. There are many, many ways we could have made a fortune off your untimely death. Do you get what I'm sayin', Tommy?

Tommy was stunned and transfixed in silence.

"Do you get it?" screamed Paul.

Tommy jumped back from the impact of Paul's bombastic verbal attack, his words coated in the rancid stench of partially digested rum and steak.

"I get it, Paul. I get it."

"So, starting tomorrow, you're going to meet with several producers and songwriters I'm going to send your way. You're going to work with at least one of them to give me the album that I need. You know ... the one that's going to sell millions of copies like all your others have. Not this mess of measly concoctions you've thrown together. And if you don't live up to my expectations ... well, let's say that Joe Joe and Ricardo don't like loose ends and they know where to find you. Now nod your head in agreement and let's get this thing back to the dock, okay?"

Tommy hesitantly nodded in reluctant acceptance as Ricardo climbed back to the helm and throttled the engines forward, setting a course for Long Beach.

CHAPTER SIX

AFTER A NEARLY SLEEPLESS NIGHT and two showers, Tommy's eyes still burned from the saltwater and blood that had engulfed him only a few hours earlier. Unsure as to what time Paul had scheduled the procession of producers and songwriters to start arriving at the studio, Tommy was out the door by 7:00 a.m. to be safe.

He arrived at Junebug some twenty minutes later, but to his dismay, the gate of the enclosure surrounding the studio grounds was still locked. To clear the sidewalk, he inched his car up the driveway as close as possible to the chain link fencing. He then turned off the purring engine, leaned back against the headrest and closed his eyes. Completely exhausted from the debacle of the evening before, it wasn't long before he was asleep.

What seemed like only a few minutes, turned out to be two hours when Tommy was awoken by someone knocking on his driver's side window. Still gun-shy from his recent assault, the sound startled him as he lifted his head to see the studio manager standing beside the car.

"Good morning, Mr. Model. I wanted to let you know I'm opening up if you want to come in."

Tommy nodded in agreement, still groggy from his nap. He rubbed his eyes forcefully and slapped his face before starting the engine and pulling into the parking lot. In his reserved parking spot, he once again sat silently in the car, thinking about what was to come. It just wasn't possible that his life had been threatened as it had been a few hours ago. His fiery soul searched his brain for a way out of the forced agenda that was heading his way.

Inside Junebug, Tommy made a cup of coffee and waited for the first mystery arrival. A short time later, following a gentle rap on the control room door, producer Jason Silverman walked in. After exchanging pleasantries, the two sat down to talk.

"So, Paul told me Bizzy quit and you're looking for a great producer to help you finish your newest album project."

"Actually, I wanted to self-produce this one all along, so Bizzy's departure was no big deal. But Paul is intent on me getting some help, so here you are. I know you're an awesome producer, so I realize if we work together, it could turn out to be a really good thing. However, just so I'm completely up front ... this wasn't my idea."

"I understand," replied Jason. "Speaking of Paul ... that's really crazy what happened to him last night, isn't it?"

Tommy shifted in his chair and leaned heavily on his armrest. Did Jason somehow know what had gone down on the boat? Was he part of the plan? Tommy's mind reeled before feigning denial.

"I'm not sure what you're referring to. What happened to Paul?"

"Man, I'm sorry ... I thought you knew. He dropped dead of a heart attack. They say he was under crazy pressure to deliver for the label since every artist other than yourself has been bombing lately. Financially, Honeycutt Records is in the toilet. It's a big mess. But I'm not telling you anything you didn't already know."

Tommy hesitated, shocked at the news. The head of his label, who he had learned was also a gangster-style extortionist, after threatening to kill him only hours earlier, was now dead. On top of that, according to Jason, Honeycutt was about to go under. Tommy had no idea the label was struggling as Jason claimed, although he had no intention of admitting his ignorance.

"You okay, Tommy?" Jason asked in a concerned tone.

"Yeah, of course I knew about the label's financial issues, but Paul ... wow, it's mind-blowing that he's gone. Did he pass away at home?"

"On the news, they interviewed two bouncer-looking dudes who found him. He was apparently sitting in the fighting chair of his big, fancy sport-fishing yacht docked out in Long Beach. They said he had an empty bottle of rum in his lap so that probably didn't help. Seagulls had pecked his eyes out apparently. Terrible way to go if you ask me."

"Yeah, I agree," replied Tommy, dazed and staring completely through Jason. His paranoia peaked, assuming the two guys who discovered Paul must have been Ricardo and Joe Joe. Had the hired thugs killed Paul after Tommy left last night? If so, why? Was he suddenly off the hook with Paul out of the picture, or was he now just a loose end? Should he call the police? Should he even admit that he had been with Paul last night? Would he be implicated if he did? What should he do with Jason and the rest of the day's producer lineup? His mind raced.

"Jason, this is a lot to take in, so you'll have to excuse me. I need some time to clear my head. Thank you so much for stopping by. I'll be in touch."

Tommy patted Jason on the shoulder as he stood and walked out of the control room. He quickly exited the studio and jogged out to his car. As Tommy sat in the driver's seat, he could hear his heart pounding in his head. Whatever had happened to Paul, he knew that he desperately needed to get out of town and lie low for a few days, and his Malibu beach house would provide the perfect escape.

TOMMY STOPPED BY MODEL MANSION TO GRAB A BAG and a few changes of clothing. Inside, he called his good friend and surfing instructor Skip Chadwick to see if he was free to hang out and catch some waves. Tommy offered to pay handsomely for his time, but Skip refused the money. The two planned to meet on Tommy's back deck overlooking the Pacific as soon as Tommy could get there.

Tommy threw his bag in the back seat of his souped-up, red, four-wheel drive jeep. All of the doors and canvas coverings had been removed for that full summertime effect, and Tommy's custom, nine-foot longboard was strapped tightly to the roll bar above. He had only recently started surfing after buying his oceanfront bachelor pad in nearby Malibu last year. Since then, the sport had quickly become one of his favorite passions outside of music.

As Tommy drove, his mind continued to replay the events of the night before. On the one hand, he was sickened and afraid. On the other, he was somewhat relieved that Paul was out of the picture. After all, what kind of person threatens to kill someone over the quality of their music? It made no sense.

Nearing the beach, he questioned the thought of getting back into the water, especially considering that the ocean had almost taken his life a few hours earlier. But with his writer's block so heavily consuming his abilities as a songwriter and artist, he refused to allow one more fear to take root in his mind. Even with the ever-present possibility of sharks, he wanted to nip his growing anxiety in the bud.

Tommy parked directly in front of his beach house. He unstrapped his surfboard from the roll bars and carried it along with his duffel bag into the house. The busy noise and flow of the nearby PCH disappeared as he entered and closed the door behind. The view through the full wall of glass windows and doors at the back of the house was stunning, with the sunlit blue horizon stretching endlessly beyond his field of view. He threw his bag on the living room floor and continued with his board underarm, navigating its huge length between the furniture and doors, and out to the deck. There, Skip sat studying the wave sets rolling in.

Skip Chadwick was the quintessential surfer-dude. He sported long, curly, sun-bleached hair, well-tanned skin, and wore Hawaiian-influenced baggies, while proudly displaying a thick coating of white zinc oxide on his nose and lips. He warmly greeted Tommy with a man-hug and a series of well-coordinated handshakes.

"Dude, it's awesome to see you!" said Skip in a heavy, surfer-style inflection. "The waves are jettin', man. We gotta get out there. A minute ago some magazine surfer went over the falls so bad that I almost threw up my chuck-wagon laughing so hard."

Tommy expressed a diffident look. "Well, I might be joining him, so I hope you don't puke on my account."

"Ah, dude ... you smoke this guy. He needs to sit on the beach with his pretty, little poser board and watch the real men show him how it's done. You ready, Tom-tom?"

"Yeah, let's get out there, mate. I really need this."

Tommy followed Skip down the back stairs leading to the sand below. They both ran to the water like two teenagers on summer vacation. Skip tossed his board, sliding it smoothly across the surface. Like an acrobat, he jumped on top with absolute perfection and skimmed into the oncoming foam ball of the final remnants of a wave. He popped up the nose in perfect timing, clearing the back side of the surge, then laid flat on the board and began paddling through the crashing surf.

Tommy paused at the water's edge as if his thoughts were going to get the best of him. Skip looked back and waved him on, giving a loud "Ahaaa!" as the final encouragement Tommy needed to plunge in.

Arriving to the *outside* between sets, Tommy and Skip sat straddling their boards in silence. The only sound was the low roar of the breaking waves behind them. The distant horizon began to undulate. Skip paddled hard left to position himself for the solid looking wave he knew was coming. Seconds later, he beautifully executed his takeoff, and with a series of classic moves, he rode the wave all the way to shore before kicking out backside. He landed face down on his board and headed back out for another round.

Tommy was completely alone for the moment. He stared into the blue depths, mesmerized by the sun's rays cascading downward. His mind began to build anxiety about what lie beneath. Calming himself, Tommy looked skyward and asked, "What are you doing to me, Lord? I don't know what you want from me. And why does all of this bad stuff keep happening? It has got to stop. Please, make it all stop."

Skip paddled to rejoin Tommy. He smiled and jokingly asked, "So, are you just going to sit here or are you going to shralp one, brother?"

Tommy smiled, pivoted his board toward the beach, and began his fierce paddle to catch the approaching wave. With the confidence of a rock star kicking in, he calmly popped to his feet as he took off right, elegantly applying his goofy-foot style. He walked to the front of the board and did his best version of a hang ten. His toes gripped the nose and his body arched into a "C" shape, a traditional, old-school move he had learned from Skip. As the wave closed out, he shuffled back to the center and pumped past the foam until the surge regenerated allowing him to complete his ride to shore.

He jumped off into the shallows and grabbed his board to keep the fins from digging into the sand. He looked back to where he knew Skip, the patient friend and teacher had been watching. With great pride, Skip raised his arm high in the air, giving Tommy the hang-loose, *shaka* sign. He rotated his wrist back and forth in ultimate approval. Tommy beamed with accomplishment. For the moment, at least one demon had been put back in its cage.

CHAPTER SEVEN

TOMMY WAS EXHAUSTED from the surfing session. Back in his beachside home, he showered the salt and sunblock from his body, then crashed on the couch and closed his eyes. A ringing phone hanging on the kitchen wall broke the silence, but he desperately tried to ignore the incessant droning. Finally, an answering machine picked up. Through it, he heard the muffled voice of his manager, Bob Walker, a distinct sound that snapped him back to the reality he had been trying to avoid.

"Tommy? Are you there, buddy? I'm getting worried about you, man. I tried the main house several times, but got the machine there too. I sure hope you're okay. I just want to see how things are going after our meeting with Milt yesterday. I guess by now you've heard about Paul's passing this morning. That's tragic news for sure, both personally and professionally. I'm going to arrange some meetings with the Honeycutt team in a few days to discuss our go-forward plans. I'll let you know what they have open. I'd love to come by the studio when you're cool with that. Give me a call when you get this. Ciao."

In his haste to get out of town, Tommy had completely forgotten to call Bob to fill him in on all that had happened following their meeting yesterday. Tommy had worked with three managers in his short, five-year career, and admittedly, he wasn't the easiest person to get along with. The first two had been completely worthless, but Bob was different. He had been instrumental in securing several lucrative opportunities for his star client, and his loyalty and determination were unmatched.

Tommy was grateful for his manager's trust and dedication, but under the circumstances, he felt it best to keep his recent interaction with Paul under wraps. Tommy made a mental note to call Bob back tomorrow, then closed his eyes and tried to regain his peace.

A few minutes later, a knock at the back door popped his eyes open again. He looked through the glass to see Skip who smiled and held up a six-pack of Tommy's favorite beer, a local brew called Beautleg. Tommy laughed and rose from the sofa to walk over and let his friend in.

"Hey, bra," Skip greeted, hugging Tommy as he entered. "I thought we could have a little happy hour before we head over to Sandpipers. Cool?"

"Yeah, that sounds good, mate."

Retreating to the deck, the two friends talked, laughed, and watched the sun melt into the Pacific horizon as they downed the pack of brewskis. As the last glow of the orange orb disappeared from view, Tommy faintly heard what sounded like the voice of a woman rising from the beach below, barely discernible over the sound of the crashing waves.

"Is someone calling your name, Skip?" asked Tommy. "Maybe I'm imagining things."

"Dude, that's probably Miss February! I asked her to bring a friend and come pick us up."

"Miss February?" replied Tommy in puzzlement.

"I can't ever remember her name. I know that's wrong, but it's something strange that won't stick in my brain for some reason. She was a centerfold this past February, but I can't remember the magazine either. I'm must be really losin' it. Too many doobies I guess."

"Centerfold ... like, nude?"

"I don't think they have too many centerfolds who pose with their clothes on, bra."

Skip laughed like a dirty-minded Spring Breaker as he stood, then steadily progressed through his standard series of handshakes with Tommy.

He leaned over the deck rail and called down to the woman. "Hey, baby!" We hear ya. We'll be right there. If you want to go back up to the car, we'll meet you out front."

Looking back at Tommy, Skip reinforced their plans for the evening. "Dude, you will love her friend. She's smokin' hot. Hotter than Miss February, for sure. So we'll head over to Sandpipers, sip a few cocktails, veg on some dinner, and see where things go from there. You're a rock star ... you know the drill."

The mannerisms of a cartoon character usually reinforced Skip's enthusiastic surfer-slang-laden accent. He was anything but boring, and Tommy loved spending time with him.

Tommy followed his friend out the front door and locked it behind. When he turned, his view was met by two of the most beautiful women he had ever laid eyes on. One was a blonde, the other a brunette. Both were well tanned and sported t-shirts casually tucked into cut-off, denim short-shorts.

"Tommy, let me introduce you to the ladies," offered Skip, carefully wording his introduction to hide the fact that he obviously couldn't remember their names.

"Angels ... this is the one and only, Mr. Tommy Model."

Both women were beaming from ear to ear as they approached Tommy, gently bumping each other while jockeying for position. Offering her hand first, the brunette introduced herself.

"Hi, Tommy. I'm Cindy."

The blonde quickly nudged her friend to the side, replacing her hand in his. "Hello, Tommy. I'm Summer."

Tommy equally charmed both women with his boyish grin and bad-boy style. He knew he was a good-looking, platinum-selling rock star with a Scottish accent to boot, so meeting women was not usually a challenge. But both of these ladies had immediately cast a spell on him, and surprisingly, he felt a bit nervous. With far too many bad experiences under his belt, Tommy was unfortunately always on guard with women he didn't know, and even with some that he did know. In this case, he trusted Skip's judgment, so he temporarily lowered his shields, and it felt good.

"Hi, Cindy. Hello Summer. It's very nice to meet you both," Tommy coolly responded. He looked around Summer to see a baby-blue bug parked behind her.

"Is that your car?" asked Tommy.

"It's mine," claimed Cindy.

"It's cute, but there's no way we're all going to fit in there. Do you guys wanna take mine?" offered Tommy holding out his keys.

"Yes, but only if I get to drive!" Summer jumped forward in excitement, snatching the keys from Tommy's hand.

As Summer and Cindy climbed into the front seats, Tommy pulled Skip in close and whispered, "So are you telling me you couldn't remember the names, Summer or Cindy? Neither of those seems too odd to me, mate. Which one is Miss February?"

"Dude, I'm high as a kite most of the time, buzzed on life and buds. It was only Summer that I couldn't remember. She's the centerfold," Skip replied in slight embarrassment.

Tommy patted his friend on the back, easing his moment of awkwardness. They both contorted their way into the back seats as Summer started the engine and released the parking brake. Letting off the clutch too quickly, she immediately began stripping the gears. Lurching forward multiple times the foursome laughed as their heads jerked back and forth. Finally, Summer reached enough speed to settle into fourth gear. Fortunately, Sandpipers was just over a mile away, and within a few minutes, they slid into the sandy parking lot.

Summer parked, turned off the ignition, then looked back at Tommy with childlike excitement and asked, "So how did I do?"

"You did great Summer," Cindy interrupted before Tommy had a chance to respond. She winked to show she wasn't oblivious to the truth. She did, however, want to protect her friend's feelings in case Tommy was in an overly honest mood.

Catching Cindy's cue, Tommy responded, "Yeah. You did awesome. I usually struggle with this big ole machine, but you drove it like a pro."

"Great! Let's go have some fun," Summer replied, giddy from her perceived accomplishment as she hopped down from the driver's seat.

Sandpipers was one of Skip and Tommy's favorite hangouts. It was an oceanfront restaurant and bar that not only offered indoor seating with a view but also tables, lounge chairs and cabanas right on the sand, just a few feet from the water. Down the coast to the east, the full moon was peeking over the distant horizon, casting its illuminating glow across the ocean. The hostess seated Tommy and his friends in a private cabana, shielded from the view of looming fans, some of which had already noticed his presence.

"This is beautiful," expressed Cindy as she looked earnestly into Tommy's eyes.

"You sure are," Tommy replied like a cheesy B-movie actor.

Cindy smiled and shyly looked downward at her toes digging into the sand. Keenly aware of the growing chemistry between Tommy and her best friend, Summer plopped herself into Tommy's lap and placed her arm around his neck. Her long, blonde hair fell around his face as she screamed, "Let's order some pitchers of margaritas and get this party started! What do you say, Tommy?"

The server stood by patiently as Tommy looked up at her and smiled.

"Two pitchers of margaritas and four shots of your best tequila. Better bring a bucket of Beautlegs too."

The order prompted a sharp, "Woohoo!" from Summer. "Now we're talkin', baby!"

As the night progressed, the fast-friends laughed, dined, and drank excessively. Unfortunately, Summer finally became overwhelmed by her carefree approach. By partaking of more tequila libations than her scant meal of chips, salsa, and a salad could combat, the outcome was now predictable.

"I don't feel so hot," slurred Summer as she leapt from her chair, making it outside the cabana before falling to her knees and letting everything go.

Cindy was quickly beside her friend, holding back Summer's hair and offering words of encouragement over the horrific sounds emitting from the petite centerfold. Tommy asked the server to bring a cool, wet washcloth and some water. He was concerned but was reluctant to offer any personal assistance. Instead, he opted to remain in his chair, pleasantly drunk and quietly looking on.

Earlier in the evening at Summer's enthusiastic urging, Tommy had ordered an entire bottle of the restaurant's most expensive premium tequila, along with a bowl of limes, several salt shakers, and a tray full of shot glasses. As fans stopped by as they always do, he offered shots to the ones he liked. This generosity endeared him to those he encountered, while also spreading the love and expanding the party. But like a kid with a candy jar sitting directly in front of her, Summer had personally grabbed the bottle one too many times.

Now, looking at poor Summer on her knees, the sexy image of a centerfold had all but faded, and Tommy was selfishly disappointed. His fantasy of spending the rest of the night with both women had been dashed. In the dim light, he poured himself an overflowing shot. He grabbed a lime, generously applied salt to his hand, then licked, sucked, and slammed it. He followed the tart burn with a cold Beautleg chaser. Skip smiled at Tommy and slid a long, skinny joint from his shirt pocket. He lit it and took a deep, intentional drag before passing it over.

"I'm sorry, bra. This wasn't supposed to go like this," profusely apologized Skip.

"I hope she's okay, mate. I tried to tell her to eat more and drink some water along the way, but she didn't listen," quipped Tommy, as he took a hit from the smoldering Jimmy.

"Hey, guys! We're uh ... right here, and can hear everything you're saying, you heartless morons," scolded Cindy.

"Chill out, baby," replied Skip, trying his best to diffuse the situation. "We mean no harm. I just wanted us all to have a great time, but your girl got a little ahead of herself. It's cool. Is she doing better?"

Cindy gently stroked the wet washcloth across Summer's brow before helping her friend back to her feet, then brushing off her hands and knees.

"Summer, do you wanna go home, sweetie?" Cindy patiently asked.

"Home? No, I'm okay. Just let me sit down. I think Tommy's right. Maybe I should eat something and drink some water. I'm not ready to go yet."

Summer sat next to Tommy and smiled like a happy drunk. "I'm sorry, Tommy. I'm a mess. But I love you. That's for sure."

Tommy smiled as he reached out and gently held Summer's face in his hand. She closed her eyes, taking in his warm, subtle touch.

The server checked in, interrupting the moment. Tommy ordered a bacon burger and fries to help soak up the alcohol that was poisoning Summer's system. He further assured her that if she could eat a little of the food when it arrived, she would feel better shortly.

Cindy sat on the other side of Tommy. He reached over to hold her hand before offering his best version of an apology.

"You can be upset with me if you want, but I don't do sympathy well. I hope you can understand that. My life's not normal, and I'm not normal. If you want normal, you need to look in another cabana, because it ain't hanging out here."

Cindy pounced from her chair and straddled Tommy's legs, sitting on his lap while passionately forcing her lips against his. He pulled her in closer and responded with the intensity that had been building since their eyes had first met earlier in the evening.

Summer looked on in frustration, never moving her gaze from Cindy and Tommy's full-on make-out session. Skip inched his chair closer to Summer and placed his arm around her shoulder like a nervous teen on a first date at a movie theater. He handed her the still lit joint. She pinched it between her fingers and placed it to her lips. After inhaling deeply, she turned towards Skip and blew the pungent smoke directly in his face. Skip closed his eyes as if in ecstasy, only to reopen them to Summer's glare staring back at him as she asked, "What in the world are you doing with your arm around me?"

CHAPTER EIGHT

∞

TOMMY AND BOB TURNED TO EACH OTHER IN DISBELIEF at what they had just been told by Honeycutt's interim label chief, Nate Augustus. Tommy looked back to Nate and squinted.

"So let me get this straight ..." began Tommy. "You are selling Honeycutt to Galactic Records?"

"That's right. They've been trying to acquire us ever since your first album blew up, and with Paul's untimely death, there's no reason to stand in their way any longer. He was determined to see Honeycutt survive on its own against the corporate giants like Galactic, and was the last holdout against any merger. Unfortunately, we've been struggling a bit financially for a couple of years now, and Paul was getting desperate to turn things around. It's best for the shareholders, the employees, and of course, the artists. Your contract will transfer to them without any issue."

"I see," replied Tommy, pausing in reflection before continuing. "The problem is, I will go from being the top priority at a record label I signed my deal with, to one of many platinum and gold selling artists on Galactic. The talent originally part of the Galactic roster will likely always receive a much greater commitment than I will."

"You're one of the highest-selling artists in the world," noted Nate. "I seriously doubt they're going to put you on the back burner."

"Well, I had lots of other labels who were interested when I signed my deal, including Galactic. But I chose to be here. And now you, and the so-called *board*, are making a unilateral decision that will without a doubt have an impact on my career. All because you and the other executives couldn't control your payroll and employee expense accounts."

"That's not exactly fair, you see ..."

Tommy cut Nate off in mid-sentence. "No, I don't have to see anything because I've made you more money than any other single artist has on this, or any other label during the same time frame. So where has it all gone? I sure don't see much coming my way. The only means I have of earning a decent living is by constantly touring. So I'd venture to say that a lot of it is buried in the bank accounts, stock portfolios, real estate, and personal playthings that you, Paul, and the other top execs have accumulated on the back of my creativity and hard work."

"Come on, Tommy."

"You come on, Nate! And I'm equally as confident that this merger will put a sweet wad of cash in your pocket. But you're sitting there in your comfy chair telling me not to worry about my contract transferring to Galactic. Do you think I'm stupid? Are you a complete tool? Let's go, Bob!"

"Tommy ... hang on a minute. Let's talk," Nate pleaded, as Tommy charged out of the office. Bob trailed behind his client, but upon reaching the door turned back to offer Nate some reassurance.

"I'll talk to him. It's been a rough week. He'll calm down."

"Bob, we need him to be cooperative and not screw this up for all of us. The whole merger deal could go south if he causes too much friction."

"I'll talk to him, Nate. That's all I can do."

TOMMY DIPPED HIS TORTILLA CHIP first into salsa, then into a bowl of sour cream at his favorite Mexican restaurant, El Gordo.

Bob returned from making a call at the pay phone in the back of the restaurant.

"I ordered you the chicken fajitas, Bob."

"You know I hate chicken fajitas. Why would you order that for me?"

"Because I'm starving and the guy came along to take our order, and that's what I'm getting. You felt a phone call was more important than feeding your biggest client. And what in the world is there to hate about chicken fajitas? It's basically grilled chicken, onions, and peppers. There is nothing in that delicious combination that can possibly be disliked."

"I got a page to ring the office, and it was about you, so I had to make the call. And for the record, I don't like the red peppers."

"You don't like the red peppers, but you're cool with the green and the yellow peppers?"

"Yeah."

"So don't eat the red peppers, mate! Blimey. What would you have ordered on your own?"

"Probably the cheeseburger."

"A cheeseburger? At the best Mexican restaurant in Los Angeles? What are you a ten year old? Anyway ... what was the call about?"

"It was Galactic. Their CEO, Jacques Morel wants to meet with us."

"How do you spell, Jacques?" asked Tommy.

"Uh ... I think it's, *J, A, C, Q, U, E, S*. Why do you ask?"

"That's what I thought. Like Jacques Cousteau. You say it like *Jock*, as if referring to a football player, but it's spelled like you would say *Jock-ez*. It's weird how some names are not spelled as you would say them out loud. It would be like someone calling me Tommy *Mod-ell*."

"Wow, are you amped up in rare form today or what?" asked Bob.

"You bet," replied Tommy, snacking on another tortilla chip dipped again in salsa and sour cream.

"Anyway ... Jacques wants us to meet with him this afternoon. I guess Nate informed him about our talk and he wants to give you some comfort that they are serious about promoting your career and making you a priority."

"Really?" Tommy sarcastically asked as if not totally buying the line they had fed Bob. "Well, here's what we're going to tell them. I want to see just how serious they are."

"Let's not go overboard, Tommy. Please."

"No, no. Hear me out. I want total control over this album project, and they have to release whatever I give them without question or hesitation. They don't even get to hear it until it's in the can."

"No label is going to do that."

"If they are serious about supporting me they will. You know this album is going to be a little different, and word on the street was Paul was not happy with the direction I was going."

Tommy was careful not to mention what Paul had told him during their still secret, last encounter.

"But if we can get Galactic to accept the album with no strings attached, I'll only have one more to deliver before I get the twenty million dollar re-signing bonus that Honeycutt would have owed me. We need to make sure that bonus is still on the table too. I have a bad feeling they will try to find a way out of that since they don't need me as much as Honeycutt did."

"Yeah, I can see them trying to wiggle out of that bonus deal, so that's a good point to bring up with Jacques. But I don't know how you can expect them to blindly accept an album they don't even get to hear before it's mastered. I wouldn't agree to that if I were them."

"Are you my manager or not? Get with Milt and make it happen. We can meet with Jacques if you want, but those are my terms. So spell it out to him," Tommy demanded.

The server arrived with two steaming, cast iron skillets of chicken fajitas that Bob promptly reached out to touch.

"Hot plate, Bob!" screamed Tommy, but it was too late. Bob's finger was singed against the scalding heat of the metal skillet.

"I told you I hated fajitas!" exclaimed Bob as he plunged his reddening digit into his cup of iced-down soda.

CHAPTER NINE

AFTER MEETING WITH JACQUES AND THE EXECUTIVE TEAM at Galactic's L.A. office, Tommy and Bob left surprised and elated. Tommy's demands for full control of his album had been accepted, and if they renewed his deal, his future mega-advance was still on the table. The problem was, it had been almost too easy, and Tommy now held concerns that he was somehow being played.

Word on the street was that Galactic was only offering twenty million dollars for Honeycutt. Tommy pondered that if that were true, why would Galactic be willing to pay a future bonus to him for the same amount they had paid for the entire record label? It was a thought he would find difficult to shake.

BACK AT MODEL MANSION, Tommy retreated to his poolside oasis with Cindy. His long-time personal assistant, Monique, brought out drinks, with a Rum Runner for Tommy and Pina Colada for Cindy. Still a bit sun-pink from his recent surfing adventure, Tommy protected his normally baby powder-like complexion by shielding under an umbrella. Cindy stood from her lounge chair and slid it slightly forward beyond the shade.

"Did you seriously just move your chair because the umbrella was blocking about an inch of sun from your arm?" teased Tommy.

"Absolutely," replied Cindy. "How weird would I look with an elbow a tad lighter than the rest of my body?"

Tommy smiled and shook his head while admiring the view of Cindy in a black two-piece. Her stunning silhouette was set against the backdrop of his sparkling, blue pool, with the expansive valley stretching far beyond towards the hazy L.A. skyline. It had been only a week since they had met. Thankfully, Tommy had not grown tired of Cindy yet, nor she of him. Still, he had no intention of getting serious with anyone. He knew that Cindy would eventually bail on him like every other woman had when the excessive demands of his rock star life finally kicked in, but he was enjoying the moment for what it was.

TOMMY HAD MADE SIGNIFICANT PROGRESS in the studio since his meeting with Galactic and estimated that the album would be ready for mixing and mastering within two weeks. Through the process, he had been amazed how quickly he had been able to complete the recording of a full song, something that used to take Bizzy days or weeks with all of his incessant tweaking. The problem was, Tommy still had doubts that the album would resonate with the outside world. He was essentially following a paint-by-numbers approach to self-production to get the project finished. Wrapping the album also meant Tommy could start preparing for his next tour. He hoped that getting back on stage and feeling the love from his fans would finally rid him of his creative issues, once and for all.

Two weeks later, Tommy had completed recording the twelve songs he had selected for the album. In total, the entire process had only taken three weeks, a time frame that was about four months less than his last album. Even though everyone was well aware the songs were not up to his usual standards, the musicians and studio team Tommy recorded with all had an enjoyable experience and made the most of what they had to work with. It helped that Tommy had curtailed his drinking and drug use during the sessions, minimizing the highs and lows that those around him normally encountered. Tommy Model in a much happier place, at least for a little while, was turning out to be a good thing.

The sale of Honeycutt progressed quickly, and by the time the album mixing and mastering had been completed, the deal had been finalized. The few employees who were staying on through the transition were relocating from Los Angeles to their new offices at Galactic's headquarters, located high on the 45th floor of a Manhattan skyscraper. Unfortunately, most of Honeycutt's staff had been laid off with only two weeks' severance. Hearing of this, Tommy personally directed his business manager to cut checks in the amount of $1,500 to each employee who had been let go, making sure that they cleared at least $1,000 after taxes. Individually it wasn't much, but collectively he paid out over $60,000.

A caring, compassionate person was always struggling to kick its way out of Tommy. It was an alternative being who usually resided just beneath the surface. Occasionally, it even got far enough along that it threatened to completely distort the image of the selfish, spoiled, and angry drug and alcohol-fueled maniac that the Tommy Model persona could often become. The appearance rarely lasted long, and the rock star always reemerged safely intact.

Tommy was relieved to learn that Honeycutt's two, top radio promotion and marketing executives had been kept on following the sale. When they called to invite him to New York to hear the new album and introduce him to the rest of Galactic's staff, he was ready.

EXCITED TO FINALLY GET THE PROCESS ROLLING, twelve hours later with masters in hand, Tommy, Bob, and Cindy boarded a private jet from LAX, and made the long trek overnight to New York City.

They arrived at Galactic the next morning, just in time for the 10:00 a.m. meeting.

Cindy hugged Tommy goodbye as she stayed behind in the lobby while Tommy and Bob were led to a large conference room with a wall of windows that overlooked the Manhattan skyline. Within a few minutes, Matt Millerson and Toby Posner entered and warmly greeted Tommy and Bob.

Having become close friends over the past five years, Tommy was elated to see them. Millerson and Posner had led the teams responsible for elevating all of Tommy's previous sixteen singles into the top five, with more than half of those making it to number one. It was a new beginning, and they seemed anxious to get started with the promotion and marketing campaigns.

Matt began the conversation by explaining that Jacques had another meeting that came up last minute, but he would try to join them soon.

"So how has the transition from L.A. to New York been for you guys?" asked Tommy.

Matt and Toby glanced at each other as if hoping the other would answer. As the stronger personality of the two, Matt was first to reply.

"It's been a real whirlwind. We're temporarily staying in a hotel while looking for a place to live. It's not as easy as one might think to find a decent apartment here in the city."

"Really? Looking out across that skyline, one would think that wouldn't be a problem," noted Tommy.

"There are a lot of buildings here, but not a whole lot of affordable vacancies. I think we've decided to expand our search across the Hudson to New Jersey to see if we'll have better luck there. Once we get a more permanent home, it'll start to settle in."

"I think we're both trying to get through the days without thinking about the personal side too much," Toby added. "Our families are still back in Los Angeles, so that's been tough. But we're not here to talk about us ... we're here to listen to some new music. Did you bring a CD of your next great masterpiece?"

"I sure did," replied Tommy handing over the gold compact disc snapped securely inside a clear jewel case. *Tommy Model* was written in thick black ink on the disk and across a piece of white tape stuck to the case.

"So what's the new album called?" asked Toby.

"Well it's not a song on the album, but I think we've landed on *Modelesque* as the title. I can't believe we haven't used that before."

"I love it," Toby replied in excitement. "What track were you thinking of for the first single?"

"Track two is what I've been leaning towards. It's a song called 'Livin' Large' that I'm really proud of."

"Okay then, let's check it out!" exclaimed Matt, as he inserted the CD into the impressive entertainment and sound system.

As "Livin' Large" thundered out of the massive speakers, Toby and Matt bobbed their heads to the mid-tempo rhythm of the song, while Tommy sat anxiously unflinching, his eyes carefully watching their every mannerism.

As the last note faded out, Matt pushed pause with the remote control and simply said, "Nice."

Internally, Tommy was taken aback. After all of his efforts and the insanity he had been through, the best word Matt could come up with was, *nice?* Surely, he could think of a more enthusiastic term than that. Before Tommy's brain had a chance to kick his adrenaline into overdrive, Toby asked, "What do you think for your next single, Tommy?"

Regaining his composure, Tommy adjusted his posture sitting tall in his chair. "I think it would be the next track called 'Horizon Line.'"

"Awesome. 'Horizon Line' it is," Toby stated, as Matt again pushed play on the remote.

To Tommy's dismay, as the second song ended, the response from both Matt and Toby was equally as cool as the first.

"Tommy, do you mind if we scan through all the other tracks?" asked Matt. "Then we can come back to discuss the ones we think would make good singles."

Tommy hesitated and looked at Bob who stared back without blinking. He knew where Tommy's mind was taking him and he dared not give him any ammunition with a supportive gesture.

Tommy turned back towards Toby and Matt and answered in a snarky tone, "Sure, if you want to *scan*, then scan away."

"Great," replied Matt as he pressed play once more.

As they whisked through the first verse and chorus of each song, it quickly became apparent to Tommy that they were unenthusiastic to say the least. When Matt stopped the final track, Tommy had taken enough and launched his attack.

"Okay, guys ... I'm not an idiot. You've never acted like this when we've had these listening sessions in the past, so what's the problem? These are great songs!"

Matt once again looked at Toby, hoping his counterpart would grab the sword, pull it in, and answer. It was a revisited move that irked Tommy even more.

"Don't look at him, Matt. Answer me!"

Matt closed his eyes and took a deep breath, then opened them again and dropped the bomb.

"Tommy, I'm really sorry. I know these songs are your babies, but we've both been doing this for over ten years now. Coming from a place of extensive experience with these situations, we don't hear a viable hit. Do you agree, Toby?"

"Yeah. There's nothing there we can work with. To be completely honest with you, we were very hesitant to move to New

York after Honeycutt was sold. But we wanted to be a part of promoting and marketing your next album. We hoped to accomplish the same level of success we did with the last sixteen singles. But we can't move here permanently if there's nothing for us to market and promote."

"Are you nuts? There are twelve amazing songs for you to work with! Take your pick. They are all great!"

"Respectfully, Tommy ..." responded Matt. "They aren't great. These are not typical Tommy Model songs, and you have to know that. And that's been the word on the street ever since Bizzy left the project."

"Bizzy never even got started on the project!" fired back Tommy.

"Well, apparently he heard what we're hearing, and that's what caused him to leave. I'm just being brutally honest with you because someone needs to be. Bob sure hasn't been."

"Excuse me?" snapped Bob.

"We all know this should be a throwaway album" added Toby. "I was hoping what we had been told was dead-wrong and you were going to knock us out with the same kind of incredible material you've recorded over the past four albums. But it's not there, man. If uprooting and dragging our families across the country didn't depend on it, I might not be so direct about it. But I can't afford to take that big of a leap for something I don't believe in. I'm sorry."

Tommy shot back. "Well, I tell you what, guys ... Jacques better have a different opinion than you two bozo's or we've got a big problem. When is he coming?"

"He's not coming," replied Toby. "He deferred to us on this. I'm sorry Tommy, but our recommendation is to ask you to please start over. Resolve your issues with Bizzy and make the album the world deserves to hear. We won't be a part of it, but for your sake ... do the right thing while you still can."

Seeing the conversation was getting nowhere, Matt interrupted, "Listen, we've got to run, buddy. Actually, this was the deciding factor for us, so we're both giving our notices today and heading back to L.A. since there's nothing for us here. We have offers with another label back home, and we'll likely take that gig. I'm very sorry, Tommy. You've given us great careers and been wonderful to work with, but business is business."

Matt and Toby stood to leave and reached across the long conference table to shake Tommy's hand. Tommy stayed seated, his arms wrapped tightly across his chest in a defensive posture. Bob did the same, making it clear he had nothing for them either. Both men pulled their hands back and turned to walk out the door, looking back one last time as they disappeared from Tommy's view.

"This is insane, Bob! I have never been so disrespected in my life. I'm Tommy Model for Pete's sake! I made those guys who they are. And this Jacques fella refusing to meet with me! What is that all about?"

"I don't know Tommy, but I'll get to the bottom of it."

"I tell you what ... you and Milt better figure out a way to shove this album down their throats. They agreed to allow me to release what I wanted to, and now they're going back on that promise."

"I know, I know."

"We've got to get out on tour to get some money flowing in. And just so we're clear ... there is no way I'm going to start writing and recording new songs with Bizzy again. Besides, he's moved on with that hack, Jackie James and his band Silverback. Did you know they are on this same crappy label with me now? How did that ever happen?"

"It's a mess, Tommy. That's for sure."

"Figure out a way to fix it, Bob. Okay?"

"We'll work it out somehow," despondently replied Bob.

As Tommy and Bob rose to leave the conference room, Tommy kicked over the chair at the head of the table. He stormed along the hall and back to the lobby where he expected Cindy to be waiting. To his surprise, she wasn't there.

Turning to the receptionist, Tommy asked. "Excuse me, Miss? Did the woman I came in with go to the restroom?"

"Uh, well ... she, uh ..." stuttered the young intern.

"Come on, honey ... I don't have all day. Where did she go?"

"She's in the executive dining room down the hall, but I ...."

Tommy interrupted in his typical chauvinistic tone, "Thank you, baby!" then barged off in the direction the receptionist had pointed.

He opened two closed doors in the hall looking for the executive dining room. One turned out to be a vacant office and the other a cleaning supply closet. Reaching a third door, Tommy didn't hesitate to push it open.

As he did, his brain burned in the image of the backside of a man's naked body, his hips thrusting forcefully between a woman's outstretched legs that extended straight and high in a "V" formation. Her face was hidden from Tommy's view, but she moaned excessively with each forward motion, obviously enjoying the experience. Tommy quickly pulled the door shut and laughed, thinking he had caught two employees in the act. He started back along the hallway to continue his search for Cindy, but out of the corner of his eye saw a plaque on the wall next to the door he had just entered. To his dismay it read, *Executive Dining Room.*

Stopping dead in his tracks, Tommy's face shifted from a smile to intense anger. He reopened the door and charged in to find that the woman shielded from view, was in fact, Cindy, who was still going at it strong with her mystery lover.

Tommy leapt forward like a wild animal and yanked the man backwards by the shoulders, pulling him off his shocked and mortified girlfriend.

"No, Tommy, no!" screamed Cindy.

In one swift move, Tommy turned the man and punched him in the face so hard that it sent his foe reeling back against Cindy still lying on the table. Breathing heavily, he looked on in disgust at his bloodied and stunned victim.

Tommy squinted and twitched his eye. "Of all people you could do this with, you had to pick this loser?"

The man stood up straight and moved in close to Tommy.

"I'm no loser! I'm the guy who's going to take everything you have. First, I got your producer, and now I just moved on to phase two by banging the crazy out of your girl. And I did it a hundred times better than you could even imagine! She'll be feeling me for weeks."

Tommy's fist once again found its mark, knocking Jackie James out cold.

CHAPTER TEN

A UNIFORMED POLICE OFFICER UNCUFFED TOMMY. He sat across the desk from Galactic Records' CEO, Jacques Morel. Bob paced in tight turns behind Tommy's chair as the tension in the room mounted.

"Would you like to sit, Bob?" calmly asked Jacques in a heavy French accent.

"No, I would not like to sit, Jacques!" retorted Bob. "What I would like to know is what kind of circus are you running around here? Your people had my client handcuffed! Are you nuts?"

On the verge of losing control, Bob tried to calm himself. "Look ... we were excited to come meet with Matt and Toby who we've become good friends with over the past five years. Unfortunately, they have obviously been brainwashed by whatever agenda you are pushing here. Completely out of the blue, they tell us that Tommy is no longer the viable superstar who made their entire careers. And you don't even have the professional courtesy and courage to show up at this fake meeting. Instead, you defer to them to deliver your predetermined verdict."

Still standing behind him, Bob put his hands on Tommy's shoulders for effect and continued. "My client built Honeycutt

Records. How that idiot, Paul Watkins, God rest his soul, was able to ruin the opportunity he had before him is beyond me. But what's even more idiotic, is that you knew full well that our producer on the past four albums, who was also one of Tommy's best friends, left him to go work with Jackie James and his no-count band, Silverback. Yet you apparently had the audacity or stupidity ... I'm not sure which, to apparently schedule a meeting with Jackie at the same time Tommy is here? Unless he just randomly comes to the office and hangs around. Are you insane? Did you ask him to have sex with Tommy's girlfriend too?"

Bob paused, concerned that in his attack on Jacques he had been insensitive to Tommy. "I'm sorry, Tommy. No offense."

"It's okay, Bob. Let's get this over with. I'm completely numb about the whole thing," replied Tommy.

"Look what you've done to my client," said Bob. "If it were to get out, this debacle would no doubt irreparably damage Jackie James' reputation. When fans find out what he did to Tommy, it'll be chaos for him. So if you don't want me to go to the press to make sure the entire world knows what went on here today, then you'll agree to stop messing around and release the album as it is. Just uphold your promise. And oh yeah ... while we're at it, you'll agree to promote at least two singles spending no less than a million bucks on each. We're not dumb. We know this isn't the best album he's ever created. But he's Tommy Model, man! You better wake up to the opportunity you have with him on your roster."

"Are you through?" sternly inquired Jacques. Bob shook his head up and down and nervously swallowed hard as the label exec returned volley.

"Sure ... we'll release the album and promote two singles at a million dollars a pop to keep the story under wraps. But know this ... Tommy Model is in the sunset of his career, and as far as I'm concerned, he's done here. We paid Bizzy quite well to leave your miserable little project behind. There was no way he could refuse us resolving his gambling debts and burying him in enough drugs to keep him happy while he works his magic on Silverback's next album. Addictive personalities are so easy to manipulate. Beyond that, it didn't take much. And Paul ... well, he kept holding out on us, trying to find a way to make it work without selling Honeycutt. We really couldn't afford to keep waiting. Let's just say, that perhaps we helped things along a little. Remember that when you think you know who you're dealing with here."

Tommy interrupted, "Are you saying that you had something to do with Paul's death?"

Jacques returned a sinister glare towards Tommy. "We bought Honeycutt to put the last nail in the Tommy Model coffin. Doing so will get you out of the way for the next big wave of music we're bringing to the world. It's a massive rising tsunami called *grunge*. I'm sure you've heard of it."

"It's total crap," replied Tommy.

"No, it's infectious, and the world is going to embrace it like a crazed lover. Being a grunge artist himself, that's why Jackie James can invite a sweet, young girl for an innocent cup of coffee in the executive dining room. Then, the next thing she knows, she has her legs in the air experiencing the same intensity and fever that the world is about to."

Jacques laughed loudly like an evil villain projecting his menacing presence from an old-time Vaudeville stage.

Tommy growled with pent-up rage, leapt to his feet, and began to climb across the desk going after Jacques. Bob grabbed him by the legs and pulled back with all his might. With Tommy on his feet again, Bob wrapped his arms tightly around from behind and across Tommy's chest. He squirmed and lurched to break free, but Bob had the leverage and pulled his client towards the door.

Breathing heavily, Tommy dug his boot in firmly enough to stop Bob momentarily. It gave him a chance to cast one parting verbal blow at Jacques.

"One of these days, when you don't see it coming, I'm going to ruin your world, you scumbag. And you'll definitely know it was me who has destroyed you. You can rest assured of that. Release the album, and spend the money to promote the singles, but don't ever expect another song out of me! You got it?"

Jacques smiled. "Thank you, Tommy. That's exactly what I hoped you would say. Now get out before I have you thrown out."

Bob pulled Tommy out of Jacques' office and finally let him go as he closed the door behind.

"All right ... calm down," instructed Bob. "I know you are upset, but let's just go. Do not do anything crazy on the way out. Okay?"

Tommy took a deep breath and began walking the long hallway towards the lobby. When they reached the large open waiting room, Cindy was sitting in the corner sobbing. As Bob and Tommy passed she stood to follow them out. Quickly catching up, she reached out to grab Tommy's hand. He jerked away as her fingers touched his, then he stopped and turned.

"What are you doing? Leave me alone," scolded Tommy.

"But Tommy."

"You know what? I really liked you. I'm usually the person who destroys a relationship. So thank you for beating me to it this time."

"Tommy, please," begged Cindy. "I swear I think Jackie put something in my coffee because I had no intention of doing what I did. I know that sounds unbelievable, but I can't explain it, because I do care about you. Please give me another chance."

"You know, you're probably right that he drugged you. That's the kind of degenerate Jackie James is. Jacques probably even orchestrated the whole thing. But the image of you two together is so scorched into my mind now that it can't be erased. I despise that little punk more than you can ever know. When I look at you, it makes me think of how much I hate him, and I literally want to vomit. So go and live your beach-bikini life back in Malibu. We're done. Now excuse me, but Bob and I need to go."

Cindy grabbed Tommy's hand and held it to her face. She kissed his palm in one last desperate attempt to change his mind.

"Please, baby! I don't even have enough money to get back home. You can't abandon me like this!"

Tommy reached into his pocket and pulled out a thick, folded-over block of cash. He peeled off a thousand dollars and handed it to Cindy.

"Here, this should do it. I should have just paid you in the beginning like every other whore I've been with."

Cindy reacted without thinking and slapped Tommy's face, then quickly reached out to console his reddening cheek. Tommy dropped the cash and turned towards the open elevator as the bills slowly floated to the ground landing around Cindy's feet.

"Tommy please!" pleaded Cindy as tears continued to stream down her face.

The elevator doors closed and Tommy and Bob stood in silence as it began to drop. Bob was somewhat relieved that Tommy seemed so calm considering all that had just happened. Then suddenly, without warning, Tommy reached out and opened the emergency phone door inside the elevator wall. He ripped the phone from its cord and began hammering the shiny metal door. He attacked his reflection with all of his might until finally, the phone shattered. The elevator door was heavily cratered from the attack, and Tommy now stood staring back at a carnival funhouse mirror version of himself.

Bob put his hand on Tommy's shoulder and forced a half-hearted laugh. "So should you finish off that mean old Tommy Model reflection? I hear he can be a real jerk sometimes."

Tommy finally cracked a smile, then began to cry uncontrollably ... the emotion of so much gone bad so quickly, finally overcoming him.

The elevator stopped, and the door opened. Two businessmen in suits and ties tried to enter as Tommy turned his head to the back to hide his anguish. Bob held his hand out to stop their approach.

"Get the next one," he directed.

Ignoring his demand, they continued to try to push past Bob who reached out and grabbed the collar of the one closest to him. "I said, get the next one!"

Lifting his hands in the air as if being held at gunpoint, the man backed out of the elevator with his friend following his lead, as the door closed behind them.

The elevator finally reached the lobby floor, and Tommy wiped the watery remnants from his face. He tilted his head to shield his red eyes from view as they walked out past a flood of people who entered as they exited. He and Bob pushed through revolving doors and stepped out to the bustling Manhattan sidewalk where their limo driver stood awaiting their departure.

Tommy turned and looked skyward, following the line of the side of the enormous building towering above him. He paused, clenched his teeth, and shook his head in disgust, then turned to Bob and said, "Call and get the plane ready. We need to get back to L.A. and prepare for a tour."

CHAPTER ELEVEN

TOMMY STOOD CENTER-STAGE fiercely pounding the strings of his guitar while belting out the ending chorus of his hit song, "Luxury." With the final drum crash, he tilted his head downward and stood silently with his eyes closed. He slid the strap of his guitar off his shoulders and with an outstretched arm, handed it off to his tech. All the while, he never opened his eyes or moved his head from its bowed position.

Tommy's bass player, Eric Tucker cut through the awkward silence, asking what was undoubtedly the question on everyone else's mind.

"Are you okay, Tommy?"

Tommy raised his hand, index finger pointing slightly upward as if saying, *Just give me a minute.*

He finally lifted his head, grabbed the mic from its stand, held it to his mouth and turned to face his band.

"Mates, that was one of the worst rehearsals I think we've ever had. I'm trying to rack my brain to figure out what the problem is. Is it me? Are you hungry? Are you hungover? Do you need to get laid? What is it? I honestly don't think it's me because I actually know how to play my music. But that ability is light years ahead of where each of you are right now."

Tommy paused and signaled to the sound engineer to raise his volume. He continued his rant while escalating his fervor with every word that ripped from his mouth.

"So do we need to get some food? Perhaps some more beer and liquor, or maybe even some girls up in here ... whatever it takes to fix this? You tell me. It's as if we were performing five different songs at the same time, and the last I checked, we aren't a jazz band. So I really need you to give me some idea as to what the problem is ... and I mean, right now!"

With his final words, Tommy kicked over the mic stand, and it violently crashed to the stage floor.

The band members stood in silence, shell-shocked at Tommy's outburst. Their boss was well known for often berating those who irked him outside of their close-knit inner circle. But other than some occasional constructive criticism, being on the receiving end of this level of rage was a new experience for most of them.

"Does anyone have an answer for me?" Tommy hammered home the pressing question.

Eric finally took the bait.

"Tommy, I don't want to upset you any worse than you already are. We've all been together for a long time now, so I have to tell you that we're concerned about earning enough money to support our families if this tour doesn't go well. Just before rehearsal, we heard that most, if not all of the venues we'll be performing at, are smaller theaters instead of the arenas we normally play. You've always paid us handsome bonuses when attendance at a show has exceeded ten thousand seats, so we're assuming that extra income probably won't happen this time around. If not, that will be a big hit for us, financially."

Eric took a long, nervous sip of beer from a red plastic cup and then resumed his assessment.

"Anyway ... it's hard for us to believe that the first single not doing so well can have this big of an impact on a tour so quickly. What other explanation could there be for only getting booked at small venues? Then again ... maybe the rapid decline in fan interest is more related to external factors. There's the huge shift in musical tastes, coupled by much higher ticket prices across the board, plus the economy is down, overall."

"Really?" asked Tommy, sarcastically feigning interest in what he recognized as one of Eric's frequent, drug-fueled rambles.

"Yeah. You see, fans don't have as much expendable income as they did a year ago. And what they do have, they are spending to go see ultra-poppy artists and grunge bands. I'm not sure anything can be done to fix that. A big hit record would obviously help, but I don't think we have one of those right now ... at least not from the new songs we've heard so far."

Tommy slowly moved towards Eric, his face holding the intensity of a stalking cheetah.

"So do you speak for the entire band?" inquired Tommy.

"In this case, I believe I do."

"And you have become some sort of analyst on the state of the economy, ticket prices, and worldwide musical interests as a whole? questioned, Tommy. "I'm trying to make sure I understand."

"I wouldn't call myself an analyst. I'm just explaining to you that we're a little spooked right now because there seems to be some things happening outside of anyone's control. As a result, our livelihoods could ultimately be affected. And that fear is magnified by the new music not resonating like we all expected it would. Without any hope of things improving in the short term, all of that worry is affecting our playing, for sure."

Tommy stared intently into Eric's eyes and was unable to hold back any longer.

"Actually, all of that mumbo-jumbo sounds to me like you think you're an analyst. You know, I hear Wall Street is hiring, and I sure don't want to stand in your way. Why don't you pack your gear, hop a plane to New York, and give it a shot? You sure couldn't do any worse than you are as a bass player right now."

Eric swallowed hard fearing he had crossed over into the land of no return.

"That's crazy, man. You know I want to be here with you, Tommy. What is this Wall Street stuff? I'm just saying ..."

Tommy moved so close to Eric that their chests touched. With all of the seriousness he could muster, he pulled the trigger.

"Get out! I never want to see you again! You hear me? You're as ungrateful as Bizzy. I took you from nothing and gave you a gig when no one else would. Now you live in a seven thousand square foot home, drive a six-figure Italian sports car, and have three girlfriends in addition to your swimsuit model wife. And you want to come up with a bunch of nonsense as to why you can't perform when the truth is you are bouncing off the walls, high on coke all of the time. That's the real problem here."

Tommy turned towards the other band members and continued. "You know, it's pitiful that the first time things get a little rough, you blokes want to bail on me like everyone else has lately. Well, I'll save Eric here the trouble of figuring out when he's finally reached his breaking point. Like I said ... get out!"

"But Tommy, please ..." begged Eric.

"Leave!" screamed Tommy.

Eric unplugged his bass, turned and walked off the stage. He moped down the stairs and across the open space in front of the risers, finally exiting the rehearsal hall. No one said a word during Eric's march of shame.

When the door finally closed behind Eric, Tommy held the mic back to his mouth and asked, "So does anyone else want to make a stupid comment?"

Silence consumed the room until Tommy repeated his question.

"Guys, I'm looking for some confirmation here. Does anyone have aspirations to be an analyst, a soothsayer, a weather forecaster ... anything other than a musician?"

Each of the three remaining band members shook their heads *no*, looking on in complete fear of what Tommy might do next in his unpredictable state.

"I didn't think so," replied Tommy. "Now, I want to hear the songs performed the way they are supposed to be or I'll find other players who can get the job done. The tour will be fine. Just get all of this silly worry out of your heads. I realize that radio singles drive everything in this business, and I knew this first one wouldn't be a big hit because I'm trying out some new things. That being said, our fans will love this new music on tour, trust me. It'll be great live."

Tommy paused as if deep in thought, then finding the inspiration he was seeking, he continued.

"Look ... if you guys give me one hundred percent, I'll pay each of you what you earned in total over the last tour, regardless of what happens. Small venues, large venues ... it's all the same. Just commit and stop bringing negativity around me. I have enough of that already. Sound good?"

The band members collectively nodded their heads in silent approval.

"Great! Let's take ten and then we'll try 'Luxury' one more time. I'll handle the bass parts for now."

Tommy purposefully dropped the mic to the floor in disgust. Landing with a loud thud, it echoed and quickly progressed into squealing feedback. The sound tech frantically jumped back to his mixing board to cut the volume on the dejected mic. Tommy hopped off the front of the stage and marched over to Bob who stood with his arms crossed and shaking his head side to side.

"That was nuts, Tommy," said Bob.

"You think I was wrong?"

"No, Eric was nuts, not you," responded Bob.

"Listen ... I want you to find out who told them we are getting booked in smaller venues. Only you, me, and my booking agent should know that at this point. Those dates haven't even been locked in yet, so we've got a leak somewhere."

"I agree. I'm on it."

"I also want you to see if Eric has been receiving any side-money lately. I know I'm a bit paranoid, but I have a suspicion some of these guys may be getting paid by Jacques to purposely sabotage this tour. They've never played this bad before, and I'm not buying that nonsense from Eric. They could have asked me about their bonuses. Instead, they get so depressed that they can't get through a single song without someone screwing up? Give me a break."

"Yeah, it does seem a bit odd."

"Right? So if they are part of Jacques' plot, I've got to weed them out before it's too late. In fact, look into every person in the band and crew, my booking agent, the promoters, the sound and lighting company ... anyone you can think of that will touch this tour. I don't care how much it costs! I'm sick of this lack of loyalty."

"I know this great P.I. who will get to the bottom of it for us," replied Bob.

Tommy's eyes brightened as if he had a great discovery.

"You know what ... since we're going to hire a private investigator, let's dig into Jacques and get some dirt on that scumbag while we're at it. He's obviously not going to quit coming after me, so we've got to find something to stop him. I don't understand why this bloke hates me so much. And what is with this crazy agenda he has pushing grunge music. That garage-band crap will never be mainstream."

"Maybe you're the only real threat to what he sees as his vision for a new music revolution. With nothing else unique on the scene right now, he's latching on to grunge, I guess."

"I'm one artist. What is he so worried about?"

"You're not just any artist ... you're Tommy Model. He seems to be desperately trying to get his name marked in the history books as the guy who changed music. In his lunatic mind, maybe if you retain your popularity that continues to leave the door open for more straightforward, rock-inspired artists who have a similar sound and style to you. He's cutting off the head of the snake, so to speak ... not that you're a snake. You know what I mean. Please don't fire me for saying that."

"What? I'm not going to fire you. Stop being ridiculous. So you think it's all about Jacques being seen as this brilliant agent-of-change, and making a fortune in the process if he actually pulls it off?"

"Maybe. What else could it be?"

"I've heard of new and developing artists being signed to dead end record deals to reduce competition for a label's top acts. I've never seen someone trying to destroy a successful artist's career to make way for a big unknown like this guy is doing. I just don't get it."

The door to the rehearsal room exploded open as Eric came charging back in a violent rage. He was moving so fast his long, wiry hair was sticking straight out behind his head like the tail of a wild mustang. Eric's nose and upper lip were covered in a white residue as he searched the room for Tommy. Obviously hopped-up even more than before, he seemed intent on delivering some payback. He reached the side of the stage before turning and finally spotting his target across the room.

Eric adjusted course and made his final run towards Tommy who inconspicuously reached into a large road storage case directly behind him. He strengthened his grip on the contents inside while never breaking focus on a fast-approaching Eric. Within a few feet of reaching his intended victim, Eric clenched his fist and raised it high, ready to cast his blow. Seemingly, out of nowhere, one of Tommy's massive security guards intercepted the cocaine-crazed bass player. He grabbed Eric from behind and placed him in a full nelson headlock.

Not ready to give up the fight, Eric leapt into the air and extended out both feet in his best effort to deliver a kick to the face. Tommy was fully prepared. Having unsheathed a large, golden drum cymbal from its case, he swung with all his might and swatted away Eric's foot like an annoying little gnat.

The security guard quickly dragged a screaming Eric out of the room while the other band members and crew stared on with mouths wide open. Tommy sighed in relief that his idea to beef up security around him had paid off. He turned to Bob, smiled, and nervously joked, "Well one thing is for sure ... Eric is never gonna make it on Wall Street acting like that."

CHAPTER TWELVE

Butch Remington had a stellar reputation for being the P.I. to the stars. He was tall, stylish, and charming. And whether real or made up, he had a cool name that perfectly fit his image and profession. Above all else though, he delivered high-level results in a confidential and timely manner, and that's exactly what Tommy wanted.

With every unusual event that had recently transpired, Tommy was growing more and more paranoid. Bob had already contemplated hiring Butch after their meeting with Jacques in New York, so when Eric Tucker lost his mind at rehearsals, he was already fully prepared to pitch the idea to his rock star client. What Bob didn't expect was how many people Tommy would want to investigate all at once. He now struggled with the logistics of that demand while meeting with Butch.

"Look, Butch ... I totally understand that you normally focus on one target at a time, but Tommy is extremely concerned that there is a major conspiracy afoot, likely being orchestrated by Galactic Records' CEO, Jacques Morel."

"I see," replied Butch.

"Maybe he's wrong, or maybe he's right, but Tommy's last tour generated north of one hundred million dollars. We're now looking at estimated earnings of about a third of that for the upcoming tour if something doesn't change soon. There are several reasons why that may be the case, and I don't want to lead your investigation down a path with my own suspicions, but just know that we believe there is a plan in action designed to completely derail Tommy's career, and that's why we need your help.

"And you think this Jacques Morel is the main person behind it?" asked Butch.

"Without a doubt. But we also think it could extend to several other people who are very close to Tommy, and that's why the list I'm giving you is so long."

"Well, Bob ... looking into so many folks at the same time is going to be a challenge. I'll have to re-prioritize my team, so it will definitely cost you."

"I understand. How much are we talking about?" asked Bob.

"Two hundred grand ought to do it. You guys willing to go that deep?"

"Including incidentals, yes. I just don't want to get into paying a bunch of additional expenses on top of that."

Butch sat silently thinking for a few seconds, then shot his arm across the table to shake Bob's hand.

"You got a deal. Tell Tommy I'll have a report to him within two weeks."

"Wow, that's fast. I hope you're as good as they say you are."

"Actually, I'm better," confidently replied Butch. "I'll be in touch."

LATER THAT AFTERNOON TOMMY HUNG UP THE PHONE after getting an update from Bob. He sat silently considering the weight of what he had put in motion. Tommy realized that not everyone he was concerned about would prove to be working against him. And through the process, he may even find out things he didn't really want to know. But it was a necessary evil to preserve his popularity and minimize the signifcant blow his fortune was preparing to take, especially if he had to cover a significant tour shortfall, or even cancel several dates altogether.

Feeling depressed, he pulled a clear plastic bag from his pocket. After pouring its contents onto the granite countertop, he cut the cocaine into two, tidy, thin rows and wasted no time jetting them up his nose. Feeling the burn of his immediate high, he called out to his assistant Monique, who entered the room wearing nothing but a tiny, red, two-piece bathing suit.

Monique's beautiful face, framed by her long, curly, dark hair, was well-matched by her toned, tan body. It was a combination that was often more than Tommy could resist. She was one of the most loyal people in his life, so for the past three years, he had controlled the temptation of making any advances towards her, other than casual and mutual flirtations. Her dedication and friendship was far too important to ruin with short-term ecstasy, even though he was sure it would be an unforgettable experience.

"Hi, Tommy. What do you need, darling?" asked Monique as she slowly moved towards him, strutting gracefully like a model on a catwalk.

"Have you been out at the pool, or is that what you're going to start wearing around the house now?" joked Tommy.

"I was catching some rays for a minute, silly. What can I do for you?"

"I want you to call and see if those two escorts you got for me after the last awards show are available tonight. I need a little escape."

"You want both of them at the same time again?" casually clarified Monique.

"Yeah," replied Tommy, vibrating his head like a dog shaking off water with the buzz starting to rattle his brain.

Monique peered behind Tommy to see the remnants of his binge on the counter and forced a smile.

"That stuff is gonna kill you, baby. You don't need it. You need to find love. All of the bad things that are happening right now are because you are only focused on Tommy Model."

Tommy forced a smile and turned his eyes downward in embarrassment.

"I know, you're right. But that's a quick fix, and the other isn't. So, for now, drugs, drink, and escorts will have to do the trick until I get beyond all of the craziness. You're killing me with this bathing suit, you know? I don't think it's a good idea you walking around here with only that on. After all, I am a rock star, and we're not known for fighting back our temptations."

Monique slowly slid towards Tommy until the space between them was just inches apart. Her large, mostly exposed breasts nearly touched the top of Tommy's abdomen. The seductive aroma of coconut oil filled the air as heat emanated from her still sun-charged body, doing its best to melt what was left of his resistance.

Monique looked up into Tommy's eyes and whispered, "So you don't trust yourself with me?"

Tommy leaned down and hovered his lips so close to Monique's that he could feel her sweet breath. They stared intently into each other's eyes as Tommy fingertips glided along the soft skin of her arms, beginning at her shoulders and pausing at her elbows. Tommy could feel chill bumps form against the slight pressure of his fingers. Monique sensed herself tremor in anticipation that they might finally, physically connect. It was a scenario they had both extensively fantasized about since the day they met. Tommy smiled again and finally answered her question.

"No, I don't trust myself with you. And as much as I'd like to rip off this little swimsuit, throw your sexy body on this counter and do things that would send you into such shock that it would ruin you forever, I can't do that, because I love you and I don't want to lose you. I couldn't bear the thought of not having you in my life."

Monique grinned, then moved her lips slightly to the side of Tommy's and gently kissed him on the cheek.

"I know. And I love you too. But don't be so sure I couldn't handle it. I probably know you better than anyone does right now. I realize you're not going to stop being you, so I wouldn't expect that. Just know you don't always need to call escorts when you want to get away from it all. And don't be so confident that I wouldn't be the one who would ruin you. I have some talents and skills that would make you never want to touch another line of coke or bottle of liquor, ever again."

Monique softly patted Tommy's face, then turned and walked away, swaying her hips from side to side and giving Tommy one more tempting view of what he had passed on.

Without turning, Monique said, "I'll make sure the ladies will be here at 11:00 p.m.," then strolled back out to the pool deck and into the bright California sunshine.

CHAPTER THIRTEEN

TWO WEEKS LATER, Bob and Butch Remington sat on the back deck of Tommy's Malibu beach house. Tommy emerged from inside with a metal tub full of iced-down Beautleg beer. He placed it in the middle of the table and sat to join his guests as they all reached for a bottle at the same time.

Bob and Butch engaged in meaningless small-talk while they nursed their beers. Tommy listened in but was much too nervous for idle chit-chat. He tipped up his bottle and continued guzzling until the last drop of foam had emptied from the bottom. Tommy retrieved another, popped the top, and took a long swig before setting down the half-empty beer on the table. He belched and interrupted the conversation.

"Okay, guys. Enough about baseball and the weather. Can we get to why we're here?"

"To the point, Tommy. I like it," replied Butch. "Well, as crazy as it may seem, you were completely right about your suspicions of a plot against you. But I think you'll be surprised to hear how it all came about, and how far it's traveled to get where it is."

"I'm feeling surprised already. Well, let's have it, Butch."

"Okay, so here's the deal. About two years ago after your concert in Hartford, Connecticut, you met an attractive, forty-one-year-old redhead who came on to you backstage. Three people who were there recall that after several drinks and more than a few lines of cocaine, the two of you retreated to your tour bus where ... let's just say you hooked up. During that encounter, apparently, the sounds coming from inside your bus were so loud and vocal that members of your band and crew huddled outside to listen."

"You're kidding me?" Tommy said.

"Unfortunately not. All three had quite vivid memories of the events that transpired that night, and one apparently even remembered some of the woman's verbalizations. Would you like to hear what he said."

"Sure ... why not?"

Butch flipped open a notepad and donning his glasses, began to read in a monotone fashion.

"And I quote, 'Yeah baby! That's it. Give it to me! Oh, that's so much better than my tiny, little husband could ever do.'"

Tommy held out his hands and shrugged his shoulders, momentarily proud of his accomplishment. Bob laughed at the gesture as Butch continued.

"There's more, but I'll spare you the details. You get the point though. All of that dirty-talk must have inspired you even more because allegedly the bus started rocking so hard the crowd outside joked that it might actually lift off the ground."

Bob and Tommy laughed again.

"It all concluded with ... and I quote once again, 'a loud, drawn-out cry of ecstasy after which the woman moaned, 'Oh, Tommy. That was incredible. I don't think I'll ever be the same.'"

Tommy shook his head in slight embarrassment, then said, "You know, as many times as that same scenario has played out over the past few years with an endless number of women, I remember that lady because she was a bit older. She was sexy as all get-out though, and was really, really into me. But how in the world does that all relate to anything?"

Butch stared at Tommy and removed his glasses, placing them on the table. He turned to look at the sun sparkling on the water and quenched his nervously dry throat with a long drink of beer.

"I'm trying to figure out the best way to tell you the rest of the story, Tommy. It's a doozy. There's no easier way, so I'll just get on with it."

"Is it that bad?" asked Tommy.

"Yeah, it is. Because apparently that fiery, little redhead you slept with, was none other than Angela Morel ... Jacques Morel's wife."

"What? Jacques wife! I had no idea. I thought she was a groupie."

"I wish she had just been a groupie, but that's not the worst of it. Are you sure you want to hear all of this?"

"Yes, yes. Continue."

"Okay. Well ... she didn't have many close friends, but two that we did speak with confirmed that soon after that night, Angela began sliding down a long, dark path. It started with having a series of affairs with much younger men. Most were musicians like you. Although Angela kept most of her personal life private, one of her friends speculated that she must have become obsessed with trying to recapture the emotional high she experienced with you. Jacques is a workaholic, and the affection had been gone from their relationship for years, so he was no help. Unfortunately, it all came to a head one day, when Jacques came home early from work, and he found Angela in their bed having sex with all four members of the thrash-metal band, Gypsy."

Tommy interrupted, "Gypsy? Those guys are as gross as you can get, man. What was she thinking?"

"She obviously wasn't thinking, because she ended up contracting HIV from one of those idiots. Fortunately, her doctor caught it before it could develop into AIDS and she began treatment. So unknowingly you sparked a sexual addiction in Angela, who by the way had supposedly never slept with another man other than Jacques before you rode into town."

"How was I to know all that would happen? We were just having a good time," replied Tommy.

Butch downed the rest of his beer, and after a deep breath, he resumed his report.

"The general consensus seemed to be that the Morels were a dynamic duo who many people thought to be the perfect couple. But it turned out that they weren't at all how others believed them to be. So after an incredibly ugly divorce, and what would have been a lifelong cover-up of what really happened, it all got even more intense from there."

"How can it get any worse, Butch? I mean, I never would have spoken to her if I knew all of this would happen."

"Well, you have to understand that she was never going to have a normal relationship again. She couldn't fulfill the desires of the sexual addiction she had developed for fear of infecting someone else with HIV. So she tried to numb her feelings with various forms of prescription and illegal drugs, and before long she was a homeless, full-blown junkie who had lost everything. Still scarred by the betrayal he felt, Jacques wouldn't support her financially or get her any help to beat the addictions. Eventually, when the mental anguish became too much to bear, she took her own life."

"What?" trembled Tommy, shocked by Butch's ultimate revelation.

"Yeah. And that was about six months ago. When they found her two days later in a house she was squatting in while some friends were out of town, a cassette of your last album was playing in a continuous loop on the stereo."

The three men sat in silence. Tommy's eyes teared up as he looked at his beer bottle and picked at the wet, peeling label. He sighed deeply in efforts to relieve the tension in his chest as he responded to the tragic news.

"It all starts to make sense now. But as incredibly sad as that makes me, I am what I am, and I don't apologize for that. If I had that specific situation to do over, knowing the eventual outcome, I would take it back in a heartbeat. But Angela obviously needed something she wasn't getting at home, and I gave her the excitement she was looking for. In my world, that happens all the time. I'm a fantasy for a lot of women, and that night seemed like good fun to me. Until now."

"You can't take this on your shoulders, Tommy," interjected Bob.

"I know. You're right. And I don't mean to sound callous, but the decisions she made that led to meeting me and everything that came afterward, is not something I am willing to accept the burden of. We're adults, and when you play with fire ... well, you know the rest of that saying. Still, it's extremely painful to hear all of that."

Tommy finished off his beer and grabbed another from the watery pool of melting ice. He popped the top, gulped down half the bottle again, then continued.

"So, Butch ... with all of that being said, am I to assume that Jacques wouldn't agree with the assessment that I don't bear complete responsibility for everything that happened?"

"That would be safe to say," replied Butch.

"And now he's in full-on Tommy Model destruction mode. I guess illogically, in his mind, she's dead because of me, right?" asked Tommy.

"It appears so."

"It's not that he wasn't taking care of his wife or that he didn't help her when she really needed it. If he had been a better husband all along, she never would have pursued me, or anyone else for that matter. But he'll never see that. So since he's intent on blaming me, what's his big plan to take me apart completely? He's obviously off to a running start."

Butch put his glasses back on and flipped through the pages of his notepad. Finding the information he was looking for, he did his best to answer Tommy's question.

"That has a long, twisted answer in itself, but here goes. And just know ... this might be even more upsetting than what I've already told you, so prepare yourself."

"Are you for real? This is nuts!" said Tommy.

"I know. It's really jacked. To start with, Jacques paid Bizzy-B Jonson a million dollars, and that was on top of eliminating all of his drug and gambling debts. In return, he had to leave you and work with Jackie James and Silverback instead."

"Jacques had basically told us that when we had our falling out in New York. I didn't know it was a million dollars though!" raged Tommy. "After everything I did for Bizzy. I'm so gonna get him back for this!"

"Hang on. That's not all."

"Great! What else?"

"Well you probably didn't know this, but Jacques recently became one of the key investors in Honeycutt Records. It turns out that he called-in a multi-million dollar loan he had given Honeycutt to help keep the company afloat until your new album dropped. Jacques wanted it all back immediately. That's what sent Paul Watkins into a tailspin the day he came to the studio and spoke with you. I don't mean to let the cat out of the bag because from our discussions I'm guessing you never told Bob about your little boat ride with Paul the night before he died."

Bob interrupted, "Boat ride? What boat ride, Tommy?"

Tommy waved his hands in an effort to hold Bob at bay.

"I didn't want you to freak out, Bob. Let Butch finish, and I'll fill you in later. Go ahead, Butch."

"I'm sorry, Tommy. I have to tell the entire story, or it won't make sense," explained Butch.

"Whatever. Just get on with it."

"Anyway ... Paul needed to make sure the label was going to generate the level of sales your past albums had. Doing so would have allowed him to pay off the loan and hopefully get Jacques off his back. But when Bizzy quit and word got out that the songs were sub-par, Paul became desperate. That's why he threatened you. I'll skip the whole Catalina Island experience for you to share with Bob later, but after the boat docked back in L.A. early that morning, and you high-tailed it out of there, Jacques was waiting on his own yacht docked nearby. Seeing Paul return, he paid him a visit to ask about his money."

"So do you think that Jacques knew Paul had taken me on the boat the night before?" asked Tommy. "Otherwise, how would he know where to find him?"

"Oh, he definitely knew about it. Apparently, acquiring Honeycutt was always Jacques' intention when he gave Paul the money. Unfortunately the conversation that morning did not go well. When Jacques wouldn't back off of collecting the loan, or Paul selling him the company, Paul threatened to go to the Galactic Records' board of directors and expose Jacques' extortion plot. A massive argument ensued, but Jacques eventually left, and Paul commenced to drowning his troubles in a bottle of rum."

"This is headed in a very scary direction, Butch."

"Unfortunately it is. We have it from a very reliable source that it was at Jacques' direction that your pals, Joe Joe and Ricardo returned to Paul's boat an hour or so later. They found Paul sitting in the fighting chair, still grumbling and nursing the bottle of rum. They were there for one purpose, and that was to eliminate Paul from the equation. So they allegedly injected him with enough adrenaline to kill a bull, which basically exploded his aorta, and made it look like he had a heart attack."

"Wait a minute, I thought Joe Joe and Ricardo worked for Paul?"

"Who are Joe Joe and Ricardo?" asked Bob.

"Later, Bob!" snapped Tommy.

"It took a bit of doing, but we got Ricardo to spill the beans, and he confirmed everything that happened on the boat that morning. They also worked for Jacques, not just Paul, so you're lucky they didn't let the sharks eat you after all."

"What sharks?" screamed Bob.

"Bob if you say one more word, I'm gonna ..." Tommy stopped himself, shook his head and blew out a long, deliberate breath as Bob retreated and leaned back in his chair. "Please go on, Butch."

"As I was saying, they also worked for Jacques who had much more money to burn, so they were easily persuaded to turn on Paul when the time came. With their CEO out of the picture, there wasn't any choice but for Honeycutt to sell to Galactic. As you can see, it's all a very elaborate plan."

"I knew Jacques was behind this. And all because he thinks it's my fault that his marriage fell apart and his ex-wife died. What a sick, demented dirtbag."

"Following the Honeycutt sale, Jacques even brought Matt Millerson and Toby Posner into his scheme. He paid them each one hundred grand for the parts they played. Jacques knew you trusted them from working together at Honeycutt and they could easily get you to New York for the meeting in Galactic's offices."

"Is there no loyalty in this business? Was I not good to these people? This is sickening. So the New York meeting was all a setup?"

"Yes. Originally the plan was to humiliate you by disregarding your music, but when Jacques found out Cindy was coming, he added an extra layer to his scheme as the ultimate payback. Jacques promised Jackie James that his band would be Galactic's highest priority for the next five years, and over that time he would make him a superstar. All he had to do was roofie your girl Cindy and have sex with her while you were in the building. Apparently, Matt and Toby were asked to end their meeting with you at a certain time. I honestly doubt they knew why, but it would have coincided with exactly when Jackie was with Cindy. Jacques wanted you to find them together. Which you obviously did."

"So Cindy was telling me the truth that Jackie drugged her? I'm such an idiot."

Tommy dropped his head into his hands and covered his face in shame. He had developed strong feelings for Cindy, and he now regretted his decision not to believe what she had told him. Bob stood and asked for Butch to hold on while he went into the house to get something. Returning with a bottle of whiskey, he poured three shots. Tommy looked up and glared at Bob, but quickly downed the whiskey and asked for another, as Butch returned to his place in the story.

"If Jacques had stopped there that would have been a nightmare all on its own. But he didn't."

"There's more?" asked Tommy, obviously exhausted from the onslaught.

"Unfortunately, yes. This guy is going to a lot of trouble to ruin you. As you know, Jacques essentially controls the careers of many of the top recording artists in the world. Several are even signed with the same talent agency as you, and ultimately also work with the same concert promoters and venues. We received confirmation from multiple sources that Jacques told most of the key players involved with arranging your tour, to find ways to drive down your income.

He either directly paid or offered kickbacks totaling millions of dollars for each company or person to make it happen."

"This is unbelievable. Are you telling me that my agent is involved in this too?"

"Yup. Your agent, Harry Zackstrom purposefully started by scheduling and routing your tour in a manner that coincided with dates when larger venues were already booked for other concerts or sporting events. Using that as an excuse, he suggested you consider smaller venues, which you and Bob apparently agreed to, probably because you thought there was no other choice."

'That's what he's been telling us for weeks," added Bob in a highly frustrated tone. "It was either perform in theaters or postpone the tour to wait for a better window of opportunity, the latter of which Tommy absolutely did not want to do. Harry's strategy was to start at smaller venues, then as the tour progressed and further out in the schedule, more arena dates should open up. With everything that has happened over the past couple of months, we got a late start on green-lighting a tour, so what Harry had been telling us seemed believable. There's a lot of competition for space out there, so if you don't plan far enough in advance, these kinds of things do happen. The problem is, the current single's lackluster performance has caused a stir and led to a lot of bad press. So much so, that the larger venues available further out in the tour have been reluctant give us the dates we've requested. If the entire tour ends up with Tommy performing at two to three thousand seat venues, it will only generate approximately a third of what the last tour brought in. But go ahead, Butch ... I'm sorry I interrupted."

"It's all good, Bob. Obviously smaller venues have significantly fewer seats than what you are used to, so Tommy's income and profitability are going to be adversely impacted if you move forward with the tour. But you both already know that. What you probably didn't know is that Harry Zackstrom is the person who has coordinated much of the bad press you've been receiving. And he leaked the fact that your performing in theaters before the tour had even been announced, which has only further added to the false narrative that Tommy Model's career is on the decline. As you can see, the whole thing is planned to snowball over time, and the ultimate goal is to severely damage your brand and finances."

"I'm going to kill, Harry. Do you know how much Jacques paid him to do this?"

"Three million dollars," replied Butch. "It had to be enough that it was personally worth his while, and I think that number did it. But I've got some additional unrelated intel on Harry if you ever need it. Unfortunately, even that's not the end of the story."

"I'm gonna throw up," said Tommy.

"Do you need a minute?"

"No, go ahead."

"I'm sorry, Tommy. I know this is tough to hear, but on top of everything else your band was a part of this as well."

"I had a feeling something was going on with those guys. They've all been acting really weird."

"Well, your bass player Eric Tucker's meltdown was not supposed to happen. It was likely that the guilt of taking money from Jacques became too much to bear, so he lost it and blew their little secret. All four guys in your band, as well as your road manager, were on the take. We found that payments of five hundred thousand dollars each have been recently deposited into their bank accounts."

"This never ends," remarked Tommy, his face now sullen and pale even in the bright glow of the afternoon sun.

"We spoke to Eric, and he came clean. Supposedly they were to wait until the tour started before initiating their coup. The plan has probably been changed by now, but they were going to play horribly at the first show. Then when you surely reamed them out afterward, they were all going to quit at the same time. That would leave you in the middle of a tour completely without a band. Even if you were able to quickly put another group together, once you got that in order, your road manager was going to walk out and take his entire team with him, essentially grinding the tour to an abrupt halt."

"Okay. I've heard enough. I'm numb and lost for words, and obviously, I have to fire everyone."

"Well, there's one more thing you should know, and that's it. Do you want to hear it?"

"Sure. Why not? We've come this far."

"If you do continue without doing anything, Jacques also has two women lined up to accuse you of raping them backstage after the first show in Boston. Accusations by the two women will undoubtedly generate a firestorm of bad publicity. As a result, all of the remaining venues on the tour will probably pull your dates and have to refund money to thousands of angry fans. It would likely be a career-killer, or pretty close to it."

Tommy shook his head in silence while Bob intervened.

"And all because Tommy unknowingly slept with Jacques' wife? This is insane. I can't believe he got to so many people. I guess money talks, and he's thrown a lot of it around. So where do we go from here, Butch?"

"Well, this might be tough to consider, but I would suggest canceling the tour. It's going to end in disaster one way or another. If you do it, at least you're the one who shuts it down, and you can manage the narrative in the press. I'd also recommend trying to get out of your deal with Galactic, because based on the profile we developed on Jacques, he is never gonna give up. He lost who he believed to be the love of his life, and he's blaming that solely on you, Tommy. It doesn't matter if that's sane or not. All that matters is he has the power to destroy you, especially in his position of influence leading a corporation with an unlimited supply of money."

"I hate to see us give in to this guy," emotionally expressed Bob. "This is what he wants."

"Well ... you could consider having him taken out," stoically suggested Butch.

Shocked at the suggestion, Tommy fired back.

"What? As much as I would like to right now, I'm not going to have someone bumped off. Why would you even mention that, Butch?"

"I'm just saying it's an option. You're giving up a lot because of one person's vendetta, and many people would hire a hit-man for far less. It's your call though. You either give in or do something to stop it. Those are really your only two choices."

Tommy shook his head in silence again as Butch concluded their discussion.

"Give it some time to sink in and let me know if you want us to look into anyone else, or if you decide that other idea isn't as crazy after all. I don't do that kind of work, but I know people who do. This is a dangerous game Jacques is playing, and I don't know how far he's willing to take it. He's already apparently behind the death of one person, and that's the only reason I mentioned going to an extreme."

Butch looked at his watch, surprised at the time.

"Shoot! I have to run, guys. You have my number. Let me know if I can be of any further assistance."

Butch stood and shook Tommy's hand. Bob walked him out while Tommy remained behind on the deck. He stood and placed his hands on the wooden rail, peering out into the endless blue of the Pacific. A pod of dolphins swimming by erupted through the calm surface and attacked a school of baitfish that collectively attempted to flee. For at least one frantic straggler, his time had come to an end. Over and over again the same scene played out, until bored of the easy pickings, the dolphins moved on, further along the shore.

With all he had learned from the investigation, Tommy knew Jacques would never stop or tire of trying. If he didn't want to end up like a hapless fingerling chased by a relentless dolphin, he knew he had to make some difficult decisions. Some major changes were in order if he had any chance of saving his career, and quite possibly, his life.

CHAPTER FOURTEEN

TOMMY MODEL WORLD TOUR CANCELED

THE HEADLINE of the entertainment section of the Sunday newspaper was bold and definite. As Tommy skimmed the article beneath, he noticed it followed nearly word-for-word the press release his publicist had issued. It read:

Model stated that his talent agency and record label were determined to see him tour in support of his current album, but those were never really his plans.

"After wrapping up my last world tour only a few months ago, then immediately heading into the studio to record and release the new album, I was hoping I could catch my breath before heading back out on the road again," Model explained. "Unfortunately, I guess somewhere along the way my team and I got our signals crossed, because the next thing I knew, my agent Harry Zackstrom, informed me that he had already tentatively committed us to more than twenty dates here in the states. And for some reason, he thought it would be cool for us to embark on a theater tour instead of performing in arenas as we normally do. Fortunately, I was able to

resolve the confusion before tickets went on sale, and we've canceled those shows for now."

Tommy scanned down further:

As a result of the communication breakdown, Model has parted ways with Zackstrom and his agency, WCA. With all dates now officially off the books, after a few months of R&R, Model plans to begin work on his next album, with the delayed world tour to follow its release.

"I'll be missing my fans terribly by then, but hopefully everyone will understand that I just need a little holiday, and they'll look forward to our next time around. We rushed the current album, most of which was written while I was still on the road. Unfortunately, I think that shows in the recordings. I'm still very proud of Modelesque because I was trying out some new things, but it probably won't go down as one of my best."

Tommy finished reading the article and closed the paper. What the press didn't know is that behind the scenes Harry Zackstrom had been forced into a corner. During Butch Remington's investigation, the P.I. had stumbled onto what had now become invaluable dirt.

It turned out that Harry was not only having an affair on his wife of eight years, whom he also had three children with, but he was doing so with an executive from another talent agency. Not ready to come clean on his own, and possibly lose his marriage and career in the process, Harry took the fall. In his actor's role, he was merely the over-eager, rogue agent who booked a tour without consulting his client. While that admission alone would leave a sting on his reputation, it was nothing compared to the financial and personal costs revealing an affair with a business competitor would have leveled. That, in addition to the three million dollar payday he had personally received outside of the agency from Jacques Morel, would have surely pulled the plug on his career.

Many within the music business would likely realize that a tour could not be planned or booked without Tommy's pre-approval, but the goal was to console his fans, not industry insiders. In one press release printed by hundreds, if not thousands of publications worldwide, Tommy had eliminated several co-conspirators and temporarily thwarted Jacques efforts to destroy him publicly. It felt good to be on top of the situation for once.

There ... it was done, but now what? Tommy pondered in his mind.

He sipped a hot cup of coffee and savored the flavor, finding himself strangely a bit relieved about his decision. His momentary lapse of positivity was quickly sabotaged by the thought that there was no way he was going to give Galactic another album, even if his contract required it. The question was ... how does one get out of a record deal if the head of the record label is intent on ruining your career at all costs?

TWO DAYS EARLIER, Bob had informed Jacques Morel that Tommy did, in fact, want to be released from his agreement with Galactic Records, conceding that the CEO had finally won his vengeance. To celebrate his victory and rid himself of Tommy forever, Bob suggested that Jacques simply *just let him go*. As anticipated, however, Jacques refused the offer and instead expressed his intent to exercise Galactic's option for Tommy's next and final album. Unfortunately, what sounded like a change-of-heart and positive interest in Tommy's career was nothing more than a sneaky chess move to derail it even further.

Tommy was confident that no matter how incredible the music might be on his next album, even if he did begin working on one, Jacques would never accept delivery of his master recordings. Him doing so, or not, was a key term of Tommy's agreement which had legally transferred to Galactic as part of the Honeycutt merger.

Instead, the label-head would likely keep demanding changes or completely new material, over, and over, and over again. By doing so, he would tie Tommy up indefinitely under the guise that the recordings weren't commercially viable, an opinion entirely within the label's control. Jacques had already shown that money was no object in his efforts as a saboteur. Even if the recording and video production costs stretched into the millions, Tommy doubted that anything could deter Jacques from his ultimate mission to dismantle the Tommy Model empire.

AFTER RECEIVING JACQUES' REFUSAL to release him from his contract, and with the anticipation of future events to come, Tommy met with Bob and Milt Hamstein to discuss fighting the matter legally. During their meeting Bob suggested they wait until Galactic rejected a new album for better evidence of wrongdoing. Hopefully, that could help force a renegotiation and free Tommy from their stranglehold.

To counter Bob's assertion, Milt speculated that since the current album's sales were off to such a bad start, with no signs of improving, the financial impact could later bolster Galactic's case against Tommy. Not wanting a repeat failure, the label's legal team would likely try to show they were justified in not approving any future recordings they deemed insufficient. This position would be supported by the fact that they were forced to accept and release the current album without any input. Waiting for the rejection that was sure to come would likely just waste time and not help their strategy in any way. Instead, Milt wanted to use the struggling sales figures to their advantage now, rather than risk it working against them later.

With touring indefinitely on hold, Tommy would not be generating the millions of dollars he had earned over the past four years. It was income he would ultimately need to maintain his lifestyle unless he was to seriously cut back on his spending, dip into his investments, or dispose of assets. Tommy's financial business manager had developed a strategy whereby Tommy could sell most of his sports-cars, motorcycles, boats, and even an airplane, along with all of his homes, except one. This would not only give Tommy much needed cash but would also reduce the significant ongoing costs that accompanied each luxury item and property.

If Tommy could make the necessary adjustments, and remain smart and controlled in his spending, he could afford to live comfortably for several years if necessary, while holding out on recording a new album. Hopefully, Jacques would soon tire of the game and possibly resign, or be fired by Galactic's board of directors, all scenarios that could resolve the matter without any legal action. From a P.R. standpoint, this was the much-preferred approach to minimize public exposure.

Unfortunately, Tommy was impatient and far from disciplined when it came to money. Such a plan would essentially put him in retreat mode, and since he knew the real reasons his career was tanking, it was definitely not a position he wanted to operate from. Giving up everything without punching back, was nothing more than falling into the trap that had been set.

AFTER CAREFUL CONSIDERATION, Tommy, Bob, and Milt decided to swing for the fence and file a lawsuit against Galactic Records for damages and lost income. The suit claimed that the financial failure of Tommy's current album and its singles was solely Galactic's responsibility. It alleged that the label was unable to properly promote and market Tommy due to the demands of their existing roster when coupled with the needs of artists they had acquired through the Honeycutt merger.

The suit further stated, that as a result of Galactic's inability to generate sufficient sales, radio chart success, and fan engagement for Tommy Model, as one of the top recording artists in the world,

Tommy had been forced to cancel his entire tour. It explained that this decision had been reached based on the fact that smaller, less profitable venues were apparently the only option according to his former agent's bookings and recommendations, which ultimately stemmed from a lack of marketing and promotion from the record label. This approach would use part of Jacques' own plan against him, and according to Milt, was the best way to proceed.

After much deliberation, it was agreed that there would be no mention of Jacques' plot against Tommy. Milt felt that bringing Butch Remington's findings into the matter would likely only result in a criminal investigation that could implicate Tommy personally, and would only take the focus off of the end goal of gaining his freedom from Galactic Records. Paul's unfortunate death was partially of his own doing, and there would always be time later to seek justice on his behalf if the right opportunity presented itself.

One year earlier, Tommy had personally netted more than fifty million dollars in royalties and touring income, but now his annual outlook seemed minimal at best. With no indication that the label was prepared to manage his next album more effectively, the legal filing stated that he felt it necessary to prepare for the high likelihood that at least two more tours would be non-existent, or significantly impacted. Due to the risk, he was suing for three hundred million dollars, an amount double his estimated three-year net touring loss, and justified by the immeasurable cost and negative impact to his overall career.

The basis of the lawsuit seemed legit from a common sense perspective, but in legal reality, it was a stretch. Ultimately the end-goal was not money, even though it asked that a significant amount be awarded. Instead, it was merely an effort to push the label to settle by releasing Tommy from his contract. Doubling down, Milt also demanded that the ownership of all master recordings be reverted to Tommy so he could take them with him to a new record label if he so desired. It was a bold plan and would likely cost Tommy hundreds of thousands of dollars to stay in the fight. There was no guarantee of success, but the alternative of doing nothing seemed grim.

CHAPTER FIFTEEN

Several months dragged by before the trial commenced. While hanging in limbo, Tommy had accomplished little more than the relentless cycle of getting blitzed on cocaine, followed by rounds of excessive drinking or smoking pot to bring himself back down. He slept very little, and worry consumed nearly every waking minute.

Even though Tommy felt justified in his claims against Galactic, he knew that the label's legal team would reveal or concoct information that could adversely impact his image in their attempts to position the label as the victim. Fear of the world seeing him in a negative light hovered like a black cloud, and drugs only intensified the experience. As a result of his ever-growing paranoia, his confidence slowly eroded away. On his worst days, Tommy considered dropping the case altogether, but Bob and Milt had held him intact during the long wait. Now, within twenty-four hours, opening arguments would be heard.

Trying to get his mind off the following morning's events, and to stave off his mental exhaustion, Tommy had just indulged a line of coke he had laid out on the kitchen counter when the phone rang. Holding her hand across the receiver, Monique whispered, "It's your sister, Belle calling from Scotland."

Tommy jumped off the barstool and ran to take the call, fearing something was wrong with his parents.

"Hi, Belle. Is everything okay?" Tommy frantically asked as the effects of the blow began to take hold.

"Hey, Thomas. Yeah, everything is fine. You doing well?"

"Sure, of course. I have a trial starting tomorrow for a lawsuit I'm involved in, but other than that, I'm fantastic," replied Tommy with heavy sarcasm in his voice.

"Yeah, Dad told me about that. I sure hope it works out for you."

Belle hesitated as if reconsidering the real purpose of her call. Regaining her courage, she continued.

"Look, I hate to bother you about this, and when I dialed your number I didn't realize that tomorrow was the big day for you, but I've got nowhere else to turn."

"What's wrong, Belle?" Tommy asked, shaking his head trying to fight off his amped-up high.

"You helped us get it off the ground, so of course you know my husband Richard and I have owned a restaurant here in Edinburgh for nearly two years now."

"Sure."

"And I put my fashion design career on hold after school to raise our little ones, so I haven't been able to financially contribute other than occasionally helping out with the restaurant."

"Right."

"Well, Richard has hit some choppy waters with the business and incurred a lot of debt in the process. I had no idea all of this was going on, but he had a bit of a meltdown last night and spilled his guts to me."

"I'm so sorry, Belle. Are you guys gonna be okay?"

"To be honest, Tommy ... I'm not really sure. You know I appreciate everything you did to help us get the business started in the first place, but if this thing goes under, we will have no income, so I'm a bit desperate for help."

Tommy winced at the ask he knew was coming. He loved his sister with all of his heart, but her husband, Richard Sinclair, had a history of get-rich-quick schemes that never seemed to pan out. Originally from Topeka, Kansas, Richard met Belle only four years ago when she was studying abroad in the United States. They fell in love and became a package deal upon her return to Scotland. A few months later they were married and immediately set about making babies, even while Belle was still working towards completing her BA in fashion design at the University of Edinburgh.

Two children and three failed ventures later, Richard's plan for a surf-and-turf restaurant in Edinburgh seemed like one more crazy idea at first, but now a year and a half in, it consistently rates as one of the best restaurants in town. However, without a one million pound investment from Tommy, the thought would have never become a reality. He had reluctantly made the commitment in hopes that Richard would finally stop chasing flighty ambitions and properly support his sister and their growing family. It worked for a while.

Now, the day before his civil trial against Galactic was set to begin, Belle was calling to say that she and Richard needed more money, or apparently, they could lose everything. Having already paid a significant amount in legal fees, with a possibility that the number could easily triple before the case could be concluded, Tommy was in no giving mood.

"So how much do you need, Belle?"

"Well, let me tell you what happened. We were already considering opening two additional locations for the restaurant when a real estate developer convinced Richard he could get him an amazing deal on some prime spaces. One was downtown, and the other in an area of Edinburgh they're transforming to a more upscale vibe. On the surface, it seemed like a great opportunity."

"But?" questioned Tommy.

"The developer invited Richard to dinner to discuss the two locations and what would be involved with building them out. Unfortunately, through their conversation, Richard also learned about some other properties the developer was involved with. This bloke has a big mansion and all kinds of high-end playthings, so of course Richard's old personality kicked in, and he started wondering why he couldn't have all of those luxuries as well. As a result, he got greedy again instead of focusing on his original goal."

"He never learns, does he, Belle? So exactly how big of a mess did he get you into this time?"

"This is so crazy, Tommy. The developer suggested Richard hold off on opening the new restaurant locations. Instead, he asked my easily influenced husband to consider investing in a block of abandoned buildings. They're planned to be turned into a trendy, new shopping center with waterfront view condos above. He told Richard that the return on investment would be, and I quote, 'astronomical.' That's all Richie wanna-be rich needed to hear, and he jumped in head-first."

"What the ..."

"I know, I know. He didn't have enough cash to put in, so he leveraged our restaurant for a million pounds and promised to pay the full investment within three months. I have no idea where he thought he could get the money, especially as much as it was. But he made the deal and signed a contract. The problem is, the shopping center and condo development are projected to be a huge success. That part was real. But as a result of the financial opportunity, the developer now has several other big-money guys in town wanting in. Whatever Richard's plan was to obtain the funding, it didn't pan out. He won't tell me where it was coming from, and I don't want to know. What I do know is the way the deal was written, if he can't come up with the cash by a certain date, then the developer gets our restaurant. I think that may have been part of this guy's plan all along."

"Richard is such an *eejit*. Just get to the total amount you're in the hole, Belle. I've got a lot on me right now, and this is the last thing I need to be thinking about," scolded Tommy.

"Well ... the way it all worked out, we now owe one and a half million pounds, and if Richard can't deliver in a week, we're out of the deal and lose the restaurant."

"What? So let me get this straight. I gave you guys a million pounds to open the restaurant. And now you need one and a half more to get out of this debacle, and keep what I gave you the million for in the first place?"

"More or less, yes. But with the full investment, we also stay in the development deal, and that could bring a huge windfall."

"For Pete's sake, Belle ... you sound like your husband, still thinking about the upside of a bad deal. This is really not okay. I can't afford to do this right now. I bought you the house, the restaurant, your cars, and I paid for you to go to university ... and I'm still paying for Duncan and Fiona. I think that's more than most brothers would ever do. At some point, I have to be done trying to fix your husband ... who I told you not to marry, by the way."

"Tommy, please! The complete truth is, the original total investment requirement was two million pounds. Richard already mortgaged the house for five hundred thousand, so if this falls apart, we'll eventually lose our home as well. I'm so sorry. I swear I had no idea all this was going on."

"So even though you put the restaurant and cash from your house on the line, if you don't reach the entire two million dollar investment level, does the developer really get to keep what you've put in? Shouldn't he give back the cash and the restaurant if you're out of the deal? If not, something about that sounds illegal."

"No. It's sort of like if you put an earnest money deposit on a house you're buying, then you back out of because you can't get financing. The seller can sometimes keep the deposit. That's oversimplifying this situation, but it's the way the contract Richard signed was structured. He should have hired an attorney, but he didn't even tell me, so ..."

"Unbelievable! Nope. I can't do it. My career is in the crapper, and I have no idea how much I'm going to lose financially trying to get it back on track. You're on your own this time. You need to leave that goon before he destroys your life, Belle. I've always told you that, but here we are again."

Belle started sobbing uncontrollably, partially because her emotions had finally welled over, but mainly because she knew she was going to have to work harder than ever to turn Tommy around.

Unfortunately, it was not a day when the persona of Tommy Model had sympathy for anyone. After repeated attempts to win him over, Belle finally knew she was out of luck. A flurry of disparaging remarks flew from her mouth. When the term, "whore bag" was thrown out, Tommy slammed down the phone, hanging up on his sister and leaving her to fend for herself. In Tommy's mind, it was an event that was long overdue.

Fifteen minutes later the phone rang again. Assuming it was Belle calling back to apologize, he told Monique to tell whoever it was, that he was not here.

When Monique answered, she wasn't greeted by what she expected to be Belle's sweet, slightly-Americanized, Scottish accent. Instead, the stern, thick, old-school tone of Tommy's father, Frank Maddock returned her hello. She tried to engage in small talk to lighten his obviously foul mood, but Frank curtly was having none of it.

"Put Thomas on the phone, Monique. Now, please!"

Monique held out the receiver in Tommy's direction while carrying a despondent look on her face. Tommy marched over and grabbed the phone, fully aware of why his father was calling.

"Dad, look ... don't even get started on me today. Belle needs to get herself out of her own mess for once. You hate Richard as much as I do, and if this leads to her losing everything to see she needs to leave that deadbeat, then so be it. I'm not going to give them any more money. I can't right now, even if I wanted to."

Cutting Tommy off, Frank jumped in with the furry of a father protecting his baby girl.

"You are going to help her because she is your sister. I've never asked anything of you, but this I'm telling you, you're going to do. I'm not gonna have my grandchildren living on the street. Or heaven forbid they all want to move in with your mother and I. We don't have the room. You have the money, so stop being a dobber and give it to them!"

"I can't, Dad. It's not a good time right now."

"If you don't do this, then don't call me wanting advice ever again because that well is closed. You hear me?"

Finally losing his cool following his father's threat, Tommy retaliated.

"Oh, you mean the great advice that has basically ruined my career, and is the very reason I can't afford to help Belle right now? Well, don't worry ... I won't be asking again because I'm going to be paying for that sage wisdom for years to come."

"You're blaming that on me, Thomas? I told you what you needed to hear, and quite honestly, what you wanted to hear. What good would it have done to tell you to throw away the songs you had written and start over? You wouldn't have done it anyway. I was trying to help motivate you to work with what you had. And now this is all my fault? Are you daft?"

"No, and another thing ... I've been taking care of this entire family since I was seventeen years old because you couldn't earn enough at the shipyards. And what you did make, you drank half of it away. So in essence, I enabled you to screw off and not take full responsibility just like Belle and Richard are now. But all of this is going to stop today. If that's not okay, then we don't ever have to speak again, as far as I'm concerned."

"Are you calling me a deadbeat, boy? I did the best I could so you and your brother and sisters could have a good life, and so you could flit around playing the guitar. I gave up a lot of my own dreams for yours, you ungrateful wretch. So if I got a bit tanned every once and a while, it was to give me a release so I could hold it all in perspective and keep going. And you were the one who insisted on supporting us, which I never asked of you."

"Yeah, but you sure took it without hesitation, didn't you?"

"Well, Thomas ... if that's what you think of me, and you aren't going to help your sister, then I think it's probably best we don't speak for a while. I am very disappointed in you, Son."

"That's fine with me. But why don't you give Belle the money? Oh, that's right ... because you don't have it to give either. You are unbelievable to ask this of me right now when I'm going through a career-defining lawsuit."

Tommy stopped and bit hard on his lip, knowing full well had no choice, but to give in.

"I'm going to go ahead and wire the money to her today, but you and me ... well, we're done. So don't call, don't write, don't even claim to be my father when people ask you if you are Tommy Model's dad."

Tommy stopped his scathing attack in anticipation of a response, but instead, he only received silence ... then the finality of a click, followed by a dial tone. He threw the phone across the room where it shattered against the wall. Monique knelt to gingerly gather the remnants. As she stood, Tommy charged at her. Uncertain of his intentions, she flinched as he approached. Tommy grabbed Monique by the arms and pressed his lips hard against hers, intensely kissing her, with more anger than passion. He pulled away and looked at her, breathing heavily.

"I want you on your knees right now. I need you to erase all of this insanity for me. Please! I'm begging you. I can't deal with this!"

Instead of succumbing to his demands, Monique wrapped her arms around Tommy, sheltering him in the cocoon of her embrace. As his platonic best friend and live-in personal assistant, no one had a more visible perspective on how significantly Tommy's life had been transformed since his career began to tumble. His drug-induced mind screamed out for sex, but she knew that true love, understanding, and friendship was what he needed in the moment.

Tommy began to weep as he pressed his muffled cries into her shoulder.

"I'm sorry. I'm so sorry. Please, forgive me. I didn't mean to do that. Please, I can't lose you too," Tommy pleaded.

"You're not going to lose me. Just relax. It's all going to be okay."

CHAPTER SIXTEEN

THE COURTROOM WAS EERILY SILENT except for the occasional pop of the floor or creak of a chair. The judge adjusted his glasses and carefully examined the verdict in front of him. Tommy looked towards the jury for some indication of the outcome, but all eyes quickly turned away from his gaze, and the entire panel looked in the direction of the judge. It was a move that Tommy undeniably accepted as confirmation that they had not ruled in his favor.

Shock overcoming him, Tommy's ears began ringing, and he zoned into what seemed like an out of body experience as the judge read the verdict. It had been a long-shot to hope he could force Galactic to settle outside of court and allow him out of his deal. But Jacques never took the bait. Instead, he was all too happy to take the matter to a jury trial and publicly humiliate Tommy in the process.

During testimony, Tommy had been painted as an eccentric, egomaniacal, sex-crazed, drug addict who had wonderful talent, but had squandered it all away through excesses that had destroyed his creativity and commercial viability as an artist. Although Milt Hamstein and his team vigorously defended Tommy's case, in the end, the terms of the contract had prevailed. As a result, Tommy would be required to fulfill the completion of one more album before he would be free of his professional relationship with the label.

Tommy stared at the grain of the worn-out wooden table at which he sat. As if his ears had clogged, the judge's voice seemed a million miles away and muffled by the incessant ringing in his head.

"Do you understand the verdict, Mr. Maddock?" asked the judge.

When Tommy failed to respond and instead continued to fixate on the table, the judge repeated his question in a much more forceful tone.

"Mr. Maddock! Are you with us? Do you understand the verdict as I have read it here today?"

Milt bumped Tommy with his elbow, snapping him back to reality.

"Huh? Uh, yes. Yes, judge ... I think I understand." Tommy humbly replied.

"Good. Even though the verdict is in Galactic Records' favor, I would like to encourage you, Mr. Morel and you, Mr. Maddock to work things out. There has been a lot of mud-slinging during this trial. I think most people in this room would agree that Mr. Maddock holds considerable abilities and talent, but without the proper support of his record label, it may never again see its true potential. I for one would hate to see that happen. So whatever the real beef is here, I urge you both to get through it, and I look forward to seeing Tommy Model at the top of the charts once again. With that being said ... court is adjourned."

The judge slammed his gavel against the small block of wood sitting atop his bench, finalizing the proceedings, and leaving Tommy emotionally heavy and uncertain about the future.

Across the room, Jacques Morel and his army of attorneys shook hands and patted each other in an over-the-top manner. Utterly defeated and flanked by his somber legal team, Tommy made his way out of the courtroom and into the main corridor, where he exited the building and descended a short set of stairs towards the sidewalk below.

The paparazzi swarmed around Tommy like a flurry of flies, and news reporters hurled meaningless questions, all of which he ignored. Feeling a pull on his arm, he jerked away from what he believed to be one of the many photographers encircling him. Hearing his name called again in a heavy French accent, he turned back to see Jacques standing amongst the crowd. The label-head reached out his hand, but Tommy defiantly refused to accept the gesture.

"What do you want Jacques?" asked Tommy, as the cameras furiously clicked and flashed all around them.

"I want to extend an olive branch here today, and let you know that we look forward to working hard to ensure your next album is a huge comeback success for all of us. Let's heal the wounds and move forward. What do you say?"

Jacques extended his hand once again as the intensity of the onlookers grew even more heated.

One of the reporters screamed out, "Come on, rock star! What else do you want? Shake the man's hand and stop being a crybaby!"

The crowd cheered, but Tommy hesitated. His gut was telling him to run, but his mind fully understood how this scene would play out in the court of public opinion. Giving in to the pressure, Tommy shook Jacques hand, presumably ending their feud and giving hope to the future. Jacques smiled, and his yellowed teeth repulsed Tommy. He wrapped his arm around Tommy's shoulder and pulled him in for a hug. Now cheek to cheek, Jacques whispered in Tommy's ear.

"And if you believe I will ever help you rebuild your career, you're even a bigger fool than I made you look in the courtroom.

You're done, Tommy Model. But take your chances, and when I pull away, smile really big like you mean it."

Jacques released his grip, leaned back and grinned, once again exposing his wide set of cream-corn colored choppers. The crowd cheered, and he shook Tommy's hand a second time, perceivably sealing the deal on their renewed alliance.

Tommy stared at Jacques and was now even deeper in shock at the audacity of what had just happened. He could no longer let it go. He was tired of losing. In true Tommy Model fashion as anger took hold, he reared back, then let his fist fly, punching his antagonist square in the face. Jacques' body pivoted, reeling from the blow as a chorus of groans erupted from the mob.

Quickly regaining his composure, Jacques turned back to Tommy, standing tall and boldly laughing as blood oozed from his nose. He cautiously touched his upper lip and looked down at his crimson colored fingertips. Jacques smirked and patted his attacker's shoulder, then wiped his hand down the sleeve of Tommy's jacket leaving a blood trail behind. He turned and casually walked away, knowing his mission had finally been achieved.

CHAPTER SEVENTEEN

T OMMY STARED AT THE TELEVISION hanging high on the wall across the room. Its sound blared through the tiny speaker in the hospital bed's dual-purpose remote control and emergency intercom. The entertainment news show had teased a full report before the commercial break, and now Tommy watched intently for what he knew was coming. As the segment began he held the remote to his ear to listen:

Many of you may not even remember him, but for those who do ... rock star, Tommy Model was rushed to the hospital last night after an apparent suicide attempt. Sources close to the singer say his long-time personal assistant found her boss unresponsive in the bathtub with an empty bottle of sleeping pills on the bathroom floor.

The overweight, bearded, and somewhat disheveled looking, Tommy Model, pictured here in a recent photo, is a stark difference to the sex symbol who wowed legions of fans some three decades ago. With his infectious blend of rock, pop, and new wave, Model sold over one hundred million albums worldwide. He disappeared into relative obscurity in 1990, after losing a legal battle with his record label that ended with the often temperamental rocker

punching out Galactic Records' CEO, Jacques Morel, on the
courthouse steps.

Video footage from Tommy's historical fisticuff filled the large wall screen behind the show's co-host, then replayed in slow motion in full television view for added effect. For all that Tommy had accomplished throughout his short-lived, but highly impactful career, that one moment, now so many years ago, had come to define his legacy, and it sickened him as the report continued:

Ironically, Morel passed away just last week following a long battle with cancer. As for Model's current condition, sources say he is doing well, is expected to recover fully, and should be released from the hospital sometime tomorrow. Now if he could only dig up another hit, maybe he wouldn't feel like killing himself ... right, Jessie?

"Ha ... that's right, Tom, " the co-hosts heartlessly bantered back and forth at Tommy's expense.

Tommy stabbed his finger on the remote to shut down the TV, but it failed to work. He continued to press what he believed to be the *off* button, but when a nurse called over the intercom, he realized his mistake. He dropped the remote in despair as the show continued, finding other celebrities to pick on and leave in its wake.

After his altercation with Jacques nearly thirty years ago, Tommy was arrested for assault. Surprisingly, Jacques didn't press charges, so no jail time was ever served. Tommy had always believed he was let off the hook because Jacques felt he had finally achieved the revenge he had ultimately been seeking. There was simply nothing more to prove. He had not only ruined Tommy's career, but he had publicly humiliated and wounded him to the point where he could just sit back and watch Tommy slowly bleed-out into obscurity.

Even though he never again recorded for Galactic Records, Tommy finally emerged from his writer's block. During the late

1990's he grew into high demand as a songwriter and producer for other artists, all work Galactic could not legally control. He earned nowhere near the same level of income, but the combined royalty streams he did garner, allowed him to maintain several of the luxuries he had grown accustomed to, albeit at a significantly diminished version of his former rock star lifestyle. Most importantly to Tommy, he was still able to afford his never-ending habit of drug and alcohol indulgence, the extent of which ebbed and flowed with the levels of emotions he experienced at any given point in time.

As the new millennium dawned, Tommy felt it was finally time to pen a tell-all biography to reveal the full story behind what led to his fall from stardom. He was offered a million dollar advance by a major publishing house and set out to *write* the wrongs he believed had been unleashed upon him.

Unfortunately, when word of the book got out, Jacques Morel and Galactic's legal team, put the wheels in motion to block the story's release. Galactic was able to easily prevail in the matter based on the fact that Tommy's original recording agreement also included any literary rights during its term. Tommy was still beholden to those legalities since he had never delivered his final required album. More than ten years later at the time, Jacques remained a thorn in Tommy's side.

With the book's release no longer an option, Tommy was forced to return the advance to the publisher. Unfortunately, most of the million dollar paycheck had already been squandered away or used to pay off old debts. To secure the necessary funds, Tommy had no choice but to sell his beloved Malibu beach house.

Malibu was the last of his get-a-way homes. Over time he had parted with his New York City apartment, Aspen chalet, Miami condo, London flat, and the ultimate escape, his bungalow in Mykonos. They were all purchased during a much better time when he didn't know what else to do with the millions of dollars he was earning early on in his career.

With Jacques intervention once again setting Tommy back, and ultimately blocking the opportunity to tell his side of the story, depression set in on a major level, and for most of the first decade of the twenty-first century, Tommy lost himself again in a spiral of drugs and alcohol.

Eventually pulling himself out of his dive to the bottom, a chance meeting with a wealthy investor, who was also a big fan, put Tommy in the driver's seat of running his own record label. The company signed half a dozen artists, all hand-picked and groomed by Tommy, and over the course of a five year period, many achieved modest chart and sales success. Unfortunately, the financier eventually grew bored of the music business and tired of waiting for a return on his money that never seemed to come.

With no positive forecast on the horizon, at the end of the sixth year, the money-man pulled the plug on funding, and sold his share of the company to Tommy for a dollar, just to move on. Desperately needing something to hold onto, Tommy kept the label afloat with his own cash for two more years before it finally reached a dead end. He closed shop, set the artists free by assigning their masters and related rights back to them, then once again became a recluse in his Beverly Hills compound.

Through everything, Monique had held on as Tommy's personal assistant. Even though they were the same age, she had evolved into a mother-figure for Tommy since he no longer interacted with either of his parents following the fateful argument with his father in 1990. It was a rift that Monique had often desperately tried to repair, but Tommy always ignored any suggestion of a reconciliation.

Bob Walker had also continued on as Tommy's manager, even though there was little interaction between them, and Bob had long since stopped pulling a commission from his struggling client.

TWO DAYS BEFORE the events that led to his admission to the hospital, Tommy had finally heeded all warnings from his manager and business manager. He would run out of money within a year if he failed to sell most of his few remaining assets and make significant financial cuts. But saving himself meant letting go of his housekeeper, Sissy and his landscaper, handyman, and defacto auto mechanic, Emilio. It was devastating for Tommy because they had also become his family. But most painfully of all, it meant parting ways with Monique who had been by his side for thirty-some years and was undoubtedly his best friend.

A week prior, his Beverly Hills estate had been put on the market for nineteen and a half million dollars and already had a full-price offer under contract. When the sale closed, Tommy would only net approximately seven million dollars after paying off the mortgage and home equity line of credit. He also had reluctantly auctioned off all except one car from his stable of rare collectibles. Between the seven million for the Beverly Hills mansion and approximately one million for the cars, his business manager estimated that Tommy could live comfortably for several more years, even after taxes stripped away their share of the profit. What would surely seem like a lot of money to the outside world, would likely only provide Tommy with a three to five-year window, even if his spending habits were better controlled. It would only be possible if he remained disciplined, eliminated his staff, reduced other extravagant costs, and moved to a modestly priced home, preferably far away from the excesses of Los Angeles.

With all of his difficult decisions finally in motion, Tommy struggled mentally to find a way to keep Monique in his life, as he informed her about the necessity of his actions.

"We both knew this couldn't last forever," explained Monique, as she sat sideways on the sofa, facing Tommy, and holding both of his hands in hers. "I've probably set some sort of a record for the longest tenure as a personal assistant, and I've been very fortunate to be with you as long as I have. It's been a bumpy ride at times, but hey .... we're both still here. It has to be done, and you'll never lose me as your friend, so please don't let this consume you."

Tommy's eyes welled with tears as he struggled to respond. "I don't know how I'm going to live without you in my life every day. You've seen me through all of the highs and lows. I'm a miserable wretch with no one to love. And now without you, I'll be completely alone. That really scares me."

"I understand, but maybe in some strange way, you always had me to fall back on as a friend. So it may have been easier to walk away from all those relationships that could have turned out to be the one you were looking for. This may be exactly what you need to finally find happiness. Just open your heart and give the next girl more of a chance. Okay?"

Tommy wiped away a stream of tears that had finally overflowed from his left eye as he shook his head up and down in agreement.

"I will, Monique. I promise. Look, I don't want you to worry about money, so I'm going to find a way to keep paying you without my business manager knowing. I can't cut you off like this."

"Tommy, you have been so generous to me all these years. I've saved and invested my money wisely, so I'll be more than fine. Stop worrying about me. Focus on you and finding your joy again. You deserve to be happy."

Monique looked away and tensed her lip as if holding back a secret. Tommy noticed her abrupt change in facial expression and asked what was wrong. She hesitated but knew she had to reveal what she had learned, even if it temporarily devastated Tommy even more than he already was.

"You know I've been your defender and protector, and I would never tell you anything to hurt you intentionally, right?"

"Of course. Okay, what's going on? You're scaring me," nervously replied Tommy.

"Well, you're all too well aware that Jacques Morel passed away last week. What you don't know is that he sent you a letter right before he died. I've struggled with giving you this, but it's probably best if we go ahead and rip the band-aid off while I'm still here with you."

Monique handed Tommy a white envelope. His name was handwritten on the outside along with the words, *From: Jacques Morel*. Tommy held it loosely, unsure if he should read it or burn it. He looked at Monique, and her eyes reassured him to open the envelope. He did and slowly slid out the folded letter inside. Reaching for his black-framed glasses, Tommy adjusted himself and leaned back into the cushions of the sofa before taking a deep breath and beginning to read.

Tommy,

If you're reading this, you are obviously finally rid of me. Congratulations! You ultimately won the war.

About three years ago when I was first diagnosed with lung cancer, I realized that the guilt for the horrible way I had treated you all these years had finally caught up with me. It's a karma thing, for sure.

I should have told you this sooner, and face-to-face in person like a real man, but I was so embarrassed. I just didn't know how. So here goes now ... I guess, better late than never.

Recently I ran into my deceased ex-wife's old friend, Heather. I was struck by how much Heather reminded me of Angela, especially her facial features, and the style and color of her red hair. When they were best friends and used to hang out together, everyone saw the uncanny similarities except me. I suppose when you really love someone as I did Angela, you see that person in the best light possible until they give you a reason not to. I always considered Heather a bad influence, and the person who ultimately led Angela down the wrong path. So when I looked at Heather back then, I didn't see someone who resembled my wife. I saw a demon who I believed was destroying my angel and the love of my life.

When we crossed paths again a short time ago, she cautiously greeted me but said that she was glad we bumped into each other because she needed to clear the air about something. I really didn't want to hear anything she had to say, but it was apparent I wasn't going to stop her even if I tried. So she preceded, and I reluctantly listened. What she told me, ripped to shreds what was left of my soul, and is why I'm bearing myself to you in this writing.

You see ... it turns out it was Heather, not Angela who slept with you that fateful night so long ago. When word got back to me about a redhead that everyone said was my wife hooking up with Tommy Model on his tour bus, I never once stopped to think about the fact that she had gone to your concert with Heather, or that they could have possibly mistaken Angela for her best friend.

When I later accused Angela of the infidelity that I believed to be true, simply because a bunch of roadies said it was, she desperately denied the accusations. According to Heather, Angela feared that if she had exposed who had actually slept with the great Tommy Model, I would have finally been enough ammunition for me to demand that she cut off ties with Heather once and for all. Angela was a lonely woman and Heather was her only true friend, so it would have devastated her to lose that relationship in her life.

So other than repeatedly claiming her innocence, Angela kept quiet about Heather, thinking my rage would pass, or perhaps I would finally come around and believe her. What Angela didn't anticipate is how deeply I was angered and hurt by what I thought was an unrepairable disloyalty to our marriage. I shut her out completely.

According to Heather, it was my actions and my inability to listen and believe Angela as someone who had never lied to me ever before, that ultimately led to her seeking out other men and the drugs that eventually consumed her life. Apparently, she felt that if she was going to be accused of being reckless and unfaithful, she should at least experience the excitement of the person I had painted her to be. If I had only taken Angela at her word, she would still be with me today, and for that, I am terribly heart-broken and ashamed.

But I am even more deeply saddened and disappointed in the way I have falsely accused and blamed you for my Angela's death. I purposefully ruined your life, and now I realize it was all based on a false reality. For that, I am truly sorry, Tommy. And although I don't expect you ever to forgive me, I do hope that you can put all this behind you and find your way back to the incredible superstar we all know you can be. I destroyed that, and I regret my actions. I had no right to do so, but my death will hopefully serve as some penitence for the pain I have caused you.

Please use your talent to bring joy back to the world. If I am fortunate enough to see you on the other side, I hope we can embrace and you can find forgiveness in your heart for me.

Respectfully,

Jacques Morel

P.S. Please go see Galactic's new CEO, Peter Kirkinour. I have filled him in on everything, and I've asked him to work with you to find an amicable resolution to your relationship with the label. He is expecting your call.

CHAPTER EIGHTEEN

As Tommy drifted in and out of sleep while lying in the hospital bed, he replayed in his mind the series of events that had occurred the day before.

He clearly recalled that after reading Jacques' letter, he watched Monique packed the last of her things. He helped carry them out to her SUV, the same dream car that he had given her two years ago as a birthday present. He vividly recalled as she shut the back lift gate and turned to hug him goodbye. They both cried as they held each other tightly until Monique loosened her grip and stepped back to look into Tommy's eyes. She wiped away his tears with her thumb, then softly stroked her hand through his long, unkempt hair. Holding his thickly bearded face in both of her hands, she leaned forward to kiss his lips.

As they paused in their emotional embrace, Monique began shaking and crying all over again. To stop the pain, she quickly pulled away, turned, and walked to the driver's side door. She looked back one more time. Without further hesitation, she opened the door, sat down, immediately started the engine, and sped away along the long tree-lined drive of the compound.

This was not at all how Tommy had envisioned life at his age. With Monique's departure, he found himself desperately alone. In the moment, it was painfully noticeable that he didn't even hear the sound of a single bird in the trees, only a slight rustle of wind against the leaves.

Jacques' letter had been mind-blowing, but it did little to change the mood of his current situation. The damage had long since been done. Even with the invitation to meet Galactic's new CEO laid out before him, he was far too depressed from all of the recent events to think about reconciliation, or what that could even mean.

He retreated to the lonely, lifeless house. Inside, he aimlessly bounced from room to room, then to the pool deck, the pool house, and even to edge of his property under a shade tree. He felt like he was coming out of his skin and couldn't get comfortable anywhere. Anxiety kicked in, and he fantasized that if he were to die right now, there in the far reaches of his backyard, it was possible no one would find him for days. In fact, the famed Beverly Hills coyotes, buzzards, and insects could likely dispose of him to the point that he might never be found. The idea of disappearing strangely appealed to him for a second, but the gruesomeness of how that would occur, snapped him from his delusional daydream.

Tommy's breathing and heart rate increased as his body began to feel like it was on fire. He sweated profusely and became gravely concerned that something terrible was happening. *Was it a heart attack ... a stroke?* He needed to cool off and calm down fast.

Re-entering the house, he cranked the A/C, stripped off all of his clothes, and made his way to his elegant, spa-like master bathroom.

He filled the over-sized, white-marble tub with cold water and sat on the edge cooling his feet. Still rattled with fear, he desperately needed to bring himself down. He turned and stood, walked over to the cabinet, and began rifling through a bevy of pill bottles in search of his anxiety medication. He couldn't locate the prescription he knew should be there, but he did find a vial with one sleeping pill left inside.

With no better alternative in his clouded mind, he unscrewed the lid and turned up the bottle into his open mouth. Angered that it possibly wouldn't be enough to make him feel better, he threw the empty plastic container against the wall. It bounced back and hit the edge of the tub where it came to rest on the tiled bathroom floor

The cool water of the tub beckoned Tommy like a siren, and he made his way over to the edge where he stood and thought for a second. *Will I drown if I fall asleep from the pill? I surely don't want to drown, but I'm so blasted hot. It's like I'm walking through fire. What is going on with me?*

The intense urge to reduce his temperature overruled Tommy's fears, so he stepped in the tub and immersed himself into the cool water. He immediately felt a calm and peace overcome his mind and body, not sure if the water or the sleeping pill was to thank. He drained out a few inches from the basin to minimize the possibility of slipping under if he did fall asleep, then laid his head back, and closed his eyes to relax.

The next thing he knew, paramedics were standing over him as Monique huddled in the corner of the bathroom crying uncontrollably.

"What's going on, mates?" asked Tommy in a groggy, half-asleep voice.

"Sir, we need to get you to the hospital! We're going to lift you out of the tub and place you on this stretcher. You're very lucky your friend came back to get some things she had forgotten from the house, or you might be dead. Really, sir ... taking a bottle of sleeping pills is a selfish coward's way to go. Look at how devastated your friend is."

"What? No, no! I didn't take a whole bottle of sleeping pills! I only took one to calm down. I didn't have anything else. Monique, I swear! Please believe me."

Monique grabbed her mouth holding back another round of emotions and ran out of the bathroom.

Tommy continued to protest to no avail, as the paramedics lifted his dripping-wet, naked body from the tub and laid him on the stretcher. They placed a white sheet and blanket on top, strapped him in, lifted the gurney to waist level, then carried him out of the house to the ambulance waiting in the driveway.

The sleeping pill had zapped Tommy just enough to subdue the fight he would have normally given in response to such a misunderstanding. As the ambulance sped out of his compound and the driver engaged the siren, Tommy gave in to the fact that there was nothing he could do to stop them from taking him in.

Two hours later, with an I.V. in one arm and blood pressure cuff on the other, the emergency room doctor stepped into Tommy's room.

"Well, Mr. Maddock, your toxicology reports revealed a minimal level of nonbenzodiazepine in your system. That would confirm your assertion that you only took one sleeping pill. However, since you were found in a manner consistent with attempted suicides, it's hospital policy and best for your overall safety, to admit you overnight. It's just a precaution to make sure you're not really thinking about taking your life."

"Doc, I've had a lot of bad stuff happen to me that would make any sane person a little crazy, but I'm definitely not suicidal. As I told everyone who will half-listen to me ... I was having an anxiety attack because I had just terminated my entire staff. I got overheated and needed to relax, so I took a sleeping pill and hopped in a cool bath. That's all. So I'd really ..."

Tommy abruptly stopped in mid-sentence. He was about to say that he wanted to go home, but what was there? Only the same empty house and memories that had essentially put him where he was now. *Why go back into that same situation?* Tommy thought to himself.

"You know what, Doc ... if it's hospital policy, it's hospital policy ... so whatever you need to do. I would like to request a private room because of the whole celebrity thing."

"Oh, are you a celebrity?" asked the doctor.

"Yeah ... I'm a celebrity. Or at least I used to be. A long, long time ago I was somebody much different than the miserable bloke you see lying here now."

CHAPTER NINETEEN

TOMMY SAT PATIENTLY IN A WHEELCHAIR as an orderly pushed him through the exit doors of the hospital. The glow from the warm sun greeted his face. He closed his eyes and soaked in the energy before standing to his feet as Monique pulled up in her SUV. He turned to shake the orderly's hand and thanked him.

As he pivoted back towards the vehicle, a man walking towards Tommy carrying a bouquet of flowers seemed vaguely familiar.

"Tommy? Tommy Model?" the hip looking thirty-something inquired as he stopped and slid his sunglasses below eye level. "Tommy! Is that you, man? Wow, I barely recognized you with the beard and longer hair. How are you? Is everything okay, brother?"

"I'm sorry, you look very familiar to me, but I can't place where I know you from," stated Tommy.

"Well, I sure know who you are, man. You're my hero. I'm Matty Thorpe, lead singer of the band, *Hector's Folly*."

Tommy's mouth dropped open, and he reached out to shake Matty's hand.

"Matty Thorpe! It is a real honor, mate. I love you guys," replied Tommy like a giddy fan.

"You're messin' with me, Tommy Model. That's amazing because from the second I heard your first album, I knew I wanted to be a rock star just like you. It's so cool to meet you. I saw the news last night that you were in the hospital. If there is anything I can do, please let me know. We sure don't want to lose you, pal. You're the king in my book."

"No, no. It was a big misunderstanding. I didn't try to do what they said I did, but these doctor's want to cover themselves by forcing you to stay overnight and make sure you're not lying to them. But all is good. Seriously. How about you? Are you here visiting someone."

"Dude, yeah ... my wife and I just had our first baby. We're elated. She's a healthy baby girl."

"Congratulations! That's awesome news. Please give your wife my regards."

"I sure will, Tommy. She's going to freak out that she couldn't meet you. Hey ... I know this sounds crazy, but it almost feels like it was meant for us to run into each other because, in two days, we are flying out to start our European tour in Glasgow, Scotland. You're from around there, right?

"I'm from Edinburgh, about an hour away from Glasgow."

"Cool. We play Edinburgh two nights after Glasgow. We had to postpone a couple of shows for the baby to get here, but we're ready to rock now. It would be incredible if you could come with us. We'll pay for everything, man, and we're flying private. Just to have you along would be so inspiring."

"No, I really couldn't, Matty. I've got some things planned and ..."

Matty interrupted, determined not to take *no* for an answer. "Please, Tommy. It will give you a chance to go home for a visit. How long has it been?"

Tommy paused and sighed before responding. "Actually, it's been a really long time. I should have gone home ages ago, but life got away from me."

"Well here's your chance. How 'bout it? It will be amazing to spend more time with you. And I know you'll love the rest of the band."

"Well ... you guys are seriously my favorite group right now, and have been ever since the first single came out. What has it been five years now?

"Exactly, five," responded Matty.

"That's about the time frame when my career fell into the loo, but you seem to be going strong. That's good to see."

"Yeah, it's tough, but we're finally doing some stadiums this year, so I think we'll hold on for a while longer," Matty chuckled as he nervously joked, not sure if he should respond to Tommy's mention of his career derailment.

Matty looked at his watch and realized he was late for a doctor's scheduled visit to see his baby. "Shoot, Tommy. I gotta go. How about it? Will you come with us?"

Tommy hesitated and swung his head back and forth as if trying to force himself to say *no*, but he really did want to go. Getting back to Scotland would surely do him good. It would also give him a chance to escape the relentless paparazzi who were stampeding towards him from across the parking lot.

"Ah, what the heck. That sounds like fun. Let's do it!"

"Awesome, dude. I'm so happy. You have no idea. My first baby, and now meeting my hero. I'm so pumped, man!"

"Me too. I really appreciate the invite."

Tommy and Matty shook hands and quickly exchanged cell numbers. They agreed to talk the following day about the specifics, and then Matty rushed away through the sliding electronic doors of the hospital. Tommy turned to a waiting Monique who smiled and gave him the thumbs up, having rolled down the window and eavesdropped on the conversation to make sure he wasn't being imposed upon by a crazed fan.

The surging paparazzi had finally arrived, and they encircled Tommy as he tried to push through them to get into the SUV.

"Tell us why you did it, Tommy! After all you've been through, why try to kill yourself now? Was it Jacques Morel's death that sent you over the edge?" screamed a so-called reporter.

Finally to the door, Tommy pivoted his body back towards the anxious crowd and said, "Get this and get it good ... I didn't try to kill myself. I took a sleeping pill to relax, and because it was the last one in the bottle that I dropped on the floor, the wonderful people who found me feared the worst. That's all there is to it. Now, I'd appreciate it if you'd please back up so I can open the door."

A flurry of additional questions spewed at Tommy in a garbled chorus of chaos as cameras clicked at a frenzied pace. Tommy opened the door and pulled it into the mass of bodies as he squeezed through the small opening.

"They better not scratch my car!" yelled Monique. "I will choke someone out if they do!"

"Pull away slowly," instructed Tommy.

Monique did as Tommy directed. When the last of the eager followers dropped off from the side of the vehicle, she punched the gas and sped away. Tommy looked back in the side-view mirror and shook his head in disgust.

"I'm so glad I'm going to get out of this town," remarked Tommy.

"You mean your trip to Scotland?"

"Yeah, that initially ... but I'm thinking about leaving permanently too. There's nothing left for me in L.A. I can't breathe here anymore. There are too many painful memories."

Monique smiled as she looked at Tommy, then quickly turned her head back as she swerved to avoid a pothole.

"You know, Tommy ... I think that's a great idea. Get a fresh start somewhere else. Maybe we should have done that a long time ago. Where are you thinking?"

"I have no idea ... maybe somewhere peaceful where I can dream again. I never think about the future anymore." Tommy pulled down the sun visor and looked at himself in the mirror.

"Even though I don't look like it at the moment, I'm still fairly young. We're both still young."

"Ha, speak for yourself. I don't feel young. I'm thinking about getting a nose job. What do you think?"

"What? Pull over!" Monique looked at Tommy and smiled, but didn't immediately react. He repeated his demand. "Pull the car over!"

Monique calmly steered the car to the side of the busy street and came to a stop with her foot still on the brake.

"Why are we stopping, Tommy?"

"You listen to me. You are perfect just the way you are. Don't you dare go messing up that beautiful nose or any other part of you. It's this town that gets in your head like that. You need to get away too. So I want you to think about where you would like to move, and I'm going to take some of the money from the house sale and buy you a nice place somewhere."

"No, Tommy. You can't do that."

'I'm not listening to you. I'm going to do this. You just need to figure out where. Okay?" Monique turned away and stared out the window as Tommy repeated his question. "Okay?"

Monique nodded her head in agreement as she fought to hold back the tears that were beginning to brew beneath her sunglasses. She knew the Tommy Model that most of the world never got to see, an extraordinarily dedicated and compassionate man, who although a lost soul, cared about others more than himself. It was his massive early success, mind-numbing fall from grace, and the constant fight to hold on to a sliver of fading fame that often made him seem self-centered and heartless. But most of his outward arrogance was merely a put-on to protect his heart and divert attention away from a less than exceptional reality.

Monique wasn't sure she could ever leave Los Angeles, but keeping hope alive for Tommy had been her life's work. Even though no longer employed in an official capacity, she wanted to see him happy again. So she played along for now.

"What do you think about Charleston, South Carolina?" Monique asked. "I hear it's beautiful there this time of year. It's has a lot of history, and the people have such wonderful Southern hospitality. It's super laid back, and they have all of these great restaurants and shops there. Doesn't that sound nice?"

Looking straight ahead, Tommy smiled and replied, "I think that sounds glorious."

CHAPTER TWENTY

NEARLY TEN THOUSAND FANS shook the foundation of the famed Edinburgh Castle as Hector's Folly blazed through their raucous set-list. Tommy stood stage-left, bobbing his head with the thunderous rhythm, while Matty engaged the massive crowd. A collective soul sang in unison with every lyric, creating a wall of sound that often overpowered Matty's own vocals.

Before leaving for Scotland, Monique had insisted that Tommy shave his beard and cut his hair. He now once more resembled the Tommy Model of old. Two nights earlier he had stood in a similar location in the wings as the band performed in nearby Glasgow. But tonight's performance, solidified by the adrenaline bubbling in his veins, made it apparent that the desire to take the stage was once again consuming him.

With only three songs to go, Matty Thorpe paused and consulted with each band member before returning to his microphone.

"Hey, Edinburgh!" he screamed as the masses roared back like an army of lions. "We've got a special treat for you tonight ... oh yes, we do! Straight from this amazing city, it's the King of Bling, the Master of Disaster, the Roller in every Rocker; and I have no idea what any of that made-up stuff means. But it's difficult to properly describe the greatness that is my all-time hero. So here he is, folks. The one ... the only ... Tommy Modellllllll!"

The shocked onlookers broke out in an explosion of applause and chants. Tommy stood dumbfounded shaking his head *no,* while Matty beckoned from center-stage. The chaos of sound quickly evolved into a coordinated chorus of "Tommy, Tommy, Tommy, Tommy Model." Tommy's fear subsided, and he grinned, elated by the overwhelming response.

He needed this experience more than anything, but they had not planned it. Normally he would have been concerned he hadn't warmed up his voice, but at this point, what else did he have to lose? Pushing past his hesitation, he marched on stage waving to the crowd who elevated their song with his appearance.

"Hey, Tommy?" asked Matty as he handed him a mic. "How about we get a little 'Luxury' up in this place?"

Tommy smiled as the drummer kicked into the highly recognizable beat of his 1987 hit song, "Luxury."

The performance went off without a hitch, and Tommy worked the crowd and sounded as incredible as ever. Through one act of kindness and respect from a new-found friend, the rock star in Tommy had stripped away the cocoon that had held him captive for so long. And the throngs of joyous fans made it clear that there was still a place for Tommy Model, even if it was in his hometown.

After the show, Tommy, Matty and the rest of the band retreated to a downtown pub famous for being in business for over one hundred years and still going strong. Earlier in the day, Tommy had called five of his closest childhood friends to invite them to the concert and a reunion at the pub afterward. All, but one had shown up, and Tommy was excited to reconnect with his old pals. The large group of rowdy rockers and Scots sat around several tables pulled together in the back corner of the pub. There, they spent the next two hours downing pints while Tommy's old friends revealed funny and often embarrassing stories from his youth.

At 1:00 a.m. when the pub closed for the night, Matty and the other members of Hector's Folly excused themselves to head back to the hotel to get some sleep. Matty and Tommy made arrangements to meet for breakfast the next morning before they would part ways, as the band continued on its UK and European tour. Since he hadn't been home for so many years, Tommy planned to spend a few more days in Edinburgh.

For Tommy's friends, hanging out with a world-famous rock star and free for a night on the town, the evening was far from over. Tommy and his mates headed over to one of his pal's restaurants overlooking the Forth Rail Bridge which spanned the Firth of Forth. The view from the outdoor patio of the well-lit bridge and its reflection in the glassy water was stunning. Staring into the scene and surrounded by his friends, Tommy questioned why he had ever been so determined to leave this place. He held his pint of ale high above his head and toasted his companions.

"Charles, Angus, Richy, and Max ... here's to you mates. It's a real honor to spend time with you again."

"Here, here," the group replied in unison, then drank healthy swigs all around.

Angus returned his glass to the air and exclaimed, "And a toast back to you, Tommy. I'd usually recite this in Gaelic, but I'll do my best to translate this for your Americanized ears."

"May the best you've ever seen
Be the worst you'll ever see.
May the mouse never leave your pantry
With a tear-drop in his eye.
May you always keep healthy and hearty
Until you're old enough to die.
May you always be just as happy

As we wish you always to be."

Tommy cheered the toast, but intent on proving he was still a full-blooded Scot at heart, he replied, "I'm not as far-gone as you might think, gentlemen. If you believe I'd forget that one, you've got another thing coming. Let me repeat that back as a real Scotsman would."

"May the best ye hae ivver seen
Be the warst ye'll ivver see.
May the moose ne'er lea' yer girnal,
Wi' a tear-drap in his e'e.
May ye aye keep hail an' hertie
Till ye're auld eneuch tae dee.
May ye aye be juist as happy
As we wiss ye aye tae be."

The table erupted in laughter and high fives all around. The men were so excited they forgot to drink, and Max quickly reminded them to hit the pint to avoid any bad luck that might befall them.

"You know guys ..." Tommy began to speak but stopped to take another sip of beer. "I have to say that I'm a bit jealous of you blokes. I gave up a life here to chase a dream that gave me great success and fame, at least for a little while, but eventually, it only brought me heartache."

"Yeah, but what a life it's been," answered Angus.

"I don't know, mate. Hearing about your wives and children, and your thriving businesses, and seeing Edinburgh again, I wonder if I made the right choice. All I ever wanted to find was someone to love. While I have a true passion for music, which has definitely been reignited after tonight's show, it's taken away any chance for a stable relationship. So here I am, lost and alone, and waxing nostalgic that I should have pursued a more normal existence."

Seizing the moment, Richy spoke up. "Tommy, Tommy, Tommy. Our lives are far from perfect. I want to strangle my kids some days, especially now that they are teenagers. I love my wife dearly, but she busts my balls constantly, and we're always at risk of something going awry with our businesses. We don't have millions to fall back on, so it can be nerve-racking standing on the edge of that slippery slope. Besides, as we Scots say, *whatever is meant to happen to you will happen to you.* My point is ... we all have challenges in life, and I think at times we all wish we had maybe taken a different path. But at the end of the day, I don't think any of us would make a single change if we could, right guys?"

Max and Angus who shook their head in agreement, but feeling the urge to lighten the mood Charles exclaimed, "Nah, I'd rather be Tommy Model any day of the week. Here's to Tommy!" The four friends lifted their nearly empty glasses to their mate once again, putting a nail in the sad-sack discussion.

"So, Tommy. Are you going to see your folks tomorrow?" asked Angus."

Tommy looked down and wiped the condensation from his glass mug. He was a bit embarrassed to admit the falling out he had with his family.

"I haven't spoken to my folks, or any of my relatives for about thirty years now, so I probably won't be popping in for a visit."

The four pals all nervously looked at each other as Angus continued the conversation.

"You should probably stop by and see them, Tommy. All that is in the past, right? You're a *long time deid,* and you sure don't want anyone in your family leaving this world without making peace with them."

"I don't know, Angus. Sometimes it's best to let sleeping dogs lie."

"*Yer at it now,* Tommy. Don't be a *choob*. I'm telling you, mate ... go see your parents," scolded Max.

"You guys are being a little pushy. You have no idea what happened back then. It was a bit unforgivable. Why are you're so intent on me seeing them after all this time? Is there something you're not telling me?"

The group silently stared at Tommy, who interrupted before anyone could answer. "Sure, I'd like to put everything behind us, but my mum is probably so mad at me she won't even let me in the front door. Actually, to be completely honest ... now that I think about that, I'm afraid of the possible rejection. It's risky at best to chance that they'd even be willing to see me."

Richy intervened. "Stop your ramblin' and go visit them tomorrow. Trust me ... you need to do this."

"You guys are freaking me out. If there is something I should know, you need to tell me now."

"Just do the right thing, old friend. You'll be fine," replied Max as he raised his mug to toast one last time while also changing the subject. "To Thomas Maddock, the greatest rock star I know! Then again, he's the only rock star I know."

Laughter picked the somber mood back off of the floor. The men held their glasses high for the last round of the morning, as the faint glow of sunrise began to permeate the dull gray sky. Tommy smiled half-heartedly. He was still concerned about what a visit to his family might entail and the painful emotions that would get stirred back to the surface. But if he ever was going to take the chance, the time was now.

CHAPTER TWENTY-ONE

Tommy took a long, deep breath. Willing forth his courage, he raised his clasped hand to knock on the white, wooden door securing the entrance he had passed through so many times as a younger man. He could hear the muffled sounds of his mother's voice getting louder as she approached from inside. He swallowed hard and mentally prepared for the worst as Davina Maddock unlocked, then opened the door.

"Yeah, what is it?" she asked in a highly irritated tone, expecting one more in a long line of salespeople who banged on her door day and night. When Davina realized her mistake, her ire quickly turned to bewilderment as she tried to reconcile the matured image of her son who stood before her.

"Thomas? Is that you?"

"Yes, Mum. It's me. It's your long-lost son come home at last."

Tommy forced a smile as his eyes welled with tears. He fought to choke back his emotions as the familiar smell of his mother's lilac perfume, mixed with what he was sure was beef stew simmering on the cooktop, propelled his thoughts back thirty years.

Davina stood dumbfounded at the sight of her son standing on her front stoop. Entirely unexpectedly her hand moved with the lightning stroke of a champion prizefighter as she slapped Tommy hard across his face. Just as quickly, she reached through the door with both arms outstretched and grabbed her son by his jacket. She pulled him close and embraced him with all the strength her tiny frame could muster. She wept deeply into Tommy's chest, as he gently patted her back in his best attempt to console her conflicted mind.

Davina looked into Tommy's eyes as he reached down to wipe the tears from her face.

"I'm sorry, Mum. I've been such a fool. I hope you and Dad can forgive me," pleaded Tommy, with all of the years he had missed with his parents hitting heavy on his heart.

"Come in, Son. It's good to see you."

"Mama, is that Thomas?" hollered Tommy's father, Frank Maddock, from the comfort of his recliner in the nearby living room.

Tommy was anxious to see his dad as his mother pulled off his jacket from behind and turned to hang it on a rack by the door. Tommy swung back to look at her as if asking approval to progress forward to meet the king. She nervously smiled and shooed Tommy along with both hands, giving him the reassurance he was seeking.

Tommy casually strolled into the living room where he saw a much older version of the man he had so revered as a youth. He struggled to adjust to the visual that a hard life, plus three decades, had tolled on his father.

"Hi, Dad," Tommy meekly said as he walked over to shake hands.

"Hello, Thomas," Frank replied as he extended his hand in return.

Tommy placed the closed fist of his free hand to his mouth and clenched his fingers together tightly in an effort to mentally cut off the agony he was feeling.

"How are you doing, Dad?" Tommy asked as if not even a day had passed.

"I'm feeling pretty good today, Son. How about you? You been practicing with the band?"

Tommy was pleasantly surprised that the conversation was flowing so freely with no bitterness or anger from his father. He was caught off guard that his dad was somehow aware that he had performed with Hector's Folly the night before.

"Yeah, I played with an amazing band last night. That was the first time in a while, and it was like a dream. How did you hear about that?"

"What do you mean? You're with your band every afternoon. Don't be silly. Those mates of yours are going to take you away from your mother and me eventually, but I'm glad it keeps you focused and out of trouble."

Tommy was confused by the conversation that didn't seem to make sense, at least in the present moment. He gazed back at Davina who suggested Tommy sit in her recliner positioned beside Frank's chair. The low sound of a soccer match commentator emanated from the television sitting on the chest across the room. His father became momentarily lost in the game when the opposing team scored a goal.

"So when did you get a flat screen, Dad?"

Tommy's mother interrupted to answer. "Your sister, Belle bought that for us last Christmas. We finally got rid of that big box set we had for so long. It's nice, isn't it?"

Tommy nodded his head in approval. He was anxious to ask about his sister, but the gravity of the moment was too intense to turn the attention elsewhere.

"Dad, when you mentioned I'm with my bandmates every afternoon, what did you mean by that?" asked Tommy, getting back to the concern at hand.

"Have you lost your mind today, Thomas? You and those boys in Velour have a record deal in the works. You're with them every day about this time. You go to school, then on to rehearsals, come home, eat, go to sleep, then get up and do it all over again. You're gonna be famous, my boy! Your mum and I are very proud, and you've worked so hard to get to where you are. You deserve it."

Tommy looked back at his mother whose face now carried a somber message.

"Thomas, why don't you help me in the kitchen for a bit so we can get supper ready."

Tommy patted his dad on the knee, then stood and followed his mother into the kitchen, separated from the living room by a wall.

"Mum, what's going on? Why is Dad acting like it's 1984?"

Davina stared at the hardwood floor beneath her feet and bent over to pick a crumb. She looked at Tommy, then down again, this time fumbling with the pocket on her apron. Tommy repeated the question.

"Mum, what's going on here? Why won't you talk to me?"

Davina returned her eyes to Tommy's. With frustration and sadness consuming her, she slapped her son across the face again.

"You have the audacity to abandon us for thirty years, and then you think you can just stroll in the door as if no time has passed ... like you never did that to us? Well, I've got news for you ... it's not going to be that easy, Thomas!"

"Mum, please. I'm sorry. I was out of my skull and high on drugs the day Dad and I got into our argument. There was so much pressure on me at the moment. I had a lawsuit trial starting the next day, Belle was asking for a lot of money I didn't have to spare, and Dad was coming down hard on me for not giving it to her. After everything I had done for you and Dad, and my brother and sisters, I needed a moment for me. But I didn't handle it right. I know that now. I've known that for a long time. I was embarrassed and didn't know how to fix it."

"All you had to do was pick up the phone, Thomas. Or come home, for goodness sake. Your father has been sick with worry about you for years. He eventually had a heart attack that fortunately didn't take him from us, but a few months later it was obvious his memory was fading fast. We got him on medication right away, and it's not a cure, but it's slowed the progression."

"So does he have dementia, Mum? Is that what you're telling me?

"Yes, he has dementia, but there's no candy-coating it. It's full-blown Alzheimer's disease."

"What? I don't understand. He just seems a little confused."

"Today is a really good day, so you're lucky. This evening or tomorrow, he might not even remember who you are, so you need to prepare for that? Specific reactions to the disease and medication are completely different from person to person. Some get extremely angry and have a complete personality change, but fortunately, so far your father hasn't gone through that. Normally he can remember certain events from several years ago, but he can't recall what has just happened a minute earlier, so it's a constant loop of confusion. That's why he thinks you are still in Velour. He remembers 1984, but not when you walked into the room."

Tommy leaned back against the countertop doing his best to mentally process what his mother was telling him. He had somewhat zoned out when she uttered the word Alzheimer's, and he was still trying his best to catch up.

"So how long has he had this?" Tommy asked.

"It's been five years. It got bad very quickly then the medication leveled it off a bit. But over the past year, it's progressed much faster. It's not good, Tommy. It will eventually kill him, and you need to understand that."

Tommy leaned back and braced his hands against the cool, tiled counter. He shook his head in disgust, feeling the full weight of the reality his mother and father had been living without his support.

"Is there anything I can do, Mum. I'm selling off everything, so I'll have a a lot more money soon. Is there somewhere I can take him to cure this? I'll give my last dime to make it better. Just tell me how."

"It can't be fixed, Tommy. At least not yet. Doctors and scientists are working to find a cure, but they've got a ways to go. Unfortunately, it's a disease older people typically get, although not always. I've learned that sometimes even younger people in their forties or fifties can have a health event that triggers it, but they're more the rarity. Since the elderly are perceived to be nearly through with life, there's not as much effort put towards finding an Alzheimer's treatment that either reverses the course of the disease or prevents it altogether. I've remained hopeful that something would come along before we lose him, but it's not looking good."

"I still don't understand. If it's only memory loss, how will that eventually take him from us? I can't bear thinking about that."

"Well ... I've had to learn a lot about this by default. Basically, the brain eventually becomes so damaged that the body can't function normally. Once that happens, there are several scenarios than can lead to death, and none of them are pretty."

Davina looked away fighting back the tears at the mere thought of losing her beloved, Frank. Tommy stood and walked over to the doorway leading back to the living room. His father carefully studied the soccer match. With the final whistle, he lurched forward with a victory cheer. Unaware of his error, Frank raised his fist high in the air as the commentator announced that the opposing club had beaten his favorite team, 2-1.

CHAPTER TWENTY-TWO

TOMMY LISTENED INTENTLY as the doctor asked his father a series of questions designed to determine the extent of his Alzheimer's progression. The answers, or lack thereof, along with Frank's deep frustration of not being able to conquer the relative simplicity of the quiz, was painful to watch. Tommy felt compelled to intervene as if doing so would somehow make it better.

If the questions could be answered, then maybe Dad doesn't have Alzheimer's after all, Tommy thought to himself. *Perhaps his memory loss is due to a bad combination of one of the many prescription drugs he's taking? If so, maybe that can be fixed.*

It was an unrealistic notion and he knew it, but he was desperate. Unable to hold back any longer, Tommy tried to coach his father following one specific question. The neurologist slowly raised a finger to her lips, silently asking Tommy to refrain and let the chips fall where they may. The outcome was obvious, and the doctor's confirmation of mid-stage Alzheimer's was no surprise.

Frank's friendly inquisition of strangers would always start the same way, and with the exam complete he launched into to his usual routine, "So, Doc ... where are you from?" he inquired.

Tove Lund had been born and raised in Oslo and had earned her Ph.D. in Neuroscience from The University of Edinburgh, one of the top research institutions in the world. She had been married for ten years, had two wonderful children, and a French bulldog named Morton. Even though Doctor Lund had previously relayed all of these facts to Frank, he couldn't recall that she had done so eight times over the past thirty minutes. If Tommy had not interrupted, she would have likely patiently replied to each question once again.

"Doctor Lund," Tommy paused, reassuring himself it was okay to show some vulnerability under the circumstances. "I realize that with me being from here in Edinburgh, you may have heard in the local press or rumor mill over the years that I don't have as much money as I used to. The media loves to share anything negative they can find on me. Just please know that I'll have significantly more funds available here shortly after some property sells back in the states. I'll pay whatever I have to get him better. I know there supposedly isn't a cure, but I also well know that money talks. Is there maybe a medical trial that someone is working on behind the scenes? I hear you just have to ask the right questions and offer enough cash to get into the more secretive ones. How about stem cell injections? I'm willing to do whatever it takes. Just please help him."

Tommy despondently looked at his father who smiled back at Tommy and interjected. "I don't know what all the fuss is about, Son, but I'm sorry it's upsetting you. If you're thinking about spending your money on me for some reason, I won't have it. No, mate ... I surely won't. You have your whole life in front of you, and you've got to save your money for the future, my boy."

Tommy turned back to the doctor and shook his head. He was perplexed at how his father could not know the gravity of the situation he was facing. Yet somehow, he could be so caring and concerned for Tommy's well-being, even if his perception was a scenario now three decades old.

Hoping to help Tommy ease his mental burden, Doctor Lund replied. "There isn't an approved treatment that your father isn't already taking. It's a tough disease. We know that an abnormal level of certain proteins in the brain clump and tangle together. They eventually block the nerve cells from communicating correctly and receiving the proper nutrients necessary for healthy brain functions. Unfortunately, we don't know what causes these proteins to get out of control in the first place. Stopping that process before it becomes a problem is a code that has yet to be cracked. I wish I had better news. We are researching stem cell therapy, but we're not to a point where we can say it makes a difference."

"Well, what can we do, Doc?" asked Tommy, struggling for some semblance of hope. "I can't sit back and watch him go through this. He's only in his seventies."

"I know this is not the answer you're looking for, but it's a realistic one. I would honestly recommend that you all try to enjoy your time together. Get out and do things. Don't sit in the house and wallow in depression. Even if Frank can't recall what you just did a few moments earlier, the happiness he feels while living that experience does have a positive effect on the body and soul. You don't want to look back on this later with any regrets. Doing your best to keep Frank, your mum, and yourself busy is a great way to work through this."

Frank jumped into the conversation. "Hey, Thomas?"

"Yes, Dad."

"You two are talking about us doing things together, which sounds really nice because, you know, Doc ... my boy is leaving us soon for a life in the spotlight. He's going to be a big-time a rock star! Anyway ... I realize you're a wee bit old for this, Thomas, but if you're not opposed to it, I'd like to go to the zoo sometime."

"The zoo? Where did that come from, Dad?"

"Well, I haven't been since I took your sister a few years back and I loved seeing all of those amazing animals. I probably never told you, but I always wanted to go to some faraway land and see exotic creatures in the wild, but your mother and I haven't gotten around to that yet. It's hard to get away, especially with all the work I have at my job over at the shipyards. A good visit to the zoo always makes me think that's still a possibility we can explore someday. So how about it? Can we go sometime?"

"Sure, Dad. That sounds fun," Tommy replied, not sure whether to laugh or cry at his father's joyous innocence.

THREE DAYS LATER, the twin-engine propeller plane touched down on a remote airstrip in the heart of the Serengeti National Park. After coming to a stop on the hard-packed dirt runway, Tommy, along with his mother and his father, carefully navigated the stairs that extended from the door to the ground. The endless Serengeti plain stretched in all directions as far as the eye could see.

Tommy's father spun his body in a circle, overjoyed at what he was witnessing. The memory of the moment would be fleeting, but Frank temporarily knew precisely where he was, and the excitement of experiencing something that had long been on his bucket list gave him great contentment.

Their guide, Jalali was born and raised in nearby Mugumu, Tanzania just beyond the park's borders, and was one of the most respected guides in the region. He had a knack for tracking some of the rarest animals on the Serengeti in areas not so heavily inundated with tourists. After some brief pleasantries with Tommy discretely explaining his father's situation to their new acquaintance, the group loaded into their waiting four by four and set off for lunch at a nearby safari camp.

After a simple, but delicious meal, the foursome re-boarded the open-top SUV and headed out to get their first glimpse of *the great migration*. Along the way, they passed a small herd of giraffe, the tallest of which were nibbling the leaves from the upper branches of an acacia tree. Frank grinned from ear to ear at the site, and Tommy snapped a photo of his father looking onward with the giraffes in the background.

Jalali steered the vehicle beyond the last grove of trees, and the vast Serengeti opened up before them. As far as the eye could see, what must have been thousands of wildebeest grazed across the grasslands, with an occasional zebra or two peppered in amongst the throngs.

Jalali pointed the long lens of the spotting scope towards a small clump of trees and bushes at least a half a mile away. Letting Frank view his finding first, he was surprised to see a pride of lions resting in the shade scanning the massive expanse of prey opportunities before them.

Jalali guided the Maddocks across a large area that followed a sweeping circle. Their path eventually led back to camp as the sun began to set against a range of hills and kopjes in the distance. Along their trek, they experienced a wide variety of animals including African buffalo, elands, a nervously alone jackal, gazelle, hyenas, impalas, a cheetah family including a mom and two cubs, and a small pack of endangered wild dogs chasing a warthog. As they reentered the scrub area lush with trees, they encountered one of the Serengeti's rarest animals, the caracal, a gorgeous lynx-like cat with enormous ears and long tufts of hair extending beyond their tips. It made a quick appearance then disappeared like a ghost behind a tree.

Back at camp, Tommy reflected on what had been a glorious day while he, Davina, and Frank all relaxed eating dinner around a warm fire as the African night cooled considerably.

"Did you have a good time today, Dad?" asked Tommy.

Frank stared back at Tommy, seemingly confused on how to answer.

"Well, Son, I think so. I don't quite remember what we did, but these beans sure are tasty," he replied.

Davina reached over, rubbed Tommy on the shoulder, and smiled, consoling his heart as only a mother can do.

CHAPTER TWENTY-THREE

Tommy struggled to open the door to his parent's Edinburgh home with both hands full of groceries. As he entered, he heard an unfamiliar female voice in the living room speaking with his father. His sister Belle had been away on holiday since Tommy's return to town but was scheduled to come home today. Thinking the voice might be hers he rushed through the entryway with anticipation.

Standing next to his father in the small, cozy living room was not his sister, but instead one of the most attractive women he had ever laid eyes on. He stared awkwardly while the weight of the sacks began to burn into his arms.

Frank looked up from his recliner to see Tommy. Stopping his conversation, he greeted his son.

"Thomas, my boy. What do you have there? Some food? Well, don't just stand there, go set those bags in the kitchen and come meet, uh ... uhmmm. I'm sorry, what's your name?"

"It's Amanda. Hi, Tommy," she replied in a smooth, classy Scottish accent.

"Yes, Amanda. I knew that," responded Frank, cleverly sliding over his forgetfulness. By becoming highly adept at covering his memory loss, he sometimes seemed less besieged by the disease. Ultimately though, it was just a trick.

Tommy nervously fumbled with the niceties. "It's amazing to meet you, Amanda. Let me go put this in the kitchen, and I'll be right back."

Amazing? Tommy thought to himself as he walked away. *That word was a bit over the top, don't you think?* Tommy mentally scolded himself for not being cooler.

He rubbed down his hair and tucked in his shirt before reentering the room. He focused his gaze back on Amanda as her straight, shoulder-length, golden hair caught the light from the window creating a halo effect around her face. *That perfect face,* he thought. Her eyes mesmerized Tommy. She nervously smiled as he stared on like a deranged stalker. The superficial Tommy Model desperately scanned from head to toe in efforts of confirming that her body matched the quality of her profile, but her blue medical scrubs were much too baggy to make the final determination. That would have to wait.

"So, what are you guys up to?" asked Tommy.

"I'm a registered nurse and friends with your sister, Belle. She hired me a while back to check in on your dad a few times a week to make sure he's doing okay health-wise. Your mother was telling me that you took him to the doctor last week. Was everything okay? And then you whisked them off on a safari! That had to be fun."

"Yeah, the trip to Africa was for him, but the doctor's visit was more for my sake. I had to hear the Alzheimer's diagnosis for myself, I guess. And I wanted to find out how far along things had progressed. I knew it was going to be what it is, but I had to get confirmation in person. That's all."

"That's totally understandable. Your father is a tough cookie, and he's doing really well, considering. How are you holding up, Tommy?"

Tommy felt as if he had been hit by a sonic boom. Someone other than Bob or Monique actually cared about his feelings for a change ... and it just happened to be an incredibly gorgeous woman. The events of the past week had been a significant impact on his mind, and inside he was still consumed by guilt and remorse. He was desperately struggling with the fallout from his own life. And now, with his father's condition layered on, Tommy was challenged in his private moments with staying off the drugs and booze.

"Thank you for asking," Tommy responded. "It's been a shock to the system for sure. Mum and Dad are the ones directly dealing with this though, so I really can't complain."

Frank looked at Tommy then turned his head back to Amanda, then back to Tommy, and once again to Amanda.

"I don't know what in the world you kids are talking about. Sounds like gibberish to me. I'm going to go see what your mother is into and let you two chat."

Even with Alzheimer's robbing his thoughts, Frank still could recognize there was undeniable chemistry between Tommy and Amanda, and he cleared the path for his son. As his father disappeared into the kitchen, Tommy quickly took his place in the recliner sitting beside Amanda.

"What's your last name, Amanda? You seem very familiar to me?"

"Perkins,"

"Amanda Perkins? Amanda Perkins, the singer?"

Amanda smiled and shyly shook her head *yes*, in confirmation. Tommy progressed into lovesick meltdown mode.

"Amanda, you have no idea how much I love your music. I'm a huge fan, or at least I was. What happened? You were so successful and then ... what has it been, maybe ... six years ago? You were suddenly nowhere to be found." Tommy caught himself. "Oh, my ...

listen to me. Of all people, I shouldn't be asking you how that happened. I'm sorry. I'm just glad to get to meet you."

Amanda smiled again pulling Tommy even deeper into the depths of her dark, brown eyes.

"Actually, the pleasure is all mine. I'm a huge fan of yours as well. It's hard to find someone in Edinburgh who isn't. I was very inspired by your music, and growing up here as you did, your success gave me the confidence to pursue my dreams."

"Come on. You're shining me on now."

"No, no. It's true. Like you, I had a meteoric rise to the top, and then I held on for dear life the three years thereafter. My second and third albums never matched the success of the first one, so the label dropped me. I was really lost for about a year, but I eventually decided to go back to school and get my nursing degree. After working at a hospital for a while, I started my own home health services company."

"That's so cool. I wish I would have transitioned to another career. I'm so glad to hear you've been keeping an eye on my dad."

"I've enjoyed getting to know your folks. Unfortunately, as things have intensified, I stop by more frequently now, to make sure you dad is doing all right. It also gives your mum a break for a little while. I visit with him for an hour or two, and she sometimes can get out for a cup of tea, or the store, or just hang out with some friends for a bit. I don't know if you realize it because she handles it so well, but the real burden is on her. She's very patient and caring for your father, and I'm sure fear of the inevitable is agonizing. She's a special person, for sure."

"I know. Mum is pretty amazing, isn't she?" said Tommy. "But, hey ... wow! It's impressive that you've been able to take your career in a totally different direction. And now you're giving back, helping others in a meaningful way. I wish I could say that. I should have been here for my folks, but I was way too wrapped up in my own world to know all this was going on."

"I completely understand. Most people never experience what we do as celebrities, Tommy. I had allowed the fame to change me too. Not significantly, but enough to where I didn't like the person I was looking at in the mirror anymore. I always thought I would use my money and notoriety for good, but the chase of continued success is relentless."

"It sure is. Fans don't have a clue how crazy it makes you feel."

"No, they don't. It's so difficult not to get trapped constantly trying to top yourself, especially when people are always telling you how wonderful you are. But ultimately, the decision for a career change was made for me. So in that sense, I had a little help."

"Whoever made that decision was a fool."

"Thank you. I'm much happier now, though. I still sing and perform my own music and covers with a full band at a club called Hops every Friday and Saturday night. It's a good time and no pressures. You'll have to come see me sometime."

"I'd love to. That sounds like fun."

"Listen ... don't be so hard on yourself. You're here for your folks now. And your sister is going to be so happy to see you."

"I seriously doubt that. The last time we spoke, she had some pretty choice words for me."

"Please don't tell her I told you, but she carries around a huge sack of guilt about what happened. You do know that giving her the money saved her marriage and changed both her and her husband's life forever, don't you?"

"No, I didn't. I just assumed Belle would blow through it like she had several times before. Or actually, it was her husband, Richard who always did that. But still ... I figured they were a hopeless package deal."

"Do you want to hear what really happened?"

"Yeah, I do."

"Well ... when you and your father had your falling out, and you wired the money, she told Richard she was in charge of their finances going forward. She also made it crystal clear that she would make all business decisions, and if he didn't like that he could leave. She threw down the gauntlet and set some demands on him that changed him in a big way. She then went and met with the developers that were trying to extort your brother-in-law and take their restaurant away in the process."

"I'm shocked my sister got some courage."

"Oh, she got more than that. She set the developers straight. Even though she had the money you sent to fulfill their required investment, they still tried to block them from the opportunity. She told them that if they wanted bad press about how they had destroyed the marriage and family of Tommy Model's little sister over their greedy, dirty business tactics, she would make sure they got what they were asking for. You probably have no idea how much you are still loved here in Edinburgh, and back then they were terrified of the thought of tenants and customers boycotting their shopping and condo development."

"You're kidding me. My sister seriously did that?"

"Totally. And the end result was that Belle and Richard held on to the restaurant and their share of the real estate deal. It became an enormous success, and in the process they became multi-millionaires. After that, your sister started her own real estate development company called, Model Holdings. It's named in your honor, of course. With Richard's ongoing understanding that she's the boss, they've gone on to build an enormously profitable company. He's the idea guy while she's the final decision-maker and voice of reason. They just had to figure out how much they needed each other. And now they give back to the community in incredibly wonderful ways. I think they consider themselves more philanthropists than real estate moguls at this point. It was quite a transformation."

"I'm blown away, and I'm so proud of her. But it saddens me that I wasn't around to see it as it happened."

"You've got to stop beating yourself up, Tommy. You saved a marriage and a family from being torn apart. As a result, you helped Richard become a better person and gave him and Belle a united front to fight for. They've had the financial means to live a wonderful life, and thanks to you, their kids got great educations and are highly successful and happy in their own right."

"My niece and nephew are doing well too? They were only babies when I last saw a picture of them."

"They sure are."

Tommy smiled like a proud uncle. "That's so good to hear."

"Yes. And now the city and its residents are receiving countless acts of kindness in return. Your sister even gave me a loan to start my company. I've paid it back, but I could never have done it without her help. So without you, I may have still been nothing more than a very lost, former pop star. You've touched a lot of people's lives, Tommy Maddock."

Humbled by Amanda's revelations, Tommy smiled and struggled to hold back his emotions. He heard the front door open. As it swung inward, it hit hard against the wall. Footsteps on the hardwoods in the entryway rapidly approached the living room. Belle appeared and ran towards Tommy who stood and beamed with exhilaration as his sister leaped into his arms and cried with joy.

Belle pulled her face back, looked into Tommy's eyes and said, "God, I've missed you!" She kissed him on the cheek and laid her head back on his shoulder, holding on as if she would never again let go.

CHAPTER TWENTY-FOUR

TOMMY AND BELLE SAT AT THE BAR of a local pub. Belle reached into her purse and pulled out a folded sheet of paper. She gently opened it and laid it flat on the counter in front of her brother.

"What's this? Tommy asked."

"It's your investment portfolio statement."

"My investment portfolio? I don't understand."

"It's for an account I opened for you several years ago. When Richard and I got back on our feet, and things started going in a much more positive direction, we knew we wanted to pay you back for everything you had done for us. So we took the combined two and a half million pounds you had given us for the restaurant and the real estate development deal, and we placed it in an investment account that's set up in a trust for you."

"Really! I had no idea."

"I wanted to tell you all along, but Dad insisted that when you were ready, you would come home, and we shouldn't bother you before then. So we patiently waited. I think he thought it would be months, not years."

"Me too," replied Tommy in a somber, reflective tone.

"That probably wasn't the right thing to do in hindsight, but we wanted to give you your space. So, two-point-five million pounds sterling invested smartly over the past thirty years gives you that."

Belle pointed at the balance of the statement. Tommy swallowed hard and began choking on a sip of his Old Fashioned.

"That says twenty-eight million pounds, Belle! Are you kidding me?"

Belle shook her head acknowledging *no* ... she was not kidding.

Tommy stared at the statement in disbelief, then leaned over and hugged his sister.

"We'll get it released from the trust this week, Tommy. We just wanted to keep it safe. If something would have happened to us, you were in our will and would have received it from our estate. I want you to know we weren't purposefully keeping it from you. Time flew by, and we kept hoping you would reach out."

"I never would have thought you were purposefully keeping it from me, Belle. Wow ... I appreciate this so much! It's going to make a big difference in my life right now. Things have gotten so bad financially that I've had to sell off everything."

Belle grabbed Tommy's hand where it rested on the wooden bar top.

"If we had known things were that bad, we would have given it to you sooner. We had no idea."

"It's all right, Belle. Stop fretting."

"Tommy, just promise me that you won't go crazy and do something silly with that much money. You rocked our world with that suicide scare. I reached out to Monique to make sure you were okay, and she told me it was all a big misunderstanding. But we were sick with worry when we first heard. If something bad happens because of all this money, I couldn't live with the guilt. So please."

"Don't worry," Tommy consoled Belle. "When you're brought to your knees as I have been, if you're smart you'll never let that happen again. And I certainly don't plan on repeating the past. I have a vision to turn everything around and do some good along the way. But this will make that dream a lot more possible to accomplish."

"Well, we're happy we can give something back to you because you changed our lives forever."

"So tell me," asked Tommy. "How are your children, and our younger brother and sister doing?"

"Well, our babies are all grown up and married, and looking forward to starting their own families soon. Duncan moved to London and owns a P.R. firm that works with high-end celebrities in sports and entertainment. You should think about hiring him. He's yet to settle down, but I think he finally has a serious girlfriend. Our wonderful baby sister, Fiona got married and moved up the coast to Aberdeen. She and her husband have two girls who are both at university now, and they have always been the perfect little family. He's an electrician who owns his own company and apparently makes a boatload of money, so she's got no worries."

Tommy smiled, glad to know that his siblings were doing so well, but guilt quickly crept back into his mind, saddened by the thought that he had missed so much of their lives. He took another sip of his drink then shook it off, determined to make the best of it going forward.

"Belle, I want you to know that I'm not trying to charge back in and take over with Dad. I know you've been handling things fine without me, and I appreciate that so much. When I took him to the neurologist while you were still away on holiday, I had to hear the diagnosis for myself. It's all been an enormous shock to me, and I wanted to fix it, but I guess that's not possible."

"I totally understand, Tommy. I'm glad you want to be involved. It's been a lot for me and Mum to handle alone. I know you'll probably be heading back to the states soon, but the more time you can spend with Dad before you go, I think that would be great."

"Well actually, I've been giving it a lot of thought to moving back here. I've got nothing keeping me in L.A., and being home in Edinburgh just feels right. What do you think?"

"Oh, Tommy ... that's wonderful news! That would make me so happy. I want you to get to know the improved Richard and our kids. You've never even met your niece and nephew and their all grown up now. It's scary how much they look like you and I did when we were younger. And I'm sure Duncan and Fiona would come home for more visits. We can go see them sometimes as well. This is so exciting!"

"It's settled then. I'll just have to find a place to live. I also want to start writing and recording music again. Strangely, I'm feeling very inspired being back here, even under the dark cloud of Dad's situation. It's so funny, because he thinks I'm still in Velour and that I've got my whole career in front of me. If I could only go back to that point in time, I would change so much. Obviously, that's not possible, so we'll have to see what the future brings."

"I know a great real estate agent who could show you some properties. She's incredibly intelligent, extremely good at her job, and quite attractive, I must say."

"Great! When can I meet her?"

"You already have. You're looking at her."

"Ha. Incredibly intelligent might be a bit of a stretch," joked Tommy.

Belle punched Tommy in the shoulder, and he flinched from the blow.

"Just remember who made you twenty-eight millions pounds, smart aleck."

"That's true. I take it back."

Tommy extended his still throbbing arm around Belle and pulled her in close as she leaned in, still sitting on her bar stool. She laid her head on his shoulder and smiled, grateful her brother was finally back in her life.

The next day Belle drove Tommy to one of her property listings, a quaint cottage tucked away on a quiet country lane. Tommy sat in the car and stared out the passenger side window at the cute little house.

"Do you want to go in?" asked Belle.

Tommy turned to Belle and smiled. "I don't want you getting upset with me, okay?"

"Okay," Belle replied in a reserved tone.

"I'm coming from a ten thousand square foot mansion with lots of land and amenities. And that was after downsizing from fifteen thousand square feet. I obviously have to minimize and cut back, but I think if I went this far, I would be miserable."

Belle laughed like a frat girl who had just pulled off the ultimate prank as she pointed her finger at Tommy.

"I got you so good! I should have videoed your face when we first pulled in. This is one of my listings, but this isn't the one I had in mind for you. I couldn't resist. The other house is around the corner."

"Phew, that's a relief. I was so worried about hacking you off," replied Tommy.

Belle pulled out of the loose gravel drive of the cottage and continued along the lane, still laughing at her brother's expense.

A few minutes later she turned into a long, tree-lined drive that opened up into a vast meadow, beyond which a beautiful stone mansion majestically greeted the eye. Tommy was captivated by the house and the surrounding land. As he stepped from the car, he felt tranquility and peacefulness, accentuated by birds singing in the trees around the perimeter of the sprawling lawn.

"Belle, this is as big as a castle. I can't afford this."

"I think you'll be surprised, Tommy. This house and the surrounding ten acres is only two-point-two million pounds. These aren't California prices here. You'll have to hire someone to manage the grounds and maybe a housekeeper, but I think it will be a great place for you to settle down and raise a family. Look at all this land for children to play in. We would have loved this as kids, wouldn't we?"

"No kidding. We only had a narrow little cobblestone street to play on, and we have the scars on our knees to prove it."

"Do you want to see inside?" asked Belle, eager to give her brother the grand tour.

"You bet!" anxiously replied Tommy.

As Tommy and Belle toured the lavish home, Tommy was smitten with the details of the quality and craftsmanship. In particular, he thought the acoustics of one room would be perfect for a home studio. The house was vacant, and all furniture had been removed. As a result, it felt a bit solemn and cold. But Belle reassured her brother that with the right interior decor and layout, the eight thousand square feet would soon feel like home.

Back outside, they stood in front of the mansion looking up on the two-story, stone outer walls that glowed a rich, gray hue in the mid-day sun.

"So, what do you think?" asked Belle.

"If you feel like it's a good deal, then let's do it. Twenty-four hours ago I couldn't even have thought about this. But with the investments you and Richard made for me, I feel like I can start living again, and maybe not worry quite as much. I'm just a little concerned about the upkeep."

"That is something to consider. But I can honestly say this is an incredible deal. It's not even listed on the market yet, so you're getting in before anyone else sees it. In a year, if you find it's too expensive to maintain, or there's anything else you don't like about it, we'll put it back on the market. I feel confident we could get several hundred thousand more, easy. In fact ... I will guarantee that if you do decide to sell and we don't get half a million more, I'll buy it from you for at least that or give you the difference. Trust me."

"All right ... you've talked me into it. Let's do it!" agreed Tommy.

"Great! We should go in at full asking price since it's not listed yet. I'll make the offer. Now we need to find you a younger wife and you will be on your way. So how about Amanda? She's available you know. And she's always had a big crush on you."

"She does not. You're just saying that. I really don't think a beautiful, down-to-earth woman like Amanda would ever want to get involved with the likes of me."

"Oh, yes she would, Tommy. Think about it ... as a popular former recording artist, she knows what you've been through. If you do start performing again, she completely understands what that life is like and will be able to support you better than someone who doesn't get it. And she's still young enough to start a family, but mature enough to deal with you. That said ... if you ever cheat on her, I will kill you because she's one of my very best friends."

"Wow, Belle! You already have us married and having kids. We haven't even been on a date yet."

"Well, I know love when I see it. I immediately noticed the way you two looked at each other at Mum and Dad's house yesterday. We talked on the phone last night and she was carrying on about you non-stop, so you need to ask her out before it's too late."

"You've got this all figured out, don't you?"

"I sure do, big brother. It's time for you to have a serious relationship and I'm not letting you get away from us again."

CHAPTER TWENTY-FIVE

THE IMMENSE CROWD ERUPTED INTO A ROAR as the winning goal was scored in the final seconds of extended time. In the excitement of the moment, Frank leapt to his feet and raised his arms high above his head. He pounded his fists rapidly up and down along with tens of thousands of fellow home-team fans.

Following the last televised soccer match, Tommy had witnessed Frank's confusion when he cheered for the wrong club. But today, there was no mistaking that it was his father's favorite team who had just won a critical match against their biggest rivals. Standing at his side, Tommy was more elated by the joy he saw in his dad's face than the win itself.

As Tommy and Frank walked out of the stadium decked out in their home team scarfs and jerseys, they were surrounded by the organic flow of the masses. A tall, muscle-bound fan walking behind Tommy and his father leaned in and asked, "Oi, aren't you Tommy Model?"

Tommy replied in a gracious and straightforward, "Yes."

"And is this your pop, mate?" inquired the burly man.

Again, Tommy replied in the affirmative.

Quickly coordinating with his pals around him, the bodybuilder and his group of bodybuilder-looking friends, leaned over and lifted Tommy and Frank off the ground. They carried father and son on their shoulders, high above the heads of the surging crowd. Now in full view, several fans walking nearby also recognized Tommy. In less than a minute, the crowd was chanting a similar cadence to what Tommy had experienced when he had recently taken the stage with Hector's Folly.

"Tommy, Tommy, Tommy, Tommy Model!" The cheer echoed between the buildings while the parade of followers progressed along the lane, heading back to their homes, cars, and the railway station. As simple chants often do, it eventually developed into a much longer song when someone added another section. "Tommy, Tommy, Tommy, Tommy Model. Our favorite son has finally come home."

The chorus continued until the thousands had dwindled to less than fifty, as fans dispersed in various directions. Tommy laughed at the sheer spectacle of it all as he and his father continued to be carried aloft in celebration. It was an amazing tribute that could only happen in Edinburgh, and he was grateful to be back in his hometown. Here, he was obviously still widely respected as the local boy who had broken through to immense fame and popularity, albeit now many, many years later.

In the moment he wondered if perhaps there were still fans elsewhere who felt the same. After all, he had sold over one hundred million albums, so surely there were others across the globe who still fondly remembered him. If only they too could be reminded that he still existed.

When the song finally subsided Frank looked over at Tommy and asked, "How do all of these people know you, Son?"

Tommy smiled and shrugged his shoulders. He was already learning little tricks to play along with his father's memory issues.

Deflection was often much easier than trying to fight the reality of continually correcting the record, or explaining the obvious, which was a natural, but fruitless tendency.

Eventually, with their paths diverging, the four men who had carried Tommy and Frank such a great distance, gently set them back to their feet. Tommy thanked them for the memorable experience, and after a quick photo, they bid each other farewell. Tommy and Frank slowly walked the last block, along the narrow, cobblestone lane towards home.

A few minutes later, Davina greeted her son and her husband at the door. She had been anxiously watching for their return with a bit of worry surrounding how the day's outing had gone.

"Hello, my love," said Frank as he kissed his wife on the cheek. "I've got to get off these feet. My dogs are barking!" exclaimed Frank as he made a bee-line for his easychair.

"Hi, Mum," Tommy said as he leaned down and also kissed his mother on the cheek.

"So ... how did it go, Thomas?" asked Davina.

"It was great. They scored the winning goal in the last few seconds and Dad seemed to know it was his team this time. Maybe it's being around all of that energy. It was almost as if he had no memory issues at all during the match. Later though, when some highly enthusiastic fans were carrying us on their shoulders and chanting my name because they recognized me, he didn't understand how so many people knew who I was. But that was the worst of it. Alzheimer's is such a bizarre disease, isn't it?"

"It really is. I'm glad you both had a great time together. I think you being back in his life is helping him more than you may realize. He seems much happier now, even when you're not around. Speaking of which, when do you move into your new house?"

"Next week. I'm very excited. I couldn't have done it without Belle. She really came through for me."

"That's wonderful, Thomas. I'm so elated you are coming home," said Davina as she began to tear up.

"What's wrong, Mum? Please don't cry," pleaded, Tommy.

"This has been killing me, so I need to tell you. I'm so very sorry we didn't work harder on our end to resolve the rift between you and your father. I think that may have been the only serious argument the two of you ever had, but it was a doozy. Frank had no idea the extent of the stress you were under. He shouldn't have put the burden on you to bail out Belle and Richard from their troubles."

"Mum. It's okay. Come on."

Davina paused to slide a tissue from her pocket and dab the tears that had streamed down her cheek to her chin, creating faint lines in her makeup.

"On the other hand, Thomas ... look at the life that Belle's been able to have because of your love and kindness. And now it's coming back to you in a big way, perhaps when you need it the most. Then again, maybe if we would have been there for you, your life would have been much better all along."

"It's all right, Mum. Please don't do this to yourself."

"I know, I know. We kept hoping you would reach out. And you were probably thinking the same of us. I have tremendous regret for not putting my foot down to resolve the matter. Just please know that we never stopped loving you, and I'm extremely sorry it all happened the way that it did. I hope we can all focus on the present and the future, and put the past behind us."

"I agree, Mum. The past is the past, and I surely don't want to relive it. Let's look forward to the times ahead."

Tommy hugged his mother. A knock interrupted the conversation at a good place. Davina made her way to the front door, opening it to find Amanda who was stopping by for her visit with Frank. Tommy's heart raced as she entered the hallway and walked towards him, neatly dressed in pink scrubs. Seeing Tommy, Amanda lit up and smiled. Tommy took a deep breath, then exhaled as she greeted him.

"Hi, Tommy."

"Hi, Amanda. You look nice today."

"Thank you. There's not a whole lot one can do to look good in scrubs."

"Well, I'm sure you always look beautiful in whatever you're wearing."

Amanda blushed with embarrassment. She excused herself as she eased by Tommy and into the living room where Frank had fallen asleep from the exhaustion of the day.

She gently slipped a blood pressure cuff over his arm as Frank opened one eye to see what was happening. Without waking her patient completely, she took his B.P., listened to his heart and lungs, checked his oxygen level, and slowly inserted a thermometer into his mouth to get his temperature. All results were good as they usually were. Instead of having their usual chat, Frank insisted on taking a nap, so Amanda quietly packed her things and readied to leave.

With Belle's voice still ringing in his head about Amanda's apparent interest in him, Tommy was keen on testing the waters.

"Sorry I wore Dad out today."

"That's okay. It's great all the things you're doing with him. I know Belle and your Mum appreciate it as well. It gives them a much-deserved break every now and then."

"Since Dad's not good company today, do you want to go grab a coffee or tea with me and we can talk?" asked Tommy.

"Sure. That sounds nice," replied Amanda looking into Tommy's eyes and engaging with a smile.

AMANDA AND TOMMY WALKED TO A NEARBY COFFEE AND TEA SHOP and spent the afternoon discussing their former lives as celebrities as well as their hopes for the future. The conversation was easy and natural. Tommy felt a strong chemistry with Amanda that he had never experienced with anyone else before. He learned about her charity work, and how giving of herself had carried her from the sadness of losing a music career that had ended long before she was ready to let it go.

Tommy was inspired by her kindness towards others, and she encouraged him to try to be more open to sharing his time with those in need. She assured Tommy that doing so would diminish his own conflict and pain. She suggested that eventually, he would become so connected to the feeling of giving back and being grateful for all of the good things in his life, that he would no longer be able to live a self-centered existence. As a result, wonderful things would start to happen again. It all intensely resonated with Tommy and he vowed to try to escape from his bad habits.

"You know," started Tommy. He paused to reach across the table to place his hands in Amanda's. "I think it may already be working because by devoting more time to my father, I met you. You're such an amazing woman, and I'd like to spend more time getting to know you ... if that's okay with you?"

Amanda smiled and looked at their connected hands. She lightly squeezed her fingertips into his, reciprocating the feeling.

"Of course, Tommy. I'd like that. In fact ... if you're interested, we can start tonight. I'm performing with my band at Hops if you have time to stop by. I'd welcome your input on the show. It's just for fun, but I still take it very seriously."

"I wouldn't miss it for anything," replied Tommy.

Tommy and Amanda slowly walked back to her car parked in front of his parent's house. They hugged goodbye, not ready to tempt the fate of a kiss yet, and agreed to have a late dinner after the show.

A FEW HOURS LATER, Tommy was feeling a bit like a teenager going on a first date as he readied for the evening. He applied gel to spike his still-thick, blond hair which now required a bit more color to hide the gray. He dressed in a modern, youthful fashion, but still very much his own style. As he briefly stared at himself in the mirror, it dawned on him that other than a few extra pounds, physically, he had changed very little in three decades. For that he was grateful, especially having lived through all of the years of substance abuse and depression.

When he arrived at Hops, Amanda was already performing her first set which was an entertaining combination of her personal hits and unique versions of cover songs by other artists. If Tommy wasn't one hundred percent convinced that he was in love with her before, her sultry voice and captivating stage presence completely did him in. He watched in awe of her talent while he stood in the back corner of the small venue trying to hide his presence. Amanda however, didn't miss Tommy's entrance, and she soon acknowledged his appearance.

"Hey, everybody. I want to thank you all for coming out tonight and being so supportive. There's a very special person in the audience I'd like to acknowledge. He is one of my inspirations and the most successful recording artist ever born and raised here in Edinburgh. I'm also happy to say he's become a dear friend. Ladies and gentlemen, please give it up for Mr. Tommy Model!"

Amanda pointed in Tommy's direction with her hand, and the entire crowd pivoted to look. They erupted in applause, cheers, and whistles while Tommy humbly waved and mouthed "Thank you," several times before the admiration quieted.

From the stage, Amanda continued. "Sorry to embarrass you, Tommy, but there is no way I'm going to let you hide in the back of the room. I'd love it if you'd join me here on stage and maybe we can sing a song together. What do you say?"

The audience broke into a frenzy at the thought of a duet. Those standing closest to Tommy encouraged him with back pats and gestures beckoning him to the stage. Tommy shook his head and smiled. He had vowed to never again perform in a bar or nightclub, having agonizingly done so night after night for a nearly a year leading to his big break. He was now casting aside that rule for Amanda as he walked to the front of the room, high-fiving and fist-bumping fans who extended their hands in appreciation and excitement.

As he stepped up onto the small stage, he hugged Amanda and kissed her on the cheek then asked, "So what would you like to sing together?"

Amanda picked a sheet of paper off the ground and handed it to Tommy. As he looked down, he eyed the printed lyrics to the song Amanda wanted to perform. Tommy grinned and nodded his head in agreement, as the band kicked into one of his favorite songs.

Together, Amanda and Tommy exchanged verses and harmonized the chorus perfectly as if the duet had been practiced incessantly for weeks. The couple was drawn into the sensual, romantic intent behind the lyrics and their attraction was obvious. The audience also engaged in the infectious melody, and not a single body stood still. With the last word, Tommy pulled in Amanda and kissed her passionately on the lips as cell phones clicked and captured the moment.

CHAPTER TWENTY-SIX

THE BLACK SUV CAME TO A STOP on the gravel drive as the headlights further illuminated the well-lit, block-stone facade of the majestic, two-story mansion. The driver opened the back door, and Tommy and Amanda anxiously hopped out. They thanked their chauffeur, then turned to walk towards the charming, glass-paned front door with its ornate stone carving, reminiscent of angels wings, above.

"Oh, Tommy it's amazing!" exclaimed, Amanda. "A bit grand, but amazing."

"Wait until you see it in the daylight. The grounds are incredible."

"I thought you weren't moving in until next week."

"I'm not officially, but I already own the place, so I'm excited to show you. Would you like to go in?"

"Yes, of course."

A tawny owl hooted in the distance, eerily piecing the silence of the moonlit night.

"Did you hear that, Tommy?"

Tommy fumbled with the key in the lock while he responded to Amanda. "You mean the owl?"

"Yes. You know that's good luck, don't you?"

A bit resistant due to recent inactivity, the deadbolt finally gave way as the key turned. "I didn't know that," Tommy replied. "But we're in, and I'm here with you, so I am feeling pretty lucky."

"Me too," agreed Amanda.

The owl repeated its call as the couple entered and Tommy closed the door behind as he searched the wall in the dark for the light switch. Amanda gently coaxed his arm back before he could find his target. She faced him and placed her hands on his biceps, gently massaging them in the black chasm of the windowless hall. Taking his cue, Tommy slid his hand into the small of Amanda's back and pulled her body into his.

The chemistry was electric as they kissed each other. Their interaction was so intense that Amanda briefly forgot to breathe and had to break their connection to gasp some air. Tommy kissed her neck, and slowly inched down to her fashionably exposed shoulders causing Amanda to tremble from the sensation.

She softly whispered in Tommy's ear, "I want you to make love to me right here, right now. Every time we walk through the front door, we'll remember the first time we were together." She solidified her demand with a tender bite to his earlobe.

Tommy's breathing escalated as he swiftly removed all of Amanda's clothing and attentively caressed her soft skin. Against her warmth, he could smell the addictive aroma of cocoa butter. His eyes adjusted to the darkness and with the faint glow of moonlight that crept in from a side room, he could finally see and feel Amanda's unveiled body. Normally hidden under the garb of baggy medical scrubs, he found the well-toned, curvaceous, natural woman he had hoped and suspected she would be.

In turn, Amanda aggressively ripped off all of Tommy's clothing from head to toe, then stood facing him and seductively drifted her nails along his chest and abdomen. The sensation was more than he could resist and with one smooth move, he turned Amanda to face the wall as she arched her back and lifted her hips, then slowly leaned back into Tommy.

Seductively attentive to one another in dark hallway, the intensity of the passion and energy between the couple was to a level neither had experienced before. Eventually consumed by sheer exhaustion, they collapsed to the floor where Amanda laid on top of Tommy. As their breathing subsided, Tommy could feel Amanda's heart beating in rapid rhythm. It occasionally synced with his as the warmth and satisfaction of the moment comforted them to sleep.

Several hours later they both awoke, Amanda still cradled on top of Tommy and wrapped in his arms. The early morning sun had shifted the darkness of the hall to a bright orange glow. Amanda raised her head and looked into Tommy's still-sleepy eyes.

"Good morning, rock star," she said with a coy smile. "That was quite a show you put on last night."

Tommy smiled admiring the beauty of Amanda's kind eyes and responded, "I must admit ... I was pretty impressive. But you really brought down the house with that finale."

The couple laughed, and Tommy hugged Amanda tightly, the warmth of their naked bodies making the chill in the house suddenly more noticeable.

"Man, it's cold in here!" exclaimed Tommy.

"It sure is. Give me a second and I'll try to fix that," replied Amanda. She slid down Tommy's body and together, they quickly forgot about any temperature issues in the house.

Tommy knew he was hooked on Amanda, and hooked hard. Although obviously important, it wasn't merely the physical attraction that solidified his feelings for her. It was something more significant that he couldn't explain. It was an energy, a vibe, a feeling. He felt as if he had known Amanda for lifetimes beyond his own, and he was confident she felt the same. Even though it was only in its infancy, for the first time, a relationship felt easy. It should have scared Tommy, but it didn't, and he was ready to give up any resistance.

As Amanda returned her head to Tommy's bare chest, he stroked her shoulder-length blonde hair as she closed her eyes, entranced in the moment.

"Marry me," whispered Tommy.

"What?" Amanda asked as she raised her head and looked at Tommy. She knew full well what he had said, but her mind was still struggling to catch up with her emotions.

"Marry me," Tommy repeated.

"Are you serious?"

"I've never been more so," he confirmed. "I've been waiting for you my entire life, and here you are ... so marry me."

Amanda raised onto her elbows to get a better view of Tommy's eyes. "Are you sure this is not the sex talking?"

"No, it's not the sex talking. It's everything about you. You're amazing, and I'm hoping you feel the same about me."

Amanda slid up Tommy's chest to reach his lips with hers before responding.

"Of course I feel the same. This just seems a little crazy-fast, don't you think?"

"Yeah, but do you have any doubts this is right, and we're meant for each other? Just think of how this all came together. If this isn't fate, I don't know what is."

"No, I don't doubt it. I've had a crush on you forever so this is a dream come true for me. It's like a fairytale. You had me long before I ever met you, Mr. Model."

They locked lips again only stopping for Tommy to repeat his question. "So, will you marry me?"

Amanda leaned in to kiss Tommy once more. Her emotions overflowed, as she began crying tears of joy and shook her head in confirmation.

"Yes, yes, yes!" she replied. "Absolutely, yes!"

CHAPTER TWENTY-SEVEN

THE WEDDING CEREMONY of Mister Thomas Maddock and Miss Amanda Perkins neared its conclusion as the minister asked the customary question, "If anyone feels this couple should not be united in holy matrimony, speak now or forever hold your peace."

Even though he was an old friend of Tommy's, O'Shea Muldoon was a well-known troublemaker around about Edinburgh. He always had been, and likely always would be. So it was no surprise that it would be O'Shea Muldoon who would stand in a drunken stupor and interrupt the service to comment on the union.

"I have something to say!" exclaimed O'Shea.

Every guest seated in the immense sanctuary of the church turned their heads and gasped in awe that someone would actually speak up.

"Yes, Mr. Shea," replied the minister.

Having grown up together, the pastor well-knew the red-haired, freckle-faced man, who had a reputation in his youth of being a bully. As a result, he was repeatedly kicked out of children's choir for his bad behavior, and now here he was, all these years later, once again creating chaos inside the church.

"You know it's O'Shea, Reverend. Not Shea. I don't know who Shea is, and if you're going to speak to me, you should at least get my name right, okay?"

"What would you like to say, Mr. O'Shea? Let's get on with it please."

"I just wanted to say how much I love Tommy. When we were growing up and everyone else treated me like an outcast, he always showed me tremendous respect. It's a little-known fact, but he's the reason I didn't go to prison years ago."

"O'Shea. I appreciate it, mate, but really ... you don't have to thank me," said Tommy in efforts to end the interruption and move things along.

"Please indulge me, brother ... if you will. You see folks ... it was Tommy who took the rap for me when I stole a case of Scotch whisky from a liquor store when I was sixteen years old. The cops loved him so much, but everyone knew they hated me with a passion and were looking for any excuse to put me away. So when they came to question me about the theft, Tommy was there. He told those blokes it was he who had made the heist while wearing a ski mask. They knew he was fibbing, but let him off with only a warning after he gave them back the case, minus a missing bottle he said had been broken. I imagine those fellas took that booze for themselves, but after they left, we celebrated like rock stars with a shot or two from that so-called missing bottle. Tommy putting it on the line for me was a kindness I will never forget."

O'Shea began to tear up, and his voice quivered as he continued. "Then he gave me my first real job as a roadie back in the early days with his band, Velour. Remember those good times, Tommy?"

Tommy calmly smiled and shook his head, *yes* in acknowledgment. He rubbed the top of Amanda's hands with his thumbs, turning his eyes to hers in reassurance it was all going to be all right.

"Well, what you people don't know," continued O'Shea, now with the complete anguish of the memory coating his face, "is that man standing there, with that beautiful angel of a woman, is a Saint. My mother was dying of cancer when I was only seventeen years old. Tommy had just received his first record deal advance check, and he took some of that money and paid for all of her treatments. We were very poor, you see. And when she finally left this world for a better one, he was there for me like no one else. He covered all of the costs of her funeral. She would have been so proud to see you here today, Tommy. I know this isn't the right time or the place, but I want everyone to know that if there's anyone in this world who deserves happiness, it's you, my friend. And after I shut my mouth, if someone objects to the two of them getting married ... I will flat knock you out! Got it?"

O'Shea apologetically waved at Tommy as he slowly returned to his seat. The audience sat in stunned silence. Forever the good friend, Tommy smiled at Amanda and slid his hands from hers then turned to face the crowd. He applauded O'Shea's courage and kindness, even if it had been entirely awkward and out of place. Taking Tommy's queue, Amanda, the bridesmaids, groomsmen, and all of the guests began clapping and cheering as they stood and turned to face O'Shea, who was coming down from his emotional high and now sat in utter embarrassment.

When the commotion subsided, Tommy turned back to Amanda who now stood with tears of joy in her eyes. She found herself even more proud of the often misunderstood, but kind, caring soul that she knew Tommy to be. She looked forward to helping him bring that person more to the forefront of his life.

"Where were we, Reverend?" asked Tommy.

Hesitantly the minister repeated the question "As I was saying ... if anyone feels this couple should not be united in holy matrimony, speak now or forever hold your peace." Not even the creak of a pew broke the overwhelming silence as everyone hung on baited breath for what seemed like minutes, but was actually no more than five seconds.

"Great! Then I now pronounce you husband and wife. You may kiss the bride," directed the minister.

Tommy and Amanda sealed the moment with a kiss. It wasn't like most just-married couples who nervously peck each other like chickens, or don't know which way to turn their heads. Instead, they delivered a real movie star quality kiss. Cameras and cell phones clicked away in a fury, capturing the moment for all prosperity. The audience of friends and family again erupted in cheers and applause, as Tommy and Amanda proceeded along the aisle and into the sunlight that greeted them beyond the front doors of the church.

The reception afterward at a nearby Scottish castle was as magical as the wedding itself had been, as family members and old friends joined the couple in celebrating the joyous occasion. Tommy was elated to see that Monique and his long-time surfer-buddy, Skip Chadwick, had made the crossing to wish them well and share their own good news.

Apparently, shortly after Tommy left Los Angeles for Edinburgh, Skip called Monique to see how Tommy was doing. Having decided to take the life-changing leap that she and Tommy had discussed, Monique was busy packing for a move to Charleston when Skip called. Still conflicted about her pending relocation, she was looking for a distraction, so the two decided to casually meet for coffee to discuss their old friend, Tommy. Coffee led to drinks and dinner later that evening. Drinks and dinner eventually led to Monique putting her move to South Carolina on hold. That decision evolved into a full-blown relationship, and the happy couple was now planning their own wedding only a few months down the road. Tommy was ecstatic for his dearest friends and couldn't think of two people he'd rather see together.

The party continued into the afternoon, and dancing eventually turned into drunken attempts at karaoke by rambunctious, kilt-wearing friends of Tommy's. Two groomsmen eventually got into a brief, yet momentarily intense shoving match over who would sing Kim Carnes, "Betty Davis Eyes." The moment signaled it was time for Amanda and Tommy to depart and they bid their farewells, eventually breaking free from the multitude of well-wishers. A small crowd chased them to the front circular drive of the castle. Turning for a final wave, the elated duo jumped into a waiting black SUV and were sped off to the airport where they boarded a private jet for their honeymoon destination.

THE NEXT DAY, TOMMY AND AMANDA SAT ON THEIR SECLUDED PRIVATE DECK, basking in the sun overlooking the crystal-clear, white-sand shallows surrounding their over-water villa. Amanda had always wanted to visit Bora Bora, an interest she had casually mentioned to Tommy in passing one day. She never dreamed that she would actually see the beautiful island in person, especially on a honeymoon. Yet, here she was.

Amanda looked at Tommy and smiled as she sipped her pink-colored Mai Tai cocktail and took in the moment. Tommy was relaxing with his head back and sunglasses facing skyward when she stood from the comfortably cushioned chaise lounge and completely removed her bathing suit, then strolled over to the small swimming pool built into their private deck.

Catching her shadow as she passed Tommy opened his eyes to now see his wife's beautifully naked body, glimmering and coated with the sheen of sunscreen. She bent to scoop water from the pool with her hands which she drizzled over her back to cool off. It was a sight that seemed absolutely surreal to Tommy.

After all the years of loneliness and sadness, it took almost losing everything to find the love of his life. Now here he sat watching in awe, the incredibly sexy woman who was now his wife. Her curvaceous silhouette was framed perfectly by the endless expanse of turquoise ocean beyond. Unable to resist the sight any longer, Tommy joined Amanda in the pool, and they made love for the third time since their arrival early that morning.

Later that evening the newlyweds enjoyed a fantastic dining experience at one of the resort's stylish restaurants. Lightly tanned from the sun, both Tommy and Amanda looked stunning in their casual, island-wear. They glowed with a joy for each other that was further accentuated by the romantic, candlelit room. A passing couple recognized the duo from their wedding photos now garnering millions of views online. They briefly congratulated the pair, then respectfully left them to the peace of their time together.

Back at the villa, Tommy and Amanda entered the spacious living area to find a beautiful acoustic guitar resting on a floor stand in the middle of the room.

"Look at this," remarked Tommy.

"I wanted to surprise you, baby ... in case you got in the mood to play. So I asked if they had a guitar. Apparently, it's a common request from other musicians who visit the resort, so here you go. They wouldn't say who for sure, but supposedly a famous guitar player from Ireland was here last week and borrowed this same guitar. They said he always wore a skull-cap, even when he was in the pool."

"Really ... well I can't imagine who that might have been," joked Tommy. "Maybe it's got some good vibes and a new song or two left in it."

"We'll see, won't we," said Amanda beaming from ear to ear, happy she had pleased Tommy with her surprise.

Climbing to a rooftop deck separate from the one they sat at earlier during the day, they found a magazine-perfect scene. The faint glow of hanging lanterns and floor lights surrounded the perimeter, illuminating the richly colored teak wood. Towering, billowy, gray clouds were visible in the bright moonlight which shimmered off the calm water below.

A chilled bottle of the resort's best champagne rested in an ice bucket between two comfortable chairs facing the water. They sat, and Tommy poured a glass for Amanda, then one for himself. They toasted to their future together and stared into each other's eyes as they sipped the sweet bubbly, then turned to take in the view.

A lightning flash inside a cloud in the far distance further electrified the moment, and Tommy felt very inspired. He now had a muse and a purpose beyond the fragile, imperfect character he had long ago become. Tommy picked up the guitar he had carried with him. One chord led to several, and in less than a half hour, he and Amanda had written an awesome song, leaving both utterly surprised by the collaboration.

"I don't want to jinx anything, but that's the first song I've written in at least a decade," said Tommy.

"You know I love you, sweetie ... so I don't want you to think I'm just saying this, but that song may be one of your best ever. It's incredible. Seriously. What do you think?" asked Amanda.

"I honestly feel that way too. It's like it was there all along and you had to bring it out of me. It is pretty amazing. I'm shocked it was that easy. Do you want to try to write another?"

"Sure, let's give it a shot."

Two hours later, Amanda peaked at Tommy's watch. It was nearing midnight as Tommy jotted down the last lyric to the third song they had written. All were hit-worthy in their collective professional minds. Tommy wanted to continue into the morning, but Amanda begged him to come to bed, reassuring him that they could start fresh again tomorrow. In his child-like fervor, Tommy initially resisted. Amanda stood and slid the dress off her shoulders and once more stood completely bare in front of her husband. The elation of an all-night songwriting session was quickly overridden as he followed Amanda to their luxurious bed on the main floor below.

There, they made love again. Afterward, Amanda quickly drifted off to sleep, completely exhausted from the amazing day she had experienced with her husband. Tommy tucked his arm behind his head as he stared at the teak ceiling. His mind raced from the excitement of the new songs they had just created together. While he wanted to enjoy their remaining time in Bora Bora, he also couldn't wait to get back home to see how they would develop in a studio with full instrumentation.

There, with his new bride, laying on a plush bed, in a villa with ocean water flowing beneath, at a remote resort in the middle of the South Pacific, the new and improved Tommy Model was reborn.

CHAPTER TWENTY-EIGHT

THE THUNDEROUS POUNDING OF DRUMS and crashing cymbals seemed to reverberate throughout the entire house, and Amanda could find peace nowhere. She slowly opened the door to the large bedroom Tommy had converted to a recording studio two weeks earlier following their honeymoon.

Dressed in burgundy-colored scrubs she waved at Tommy to get his attention, her face displaying the anguish she felt inside. He quickly jumped from his chair while signaling the drummer to continue as the newlyweds slipped into the hall. He closed the door behind, but simply leaving the room offered little buffer against the intense volume of the drums. Tommy grabbed Amanda's hand and guided her along the hall and out the back door into the well-manicured boxwood gardens.

"I'm sorry, honey," sympathetically apologized Tommy. "I know it's loud, but we'll be done with the drum tracks today, I promise."

"Good, because after four days and nights of that, I'm about to go batty. I didn't realize it would take so long for him to lay down twelve songs."

"Yeah, me too. He's a bit of an over-achiever and perfectionist, but that's why I picked him. As always, you look super sexy in those scrubs," Tommy noted as he leaned over to kiss Amanda's neck. "Are you heading out?"

"Stop kissing me, Tommy. You're going to get me all worked up," joked Amanda as she squirmed away from her husband's advances. "Yes, I'm off to check on your father so thankfully I'll get a break from the little drummer boy for a while. Maybe he'll be done by the time I get back."

"Let's hope so," replied Tommy. "Give Mum and Dad all my love."

"I will."

Amanda started to walk inside, but stopped and turned back to look at Tommy.

"You know I love you, and I never want to be one of those nagging wives, but you told me to help you stay focused on what really matters as you restart your career."

"I did," cautiously agreed Tommy, not sure what was coming next.

"Well, I think this is one of those moments where I should gently remind you not to get so consumed in recording this album that you don't take time to visit your father. He needs to get out of the house and do things with you while he still can. So will you please find a little time to get together soon?"

Tommy smiled, grateful for the kind subtle way she had handled him. As usual, she was right, and he knew it.

"I'll call Mum tonight and see if he'd like to go fishing this weekend. We haven't done that since I was a kid, but I know he used to love it."

"That sounds nice, Tommy. He's mentioned that to me as something he really enjoyed in the past, so I think that's a great idea. I'll see you later."

Amanda leaned in for a quick goodbye kiss, but one kiss turned into two, and two turned into a much longer make-out session. Before she knew it, her scrub bottoms were off and she was atop Tommy as they made love on the smooth, pea gravel path inside the boxwood hedge maze of the garden.

It had been this way since their wedding day. One of the two of them would offer a mild passing affection, and suddenly they were entangled in each other, going at it like college kids on spring break. Tommy hoped the passion they were experiencing would never subside, but he also knew the past few weeks had been relatively stress-free without any major life challenges, so the real tests were likely still to come.

THREE DAYS LATER IN THE EARLY MORNING HOURS, Tommy steered his SUV off the main highway and onto the narrow road leading to the Drygrange Old Bridge and the towering Leaderfoot Viaduct spanning the River Tweed near Melrose on the Scottish borders. The scene was perfectly Scotland, and Tommy was anxious to get a fly in the water in hopes of catching some large salmon or trout. He popped the back hatch to begin unloading the gear while his father continued to sit motionless in the front seat.

"Dad! Are you going to just sit there or come get dressed? Let's get in that gorgeous river and catch some fish?"

There was no reply as Tommy shimmied into his rubber chest waders. Cinching his belt and slipping his suspenders over his shoulders to keep them from falling as he walked, he marched to the passenger side door and opened it to find his father staring into space as tears streamed down his face.

"Dad! What's wrong? Are you ok?"

Frank shook his head in confirmation, then said, "Ma heid's mince."

"You're all mixed up, you say? Why? And why are you crying? You love fishing so I thought you'd be excited to come back here. Are you feeling bad? Do you want to go home?"

Frank shook his head *no* but remained closed-lipped about what was bothering him.

"Dad, you have to talk to me. Please!" Tommy's voice crackled as he became emotional at the scene.

"I, I, I," stuttered Frank, "I don't remember ever coming to this place, and you told me I used to bring you here all the time when you were a wean. And I don't remember how to fly fish. It's like a word on the tip of my tongue that I just can't get out. I know I've done all this before, but I can't remember, and I'm scared as to why that is."

Tommy leaned in and hugged his father's neck.

"Hey, it's going to be fine. You taught me well, so now I'll teach you. I also brought a spinning rod so you can use that instead. It's a lot easier than fly fishing. Come on. Let's shake it off and have some fun."

Frank nodded his head in agreement and wiped the tears from his face, as he turned and stood from his seat then followed Tommy to the back where his son helped him into a set of waders. In a matter of minutes he was transformed into the epitome of a Scottish fisherman. With rod in hand, he followed Tommy along a rutted sheep path to the water.

Tommy surveyed the surface while standing with his father on the gravel bar beneath the towering arches of the viaduct that looked more like something the Romans had built two thousand years ago rather than an old, abandoned rail-line bridge constructed in the 1860's. To their right the smaller, but equally as architecturally impressive, Drygrange Old Bridge, framed the stunning views of the valley. Tommy slipped off his backpack and set it on the dry, stony surface. He unzipped the large center pocket and pulled out two bottles of white wine, then walked to the water's edge where he carefully tucked the bottles between two submerged rocks to chill them for later.

"I've always wanted to do that, Dad. We're like Hemingway's characters Jake and Bill in *The Sun Also Rises* when they went fly fishing together. Later when we get hungry, we'll have that perfectly chilled wine with the picnic Amanda prepared for us. Sound good?"

"Aye," replied Frank in subdued approval, still uncertain of his surroundings.

"Now let's go catch some fish, Dad."

Tommy and Frank slowly waded into the gently flowing current that at this section meandered more like a stream than a river. Tommy reminded his father how to use the spinning reel, and after a few practice casts he had returned to his old form.

"Dad, try casting into that stronger current on the other side. The big fish hang out right before that in the calmer section. They dart in and out of the riffles to grab smaller fish and insects, which is what we're trying to mimic with our lures."

Frank cast his line where Tommy had instructed, and they both watched intently as it slowly swept with the flow. Within a matter of seconds the rod tip jerked, then twitched again as the thin monofilament stretched taught with a thump. It tightened and whistled in the light breeze.

"Jerk the rod back, Dad! Set the hook!" Tommy screamed in excitement.

Frank awkwardly pulled the rod tip back, lodging the hook deep into the fish's jaw. Line stripped off of the spool in a frenzy, and Tommy reached over to adjust the drag to minimize the run.

"That's okay ... let him go for a bit. We'll get him."

The line cut deeply through the water as the fish first swam with the current, then arced into the calm eddy parallel to the bank, directly downstream from where they stood.

"It may be trying to wrap you on a rock, Dad. Start reeling in now."

Frank furiously cranked on the handle of the reel, pumping the rod tip up and down, scrapping for every inch of line he could muster.

"My muscles are burning, Thomas! I don't know how much longer I can go."

"Hang in there, Dad ... he's almost to us. Just another ten feet and we'll land him."

Carefully Frank slid the fish from deeper water onto the shallow gravel shelf where it flopped anxiously trying to escape its fate. Tommy knelt and quickly slid his hands under the massive salmon, cradling the beast as he lifted it for his father to see.

"That's incredible, Dad! Your first full cast and you land a twenty-pound salmon. You rock!"

Frank stood elated and gently stroked the slick side of the massive fish.

"Should we take him home and cook him for dinner, Son?"

"No, Dad. Let's take a picture together then I'll carefully place him back in the water and let him live to fight another day. Cool?"

"Okay, that sounds good, Thomas."

Tommy pulled out his cell phone, snapped a pic of father and son with their magnificent catch, then knelt back into shallows and softly laid the salmon into the water. There he grabbed it by the tail, slowly easing it back and forth to get oxygen flowing over its gills. In a flash, it erupted with renewed vigor and splashed water in Tommy's face as its tail cut the surface and propelled its body back over the drop-off into the dark depths of the river.

Tommy turned back to his father, laughing at the payback he had just received and wiping the moisture from his cheek.

"Well, I probably deserved that for dragging him out of the water. That was so awesome, Dad. Let's catch another."

"Son, I am exhausted after that. How about I sit on the bank and watch you for a while. That really took it out of me."

"Sure, Dad. You go get comfortable," replied Tommy, painfully realizing that his aging father no longer had the strength of the man he had known in his youth.

Tommy enjoyed several hours of fly-fishing, with he himself landing an impressive array of salmon and trout, but none matching the size of his father's prize catch. After releasing another fish, he looked back to see that his father had dozed off. Tommy's stomach rumbled as he looked at his watch and noticed that it was nearly noon.

He waded back to the gravel bar, then walked on to the grassy bank where Frank sat, his chin now touching his chest as he slept. Tommy spread a tartan-print blanket next to his father, then emptied all of the contents of their picnic lunch from his cooler backpack. He retrieved one bottle of wine from the crisp water. Returning to the bank, he quietly called his father in efforts of waking him from his slumber, as he pulled the cork from its grasp.

"Hey, Dad."

"Hmmm? What?" grumbled Frank, slowly opening his weary, blue eyes.

"You ready to have some lunch?" asked Tommy.

Frank stretched his arms above his head, still fighting through his grogginess.

"Lunch? Sure, I could eat a little something, I guess."

"Well, we have a bit of a feast here, so I hope you want more than a little."

Father and son sat enjoying a lovingly prepared meal of pork pies, Scotch eggs, cold cuts, cheeses, and wafers. Cookies and pastries were savored for dessert, all while listening to the rhythmic rush of water cascading over the nearby rapids. A small herd of sheep quietly grazed a few yards behind them, and together, Frank and Tommy sipped and savored the sweetness of the chilled white wine.

"So did you have a good time today?" inquired Tommy.

"Yes, I believe so. Thank you for making us lunch. I wish my son could be with us to see this beautiful place. It seems very familiar to me, but I don't think I've ever been here before."

Tommy's heart sank at his father's words, but he quickly recovered and went with the flow of the conversation.

"It is an amazing place, isn't it?" remarked Tommy.

"It sure is. You know, speaking of my son ... he's going to be a famous rock star. He's really good, and I'm very proud of what he's accomplished. I wasn't sure at first because as most parents do, I hoped he would become a doctor or lawyer ... you know ... some respectable, well-paying career. But the second he picked up a guitar a few years ago, I knew he was hooked. When he wrote his first song, I said to his mother, 'That creativity must have come from you because I know he didn't get it from me. But wherever it's coming from, it's something special.'"

Frank looked down and swirled the golden-colored wine in his glass. He thought deeply, trying to fully recall the memory he was reliving, then continued.

"Yeah, his Mum said it would pass, but it didn't. Now he's getting ready to sign a big record deal."

"That's exciting," replied Tommy.

"It is. The only thing I don't like is, he's taken on this crazy, made-up last name of Model instead of his surname, Maddock. Our family name has a lot of history and heritage, and we even go to Scottish clan gatherings every few years to celebrate the family's legacy throughout the centuries. It's going to be a lot to explain to my relatives why my son's last name is now that of someone who poses in magazines or swishes along a fashion show catwalk."

Frank stopped to down the remaining wine then extended his glass for a refill. As Tommy poured, finishing off the bottle, he pondered his father's words and wasn't sure how to respond, if he should at all. It was apparent Frank didn't know who Tommy was at the moment. The revelation that his professional stage name had been a source of embarrassment for his Dad was something he had never previously considered, but now completely understood.

"But you know what ..." continued Frank as he sipped more wine. "Thomas is still my son regardless of what the world calls him, and at the end of the day, that's all that really matters. I love that boy with all my heart. Nothing will ever change that."

Tommy smiled, then turned back to the calmness of the river as he did his best to not think about what was to come.

CHAPTER TWENTY-NINE

THE SEVEN AND A HALF HOUR, NON-STOP FLIGHT from Edinburgh to New York City gently touched down on the JFK tarmac. Tommy felt his nervousness build. The two months of hard work that had gone into the recording of his new album was finally reaching a critical test-point. So far his master-plan was working like a charm, and everyone who had participated in the recording process had been sworn to total secrecy. As he rose from his first-class seat to disembark from the plane, he could only hope they had truly lived up to their word. He called Amanda to let her know he had made it safely, and she encouraged him to stay focused and positive.

Tommy had made the long trip back to the states to meet with Galactic Records' new CEO, Peter Kirkinour. It had been six months since Tommy had received Jacques Morel's guilt-ridden, deathbed letter that suggested that Tommy contact the new CEO. However, Peter had no idea Tommy had even recorded a new album. He certainly didn't know that Tommy was coming to meet with him at Galactic's Manhattan headquarters to share the fruits of his labor. In fact, other than the musicians, no one outside of a small, close circle of friends and family in Edinburgh knew about the album project. It was a purposeful decision Tommy had kept close to the vest to preserve the element of surprise. He simply didn't want anyone to get ahead of the story he himself wanted to convey.

With Amanda's guidance as a loving wife and health professional, over the past two months following their wedding, Tommy had also undergone a major personal transformation. He had lost the extra weight he had gained over the course of several years and felt healthy, refreshed, and invigorated. He had learned to proficiently meditate, envision the person he wanted to become and zero in on what he specifically desired to accomplish.

As part of that process, he stopped living in the past and projecting his history onto his future. With all he had been through, dwelling in what had already occurred and worrying about what was to come based on prior experiences, had become Tommy's biggest challenge. Nevertheless, he worked hard to remain fully conscious in the moment and stay true to his vision. At its core, he saw himself as a sober, positive, humble man living with great joy and inspiration, and backed by a kind, giving spirit.

Tommy was making a significant departure from the careless, self-centered rocker persona, but it felt good to see himself in a different light. It was only after he took a step back and looked from the outside in, that he understood he had to chip away at the hardness and cynicism that had built up around him. They were unnatural characteristics he had unknowingly formed as a result of all of his major successes that unfortunately had been eclipsed by even bigger failures.

As part of his new approach to life, Tommy did his best not to think or worry about how or when he would meet with Peter. Instead, like a great golfer, he just visualized his next shot. Beyond that, it would all work out for the best.

Now in full-swing mode, and with his entire album saved on a flash drive tucked deeply into his pocket, he was finally ready to share what he truly believed to be the best songs of his career. It was a clarity further validated by everyone who had heard the recordings, and he looked forward to sharing his creations with the world once more.

It was mid-afternoon by the time he arrived at his hotel. Due to the late hour, he decided to wait until the following morning to venture over to Galactic. Tired and jet-lagged, he ordered room service, and after a light meal of a grilled chicken salad and bottled water, Tommy fell asleep on his bed watching an old movie.

The next morning around 10:30 a.m., he anxiously walked the two blocks from his hotel to Galactic's corporate office. Six years earlier, the company had moved several blocks from its old address. It was at that former location Tommy had experienced the horrific nightmare with Jackie James and Jacques Morel that eventually changed his life forever. Tommy was glad not to be returning to the scene of those events. In his new, stronger mindset, he only briefly allowed those old memories the thought space and energy they would surely drain from his positivity if he gave them more credence. This was a new day for Tommy Model, and he was excited at the hopefulness he felt.

As the elevator door opened, Tommy was still pinching his nose to clear his ears from the pressure of beaming up seventy-five stories in less than a minute. The receptionist warmly greeted him as the game began.

"Hello. I'm Tommy Model here to see Peter Kirkinour."

"Do you have an appointment, Mr. Model?" she inquired.

"No, but I'm sure he'll be glad to see me. I believe he's been expecting me for quite some time."

The receptionist smiled and held the telephone handset to her ear, then called someone to whom she whispered below a volume that Tommy could discern.

As she hung up the receiver, she looked at Tommy and smiled again, then replied, "Someone will be right with you. Would you like a bottled water or some coffee."

"Sure, I'll take a water. The walk over from the hotel was a bit further and hotter than I expected."

Without reply, she opened a built-in fridge beneath her desk and handed a bottled water to Tommy wrapped in a napkin. Tommy thanked her, then unscrewed the lid and sipped the refreshing coolness as he walked to the waiting area and took a seat. Fifteen minutes stretched into forty-five while Tommy continued to practice remaining calm and focused. His mind did its best to counteract those efforts, but he held steady. It had been nearly an hour when a young woman in her early twenties finally emerged from a side hallway and called his name.

"Mr. Model?"

"Yes,"

"Hi, I'm sorry, did you have an appointment with Mr. Kirkinour?"

The old anger demon began to well-up inside Tommy. He staved it off to the best of his ability as he answered, "Well, as I told the young lady over there about an hour ago, I don't have an appointment. But if you could please let Peter know I'm here, I do believe he'll be happy to see me."

"What is your visit regarding, Mr. Model? Mr. Kirkinour is an extremely busy man, and we normally require appointments scheduled out days or weeks in advance to meet with him."

Obviously clueless to who he was, Tommy remained calm and repeated his request. "Please just let Peter know I'm here. Trust me ... he'll know who I am."

The woman smirked at Tommy and said in a condescending tone, "All right ... give me a minute," as she turned and walked back up the hall from where she had come.

Twenty minutes later she re-emerged and approached Tommy, this time with a more positive expression on his face.

"Mr. Model, I'm very sorry. I didn't realize who you were. The problem is Mr. Kirkinour is not in the office today, or for the rest of the week for that matter. He is at his beach house in the Hamptons."

"Oh, I see. Well ..."

"But I spoke with him on the phone, and he said that if you'd like to come out, we can get you on a helicopter. You can be there in about an hour. He does want to see you if that's agreeable to you. He just can't leave the house right now due to a family commitment."

"Uh ... sure. That sounds good, I guess," replied Tommy, surprised by the unexpected invitation.

"Great, I'll call the helicopter service and let them know you're on the way. One of our drivers will take you over to the heliport. Let me make the arrangements, and I'll be right back to take you down.

"Thank you," graciously replied Tommy, relieved that he had remained cool and collected when he encountered the woman's earlier reluctance. The old Tommy Model surely would have popped off, but this was a much better outcome, and it had been achieved by simply staying on course and remaining in the moment. He was confident that any issue would resolve itself. It was definitely a new approach for Tommy, but it seemed to be working, and in very interesting ways.

AFTER A BRIEF FLIGHT EASTWARD OVER THE CITY and then up the beautiful Atlantic coastline, the chopper settled onto the small landing pad of the Southampton Heliport. Across the narrow expanse of Meadow Lane, a driver stood in a sandy parking lot next to a black SUV waving at Tommy as he exited the helicopter. Still dressed in his rock star attire for the sake of his image, the mid-day heat consumed Tommy. He crossed the asphalt and hopped in the coolness of the already running SUV where he downed a large bottle of water during the short five-minute drive north.

The driver soon stopped and remotely opened a large gate, then continued up a long, curving driveway cut through the low-lying pines and oaks peppering the undulating sand dunes. The thick scrub opened into a clearing revealing a large, lush yard, beyond which the circular drive led to a sprawling, two-story shingle-clad mansion. Several cars lined the drive, and a valet jumped from his perch to approach the vehicle. He opened the door for Tommy who he emerged and cool-handedly donned sunglasses to minimize the brightness of the summer sunshine.

At the top of the stairs leading to the front door an extremely tall, bald man dressed in casual, yet stylish Hampton's day-party attire, stood beaming with a smile.

"Tommy Model, is that you, brother?" excitedly asked the man in a strong, yet charming Southern accent.

"Peter?" asked Tommy in reply, not sure if he was facing the man he had traveled so far to meet, or another go-between.

"Yes, sir. It is I. Man, it's great to see you, buddy! Get up here and shake my hand."

Tommy swiftly climbed the steps and locked hands with Peter who then pulled him in for an awkward hug.

"I can't tell you how long I've waited to meet you, Tommy," remarked Peter. "You're the entire reason I got into this crazy music business, so this is a very inspirational moment for me."

"Really? Wow ... I had no idea," humbly replied Tommy.

"I hope we can maybe work together on something soon. It would be a real honor, and I know we could bring you back to the level of success you deserve, my friend. I'm just shocked to see you. Last I heard you had moved back to Scotland and married Amanda Perkins. Beautiful girl, that Amanda. I've heard wonderful things about her. You're a lucky man, Tommy Model."

"Thank you, Peter. Yes, she has definitely changed my life. That's great to hear that you'd be interesting in working together because that's why I'm here. Is there somewhere we can speak in private?"

"Yes, yes, yes. Absolutely. We're having a birthday party for my son, Thomas. By the way ... we named him after you, no lie. Crazy, huh? Hope that doesn't make you feel too weird."

Tommy was surprised, but honored by Peter's revelation. "Not at all. That's very cool, Peter."

"Great! It would have sucked to have to change his name at this point. I want to hear what's on your mind, but I'm super-committed to my wife and kids. So do you want to come watch Thomas blow out the candles and have a piece of cake with us? My whole family would love to meet you."

"Sure, that sounds nice," replied Tommy.

He entered the front doors into the beautiful, beach-inspired home and followed Peter out to the back patio and pool deck. The vast expanse of the Atlantic Ocean shimmered beyond into the horizon. Under the pergola covered setting, a large crowd of children and parents gathered around a blond-haired little boy who sat at the head of a long, outdoor dining table. A massive birthday cake was placed in front of him with seven large candles ablaze. As the gleeful chorus of "Happy Birthday" reached its end, little Thomas strained to push himself to his feet. Once steady, he closed his eyes, made a wish and blew out the candles in one big breath.

Peter and the rest of the onlookers cheered as Tommy walked around the edge of the group, curious as to why the boy had struggled to stand. There, between the bodies, as a seven-year-old child joyously celebrated the anniversary of his life, Tommy's heart sank as he saw the braces that encased Thomas' legs.

As if sensing his presence, Thomas turned to look back at Tommy. When their eyes made contact, Thomas lit up as if seeing

Santa Claus at Christmas. He pushed back the chair to give himself room to turn. Leaving his canes behind, he anxiously clawed and grabbed at those who stood between he and his idol, as he hobbled over to Tommy. Standing directly above the boy, Tommy looked down as Thomas looked up.

The young man smiled and said, "You made it for my birthday! This is so awesome! Thank you, Mr. Model. Thank you."

The boy reached his arms around Tommy's mid-section and hugged him tightly. Tommy scanned the crowd, now silent as they watched the interaction. He placed his arms around Thomas' shoulders and returned the embrace. Finally, he locked eyes with Peter who smiled and nodded his head, then softly fist-bumped his chest, visually expressing his gratitude for the beautiful memory Tommy was giving his son. Tommy had not envisioned this, but the power of the moment made him realize it was all meant to be.

CHAPTER THIRTY

Peter closed the French doors to his home office to provide a little more privacy as guests of his son's birthday party began to depart.

"We're going to be interrupted for a bit by folks waving goodbye Tommy, but please tell me what you've got cookin'," urged Peter.

"Well actually, it's already cooked," replied Tommy. He dug into the pocket of his black jeans and retrieved the flash drive, holding it high for Peter to see.

"Is that what I think it is? Is that one of those memory sticks? Don't tell me ... you've invested in a tech company, and you need to raise some additional capital. Smart, Tommy. Diversify, that's the real key to wealth. How much do you need?"

"Huh," replied Tommy, unsure of how his big surprise got so far afield so fast. "No, no. This flash drive has my new album on it, Peter. You're the first person I wanted to share it with ... other than those who helped in the recording process, of course."

"No way! Get out of town. Are you serious, brother?" inquired Peter, giddy with excitement.

Tommy nodded his head in the affirmative as Peter stood and slowly reached towards the memory stick with eyes locked wide open as if about to touch a rare jewel. Finally reaching the small device, he carefully clasped his fingers around it and slid it from Tommy's fingers, then sat back in his chair and turned to wake up his computer.

As Peter slid the drive into the port on the side of his laptop, he turned back to Tommy and remarked, "I'm so excited my hands are shaking, Tommy. This is incredible news. I know it's been a while, but on a scale of one to ten how would you rate this compared to past albums? I know the last one didn't go so well. So excluding that one."

"It's a fifteen, Peter," confidently stated Tommy.

"Ooh, I like that number, Tommy. Most people say ten, or even eleven if they're feeling frisky, but you go fifteen. That's confidence, my friend."

Peter rubbed his hands together in quick succession like a craps player warming the dice before a big roll. He then clicked play and eased back in his chair closing his eyes to listen.

As the infectious rhythm of the first track began to course through the sound system, Peter leaned forward towards the computer and kicked up the volume even louder as his head bobbed with the vibe of the song. By the second chorus, Peter was playing air drums with his eyes still closed, as he rocked out to Tommy's creation. As the track faded, Peter pushed pause then swung his large executive chair back towards Tommy, revealing a rather serious look.

Tommy was taken aback by the expression and asked, "So did you like it? I've got eleven more on there, you know?"

"Did I like it?" responded Peter. "I loved it, man! That is so awesome, Tommy. No bull."

"Phew. You scared me there for a second," remarked Tommy, relieved he had misread the moment.

"I have to be honest with you though," Peter continued. "When I was inserting that little memory stick into my computer, I was mentally telling myself that if I didn't like it, I would be gracious to you just the same, and we'd figure out a way to make it better. I was worried it would be dated ... you know, stuck in the 80's. But brother, you have nailed it with that track. That is a monster hit, and with our endless resources behind you, there is no way that's not a winner. Can I listen to the others?"

"Sure, mate. That's why we're here."

Peter turned back and pressed play again as track two began. One by one, song by song, Peter lost himself in the incredible talent that he always knew Tommy to be. He was mesmerized by the quality of the writing and the recording, all of which had been accomplished in Tommy's home studio, albeit with the help of a great engineer, mixer, and some of the best musicians in the world.

"Who produced it, Tommy? The production quality is spot-on."

"Me, myself, and I, Peter."

"I should have known it. You are one talented dude, Tommy Model.

"I actually wrote several of the songs with Amanda. I definitely have to give her credit, because none of this would have happened without her."

"I love it. Talented and gracious. You're blowing me away, baby! Now here's a big question for you."

"Okay ... let me have it," quickly replied Tommy, amped by Peter's energetic banter.

"Can I share this with some of my key execs on the Galactic team? I'm overwhelmed, and I know they will be too. You've got at least five singles on here. This is next-level kind of stuff, and it's so *now*. We can bring you back with a vengeance, man! And you know what ... when we re-sign you for another album ... well, remember that twenty million dollar, non-recoupable signing bonus that's part of your original deal?"

"That's a pretty difficult number to forget, Peter."

"Ha, I hear you. Well, that's all yours, brother. It's the least we can do to make things right from the mess that crazy Jacques Morel created. But, hey ... that's the past. Let's get on with the future. I'm gonna fly these guys out this afternoon, and we'll make an evening of it brainstorming your comeback game-plan. Sound good?"

Tommy was ecstatic as he shook his head in agreement. While Peter called into Galactic's offices to round up his top execs, Tommy excused himself to video chat with Amanda so he could tell her the good news.

"Baby, it couldn't be going any better," Tommy expressed to Amanda as he looked at her through the screen of his cell phone. "So get this ... Peter is in there right now calling his executive team to fly out to his house in the Hamptons this afternoon to discuss a plan for my comeback. He loved the new music that much. And on top of that, he told me that I'm the very reason he got into the music business in the first place. He even named his son after me. Can you believe that?"

"You're kidding! That's great news, Tommy," replied Amanda. "I'm so happy for you. It's everything you had envisioned."

"Thank you for helping me get to this point. You're my angel, and I couldn't have done it without you."

"You're welcome, love. But it's your focus and determination that has carried you through. Just stay in the moment and don't get too far ahead of yourself," advised Amanda.

"You're right. Thank you for always looking out for my best interest. Please help me stay on track, okay? How are Mum and Dad."

"Your mum is great and said to tell you *hello*. Your father is ornery as ever. We actually had a really good day together. He got locked in on the time he took you to buy your first guitar. Do you recall that he thought it would be cool if you learned to play the banjo instead?"

"I do remember that. The music store had one banjo, and Dad became fixated on that thing. Somehow, he had seen that old American TV show, *Hee-Haw* and he loved Roy Clark. When he saw that banjo hanging there, I guess he thought I could be the next Roy Clark or something. It took a bit of convincing to buy me an acoustic guitar like I wanted."

"That's hilarious and pretty much what he recalled as well. But you do know he went back and bought that banjo, don't you?"

"What? No, I didn't know that."

"Yeah, he still has it. He showed it to me earlier. I don't understand how he remembers all of this old stuff and forgets what he said five seconds ago, but he does. It turns out he was going to surprise you with it that same year on your 15th birthday, but he overheard you joking with some of your friends about how embarrassing it was that your dad wanted you to learn the banjo. So he stored in its case, high on a shelf in the closet, and there it sits to this day. It's beautiful and looks brand new."

"That's nuts. I never knew that. It must have killed him to hear me say that. What an idiot I was."

"I didn't tell you this to upset you. You were fifteen-years-old. All fifteen year olds are embarrassed by their parents. Don't let this get in your head. Remember ... if you project your past on your future, you will always be stuck in the past."

"I know. You're right. How did I get so lucky to find you?" asked Tommy.

"Remember you feel that way when things start getting crazy again, rock star."

"Don't worry, I will. I love you, Amanda Maddock. I'll talk to you tomorrow. Sleep tight, my love."

"Have fun with the big shots from the label, baby. I love you too," replied Amanda as she hung up from the video call.

The lonely silence afterward was quickly erased, as Peter shouted for Tommy from down the hall.

"I'm coming," responded Tommy as he walked back towards Peter.

"The team is on the way. It should be about an hour. Let's listen to these tracks again. Man ... I can't get over how good they are!"

Tommy re-entered the office while Peter pushed play, launching the power of first track back out into the room. Tommy smiled as the CEO of the most successful record label in the world became immersed in his music. Peter once more began hammering away with his invisible drumsticks, which he only occasionally set aside for a brief turn at an air guitar.

CHAPTER THIRTY-ONE

SITTING AROUND A FIRE-PIT overlooking the sea-oat-covered dunes and the moonlit ocean beyond, the discussion amongst the Galactic team extended into the evening, as the plan surrounding Tommy's big comeback solidified. Peter vowed to spend whatever it took to deliver a successful career resurgence to the level that had never been seen before with any other artist.

Fortunately, except for a few faint lines extending from the corner of his eyes, Tommy still looked the part of a virile rock star. Most importantly, everyone agreed that the new music was current and chart-worthy. From a Tommy Model brand perspective, they had to find the best way to transcend time and re-engage Tommy's older fan base, while also ushering in a new wave of younger *Model Maniacs*.

Tommy conferred his dedication to the plan and his commitment to the team. But he also reiterated multiple times throughout the discussion that he preferred to take a more unique, less demanding approach to the marketing, promotions, and publicity efforts that were to come. Tommy made it clear that he was far from lazy or complacent about those demands. However, he also knew from past radio promo tours and album launches, that it was often the fast-paced, non-stop agenda of radio station visits, meet-and-greets, and television appearances that often sent an artist into an alcohol and drug-induced tailspin. Being susceptible to those vices as he was, he wanted to ensure they remained conscious of minimizing his exposure to those temptations.

"I know you realize how crazy some of the TV and radio station suits and on-air personalities can be," noted Tommy. "The last promo and publicity tour I went on was debaucherous. I think I had developed such a reputation as a wild, party-animal, that VIP's at events often wanted to experience what being around me in *Tommy Model* mode was like. That usually resulted in the label promo team dragging me out with the big shots night after night, orchestrating alcohol, drug, and sex-crazed frenzies. It was all on their expense tabs and ultimately recoupable from me, of course, so it was nothing but good times for everyone else, while I footed the bill. I went along with it all because I wanted the exposure for my music. It was the legal form of *pay to play* I guess, but it was like living in the loop of a really bad dream with the same agony, over and over, city after city, and for weeks at a time. My addictions were totally on me, but those blokes sure didn't help."

"We hear you, Tommy," replied Peter. "We've all seen it first-hand, and I can understand why it's a valid concern for you."

"Yeah, and I'm sure some of those VIP's still around from way back then are looking for something to take them back to their youth. But I ain't it! So everyone will just have to understand that there will be no one-on-one interactions beyond the actual events themselves. And I'm not paying for dining and bar tabs that are turned in as expenses by your team either. Cool?"

"Understood. We'll figure out a way to make it work," agreed Peter. "We want to support your efforts to live a healthier lifestyle."

"Thanks, Peter. I'm by no means any less crazy when I'm in my performance persona on stage. And I'll occasionally have a beer or two like we are here tonight, or a sip of something a little stronger every now and then. But the need to go extreme is completely out of my life now, and it has to stay that way."

"Noted. I think you're being very smart and mature for making those choices. From a business standpoint, we'd actually prefer this version of Tommy Model over the out of control guy of your younger days," stated Peter.

"Speaking of chilling out," Peter continued. "I think we've done all we can do this evening, so do you ladies and gents want to spend the night or head back to the city? Tommy, I'd be honored if you'd stay over if that's good with you."

The executives all opted to return to Manhattan so Peter called his assistant to schedule a car and a helicopter. A short time later when the team departed, they wished Tommy well and expressed their excitement of getting to work with him and deliver on Peter's commitments.

Finally alone together, Tommy sipped his beer as Peter dropped another log on the fire. In the silence, Tommy relaxed in the sound of waves crashing on the nearby shore. With occasional pops and the uplifting smell of burning wood, he watched the flames dance and entangle each other in the faint breeze. Feeling humbled and appreciative, Tommy finally broke the tranquility to express his gratitude.

"You know ... I never thought I'd get chance to live my passion again. I want to tell you from the bottom of my heart ... thank you, Peter."

"I should be thanking you, Tommy. This is the dream of a lifetime for me. It's gonna be awesome. I can't wait to tell the world you're back and in a big way. Hey, I almost forgot, I got us a couple of good Cuban cigars if you'd like one."

"Sure. Thank you."

Tommy reached for the cigar as Peter handed it to him along with a cutter and lighter. Tommy snipped off the cap, then methodically warmed and lit the foot, releasing the alluring aroma into the night sky. He handed the lighter and cutter back to Peter, who had already taken a more direct approach by biting off the head of his Robusto. He then aggressively fired up the end as if lighting a grill doused with starter fluid rather than an expensive, hand-rolled, quality cigar. The end result was the same as both men sat back and chilled, occasionally billowing smoky clouds into the air.

"I was so nervous and excited that I jumped right into the album discussion when we walked into your office earlier today," said Tommy. "But I meant to ask you about your son. I hope I'm not being too forward, but what's wrong with his legs?"

"No, I appreciate you asking, Tommy. He has Blount's disease. Basically, it's a disorder of the shin bones that caused him to become bowlegged."

"I'm so sorry," sympathized Tommy "Do they know what causes that? Can it be cured?"

"Well, he's always been a very active, and he started trying to walk earlier than most kids. Being new parents, we were like, 'hey ... let's help him do this.' So we did, thinking he was advancing faster than other children. Of course, any parent would normally think that was awesome. But, it turns out it's not always a good thing and apparently it can cause Blount's. The good news is he's had a couple of surgeries and has to wear the braces for a few more months, but the bones are straightening, and he shouldn't have any issues beyond this."

"That's great news, Peter. I was worried it was something long-term."

"Yeah, it's a blessing that it's not. My wife and I do a lot of charity work, and we see so many children with illnesses and diseases. Unfortunately, many aren't curable. That being said,

Thomas is such a trooper, and it's been heartbreaking to see him go through this. The surgeries haven't been a cakewalk, and quite understandably, he's embarrassed and held back by the braces. As a result, he's not always a happy camper. But you sure put a spark in his world today. He's crazy about you, so that was a very special moment."

"Well, I'm glad I could bring him some joy. Would it be okay if I send him a signed guitar and some vintage tour swag?"

"That would be nice, Tommy. I know he would love that. That's ironic because just over the past couple of weeks, he's mentioned that he wants to start learning how to play guitar, so we were thinking about getting him one. He would never play one you signed for him though. It would be too precious."

"Well, how about I send him two. I'll sign an electric guitar, and then I'll also send him an acoustic guitar that I won't sign. An acoustic is much better to learn on anyway. Will that be all right?"

"Tommy, you don't have to do that."

"I want to. You did name him after me by the way. Someday when he's a famous rock star, it'll be a terrific story for him to tell."

"Oh, please don't scare me like that. I sure hope he doesn't want to become a rock star. No offense."

"None taken. I know exactly what you mean. If I had it to do all over, I'm not sure I would go the same route."

"Well, the world would have missed out if you hadn't. Just curious though ... what would you have pursued as a career if not music?"

"Crazy as this may sound, I think I would have liked to have become a dentist. I always liked my dentist growing up, which is a bit odd for a kid, but he was such a cool character. Looking in other people's mouths may have gotten old after a while, but how respectable would that have been, right? Decent money too, I would guess."

Peter drank the last sip of his beer and tossed his cigar into the dwindling fire signaling his surrender to the evening.

"Well, Doctor Model ... I need to get some sleep. It's been a long, but amazing day. We've got you all set up in the guest house if you want to follow me over."

Tommy also tossed his cigar into the flame and rose from his Adirondack chair to follow Peter. When they arrived at the small cottage, he found it as well decorated and comfortable feeling as the main house. Tommy was relieved not to have to make the hour-long flight back to the city. He thanked Peter again for an incredible day, as they shook hands and made plans to meet for breakfast early the next morning.

Tommy pinched his shirt, pulling it to his nose. The mixture of cigar smoke, sweat, and singed firewood was as unpleasant as he suspected it would be. He quickly stripped out of his clothes and hopped into the large, walk-in shower to rinse off. Closing his eyes to wash the shampoo from his hair, he turned to face the tiled wall allowing the multiple showerheads and jets to coat his body in the warm, relaxing water.

Feeling a cool draft on his backside, he quickly turned to find a completely naked woman closing the glass shower door behind her. Likely in her early-forties, her body was tan, well-toned, and perfectly proportioned. She smiled and approached Tommy, who nervously stepped back and became trapped against the tile wall. The woman intently looked in Tommy's eyes and grabbed the removable shower nozzle that she then guided downward from his chest and across his torso. Tommy closed his eyes in the ecstasy of the sensation of the hot pulsating water, but immediately he snapped back to reality as she crossed the threshold of his waistline. He reached down to grab her hand but was already affected by the unexpected attention, and he struggled to fight off his old demons.

"Who are you? Tommy asked. "You look very familiar. How did you get in here?

"I'm one of the mom's that was at the birthday party earlier. I have always had a thing for you, and I knew this was finally my chance to have you all to myself. I used to fantasize to a poster of you that hung on the ceiling above my bed. You know that picture of you with no shirt on, and your black, skin-tight, leather pants pulled down so far there was little left to the imagination?"

"Yes, but that was a long time ago," breathlessly replied Tommy.

"Well, I can see now that what I anticipated in my imagination was actually not very accurate."

"What? Well, what in the world did you imagine?"

"Oh, I'm far from disappointed, Mr. Model. I actually should have given you much more credit."

The woman knelt in front of Tommy as the heavy flow from the rain head above cascaded over her long dark hair. She teased him relentlessly, continuing to direct the water from the hand-held wand around his abdomen and along his thighs until it was obvious he was completely under her spell.

Just when he thought he had no strength left, all of his hopes and dreams for a better life supported by his profound love for Amanda kicked in. He stepped to the side then darted out of the shower. Grabbing two towels, he busted through the front door of the guest house, completely naked, and ran barefooted across the pool deck. He streaked past the still smoldering fire pit and down the long sandy trail leading to the beach.

Tommy struggled as he ran through the soft sand above the tidal zone. When he could barely see the main house, he dropped to his knees, exhausted and out of breath. He laid in the cool sand that coated his still wet body, and covered himself in the large white towels. Looking up at the stars, he thanked God for the willpower to have made the right choice once more. His racing heart eventually calmed, then he closed his eyes and drifted off to sleep.

He awoke to the next morning's sunrise as a large seagull stood only a few feet away, his thin, stick legs appearing barely capable of supporting his well-fed, top-heavy body. The bird stared intently at Tommy, sizing him up as if he were a big fish washed onto the beach by high tide.

"Shoo!" scolded Tommy, as the gull jumped to the air and flew away. "I ain't your breakfast!" he barked.

With his comment, Tommy recalled his breakfast meeting with Peter as the bizarre events of the previous evening flashed back into his mind. He turned to look towards the house and saw Peter walking down from the dunes. Tommy was nervous as to how he would explain why he was lying on the beach, naked under two towels, instead of in the plush bed of the guest house.

As Peter approached, he waved at Tommy and shook his head, then laughed at the sight of his idol under a heap of towels with his exposed face, hair, arms, and feet all covered in sand.

"Hey buddy," greeted Peter. "I heard my wife, Jessie paid you a visit in the shower last night."

"What? Your wife? No, no!" replied an utterly shocked Tommy.

"Yeah, you met her earlier at the party, but you probably didn't recognize her with her sunglasses off and hair down. She's a like a chameleon with all of those different sexy looks of hers. I don't even recognize her sometimes."

"Peter, I'm sorry. I had no idea."

"No, I'm sorry, Tommy. She's a bit of a sex addict, and we have an open relationship, so don't worry ... I'm not upset. I figured she might try to sneak up on you at some point. But hey ... you obviously were not kidding about making a major life change for yourself. My wife is a smoking-hot babe, so if you resisted her in the buff, you do have some newfound strength. Good for you. Now ... how about that breakfast, my friend?" asked Peter as he held out his hand offering to help Tommy to his feet.

CHAPTER THIRTY-TWO

TOMMY HURRIED THROUGH THE LOBBY of his Manhattan hotel. It was half past noon as he headed for the elevators following his return from the Hamptons, and his mind reeled back on the day's events.

Following Peter's revelation to Tommy on the beach earlier that morning, the awkwardness had only worsened when Jessie joined Tommy and Peter for breakfast. During the meal, Tommy initially ate very little, consumed by his extreme nervousness surrounding Jessie's presence. To his surprise, however, she spent several minutes apologizing for coming on to him the night before, and he respectfully listened to her plea.

Seemingly unaffected by the conversation, Peter chowed down on eggs, bacon, and hash browns, while smiling at Jessie's feeble attempts to explain her actions in efforts of making peace with Tommy. It was surreal at first, but oddly enough, by the time the three of them got up from the table an hour later, all had been forgiven, and Tommy had developed an even stronger affinity for Peter. *After all*, Tommy thought to himself, *who was he to judge the idiosyncrasies of a couple's relationship.*

Now back in the city, Tommy was running late for his return flight to Edinburgh scheduled to depart JFK in just three and a half hours. He pressed the elevator call button, then smacked his forehead, having forgotten to arrange a car to take him to the airport. As he turned and made a beeline for the concierge desk, it was then that he heard a familiar voice calling his name from across the lobby.

"Tommy! Hey, Tommy! Hold up."

Tommy turned to see his old friend and manager, Bob Walker, who he had not laid eyes on or heard from in four years. A much older looking and acting Bob headed towards Tommy, weaving between the lobby furniture. Just as he was almost in the clear, he tripped on the edge of a rug. Bob stumbled and nearly went to the floor, but caught himself by grabbing the back of a sofa. Tommy reached for Bob's free arm, providing some added support, as he regained his composure and stood up straight.

"Bob? Are you okay? What are you doing here, mate?" asked Tommy as the two, long-time pals shook hands.

"I'm fine, thanks. Just a bit clumsy, as usual. I've been trying to track you down. It took a bit of doing, but I heard you were in town and staying here, so I've been camping out in the lobby for two days waiting on you. Sorry I couldn't make the wedding. I'm so happy for you. And Amanda Perkins! Wow, buddy ... you did good for yourself."

"Thank you, Bob. I am very fortunate for sure. Listen, it's great to see you, but I'm running late for a flight. Let me tell the concierge to order a car and then maybe you can come to the room while I pack. It should only take a few minutes. Then if you want to, you can ride out to the airport with me. Otherwise, I'm going to miss my flight, and I really need to get home."

"Sure, sure. Go ahead."

Tommy approached the concierge desk, but no one was there. He leaned on the granite counter and drummed his fingers nervously on the cool surface. Seeing his dilemma, Bob walked over.

"Tommy, go get packed. I'll call and schedule a car myself. Go."

"Thanks, Bob. I appreciate it. I've missed you, mate," Tommy said as he hopped backward while smiling and pointing at Bob, then turned to jog towards the elevators.

Five minutes later Tommy reappeared as the silver sliding doors opened and he shot out like a rocket, rolling his suitcase towards the front desk. He handed the guest services agent his keycard and waited patiently as she attempted to print out his folio.

"I'm sorry, Mr. Maddock. I need to change the toner cartridge," revealed the young, twenty-something agent. It'll just be a second."

Tommy's anxiety spiked as she disappeared behind a partition wall. It was several minutes before she peaked her head around the corner, then vanished again. Another minute later a tall, lanky man emerged from behind the same wall, and after greeting Tommy, he apologized for the delay. He explained that apparently one of the two printers at the front desk had quit working earlier in the day. They had been forced to use the remaining printer during a large check-out, causing the toner to become fully depleted. Unfortunately, they were out of backup toner in their supply room, so someone was running up to the executive offices to locate a cartridge. "It should only be a few more minutes," Tommy was reassured.

"Can't you e-mail me my receipt? I really need to go," explained Tommy.

"Well, we need you to sign off on the charges," noted the young man whose name tag indicated he was the *Guest Services Manager*. "The mini-bar was cleaned out, not once, but two times during your stay. When that happens, we like to get a signature on file so there are no misunderstandings later."

"What? I didn't even touch the mini-bar. I ordered room service two nights ago! That's it. How much are we talking about?"

"Well, sir ... it totals one thousand four hundred and twenty-six dollars and fourteen cents."

"You're nuts. I'm not paying that!"

"Mr. Maddock, it says right on the top of the mini-bar area that charges will be applied to your account, and there is a list of the prices for each item."

"I don't care what it says. I didn't touch the mini-bar, so I'm not paying for whoever did. And I'm no technology wizard by any means, but have you tried taking the toner cartridge out of the printer that stopped working? Do you think that might have some left in it?"

The manager paused contemplating Tommy's suggestion, then reached over and popped open the front of the printer, sliding out the hefty cartridge. He re-inserted it into the other printer, pecked around on his keyboard, then printed out Tommy's folio, sliding it to him across the desktop.

"I've credited the mini-bar charges, Mr. Maddock. I'm sorry for the inconvenience. Have a safe flight home."

"Thank you," replied Tommy as he turned and rushed towards the front, revolving door where Bob was waiting.

Together Bob and Tommy hopped into the back of a black sedan sporting heavily tinted windows, while Tommy's bags were loaded into the trunk. As the driver entered the vehicle, Bob kindly reminded him that Tommy was late for a flight and asked him to do what he could to make up for lost time. As the car lurched and weaved amongst the massive flow of other vehicles, Tommy held tightly to the back of the front seat as he looked at Bob with concern.

Trying to get his mind off of the wild ride they were on, Tommy asked Bob the pressing question he was anxious to hear an answer for.

"So why were you trying to find me?"

"Well, I think you know I moved to New York a couple of years ago to be closer to my family. What you didn't know is why. I don't want to bring you down, but I've got lung cancer, and it's finally progressing to the point that it's going to get me soon. Too many years of smoking those crazy brown cigarettes, I guess."

Tommy's head was spinning following Bob's shocking revelation. "I don't know what to say, mate. I mean ... are you sure? Is there anything more that can be done? If it's money you need, I'll take care of it for you."

Bob paused and fought back the emotion of regret behind his decision to not stop smoking when he knew he should have, then continued. "No, it's past what money can do, Tommy. Thank you for the offer though. You've always been so good to me, and I'm so glad you're finally finding happiness again. We tried for so long to get there, didn't we?"

"We sure did, Bob. And thank you for always sticking with me. I may not have told you that enough, but I couldn't have gotten through it all without you. Is there anything I can do for you or your family?"

"No, they're fine, Tommy. Don't worry ... it's gonna be all right. Maybe have a party in my memory at some point after I'm gone and raise a glass to remember me a time or two."

"You got it, buddy," Tommy replied, now fighting back his own emotions. Bob had been a mentor and confidant to Tommy throughout most of his career. Even though they had pushed pause on their business relationship due to Tommy's inactivity, their personal feelings for each other were as strong as ever. Tommy knew he would not handle Bob's passing well, but he struggled to stay in the moment.

"But hey," Bob continued. "That's not the only reason I wanted to see you. Ironically I got a call the other day for an opportunity you might be interested in. I tried your cell phone a few times, but couldn't get you. So I called Monique to see if she knew how I could find you. She got a hold of your wife, who texted and told me you were in New York and where you were staying. I asked her to let me surprise you, so I've been ringing your room for the past two days. I was worried I missed you."

"I'm sorry. I've been meaning to call you, Bob. When I moved back to Edinburgh, I got a new phone number to cut ties with some people I didn't want to ever speak to again ... mainly those leachy drug dealers and escort services. I still have my old number, but I turn off the phone and only check voicemails every once in a while to see if there is anything important. I made everyone promise they would only let me give out my new number, so I'm sure that's why Amanda didn't offer it up. You definitely need it though, so let me call or text you in a bit, and you can update my contact. It's been a whirlwind with the wedding and my dad having Alzheimer's, so it just escaped my mind. We missed you at the wedding, you know?"

"I'm so sorry to hear about your dad. Monique told me he's got it bad. And I apologize for not making it to the wedding. With my treatments I was advised not to travel, and at the time I wasn't ready to tell you about the cancer. But I do hope you received my gift."

"Yes, we did ... and thank you so much. It was very thoughtful of you and we will treasure it forever. As far as Dad goes, he's hanging in there, but it's definitely getting worse. It's a horrible thing to watch."

Tommy quickly changed the subject from the path of sadness it was rolling down. "So, what's this opportunity you mentioned?"

"Well, I got a call seeing if you'd be interested in taking part in a ten-city, mini-festival tour along with a dozen or so other artists and bands who were big in the 80's. The money is halfway decent, and they'll allow you to sell your merch through their vendors, so there's a bit more to be made on that side as well. What do you think?"

"Oh, Bob. That sounds nice, but ..." Tommy hesitated, knowing the chauffeur could hear their conversation. He was not ready for the world to know about the new album, and Bob had no idea he already recorded one. Tommy nodded his head towards the driver as he replied, "Let's chat about that when we get to the airport. Cool?"

Taking Tommy's cue, Bob nodded his head in agreement, and they turned their conversation to catching up on the past four years.

Fifteen minutes later they arrived at JFK and Tommy and Bob exited the car in the pouring rain. The chauffeur hustled to cover the men, handing them an open umbrella as he retrieved Tommy's bags from the trunk. Tommy passed the umbrella handle to Bob then walked to the back of the sedan and leaned in to speak privately with the driver. The man nodded, as Tommy slung the duffel over his shoulder, then grabbed the extended arm of his suitcase, popping it over the curb as he beckoned for Bob to follow him to the covered overhang outside the terminal.

He placed his hand on Bob's shoulder as he spoke. "Look, I haven't told you yet because it has to remain confidential for a while longer, but I've recorded a new album and Galactic is going to release the first single in about a month. I was going to call you to let you know. You must have been sensing something was going on, or we wouldn't be coming together like this."

"I don't know why, but I had a feeling something was in the works." Bob admitted. "I thought it was odd you came to New York. L.A. would not have been so strange since you used to live there, but it all makes sense now."

"The new Galactic Records CEO, Peter Kirkinour, loves me. He's crazy about the new music, and they seem to be behind me having a successful comeback. Unfortunately, I think doing an 80's tour could hurt those efforts since their plan is for me to get back to arena headliner status quickly. We'll see what happens, but that's the plan."

"I understand," Bob responded as he hung his head downward, still holding the umbrella even though he was now under the concourse awning.

"I can tell you're upset. I'm sorry, Bob. I was going the let you know after I met with Galactic. I just didn't want us to both go through another round of insanity if it didn't go well. But it did, and I want you to be excited and proud. This isn't how I wanted you to find out."

"I totally understand. And I'm not upset. I am very proud of you, and I hope it's an amazing comeback. I just thought this festival tour could be one last run together, that's all. But this is much better news even though I probably won't be around long enough to see it all come to fruition."

Bob's eyes filled with tears as Tommy hugged his old friend tightly. Tommy leaned back but continued to hold Bob's arms while trying to fight back his own grief.

"Listen, I know it's not about the money, but how much would you have made in commissions if we did this?" Tommy asked.

"I don't want a commission."

"I know, but how much?"

"Maybe seventy-five thousand. I'm not sure. But ..."

"I know you don't want it, but will you please let me donate what you would have made to your favorite charity in your honor? Please, Bob. We'll make it an even hundred grand."

Bob, clenched his mouth grinding his teeth together while he fought back more tears. He nodded his head in grateful agreement as Tommy confirmed their plans.

"Okay, mate. I'm going to call you. You decide what charity, and it will be done. I'm serious."

"Thanks, Tommy. I love you, my friend. I'm scared about what's coming. I never dreamed this would happen. I was such a fool."

Tommy wrapped his arms around Bob once more, this time lingering for a few seconds to burn the moment into his mind. With the fear of missing his flight still nagging at his thoughts, Tommy reluctantly released his embrace.

"I'm so sorry ... I have to go, Bob. With check-in and security, it's going to take a while to get through to my gate. You know how it is. Listen though ... I told the driver to wait. He'll take you to wherever you want to go and I've already paid him. I'm gonna call you in a few days and we'll make arrangements for you to come out with me on some of the promotional and public appearance dates, okay? I really want you there with me. Does that sound good?"

Bob nodded his head *yes* without saying a word, then warmly shook Tommy's hand, patted his shoulder, and turned towards the waiting car. Tommy watched as the hard pounding rain cascaded off the edge of the canopy above Bob's head, creating an even more somber mood as it fell in a circle around him while he walked. When he reached the car, Bob handed the umbrella to the driver as he climbed into the backseat and waved goodbye to Tommy. The chauffeur closed the door and Bob disappeared behind the dark window tinting.

As the sedan pulled away, Tommy could see the faint glow of Bob's open hand pressed against the glass. He watched until they were no longer visible in the chaos of the traffic. Tommy looked up into the gray sky as silhouettes of thousands of raindrops pelted his face like soft, gray bullets.

"Why does everything good have to be overshadowed by complete and utter sorrow?" he grumbled out loud as he shook his head in disgust. Regaining his composure, he turned and pulled his bag through the sliding glass doors of the concourse leaving the misery of the moment to wash away with the rain.

CHAPTER THIRTY-THREE

AMANDA SIPPED HER HOT CAFÉ MOCHA while she and Tommy relaxed at a table outside of their favorite Edinburgh coffee shop. She dabbed whipped cream from her lip with a napkin as Tommy sighed deeply, then savored the sweet flavor of his vanilla latte.

"Oh, that's good," remarked Tommy.

"You must be tired, babe," noted Amanda. "I'm surprised you didn't want to go to bed after that flight."

"I'm okay. I got a little nap on the plane."

Tommy hesitated, then took another drink of his coffee. He turned away from Amanda's concerned gaze and looked up the narrow street, shaded by an uninterrupted line of multi-story buildings, housing various shops and residences.

"What's wrong?" Amanda asked. "You seem a million miles away. Aren't you excited about how everything is working out?"

"Oh, yes. Absolutely. I just need to tell you something, and I'm worried you're not going to believe me."

"Why wouldn't I believe you?"

"Because it's a crazy story."

"Well ... go ahead and pull the cord so we can enjoy the rest of our morning. Let's hear it."

"Okay ... here goes."

Tommy looked down. Fiddling with a stir stick, he pecked it against the napkin lying flat on the table, as his mind tried to determine how best to start. Not seeing a perfect way to begin, he let loose of his fears and hoped the words would find their own path.

"So, I told you about the birthday party they had for Peter's son when I got to his house."

"Right," confirmed Amanda.

"Well, at that party I was introduced to Peter's wife, Jessie. But when I first met her she was wearing a big, white sun hat, sunglasses, and her hair was pulled up under the hat."

"Okay, so ..."

"Well, later that night after my meeting with the Galactic execs, I wanted to rinse off in the shower because we had been sitting around a fire and smoking cigars. So there I am, minding my own business, shampooing my hair, then I turn around, and a naked woman is standing in the shower with me."

"What?" snapped Amanda, as she stiffened her back and shifted in her seat.

"Yeah, so she was really coming on strong. But I ran out of the shower, grabbed a couple of towels, then took off across the pool deck and made my way onto the beach. I ran maybe a quarter of a mile, and then hunkered down in the sand hoping this woman wouldn't come after me. I must have eventually fallen asleep, but when I woke, the sun was on the horizon, and Peter was walking towards me."

Tommy hesitated, re-charging his confidence for the big finale.

"Keep going," Amanda directed in a stern voice, her eyes wide-open with intensity.

"So anyway ... when Peter gets to me, he tells me that the mystery woman in the shower was none other than his wife, Jessie."

"Peter's wife?"

"Yeah. I know. It gets better though. According to Peter, she has a sex addiction, and they have an open marriage. So I guess she thought ... here's this rock star that I've always had a crush on, and I may never have this opportunity again, so I'm going to go for it and try to seduce him. I didn't recognize her because she didn't have the hat and sunglasses on, and her hair was down. Anyway ... there I am lying on the beach, naked under two towels, covered in sand head to toe, while my new label head is casually telling me his wife tried to have sex with me just a few hours earlier. And he's cool with all that."

Amanda shook her head and fought back laughter at the mental image she held of Tommy at the scene.

"I don't see what's so funny," Tommy continued. "It scared the crap out of me. I love you so much, and I don't want to mess this up. I realize it seems a little unbelievable that with my track record, I would run away. But it's the truth. I swear!"

"Relax. I believe you. I really do appreciate you telling me. So did you see this Jessie before you left?"

"Yeah. She came and sat with us while Peter and I were having breakfast. She apologized repeatedly and said she had no idea that we had gotten married. It seemed like she was feeling more remorse about that than anything. She also partially blamed some prescription pills that apparently can affect her judgment. Who knows for sure. But she seemed extremely embarrassed and hoped that I would forgive her."

"So did you?"

"Of course. What else was I gonna do? Peter was sitting right there smirking at us like you are now."

"I understand. Just be careful when you are around her in the future. If she's tried it once, that doesn't mean she won't try again, regardless of whether she knows we're married or not. Contrary to what you may think, I do trust you implicitly. I see the lengths you've gone to in efforts of changing for the better. Keep being honest with me and we'll be fine."

"I will. Thank you for believing me. I've been a nervous wreck for hours on the flight waiting to tell you. I just wanted to do it in person."

Amanda leaned over and kissed Tommy on the lips hoping to erase any worries he still harbored. But she could sense something was still weighing him down.

"Something else is bothering you," Amanda noted.

"Yeah. The other thing is, this situation with Bob that I mentioned when I called from the airport before my flight. I'm feeling a bit guilty that I declined his offer to do those mini-festivals. Do you think it would hurt to do them and give him some happiness while I still can?"

"Honey, you don't have to be everyone's savior. I'm sure deep down Bob understands that it's not the right opportunity at this time. If you do accept that tour, you will be perceived as a blast from the past instead of being the man of the moment. You have to decide if you're going to be the greatest hits album or the exciting new release everyone has been waiting on for years. It's that simple."

"I definitely want to be in the here and now again. My old hits will always be a special part of my history, but I also want to write some new chapters in my career. This album is an opportunity to become semi-immortal through my music again. And instead of being perceived as the moody quitter, maybe this time I can romantically ride off into the sunset."

"Well, there's your answer."

"I'm not sure if he'll be able to, but I told him he could come out on some promotional and public appearance dates. If he can, hopefully that will give him a sense of being around it all one last time. It's so hard to accept that he's going to die. All of these ticking time bombs are surrounding me with Dad, now Bob, and whether the new album and singles will be successful. My anxiety is trying to take me over, but I'm not letting it."

Tommy was interrupted as two young women stopped at their table and asked, "Excuse us, aren't you Amanda Perkins?"

Amanda smiled and replied, "Yes."

"Oh, we just love you. Can we take a selfie with you?"

Amanda agreed and the two girls leaned in on both sides, while one snapped the picture. They captured the image on one phone, then switched to the other woman's phone, repeating the process. After a few attempts to get the perfect facial expressions, the women thanked Amanda, and walked away, giddy with joy and looking at their phones.

"Well, for once someone recognized me and not you, superstar," Amanda joked with Tommy.

"That's fine by me. I loved watching that. Hey, when everything gets back on track for me, what do you think about us working on a new album for you?"

"I don't know, Tommy. Let's focus on you right now. I was thinking instead that my new release could involve a little Tommy or Amanda, or maybe both. I really want to be a mom."

"For real? We never talked about children, but that is so exciting! I thought that ship had sailed for me."

Tommy slid his chair around the table and next to Amanda's so he could lean in for a hug. They released from their embrace, looked into each other's eyes, and began laughing. Tommy kissed his wife, casually at first, but the joy of the moment unexpectedly led to a more passionate display.

"Aye!" called out a patron sitting nearby. "Go get a room, you two!"

Tommy turned and stared at the heavily accented Scottish bloke. He patted Amanda's arm, then rose from his chair as if he was about to become confrontational. The man returned his coffee cup to the table preparing for the retribution that might be coming his way. Instead, Tommy merely held out his hand to help Amanda to her feet.

As she stood, Tommy smiled and replied, "Aye. Thanks for the advice, mate. I think we'll do just that. In fact, we're gonna go make a baby ... so stick that in your cup and sip on it for a while."

CHAPTER THIRTY-FOUR

TOMMY AND FRANK SAT ON THE EDGE OF THE SEAWALL at the end of Sandpiper Drive overlooking the Leith Docks Entrance Basin. The mid-morning sun delighted against the calm water. Frank stared intently across the cove to where the Royal Yacht Britannia was moored snug against the Ocean Terminal complex.

"This area sure has changed a lot, hasn't it, Dad?" remarked Tommy. "You used to work right over there."

"Did I?" asked Frank.

"You sure did. At the Henry Robb Shipyard."

"I see some ships over there, but that sure doesn't look like a place where they build them."

"It isn't anymore. About the time my career first took off in the 80's, the yard closed. It was unfortunate because lots of folks, including you, lost their jobs. And it brought an end to over five hundred years of shipbuilding history in the area."

"They fired me?"

"Well, not really. Technically you got laid off."

"I think I'd remember that. You sure they didn't fire me? People do that, you know? And for no good reason. They hand you a piece of paper telling you that you're done. They usually have a woman deliver the bad news because they know you won't punch her in the face. Cowards! They should look you in the eye if they're gonna to fire you. I did see a lady get punched one time by another lady. It wasn't pretty. You sure they didn't fire me? How did we pay for things if I didn't have a job?"

"Well ... ironically, when that all went down things were just getting going for me. But you were out of work for the first time since you were twelve years old and it hit you hard. You were so worried that you would have to sell the house and move everyone in with Uncle Owen and his family in the country. That's why as soon as I got my first royalty advance, I paid off the house to take the pressure off of you and Mum. Do you remember that?"

"I'm sorry, son. I don't. I can't believe those bastards fired me, but I do believe you about paying off the house note."

Frank turned to look at Tommy and gently touched his arm to get his attention. Tommy looked away from the water and into his father's eyes as Frankly humbly smiled and said, "Thank you for doing that. You're a good boy."

Tommy laid his hand on top of his father's and fought back the emotions that seemed to be more easily triggered nowadays since finding his peace again.

"You're welcome, Dad. I'm glad I was able to help."

The moment marked the first time his father had thanked him for saving their home so many years ago, and it struck Tommy deep. After being laid off, Frank had become extremely depressed, embarrassed and lost. Instead of returning a simple thank you when Tommy handed him the paid off mortgage note years ago, he walked away without saying a word. Neither Frank nor Tommy ever mentioned it again, but it was a reaction or lack thereof, that stuck with Tommy all this time. It was a relief to finally receive the verbal acknowledgment of gratitude he had hoped for so long ago, even if it was based on a memory his father could no longer recall.

The two men sat in silence again watching a tugboat enter the port from the Firth of Forth. Its lazy progression seemed to slow time, and Tommy treasured the moment with his father as he tuned in to all that was going on around him. Three seagulls flew by and landed on the seawall some twenty feet away, likely looking for a handout of bread or crackers they had grown accustomed to from passers-by. A large fish briefly broke the surface then disappeared as quickly as it came. The temperature fluctuated with a mixture of heat from the mid-day sun, occasionally lifted by coolness from the water below as it blew past them in the gentle breeze.

Tommy hated to break the spell of the moment, but he was there to tell his father something, and it had to be done. Even though he would likely not remember the conversation two minutes later, Tommy still believed that it was the right thing to do.

"Dad, I wanted to tell you that I've recorded a new album, and the record label will be releasing it soon. The first single is going out next week, and I have to go on a whirlwind promotional tour. I told them I couldn't be gone for more than three weeks, so they're cramming as much as possible into that short time frame. I'll start here in Scotland, head down to London, then on to a few other cities in Europe. From there I'll go to the U.S. where I think there are approximately ten major markets I'll visit there. I'll be doing radio and television ... you know ... all of the big talk shows. Then on to Australia and ending up in Japan. So it's going to be an exhausting three weeks."

"Wow, that sounds exciting. I hope someone else is paying for it though. All that seems very expensive."

"Well, the record label pays for it, but they take it back from me later when the music starts selling. It's a racket, but at least I don't have to personally shell out money on the front end. Technically, the label owns the music, so you'd think the related expenses would be a cost of them doing business. Unfortunately, that's not the way the music industry works. They take the majority of what they spend back from the artist one way or another. It's a bit crazy."

"That seems a little unfair. Don't let them take advantage of you, Son."

Tommy smiled at his father's protectiveness. "I won't, Dad. But I wanted to tell you I'll be away for a bit. Other than going to London with me, Amanda will stay here to help Mum look after things and check in on you. I just don't want you to worry. Okay?"

"I'm not worried. I don't know what's wrong with me. I don't seem to know what's going on most of the time, so if I do get nervous about something, it probably won't last very long."

"That's good ... I guess. I thought you'd enjoy sitting here. Are you having fun?"

"I don't know. Not really. I feel very uneasy for some reason. Where are we again?"

"We're in Leith, and this is the Entrance Basin where the shipyard you used to work at was located."

"You see, I don't remember that. It's pretty here, but it makes me sad for some reason."

"Okay, we don't have to stay. Do you want to go?"

"I guess."

Tommy stood, then reached down to help his father to his feet. Frank turned over and supported his body on his hands and knees, pressing against the rough concrete. He slowly slid a foot forward and with Tommy's assistance, raised himself on one leg, quickly reinforcing himself with the other. Frank groaned at the pain of his arthritis as he straightened out his legs and back. When he finally reached a standing position, he abruptly jerked his arm away from where Tommy held it at the elbow.

"Get off of me!" he screamed, suddenly in a much more pronounced Scottish accent.

"What?" replied a shocked Tommy. "What's wrong, Dad? Did I hurt you?"

"Dad? I ain't yer dad, boy! Get away from me! I don't know what yer sellin', but you aren't trickin' me with yer thievery."

"Dad, it's me, Tommy. Calm down. It's okay. You're just confused. You're having a hallucination."

"I ain't havin' no hallucination," Frank growled in an almost evil tone. "I know you ... you're that bloke frae the tele I see gyratin' around like you think yer Elvis Presley. Now you're all broke out here peddlin' yer wares to old people trying to trick us into yer Ponzi scheme."

"I don't know what you are talking about. I'm your son, Thomas. And you're Frank Maddock. Come on, Dad. Snap out of this! Please! You're scaring me."

Tommy's eyes welled with tears as the reality of the ebb and flow of Alzheimer's raised its ugly head and unexpectedly struck him like a cobra lying wait in the tall grass. The intensity in Frank's eyes was alarming, and Tommy's mind reeled on how to best handle the situation.

"You say I'm who, Frank Maddock? I know that fella too. He's a washed-up wreck of a soul just like you. Lives over there on Circus Lane, all high and mighty, in his paid for little home. I'd like to punch him right in the mouth."

"Dad. Come on! Please come back to me. It's okay. Just relax."

"Relax you say? I don't have time to relax. I've got to get back to work."

The tugboat blew its horn in the imperfect timing of the moment as it turned on its final approach to the dock across the bay.

"You see, they're blowin' the horn for us tae get back to work, and now I'm late," Frank continued. "I gotta get all the way over there and back on the line, or they'll fire me. You and yer incessant chattiness is going tae cost me my job. I got kids tae feed, ya know."

As his panicked state escalated, Frank shifted his head from side to side looking up and down the shore as if contemplating varying solutions to his perceived dilemma. Suddenly, he began to walk away from Tommy at a furious pace along the sidewalk that paralleled the seawall. The tug's horn blew a second time causing Frank to stop and turn to look across the basin. Tommy jogged to catch his father, then cautiously approached the last ten feet. The tug horn blew a third time triggering Frank to run forward past the edge of the seawall and into mid-air. He seemed to fly momentarily before plunging feet-first into the dark brown, frigid water.

For a second Tommy stood unmoving and in utter disbelief as to what had just happened. Snapping back to reality, he reacted and jumped in after his father who had disappeared beneath the swirling pattern his entry had left on the surface. Popping up to gather a full breath of air, Tommy dove back down, frantically searching the liquid darkness for his father.

Returning to the light again, Tommy struggled to catch his breath. Fearing the worst, he closed his eyes and whispered a quick prayer.

"Please, Lord. Help me."

Filling his lungs with air, he plunged back into the water, diving as deep as he could, his arms outstretched wide as he progressed downward. He felt a slight nudge against his right pinkie causing him to quickly alter course. As he reached for what he believed to be there, his hands only returned emptiness as his chest ached for oxygen. He continued to his right for another few feet when suddenly his hands bumped into what was obviously a body. Grabbing his father under the arms, he kicked fiercely to reach the surface.

The sun-lit, blue sky greeted Tommy as he gulped for air. Seeing his father wasn't breathing he quickly swam the fifteen feet to shore with Frank in tow. Fortunately, a large floating maintenance platform was tethered to the seawall. Climbing onto the wooden deck, he reached back for his father, pulled him onto the flat surface and prepared to perform CPR. He was unsure of what to do other than what he had seen in movies and on TV.

In the process of positioning Frank, Tommy inadvertently shifted his father's body to one side which forced water out of his mouth and lungs. As if an angel's hands had been placed upon him, Frank immediately awoke and screamed for air. He gathered what he could in a few breaths, then vomited what seemed to be a gallon or more of water. With his lungs nearly clear, Frank desperately continued to gasp for several minutes before he was finally able to speak.

"What happened, Son? Oh my goodness, I feel sick!" exclaimed Frank.

Hesitating, Tommy opted to fib to this father to avoid more trauma.

"It was a freak accident, Dad. We were sitting on the seawall, and when you stood, you slipped and fell into to the water. Are you okay?"

"I think so. Why were we sitting on a seawall?" Frank asked as he looked around getting his bearings and struggling for mental clarity. "Hey, are we at the Leith Docks? I used to work here, you know?"

Tommy smiled in relief that there didn't seem to be any permanent damage, and at least for the moment, the tragic experience even seemed to help his father's memory. He rubbed Frank's shoulder and replied, "Yeah, I know you did, Dad. It was at the Henry Robb Shipyards, right?"

"That's right, Thomas. But it closed a while back, ya know."

"I know, Dad. I know."

CHAPTER THIRTY-FIVE

THE LONDON RADIO STATION DJ GRABBED THE MICROPHONE suspended by the boom arm and swung it back in line with his mouth as the song faded out.

"Well there you go!" exclaimed DJ Dunphy. "That's the new single from the amazing Tommy Model. Tommy, I have to say the title, 'Big Baby' threw me a bit before I heard the lyrics. I thought maybe it was a song about all of the temper tantrums you've thrown throughout your career. There were a few, you know?"

"Yes, there were," jokingly replied Tommy. "But no ... it's about going big in a relationship, as in, not holding back. As you heard it's actually an up-tempo, rockin' love song."

"Yeah, I get that now. Interesting play on those two words Big and Baby. It's definitely a hit, mate. And thank you so much for bringing it to us for its London debut. How does it feel to be back after all these years?"

"It feels great. When I sat down to start writing the new songs, they poured out of me. I think it was just the right time. I wish it hadn't been so long, but better late than never, I guess."

"That's true. This song is fresh and modern but still has that Tommy Model flair we all know and love. Did you have a lot of help pulling that together, or was it all you?"

"I co-wrote that song and a few others on the album with my lovely wife, Amanda Perkins. But it was pretty much all me as far as the production goes. I worked with some top-notch musicians who added a lot of layers and textures that made the songs really come to life. I was worried that my music might come out sounding somewhat dated if I self-produced it. But I've stayed in touch with current trends and styles, so I think it's up-to-snuff."

"Absolutely it is."

"Thanks. It was important to bring in some modern elements to peak the interest of younger listeners without going so far that it sounded forced for commercial purposes. I wanted all of the tracks to have a very natural feel while not losing sight of the sound we had a lot of success with during the 80's."

"Plus that 80's sound has come back around to some extent, wouldn't you agree?"

"Yeah, the MTV explosion changed music in a major way because it ushered in a high level of diversity. In the beginning for me, back in 1981, it didn't matter how much you spent making a video. If you had one, MTV would typically put you into rotation because they desperately needed content. Whereas on radio, much like it is again now, you had to fit into a tight little box to get airplay. MTV blew out what the definition of a music genre was. You had rock videos playing with pop videos, playing with new wave and rap videos. Even some country stuff snuck in there occasionally."

Tommy took a quick sip from his water bottle, then continued. "So anyone who grew up in that time couldn't help but be influenced by that openness and the experimentation MTV allowed."

"It surely was a unique era. Do you think it still impacts music to this day?"

"Sure it does. Those fans went on to have children, and now those kids are the musicians and songwriters making waves. They were inspired by the music their parents loved and listened to, just like I was. In the 70's my mum was a huge fan of The Carpenters. Even though I'm a rocker at heart, the importance of a great hook and melody is ingrained in me from hearing her sing along with those Carpenters' albums, over and over again. So, to answer your original question, yes ... the 80's sound has come back around. And I fit right into that organically because I was obviously a part of the original movement."

"Well if the rest of the album is on the same level as the first single, I think you're on your way to a big comeback."

"Thanks, I'm looking forward to seeing how far this can go. There aren't any filler songs on the album. Even though streaming is the most common way of accessing music these days, I do hope that the new tracks resonate in a way that fans would still like to own the album. We're adding in some cool bonus tracks if you buy the CD or download the entire package."

"That brings up a good point because you first became popular in a time when physical record sales were crazy. What is your perspective on how streaming is changing things for better or worse?"

"Well, I personally don't think there's a whole lot of upside to streaming. Those who have tried to take a positive position, focus on the promotional aspects that hopefully leads to live performance ticket sales. But what if you're not an artist or band that has reached a viable touring level yet? It's a challenge to be seen through all of the clutter. There's simply too much to choose from online. Even if you can be found, there are still only twenty-four hours in a day and the time people have available for music is less and less because of social media distractions and other commitments. For instance, I'm a big fan of getting a good education, but it's ridiculous how much time kids have to devote to school nowadays. There's a big-time availability issue that I didn't have as a youth."

"That's very true," agreed Dunphy. "My kids spend more time on homework and testing now than I did during my entire time at university."

"Exactly. So the big question becomes when does music fit into someone's life? And anyone can put out an album or some tracks now, which is nice but also adds to the competition factor. It's almost as if you said that every kid who played a sport in college, and even some that didn't, are going to go on to compete on a professional level. Then everyone would wonder why there aren't any superstar players anymore. It's because there are too many teams, too many players, and too many games. Ultimately, it would get watered down and boring."

"So how are you planning to overcome those challenges this time around?"

"Well, Galactic Records has stepped up in a big way. We've put the past behind us, so I don't think there's going to be a lack of commitment from my record label, which is often a concern for any artist on any level. We're going a little more old-school and taking it to the fans like we're doing right now. You see a lot more of the personal touch in the states within the country music world, but how many artists have stopped by lately for an on-air chat?"

"We were talking about that before you got here this morning and I think we came up with two over the past year. That's changed a lot as well because everyone thinks they can connect with fans on social media, so we're not as necessary. But they still want us to play their music."

"Right, but the problem with social media is ... as a follower you're not typically on social media to listen to music. It's all about checking out a pic or a post, or adding your own ... and that gets back to that time-factor again. I don't care what people had for lunch or that they're getting their nails done in red rose #7. Whereas if someone is listening to us now, they are primarily interested in hearing music. Of course I'm droning on and on, but generally, you have an interested music fan in a car, or at work, or somewhere relaxing ... wherever someone can listen. And listening is the key. My record label's marketing team is going to kill me for saying this, but I don't feel like online fan engagement is as necessary as everyone thinks it is. I enjoy it to a certain extent, but at the end of the day, fans want to be entertained, and I want them to enjoy my music. Unfortunately, those paths don't always cross when interacting online."

"That's great insight, Tommy, and your thoughts are much appreciated. As an industry, I'm not quite sure where we're headed, so it definitely worries me sometimes. With that though, I know you have to run, but it's been such a pleasure meeting you, and we appreciate you spending time with us this morning. We hope the single and album are both fast number ones and I know we'll have 'Big Baby' in heavy rotation starting today."

"Thank you, Dunphy. I've really enjoyed it, and thank you for playing the new single. I hope all the fans out there like it. Please come out and see us when we head back this way on tour. It'll be soon, I hope."

"The one and only, Tommy Model, everybody! Hey let's play you out with your old single, 'Luxury', if that's cool?"

"Sure, I still love hearing ..."

Tommy was interrupted as the studio door burst open. To everyone's surprise, in charged the eccentric 80's, pop star, Nick Heatherly, dressed in a pink poncho with matching all pink pants, boots, and a wide-brimmed pink cowboy hat.

"Whoa, Nick Heatherly," yelled an excited DJ Dunphey. "What's going on? We're sort of in the middle of a show here."

"Oh, I know what you're in the middle of," replied Nick in a snarky tone. "Why are you wasting time on this washed-up loser is what I want to know? He's a crook. This nub stole the song, 'Luxury,' from me, you know?"

"Easy now, Nick," cautioned, Dunphy as Tommy took off his headphones and scooted back his chair preparing to stand. "Come on ... he didn't steal that song from you. Tommy wrote 'Luxury.'"

"Yeah, I know he wrote his version of 'Luxury,' but I had my own song called 'Luxury' that was set to be my first single from the *More is More* album. That punk released his before mine and completely tanked the setup for that entire project."

Tommy rose to his feet as anger crossed his brow. Tension spread throughout the room and beyond into the airwaves. DJ Dunphy pulled out his cell phone and began filming the encounter as Tommy started to fight back verbally.

"Look here, Nick. First of all ... what in the world are you wearing?" asked Tommy. "You look like a spaghetti western version of a bottle of diarrhea medicine. Secondly ... I told you this thirty-some years ago ... I had no idea you had a song called 'Luxury.' Your album wasn't even out yet when the label released my single. So how would we even know you had a song by the same title? And I can't help it that it was the only track on there that was worth anything."

"Well, macho boy, I'll have you know this vibrant pink ensemble is Elsie Chong. And I played you my new song 'Luxury' long before yours came out when you stopped by my flat that night, and we had tequila-lime ice lollies together. Now, don't even try to tell me you don't remember that."

"What? I've never been to your flat, you idiot! And I sure never heard your 'Luxury' before mine went number one and you started making the rounds with the press going crazy about it back in the day. This is an old, tired story that you've drummed up again for your own publicity purposes."

"Well, I'll let you off the hook on the song as I did back then. But only if you admit you came over for ice lollies, and later we played that game where you crawl around on the floor and stretch over each other to touch the colored dots."

"You are insane! I told you I have never been to your flat or had ice lollies with you. Nor did I play some contortionist game on the floor with you. Nor did I ever hear your version of "Luxury' before mine came out. Got it?"

"You're so testy, Mr. Model! Look at the veins in your neck. Those are so sexy. If I was a vampire, I'd come over and bite you right in front of DJ Dunphy."

"You little ..." Unable to hold back his frustration any longer Tommy ran around the large production table and chased Nick out the door, along the hall, and out a side fire exit. As he ran, Nick's poncho flowed back behind him like some flamboyantly styled superhero.

In the alleyway outside of the radio station, Nick turned back to Tommy breathing heavily from their short sprint. He laughed then high-fived Tommy, who hugged his old friend.

"That was awesome, Nick!"

"I haven't had that much fun in a long time, Tommy. Do you think they bought it?"

"Absolutely. Did you see Dunphy's face when he pulled out his cell phone and started recording us? Guaranteed, that's on social media already."

"I can't believe we pulled off that same stunt thirty years ago when we found out we had recorded a song by the same title. That was a bummer then, but we made the best of it with our fake feud, didn't we?"

"We sure did. We'll see if it helps us again. Thank you for doing that. This outfit is too much though."

"Would you expect anything less from me? And you're welcome. I hope this single and album are both massive for you. 'Big Baby' is phenomenal."

"Thanks, mate. I appreciate you saying that."

"Well, I mean it. Let me know as soon as you've locked in the tour dates you want me to open for you here in the UK. I appreciate you offering that. Every little bit of money helps these days. I'm going to work on putting out a new track corresponding with the shows. Maybe I'll make a bit more cash with that along with some old merchandise we've still got sitting in storage."

"You know I don't forget my real friends. You've been a good one. It'll be fun, and everyone will think we finally made up."

"Yeah, that'll be awesome. Hey, speaking of making up ... are you sure you don't want to come over for some tequila-lime ice lollies?"

"Get out of here, you nut."

Tommy and Nick shook hands as they turned and walked away in different directions. For Tommy, it was one promotion down, with three more long weeks to go.

CHAPTER THIRTY-SIX

WITHIN HOURS, the video post of Tommy and Nick's radio station spat had gone viral. By the time sunrise reached the United States a few hours later, Tommy Model's name was trending heavily online. Supported by additional efforts of the marketing team at Galactic Records, overnight Tommy had reached an audience that thirty years ago would have taken him months, if not years, to obtain.

The challenge surrounding such passive exposure was how to convert it to dedicated followers and ultimately true-blue fans who would purchase music, merchandise, and concert tickets. For now, the growing notoriety surrounding Tommy's comeback would have to suffice.

At Peter Kirkinour's urging, Tommy was now being trailed 24/7 by a cameraman who would document the events and behind-the-scenes happenings during the promotional tour. It was just one of many aspects to a multi-pronged, mass-marketing approach. Although the overall plan did not include new or groundbreaking concepts by any means, the Tommy Model team was determined to approach their efforts with a level of creativity and gusto that had rarely, if ever had been accomplished. It would be a delicate dance to *keep it real*, but everyone agreed that casting a wide net with varying strategies was ultimately the best approach for a quick career reboot on a global scale.

TOMMY AND HIS CAMERAMAN, JOEL, headed to a small, but popular London record shop. There, the goal was to film Tommy spontaneously connecting with younger fans. But not just any fans. This particular world-renowned record shop was a haven for those who were generally known to be more hard-core music lovers ... much more than the typical online streamer or digital downloader. If Tommy could win over the audiophiles and vinyl record enthusiasts, it would provide him with the critical legitimacy he needed for the new single, and eventually the album when it's released.

Nearly all heads turned as Tommy walked into the record store packed wall-to-wall with vinyls and CD's. Narrow, two-foot wide walkways separated the double-sided holding bins that ran the length of the store, front to back. A slight mustiness permeated the air as Bob Dylan crackled through an old set of wood veneer stereo speakers high on a shelf above the checkout stand. Dylan's unique voice set the tone of the room.

"Hi everybody," warmly greeted Tommy, waving his hand as if he had encountered a group of old friends. "Don't mind us. They're filming a documentary following the release of my new single. Keep doing what you're doing."

Some shoppers continued to stare at Tommy, perhaps trying to figure out who the heck he was. Others returned to their frantic search for that perfect gem of a record. Tommy greeted the heavily bearded store manager at the checkout and then turned to make his way into the thick of it all.

Randomly starting in the "F" section, he began flipping through the stacks of vinyls. He perused classics such as Foreigner's *Head Games,* Foghat's *Fool for the City*, a 12-inch remix of Frankie Goes to Hollywood's "Two Tribes," and *Reach The Beach* by The Fixx. There were also more recent releases from Fall Out Boy, Five Finger Death Punch, Flogging Molly, and the Foo Fighters. For Tommy as a true music buff, it was like being turned loose in a candy store, and he quickly gathered together a small stack of favorites.

A young woman, likely in her early twenties, inched her way towards Tommy. She frequently glanced his way above the rim of her black-framed glasses as she approached. Her slicked-down, short black hair framed her pale face. The look was attractive but felt conflicted against the flash of the silver ring pierced through the left side of her bottom lip. A small tattoo of a baby elephant holding the tail of a mother elephant laid cradled in the soft space between the thumb and index finger of her right hand. Her all-black ensemble was an obvious extension of her personality. Leery of Tommy and his cameraman, she shyly held back at first. But as a girl on a mission, she finally gained the courage to speak.

"You should check out that Franz Ferdinand album," she suggested to Tommy in a somber tone, pointing at the record he had just flipped past.

"It's good, is it?" inquired Tommy.

"One of their best, I think."

Tommy returned to the vinyl she recommended, picked it up then turned it over to read the back. The young lady nervously moved directly beside him."

"So are you Tommy Model or what?"

"You don't know? You seem to be a musical expert, so you tell me. Some days I'm not quite sure who I am."

"Yeah, you're Tommy Model. You're better looking in person, which is what was throwing me off. In most of the pictures I've seen you tend to look like you swallowed a clove of garlic."

"A clove of garlic? How exactly does that look?"

"You know ... like it was hiding in some pasta, and you accidentally ate the whole thing. It was good when it first hit your pallet, but then as it went down, it overpowered you. As a result, you second-guessed your decision about ordering what you did, especially when the reality of indigestion and bad breath for a couple of days to follow starts to kick in.

"That's actually a look?"

The woman nodded her head in agreement without a verbal response while she flipped through the albums directly in front of her.

"What's your name?" asked Tommy.

"Why do you want to know my name?"

"Well, since you know who I am it would be nice to know who you are too."

"Oh. My name's Penelope. But you can call me Pen."

"Nice to meet you, Pen."

"Same here. I have all of you albums in case you're wondering."

"So, which is your favorite?"

"Probably the *Luxury* LP. But I like all of them. So why is a cameraman following you around? He's cute, but kind of annoying. You know ... like a bee that won't stop trying to fly into your face."

"He does sort of remind me of a bee," Tommy replied, shifting his gaze to look at Joel. He quickly turned back to Pen. "I'm in the process of promoting my new single, 'Big Baby.' He's documenting the whole experience so people can see what goes on behind the scenes."

"Oh. I can't wait to hear it."

"Thanks. I hope you like it."

"I'm sure I will. So listen ... I came over because I wanted to tell you that they have this room in the back with some rare vinyls. But only certain people are allowed access. Do you want to check it out with me? The camera guy can't go with us though."

"Well if he can't go, I probably shouldn't either."

"All right. I'll probably get my pass revoked, but I guess he can come. Do I scare you or something?"

"No, he's supposed to be capturing moments like these for everyone to see. If he's not with me, he obviously can't do that."

"Okay. Well, let's go. But act cool and don't make a big deal about it."

Joel shadowed Tommy as he followed Pen to an inconspicuous door at the back of the store. Pen used her body to block the camera's view of a keypad on the wall. She punched in a four-digit code releasing the deadbolt lock with a deep thump. She opened the thick door and walked inside. Tommy started to follow, then turned back to Joel.

"Give me a sec to check this out without the camera. I know what I said, but I do want to be respectful to what they've got going on here."

Joel nodded and stayed behind as Tommy closed the door. Inside, he walked through a short hallway that opened into a small room that was even more jam-packed with albums than the main store.

"So this is the really hard to find stuff, Tommy," explained Pen. "Hey, where is your camera guy?"

"I asked him to stay behind. I'm not sure you want the world seeing this, and I appreciate you trusting me to come back here."

Pen broke her stoic expression to smile, pleased by Tommy's sincerity.

"You're okay, Tommy Model. I'm starting to like you more and more. So check this out?"

Pen handed Tommy a vinyl of U2's "Pride (In the Name of Love)" 12" single.

"This is nice," replied Tommy. "And I'm a big U2 fan, but why is this one special?"

"Carefully slide it out and see for yourself."

Tommy slowly and gently inched the white dust sleeve out of the cardboard album liner. He then slid the inner disc from its covering revealing a completely clear vinyl pressing.

"It's transparent," remarked Tommy. "I've seen colors other than black, but I don't think I've ever seen one like this. That's wild."

"It's one of only five clear copies made in Australia during 1984."

"Really! Wow. I bet that's worth something."

"You think? quipped, Pen. "That's why this room and that door are secured and fireproofed. People pay top dollar for these treasures. Here's another. Depeche Mode's *Music for the Masses* with the cover art that was withdrawn after only fifteen copies."

"Wow, that's cool. Love those guys too. What else do they have back here?"

"Oh, this is awesome. A Robert Johnson single from 1936."

"You're kidding? 'Cross Road Blues.' How much is this one?"

"They have a paper printout over here. Let me look. Uh ... it's seven thousand pounds."

"Hmmm. Hold onto that one."

"Really? That's a lot of money."

"Yeah it is, but I may seriously get that. This is crazy. Thank you for bringing me back here."

"It's all good. So are you gonna buy me something as a thank you?"

"Well sure. But let's be reasonable, Pen."

"Oh, I'll be reasonable. This David Bowie 45 is only a thousand quid, and I've had my eye on it for a while. How about that?"

"Ah. There it is. So is this what you do? Wait for rich suckers like me to follow you back here so they'll buy you your favorites."

"I'm a little insulted, Mr. Model. You make me sound like a hooker. Other than my ex-boyfriend, I've never been in here with anyone else, and that's the truth. I know I'll never be able to afford this particular record especially since Bowie died, so I was just asking. But you can say *no*."

"Don't get huffy. I was just messing with you. It's yours."

Pen excitedly hugged Tommy and kissed him on the cheek. As she pulled away, she said, "I know a lot of music vloggers and people who manage online accounts for businesses and celebrities. I'm going to make sure everyone knows how cool you really are. As cliché as this is, let's snap a pic with me, you, and Bowie so the world will believe me."

Pen quickly took the photo of her and Tommy standing side by side, as she held the Bowie 45 in her other hand. Tommy looked at his watch and realized he was running late.

"Hey, Pen ... unfortunately, I have to get to a TV talk show. But this has been an awesome adventure. Let's go pay for these before you find an old Elvis Presley or Prince rarity."

"Oh, they have those. You wanna see?"

Tommy smiled, but ignored Pen's offer and walked back along the hall to open the door. Joel resumed filming as Tommy re-emerged back into the bright expanse of the main store. Hustling to make up for lost time, at the register Tommy purchased both the Bowie 45 and the Robert Johnson single, along with a few other vinyl records he had discovered earlier in the front section of the store.

He handed the Bowie record to Pen and hugged her goodbye, thanking her again for the experience. She returned the appreciation and promised to buy Tommy's new album when it came out, but only if it was released on vinyl. As he walked out the front door,

Tommy assured her it would be. He shouted to the manager that he would see to it that they got some copies if he would hold one for Pen. The urban-woodsman stared at Tommy, still likely clueless as to who he was.

Tommy strolled beyond the window-view of the store then turned back to Joel who was still filming. "What a neat place that was?"

"It really was," replied Joel.

"I miss going into record shops. I need to do that more often. And how awesome was Pen?"

"She seemed cool."

"Yeah, and I'm very psyched to find this super-rare single from the best blues guitar player who ever lived. Most people don't realize it, but Robert Johnson influenced everything we do today in the world of music. I learned several of his licks early on when I first started playing guitar. So this is very special. But right now, I'm gonna head back to the hotel, visit with my lovely wife for a bit, then get ready for the talk show with Billy Barker. We will check in with you later. See ya, everybody."

Joel stopped filming and dropped the camera to his side. He hurried to catch up with Tommy as he quickened the pace to maximize his time with Amanda.

"So, are you a big Robert Johnson fan?" asked Joel. "I never got into his music."

"Of course. You're young, so you probably don't know the history of rock 'n' roll. When someone listens to Robert Johnson, they might think his guitar playing and singing sounds overly simple, but at the time in the late 1930's he was breaking new ground with his unique style. I believe this single was released when he was just twenty-five or twenty-six years old, but he passed away a year later. It's hard to believe that he only recorded music for a couple of years, but he has influenced musicians to this very day. Some interpret the lyrics of 'Cross Road Blues' to be about a deal he supposedly made with the Devil to achieve fame. Some even say that unholy compromise is why he died when he did because allegedly he was poisoned."

A fan walking by stopped to ask Tommy for his autograph. He obliged, and after a photo together, he and Joel continued on as Tommy picked up the conversation where he had left off.

"Anyway ... I'm excited about finding it. I probably could have gone broke buying stuff out of that little room. Ultimately, I may auction off this vinyl at a future charity benefit I'm planning. It's still just a thought in my head, so don't ask me about it on camera. Cool?"

Joel agreed as they continued to walk the final block to The Bradley Hotel.

Inside, Joel exited the elevator on his floor to return to his room where he would edit and upload the latest footage while Tommy was on the *The Billy Barker Show*. Tommy continued to the rooftop pool deck where Amanda had texted him earlier she was relaxing and trying to make the best of a partly cloudy day.

Considering the weather, the deck was busier than Tommy expected. Greek-inspired white plaster archways lined both sides of the pool, and every chair was occupied. Spotting Amanda on the far left side of the chaotic scene, he made his way around and between the chase lounges and bodies dotting the white-tiled surface.

As Tommy approached, he noticed a large, hairy-backed man sitting next to Amanda, and leaning in close as he spoke. The man's immediate proximity to his lovely wife activated Tommy's protective radar. He always tried to remain open-minded when it came to Amanda since she was also a well-known celebrity in the UK. But something about this bloke made Tommy anxious and uncomfortable.

"Hi, angel," Tommy greeted as he leaned over to kiss his wife while admiring her firm, fit body, fully-featured in an iridescent swimsuit.

"Hey, babe. How are you? Tommy this is Dmitry. Dmitry, this is my husband, Tommy. Dmitry is from Romania and is visiting London on business."

"Hello," Tommy responded, but without offering his hand to shake. Dmitry did not greet Tommy, but instead turned back to Amanda and restarted his conversation as if Tommy didn't even exist.

"So darling, as I was saying ..." Dmitry continued in a heavy Romanian accent.

Feeling disrespected, Tommy interrupted. "Okay, pal. I need to talk to my wife, so if you could bugger off, that would be much appreciated."

The thick-bodied Romanian stood to his feet and towered over Tommy by at least a foot. He faked a smile revealing a large gap between his two front teeth. He tilted his head downward and stared with intimidation into Tommy's eyes as he responded, "I was speaking to the lady, so why don't you bug off, little boy. I think she's interested in spending time with a real man today. At least that's what she told me. And this is all man ... I assure you."

Dmitry grabbed the crotch of his red, bathing suit briefs. Repulsed by the sight, Tommy looked away, but the image was already burned into his brain. Dmitry's body was as disgustingly hairy in the front as he was from behind. The fur coat he sported was only out-shined by the stench of curry and beer on his breath. The entire experience made Tommy queasy.

"All right, boys. Let's knock it off," demanded Amanda. "Dmitry you know I didn't say any such thing. I assure you, Tommy Model is all man and then some."

"Did you say, Tommy Model? Are you ...?" stuttered Dmitry as he looked again into Tommy's eyes. This time they carried utter fear while searching for confirmation that he had not just made a complete fool of himself.

Tommy shook his head and casually replied, "Unfortunately, I am."

"Oh, no. I'm so sorry, Mr. Model. I didn't know this was your wife. I mean, I do now, but ... oh, I'm such an idiot. Please forgive me. I love your music and I think you're great. Peace?"

Dmitry held out his hand seeking forgiveness. Tommy paused slightly, thinking hard as to whether he was willing to let bygones be bygones. After all, this beast of a man had just disrespected him in front of several people and was trying to snake on his beautiful wife. Besides, who knows how far he would have gone if Tommy had not arrived when he did. Tommy looked at Amanda who immediately returned a *shape up or else* expression. Snapping Tommy back to form, he reached out to embrace Dmitry's hand.

"Sure, Dmitry. Peace," agreed Tommy. Clarifying the Romanian's true intentions, he asked, "So what brings you here on business?"

"Well, I was here interviewing for a bodyguard position with a high profile celebrity. It went okay, but she seems like a real ball-buster, so I don't know if I'll take the position even if she offers it to me. We'll see."

"Well, good luck with that. We need to head back to the room to get ready for some commitments we have this afternoon, if you'll excuse us."

"Sure. It was great meeting you, Tommy. And you as well, Amanda. I hope you can forgive me for being disrespectful."

"It's all good, Dmitry" replied Amanda, as she and Tommy walked away. "Have a safe trip home tomorrow."

Tommy looked back to see Dmitry wave goodbye. Under the sun-shaded veranda, he suddenly appeared more like a lonely little boy than a hulking bodyguard. Even though Tommy was still trickling with anger from the encounter, in a glance, his ire shifted to sympathy as he waved back in return.

"You've turned me into such a softy, Amanda. Sometimes I miss the old guy who would stay riled up all afternoon after an experience like that."

Amanda rubbed Tommy's back as they strolled into the coolness of the hotel. She lovingly looked at her husband and asked, "Do you really?"

Once again, Amanda had peeled another layer of the onion from Tommy's emotionally fortified exterior as he further relinquished his resistance and humbly replied, "No, not really."

CHAPTER THIRTY-SEVEN

TOMMY AND AMANDA WERE LATE. A malfunctioning hair dryer was to blame as the dynamic duo charged through the hotel lobby and out to the curb where a car was supposed to be waiting.

"There's no car!" snarled Tommy.

"Great, now what?" retorted Amanda.

Tommy turned back to the hotel where he inquired of the bell captain. The head bellman informed Tommy that a driver had waited for approximately ten minutes, but when his customers didn't show, he left to pick up other clients and gave no indication that he would be returning. Tommy was furious.

"I'm the main guest on *The Billy Barker Show* tonight!" he exclaimed. "Who else could be more important for a driver that was hired by the show? Unbelievable!"

"Sweetie, calm down. Take a breath. You're making a scene," Amanda whispered in Tommy's ear.

Tommy inhaled deeply and closed his eyes, regathering his composure.

"All right. I'm good. I think the studio is only a few blocks away. Hey Cap ... is the Billy Barker studio a walkable distance?"

"Yes, sir. It's only two blocks. You go this way one block, then turn right, and then up to the next street. It's across from that on the right. Normally, I could hail a cab for you, but the rozzers have street closed off due to a serious collision. You can see the lights from here if you look. Your driver was one of the last cars through."

Tommy looked towards the scene of the accident, then back the other direction down the block. He scoped the distance between where they stood and the next street where the bell captain had directed them to turn. Tommy knew it was probably further than it looked, but with time slipping away, he made the decision to walk.

"Okay, we've got to go Amanda. Come on."

Tommy grabbed Amanda's hand and set off in the direction of the studio. The air was muggy, and by the time they had hurried half a block, Tommy was sweating like a brute. He wiped the moisture from his forehead and upper lip as they pushed forward.

"Oh, I'm going to look so fantastic when we get there," sarcastically remarked Tommy.

"It'll be all right," encouraged Amanda. "The makeup people will get you cooled off and looking good as new. Let's try to make it without a big brouhaha."

As they reached the turn, Tommy looked up the street leading towards the studio. It was heavily shaded between the two tall buildings and had an ominous feel, but still, he pressed on. With the focus of his attention in front of him, Tommy failed to notice the hulking figure walking nearly fifty yards behind. He also completely missed the three thugs lurking in the darkness of the sheltered side exit of a building.

It wasn't until the three, hooded hooligans were upon them that Tommy realized his incompetent error. The largest of the triad ran to head off Tommy and Amanda, as the other two closed the noose from behind.

"All right you two lovelies ... let's have the wallet, your purse, and the jewelry. My, my, my ... those are some nice wedding rings too. Oh, baby ... and that necklace. I don't want to have to snap that off your pretty little neck, so please be so kind as to remove it gently. Chop, chop! Let's go!"

Tommy turned to size up the two men behind them. One patted a stocky, black baton into the palm of his hand while the other held a large knife, both further solidifying that any valiant effort would be foolish. Without saying a word, Tommy slid his wallet from his back pocket as Amanda handed over her purse and unclasped the diamond necklace.

"Now the rings! Come on, we don't have all day," ordered the leader.

As Tommy and Amanda began to slide their wedding bands from their fingers, they suddenly heard a loud thud. The mugger in front of them dropped the purse and wallet and then turned to sprint away. They looked back to see Dmitry's massive frame squaring with the other two culprits. Having received the full brunt of Dmitry's initial attack, they groggily stumbled about trying to regain enough mental fortitude to put up a resistance.

The baton-wielding knucklehead finally went down, but the knife carrying tough guy was intent on standing his ground. He took a wild lunge with the blade, but Dmitry knocked his assailant's arm away with a perfectly positioned slap. He then finished him off with a punch that echoed against the buildings of the narrow, dark street. The misfit collapsed in a heap, joining his pal on the pavement, unmoving and silent.

Amanda turned back to see the runner still hightailing it towards the sunlit expanse of the intersection. Feeling liberated she began to run after her assailant in efforts of retrieving her necklace, a gift from Tommy following their second date.

"Amanda!" Tommy screamed. "Let it go! It's not worth it."

Dmitry was already in motion and passed the couple at a feverish pace, running after the hooded character who had nearly reached the next street. For an extremely large man, Dmitry was lightning-fast. Tommy initially thought he would never catch up, but imagined better of it once he saw the gap quickly closing as the thief finally turned the corner and disappeared from sight. In seconds, Dmitry himself made the same turn and was gone.

In the silence, the man who had intimidated them with his baton was attempting to get to his feet, groaning heavily at the throbbing pain in his head. Kneeling on one knee, he took the full force of Amanda's high-heel shoe to the face as she delivered her blow with a karate-kick scream. The man went back down ... this time knocked out cold.

"Good job, baby!"

"Thanks. I can't tell you how great that felt! Should we call the police?"

"No, we need to go. This is completely insane, but this show is very important. We'll find Dmitry and sort this all out later," instructed Tommy as he picked up the wallet and purse from the ground, then clasped Amanda's hand and made way towards the studio.

At the intersection, Dmitry emerged back into view, nearly bumping into them as they all converged on the corner at the same time.

"Dmitry! You saved us! Thank you so much," gratefully stated Amanda as she reached out to hug his thick, muscular frame."

"You're welcome, Miss Amanda."

"Yes, thank you Dmitry," added Tommy warmly shaking his hand. "We would have lost it all and who knows what else if you hadn't come along. I have to ask though ... were you following us?"

"Yes. I'm sorry. I was in the lobby when you came through, and when I saw you take off to walk here, my training kicked in. I wanted to make sure you both made it safely to wherever you were going."

"Well, I think we're both extremely glad that you did. I have to admit, I didn't like you very much when we first met, but I love you now, mate," stated Tommy.

"Hey," Tommy continued. "I know you are waiting to hear about another job, but how would you like to be our personal bodyguard. I'm going to be traveling a lot internationally over the coming weeks, and that makes me a bit of a target. I really could use someone like you with me to keep the nuts at bay. I'll also need you to hire and supervise other security people to watch out for Amanda when I'm away. What do you say?"

"Tommy, I'm fine," interjected Amanda. "I don't need security back home. Besides, I don't want to feel like I'm always on guard. Everyone loves us there, so I don't think anyone will mess with me. These idiots today were totally random."

"Okay, well when we travel together or alone, I want someone with us going forward. This is a wakeup call. It's a different world from the one we were famous in before, baby. So how about it, Dmitry?"

"Absolutely, Mr. Model! I'd be honored to accept the opportunity."

Tommy and Dmitry shook hands to seal the deal.

"Great, it's settled then," stated Tommy. "We'll talk money later, but for now let's see if we can finally get to this crazy talk show. I think that's the studio right there across the street."

"Oh, I almost forgot," noted Dmitry. "Here's your necklace, Amanda."

"Dmitry, you caught the guy? You ran like an Olympian. Thank you."

"Actually, I was on the Olympic team for Romania. Track and field ... mainly the shot put, the javelin, the hammer throw. I won a gold, silver, and bronze."

"Get out!" exclaimed Amanda. "Our bodyguard is an Olympic medalist, Tommy. Not many people can say that!"

"That's really cool. I definitely wanna hear more about this later, but right now we gotta go, guys," reminded Tommy. "Are you coming, Dmitry?"

"I'm right behind you," he replied.

Tommy, Amanda, and Dmitry crossed the busy street and entered *The Billy Barker Show* studio. After speaking with a security agent, a representative from the show greeted them and whisked the trio into an area that led backstage.

In Tommy's dressing room, a hair and makeup woman was waiting. After a brief introduction, she went to work on Tommy. She dried his sweat-covered hair, cooled his neck with an ice pack, and applied a slight bit of makeup to the corners of his eyes and forehead. After drinking a large bottle of cold water, Tommy soon looked good as new. Internally, however, he was still fired up about the car debacle that ultimately led to their mugging.

Ten minutes before the show opening, Billy Barker himself stopped by to say hello.

"Tommy Model!" Billy excitedly greeted. "I'm Billy Barker. It's very nice to meet you."

"Hi, Billy. It's nice to finally meet you too. Actually, I think you were an opening act at a nightclub I played years ago. Do you remember that?"

"I do, it was in Chelsea. I think it was called *The Fritz*, which I guess was a play on *The Ritz*. Man, that was a long time ago. You don't look a bit different. Don't say I don't either because I know that's not true."

"Awe, come on. We've both done pretty well."

"Hey, I understand there was a bit of a car mix-up?"

"Yeah, with the car it was our fault because we were late, but it went downhill from there. An accident was blocking the entire street in front of the hotel so we couldn't even get a cab. So we walked over and got mugged."

"You got mugged?"

"Yeah, but our bodyguard saved us, so it's all good."

"I'm so sorry, Tommy. I'm glad you're all okay. The manager of the car service will be hearing from me personally. None of that should have happened. Even if the street had been open, you might have been waiting a while for a cab with that convention taking place just around the corner. That's probably where the driver took off to."

"Oh, what convention is that?"

"It's a ..."

The stage manager barged into the room interrupting Billy in mid-sentence. He informed his boss that he was desperately needed to remedy an argument between two other guests. Billy apologized to Tommy and excused himself to charge off and save the day. Tommy sat puzzled and intrigued as to what convention was in town and why other guests were fighting with each other. His answers wouldn't have to wait long.

Five minutes later, the show launched while Tommy, Amanda, and Dmitry watched the events unfold from the television monitor in Tommy's dressing room. Billy's standard opening comedic monologue was a hit as usual. After a commercial break, Billy introduced his first guests. Tommy watched in stunned silence as two clowns joined the show in full makeup and attire. Apparently, both were quite famous in clown circles, and they just happened to be in town for the International Clown Convention. Billy explained that when the original guest backed out at the last minute, they got the call to fill in.

Their initial shtick with Billy eventually turned into a circus-style stand-up routine, complete with a bevy of props and audience participation. One clown was a sad-faced pierrot who took the brunt of the jokes in the straight-man role. The other was a mischievous, silly-faced jester.

Tommy had always despised clowns. But what concerned him even more, was that the audience appeared to be full of small children and their parents instead of young to middle-aged adults as he had anticipated would be the case. The enthusiastic crowd relentlessly cheered for the merry-andrews as they proceeded through their set of antics. Eventually, an entourage of twenty or more clowns engulfed the stage for the big finale, driving the kids into a frenzy.

"So this is probably why our driver didn't wait on us," remarked Tommy pointing at the television. "The entire city is busy shuttling around a bunch of clowns. I hate clowns, you know?"

"I know, sweetie," responded Amanda as she rubbed the back of Tommy's head hoping to calm him down.

The stage manager re-entered the room and asked, "Mr. Model, are you ready?"

"I guess," mumbled Tommy as he stood and lumbered after the manager. He turned back to look at Amanda who gave him a thumbs up.

After Billy's introduction, Tommy entered the set waving at the audience. It was a subdued response at best, and what little he did receive seemed to be mostly egged on by the crowd-warmer. Off-camera the onlookers were frantically directed by the warmer's signs and hand gestures, encouraging them to raise the volume and energy. Tommy reluctantly sat next to the two clowns. The harlequin immediately went about pulling the old *endless handkerchief trick* from Tommy's jacket sleeve. The children roared with laughter, entirely at Tommy's expense.

To maximize the intensity of the clown performance, the show producers had expanded the seating to within ten feet of the guests. As the interview progressed, the enthusiasm for Tommy dwindled under the short-attention span of young children. In the middle of answering one question, Tommy looked at the audience, only to see a little boy on the front row digging his index finger into his nose. Buried to the first knuckle, he finally pulled it out and licked off the tip of his finger. Tommy gagged, then began to cough and reached for a glass of water. The sad-faced clown reached for his own water, and while twisting his ear spit out a stream of liquid, once again setting the room on fire with laughter and cheers.

The interview wasn't a total bomb, but under the circumstances, it also wasn't Tommy's best performance, and the clowns obviously overshadowed him. The show's viewing audience was in the millions, and he had hoped for strong positive exposure to enhance the UK portion of his promotional tour. As he rejoined Amanda and Dmitry in his dressing room, he downed another bottle of water and sat in his chair, swiveling back and forth and seething with anger.

After the closing, Billy Barker immediately made a beeline to Tommy in efforts of apologizing for the fiasco.

"What was that, Billy?" asked Tommy. "Clowns? Really? I mean, why would you have me on with clowns?"

"I know, I know. I'm sorry. We originally had a famous actress booked, but when she canceled yesterday, we needed an easy replacement. With the clown convention in town, we were able to get them, no problem. They are famous clowns, you know?"

"Oh really? More famous than me?"

"To these kids, unfortunately, yes. But hey ... maybe you expanded your demographic. We tried to get a hold of your manager yesterday to see if you were still interested in doing the show, but he never returned our call. Once again, I'm very sorry, Tommy. I think the world of you, and would never purposefully try to put you in a bad position. But the show must go on. You know that."

"Well, I think it made me look like a fool, but we'll see how that all plays out."

"I'm sorry again, mate. I've got to run, but it was nice meeting you all."

Billy shook Tommy's hand and walked out of the dressing room. Tommy grumbled an incoherent comment under his breath, then turned to Amanda shaking his head in disgust.

"I've got to get a new manager. I love Bob, but he's sick, and this isn't going to work. I thought I could maybe do a lot of it on my own this time. But this is the kind of thing a good manager would keep from happening. We should have known about this ahead of time because I surely would have backed out."

"Let's see what happens, Tommy," encouraged Amanda. "You never know with these things. Crazy experiences like that have a way a spinning in one's favor. It's too late in New York right now, but I do think you should call Bob tomorrow and make sure he's all right. It's odd he didn't call them back."

The sound of Tommy's coughing jag and the clown's water spitting trick played through Dmitry's cell phone as he watched a video post, apparently just uploaded by the show's production staff.

"It's online already?" snapped Tommy. "Man these people are heartless. I can't believe that all of my hard work will crumble to the ground over some kid eating a booger and a couple of clowns."

Finally losing it, Tommy threw a full bottle of water at the mirror in front of him. The plastic exploded and shattered his reflection, sending water and glass everywhere. Tommy stormed out of the room and back through the hall towards the exit. Amanda and Dmitry quickly followed but were too late as Tommy approached the two clowns. They both stood, smugly leaning against the hallway wall, vaping billowing clouds of steam from their e-cigarettes. As he passed, the sad clown blew a puff right into Tommy's face, sending him into a rage.

As Tommy wrapped his hands around the clown's throat and clamped down, the other made a break for it. To his demise, the fleeing clown sprinted by Dmitry who tripped him, sending him flying face-first into the white-painted, cinder-block wall. The forceful impact was evidenced by the smudge of multi-colored clown makeup it left behind. Dmitry quickly reached Tommy and pried his fingers from their grip as the clown gurgled and flailed about. He turned a brighter shade of pancake-white as his eyes streamed tears down his face, creating a distinct furrow in his disguise.

Released from his grip, the clown struggled to regain his breath while Dmitry restrained Tommy. In between gasps, the pierrot began laughing in an ominous manner and verbally threatened Tommy, while still sucking wind.

"Oh ... I'm so going to sue you, Tommy Model!"

"Oh yeah? Who? You and your joker of a lawyer?" replied Tommy as he tried to wiggle free from Dmitry's grasp.

"Tommy, stop!" forcefully instructed Dmitry. "Let me handle this."

Dmitry released Tommy and pushed him back. He aggressively approached the clown. Towering above his target, they butted chests. Dmitry leaned his head over and nearly touching the clown's red-painted nose with his, rumbled, "You will do no such thing, Mr. Sad-Face. Because if you do, I will hunt you down and all of your clown family. Not only will I physically incapacitate each of you, but I will also expose all of your deep, dark little secrets that I'm sure your young fans should never have to hear. Maybe I'll even permanently tattoo that silly frown on your face. Hmm. I like the sound of that plan. Or you can simply apologize to Mr. Model, and we can forget this ever happened. Your choice, but I personally would choose apology. Don't you agree?"

Dmitry stood tall once again as the clown desperately shook his head in agreement and apologized.

CHAPTER THIRTY-EIGHT

TOMMY AND AMANDA HURRIED DOWN THE STAIRS leading from the private jet that had just landed in Edinburgh. They continued their pace across the tarmac, out through the VIP terminal and into the parking lot. Upon reaching his SUV, Tommy quickly loaded their suitcases in the back, shut the hatch, and hopped in to start the engine. He chirped the tires as he sped from the gated enclosure and headed towards his parent's house.

"Call Mum and tell her we're on the way," anxiously instructed Tommy. Amanda made the call and after hanging up she did her best to console her husband.

"Listen to me. Your dad's going to be all right. It's pneumonia, but they already had him on antibiotics after the water accident, so his doctor had anticipated this might happen. It's understandable that with his lungs full of water, he would have some fluid retention afterward. He should be fine in a few days."

"It's all my fault. I never should have taken him to the waterfront in the first place. I thought he'd like it. Why I thought that, I don't know."

"You can't blame yourself for this. He had no idea what he was doing, and you know that."

"I know, but ..." Tommy stopped in mid-sentence. Finally giving up the fight, he continued. "It's so frustrating that he's losing his memory. Now he's got this issue. And with the promotional tour on hold while we figure this all out, maybe I should put the entire album-launch on the shelf."

"Do you think if your father knew, he would want you to do that? Really?"

Tommy was silent as he turned the last corner and raced along the narrow lane leading to his parent's house. Years of guilt held him in conflict and the reality that his father would eventually pass away terrified him. Tommy pulled to the curb and slammed the gear shift in park. He opened the door only to pull it back quickly as a honking car passed, narrowly missing a collision.

"Slow down and turn off the car," firmly stated Amanda.

Tommy reached for the ignition button and shut off the engine as he leaned back in the leather seat. He closed his eyes and took a deep breath, then reopened them and looked carefully in the side mirror before swinging out the door. He stepped into the warm, humid, summer heat and walked towards the front of the house where Amanda was already waiting. She knocked on the front door as Tommy approached. After nearly a minute, there was still no answer. Amanda knocked again, this time starting to feel some panic herself. Still nothing.

"Where is she? Gee whiz. I'll call her again."

Amanda held her cell phone close to her ear as she hoped for an answer that came quickly. Tommy listened intently to the one-sided conversation. "Davina, where are you? On the back patio? Okay, well we're at the front door. Huh? Yes, we have a key, but we didn't want to just barge in on you. What? You and Frank are outside getting some sun? I thought Frank was ... never mind, we're coming in."

Amanda looked at Tommy in utter dismay. "You've got to be kidding me!" she said. "They are sitting outside getting some sun. Davina made it sound like Frank was on his last legs when she asked if we could cut our London visit short and come home. But they're outside basking like they're on holiday. Let's go see what's really going on."

Tommy unlocked the front door. Together, he and Amanda walked through the narrow hall. They continued into the living room and out through the back door leading to the patio where Davina and Frank sat laughing and taking in the bright and sunny day.

"Hi, Mum. Hi, Dad," Tommy greeted as he leaned down to hug them both. Amanda followed suit. "How are you feeling, Dad?"

"Oh, I'm fine. How about you, Duncan?"

"That's Thomas, Frank ... not Duncan," kindly corrected Davina. "Duncan was here earlier, so he's just a little confused."

Frank apologized. "Oh my gosh, Thomas. I'm sorry, I didn't mean to call you Duncan."

"It's okay, Dad. So Duncan was here, you say?" asked Tommy.

"Yes ... and Belle, and Fiona too. All of our children except you, Thomas. Duncan is coming back sometime today. He had a meeting to go to."

Tommy felt his frustration starting to rise, but tried his best to remain calm as he responded.

"Mum, if everyone else was here, and Dad is obviously not on death's door, why did you guilt us into coming back so quickly? If he were that bad off, you two wouldn't be sitting out here having a big laugh ... probably about how stupid Tommy and Amanda are for falling for your ruse. I've put my entire promotional tour on hold to come back here. You're acting as if because I wasn't here when my brother and sisters were, that somehow I'm being negligent."

"I don't know what this is all about, Son," Frank intervened. "But you shouldn't speak to your mother with that tone."

"You're right. I'm sorry, Dad. Mum, all I'm saying is you shouldn't scare us into thinking the worst to get us here. Just ask, and we'll come home if you need us."

"Well you not being here for thirty years is still hard for me to get over, but I'm trying. You're here now, and fortunately, your father is on the mend and headed in the right direction. We thought the sun might do him some good. Ah, there's your bother now."

Tommy turned to see Duncan step out onto the patio. The solemn look on his face was not the expression that Tommy had hoped to see from his brother after three decades of being apart.

"Hi, Duncan," Tommy greeted as he walked towards his brother and presented him with an awkward hug that was even more awkwardly reciprocated.

"Hi, Tommy. You're looking well. It's been a while."

"Too long. Duncan, this is my wife, Amanda?"

"Hi, Amanda, We've actually met, Tommy."

"Oh, of course. Did you meet here at the house when she would stop by to check on Dad?"

"Initially yes, but I'll let her fill in the rest of the story. It sounds like you two may have some catching up to do."

"No, no, no. If there's anything to say, let's get it out, little brother. Don't play games."

Duncan looked at Amanda giving her the chance to respond. Her eyes anxiously darted about, her mind pondering the best approach. With no better way apparent, she blurted out, "Duncan and I used to date, Tommy."

"What? You and Duncan?" Tommy looked at Amanda, then at Duncan who stared intently into Tommy's eyes, then looked away.

"Don't you think that would have been something you maybe should have told me?"

"Yes, probably. I'm sorry. It was a while ago, and he had moved to London, so I didn't think it was a big deal. It's not like you guys have been close."

"But he's still my brother. Is she why you moved to London, Duncan? Because you guys split?"

"You should ask her. I'm out of here."

"Hang on," demanded Tommy. "Don't run off. Answer the question."

"Yes, are you happy," tersely responded Duncan. "We broke up, and she was like family to Mum and Dad. Dad needed her around, so I decided to leave, and London seemed like a good place to go at the time. It's no big deal though. We're friends. There's nothing more too it. Just chill out because if you're anything like the Tommy I grew up with, you're getting ready to have a meltdown, and that doesn't need to happen."

Tommy clenched his fists, then stormed past Duncan, back through the house and out to the SUV. He sat inside for a moment, thinking quietly before starting the engine and driving off in a huff.

AN HOUR AND A HALF LATER, Amanda returned home thanks to a girlfriend who had given her a ride after Tommy had abandoned her without a vehicle. She found Tommy sitting peacefully in the back flower garden as bees and butterflies flitted about. He sipped on a glass of Scotch, the bottle sitting beside him in the grass next to a half-opened ice bucket.

"Sweetie?" Amanda cautiously approached.

"Hi," replied Tommy. "I feel like a real idiot, you know?"

"Why, because I didn't tell you about Duncan?"

"No, because I put you on such a high pedestal that in my fantasy mind, you've never been with another man. The best part of my life started when I met you, and I'm desperately trying to balance my old world with the new. It's really hard sometimes."

Amanda knelt on the grass in front of Tommy and leaned her elbows on his legs.

"Listen to me. You've made tremendous progress, and it's amazing to watch your transformation, but you have got to get your temper one hundred percent under control. You can't threaten people who talk to me like you did Dmitry, or beat up clowns, or go pouting off leaving me stranded because you're mad at your brother who you haven't seen for thirty years. We cannot have a child together if you are gonna keep acting like this. I'm not going to leave you, but a baby is out of the question."

"Amanda, you know my temper is not abusive or physical towards those I care about. I would never hurt you."

"I know, but I can't have our children seeing you go off on other people and thinking that's normal and okay because it's not. I realize you have a lot of anger built up inside of you. You became a spoiled and privileged rock star at a young age, and the fame and money did you in. Then you lost it all. And now you're trying to make a comeback, and nothing seems to be going right. On top of all that, your Dad has Alzheimer's, and your Mum is a bit of a nut. But that's all just life."

"I know."

"I'm trying to show you that you have to decide how you're going to deal with everything. You can handle it with grace, or you can keep on fighting every step of the way. But the latter will surely bring you more misery, and that's why I'm telling you this. So, know that I love you, but I'm going to go inside now and cool off. Hopefully, you'll give all of this some deep thought, because I am dead serious, Tommy."

Amanda rose back to her feet and leaned over to kiss her husband on his forehead before walking back towards the house. Tommy waited until he heard the door close behind her before he let loose of his tears. He knew she was right and he hated the way his anger made him feel. He had only recently begun to understand that it isn't so much a matter of controlling his temper, as it is managing the feelings that lead to his adrenaline-fueled episodes. He had made considerable progress, but it still wasn't enough.

Tommy desperately wanted children, but he agreed with Amanda. He first needed to prove he could become the husband and father who would provide peace and stability for his family. And that meant treating others with respect and dignity, whether they deserved it or not, while also letting go of the desire to always win or get retribution at all costs.

Tommy reached into his bucket and grabbed a handful of ice, then dropped the cubes into his glass. He clenched the tumbler between his thighs, and the cool condensation soaked through his pants while he poured another round. Placing the bottle of Scotch whisky back to the ground, he noticed that nearby, a bee had landed on the same flower as a butterfly. He nervously watched the two insects, both heavily coated in yellow pollen. He feared that like him, the bee might lose his head and in a greedy effort to secure all of the nectar for himself, would attack the butterfly. Instead, both harmoniously danced around each other. The bee calmly gathered pollen under his body to take back and share with the hive, while the butterfly gingerly inserted its proboscis into the heart of the flower, drinking in the sweetness.

Tommy sipped his Scotch on the rocks. The slow burn in his throat compounded the real-life metaphor playing out in front of him. It was then that he thought to himself ... *Surely, if a bee and a butterfly can get along, so can Tommy Model and the rest of the world.*

He had made up his mind. It was time to complete his metamorphosis, and nothing would get in his way.

CHAPTER THIRTY-NINE

Tommy set his smoldering cigar on top of the tee marker. He found a spot in the low-cut manicured grass unblemished by the strike of other club heads and placed his wooden tee in the ground with his golf ball on top. He walked to the back of the tee box and lined up the shot along the narrow fairway of the undulating links golf course near Edinburgh. He returned to position where he calmly addressed the ball with his one-wood. Without further hesitation, he smoothly drew the club back, then down. With near-perfect precision, he blasted his drive straight through the middle, landing slightly less than halfway into the 473-yard par 4.

"Great shot, brother," praised Duncan.

"Thank you," replied Tommy. "You're up. This is for all the money, so no pressure."

Tommy returned to his cigar and took a long draw as he watched his brother square up for his shot.

"There are two bunkers in the middle of the fairway at about 360, you know? You've got to hit your driver far enough to where your next shot will be able to carry those sand traps."

Duncan stepped away and turned to leer at Tommy.

"Do you have to cheat to win?" asked Duncan.

"Cheat? Who's cheating?"

"You, that's who. It's bad form to talk to me while I'm standing over my ball. I know you're trying to get into my head, but it's not working."

"Okay, okay. I was just trying to help."

"Save it."

Duncan returned to his line up his clubface square with the ball when Tommy interrupted again.

"All I'm saying is that you don't always seem to plan out your next shot, and on a links course like this, you have to think ahead. But you do your thing."

Duncan stepped away again. This time he took a deep breath and walked behind the tee to eye the distance. He quickly returned to position, and before Tommy could say another word, he clobbered the ball sending it bouncing some twenty yards past Tommy's, just left of center.

"Bite me," Duncan quipped at Tommy, who took another anxious drag on his cigar and began his march along the fairway as their caddies followed.

With the skilled recommendations of their professional guides, Tommy and Duncan were both on the green in three. After eighteen holes, it would all come down to a putting competition.

Duncan was away and lined up his twenty footer. He aimed his putt to the right, playing the slope of the green. Following a solid stroke, it seemed to be on target, but ultimately came to rest a foot short.

"Not enough," sniped Tommy.

Tommy squatted behind his ball and held up his club to get a bead on the best path. Seemingly, there was no variation in the green, so he carefully directed his putter straight towards the hole. Only ten feet to go and his brother would owe him a hundred quid. A gentle nudge sent the ball in perfect line towards its target. An unattended ball mark in the green kicked his effort half an inch to the left where it lipped around the cup, rolling another six inches beyond.

"Oh, tough break, Tommy. Let me show you how it's done."

An easy tap-in for Duncan put the pressure on Tommy, but with little thought, he also easily made his putt.

The brothers looked at other in shock.

"I can't believe we tied. What are the chances?" asked Tommy.

"So what do we do now? Coin toss?"

"No, let's quit while we're even. I like this. Drinks are on you and lunch is on me. Agreed?"

"Sounds good."

Tommy graciously tipped the caddies and bid them farewell as the valet stored their clubs then carted him and his brother the short distance to the restaurant next door. Tommy and Duncan had missed the lunch rush and settled into a window seat overlooking the eighteenth green.

The golf outing had come at Tommy's request, and the brothers had agreed to enjoy the day without any mention of negative things. But after ordering two pints and some hors-d'oeuvres, Tommy began the long-awaited conversation that both knew would eventually come.

"We obviously need to air out the past so we can move forward. So I'll start by saying that I had wondered why you didn't come to the wedding, but now it all makes sense. It would have bothered you to see me marrying Amanda, and I get that. I just wish you both would have told me."

"No, you're wrong there, brother. I explained to you when you called to invite me to the wedding that one of my biggest publicity firm clients had asked me months earlier to accompany him to New Zealand on a fly-fishing expedition. The trip involved a tremendous amount of planning, and it was during the same time as your wedding. I couldn't back out, or I would have risked an account that is at least 25% of our annual income."

"Okay. You see, I believed you at the time, but after finding out about you and Amanda, I thought you might have made the whole thing up."

"Look. Here are the pictures if you don't believe me."

Duncan pulled out his cell phone and began swiping through the images proving in fact, that the adventure had occurred.

"Okay, I believe you," admitted Tommy as the restaurant manager interrupted.

"Sir, we have a no cell phone policy so if you could please refrain, we'd greatly appreciate it."

"I'm sorry. I'm done," complied Duncan.

"Hey, you probably heard I took Dad fishing recently," said Tommy. "We went to the River Tweed, by the Leaderfoot Viaduct. Remember when he used to take us there as kids?"

"Yeah, that was such a cool place. And we always caught a lot of fish that Mum hated cleaning. So how did that go with Dad that day?"

"Not so well. I keep trying to do nice things for him, but they seem to get screwed up somehow. That's how we eventually got into this pneumonia mess. It's difficult to predict how he's going to react. Alzheimer's is such a stinger for anyone to have to go through. Why there isn't a cure yet baffles me. If things go well with the album, I'm going to work towards some efforts on that front."

"I know. It's difficult for me to understand too. That's the hard part about being in London. I feel guilty for leaving them, but my business has blown through the roof since I moved there, so I can't afford to abandon that now."

"That's great to hear, Duncan. I'm proud of you."

"Thanks. So can we put the Amanda concern to rest? You have nothing to worry about. We never really connected that strongly.

Don't get me wrong, she's an incredible woman as you know, but you two have undeniable chemistry. We didn't. I think it was just comfortable to have someone to hang out with for a while."

"I understand, but you moved to London, so it had to be a bit more serious than that."

"I won't lie ... after a year of dating, I was sad when we broke up, but it was because we were such good friends. So sure ... that's why I moved. Your life gets used to certain things, and when they're suddenly not there any longer, it feels easier to try to find a replacement than to deal with it. I have an amazing girlfriend now, and I'm thinking about proposing soon myself."

"Really! That's great news! Congrats on that."

"Thanks. So can we let the past stay in the past, or what?"

"Yes, Duncan. No more talk about that. Let's toast to us as brothers. I hope we can find our way back to being close again. I miss that."

Tommy and Duncan raised their pints of lager and touched the glasses together sealing their agreement to move forward.

"Speaking of getting close, I've been thinking about something I'd like to run by you, Duncan."

"Really? What?"

"Well, Bob Walker, who has been my manager nearly back to the beginning of my career, is much older now. Heck, he seemed old back in the day, but he's got terminal cancer, so it's not good. Anyway, I need to find a new manager and one that completely understands marketing, publicity, and promotions in this highly competitive world we live in now. It's more than ever about building a brand. Your business is highly successful because of your experience and knowledge in those areas. You know where I'm going, so I'll just cut to the chase and ask ... will you consider being my new manager?"

"I'm honored, Tommy. But that's a huge commitment, and I'm not sure I can afford to travel that extensively. I'll risk losing clients."

"Okay, so let's turn the whole manager concept on its head. I don't need you traveling everywhere with me like managers used to do. We can have a road-manager type person do that. I just need you to ensure I get the best opportunities and exposure while keeping me on target with the bigger-picture objectives. Oh yeah ... and please make sure I don't get booked on a talk show with circus clowns."

Duncan laughed. "Yeah, I heard. That was bizarre."

"Oh, it was. But if Bob had been able to be more engaged he never would have let that happen. I called him the next day and found out that he had gone through a bad round of treatments, and his chemo port had become infected. He was actually in the hospital and never even knew about the clown situation until I told him. It's tough watching him go through this, but at the same time, I need help. And it's crucial that promotional and publicity events reflect me in the best positive light. You can make that happen, and I'll pay you whatever you ask. It would be great to work together, and I know I can trust you. How 'bout it?"

Duncan rubbed his face and stared out the window overlooking the beautiful expanse of the golf course. Without further hesitation, he turned back to his brother and held out his hand to shake on their deal. They locked palms, and Tommy beamed, joyous that his brother had accepted.

"Please don't make me hate you," stated Duncan.

"Me? No. Why would you think that was even possible?"

"Ha."

Lunch arrived and the two brothers dined, discussing old times and future goals. Tommy was grateful he had reconciled with Duncan. Towards the end of their meal, they leaned in towards each other and snapped a pic to record and announce their professional union. Out of nowhere, the restaurant manager appeared once more, scolding them for having the cell phone out again.

"Pierre, relax. We're just taking a picture," explained Tommy.

"But as I expressed earlier, sir ... we have a no cell phone policy."

"Okay, but do you also have a no camera policy?"

"When the camera is a cell phone, yes."

"Okay, okay. I hear you."

Tommy turned his cell phone and mischievously snapped a photo of Pierre.

"Sir, please don't make me have to ask you to leave."

Tommy laughed at the suggestion, and Duncan dropped his head to his hand in embarrassment as Tommy took another pic of Pierre. This time the manager covered his face.

"Come on, Pierre. Lighten up," suggested Tommy. "We're the only customers left in here. Who are we in policy violation against?"

Tommy looked at the image and continued, "See ... that was a bad shot. You covered your face. Let's try again. Now stand straight and give me a big smile."

"Sir, please leave. This is unacceptable."

Tommy laughed again, wiped his mouth with the linen napkin, then folded it neatly laying it on the table. He reached in his wallet, pulled out a two fifty pound notes, and handed them to Pierre.

"With my sincerest apologies, Pierre. Please accept this as a gratuity and do something nice for yourself ... maybe a massage or a decent bottle of Scotch. You need to calm down, my friend. Believe me ... I know what I'm talking about."

"I don't need your money, monsieur," retorted Pierre as he placed the notes back on the table. "I just need you to leave."

Tommy looked at Duncan who shrugged his shoulders and also folded his napkin. The fire inside of old Tommy was stoked, but new Tommy held the flames at bay. He merely stood from his seat, laid two more fifties on the table, then smiled at Pierre and said, "Well then that will hopefully cover the tab. Have a good day, Pierre."

Tommy and Duncan casually strolled out of the restaurant. Once outside they burst into laughter when Tommy pulled up Pierre's picture on his cell phone and zoomed in on the surprised and frustrated expression on the Frenchman's face.

"Wow, what an uptight guy," commented Duncan. "He's gonna have a heart attack. I'm proud of you for not punching him out."

"Thanks ... me too. I made Amanda a promise to drop my anger for good, and I'm sticking to it. Actually that wasn't so hard."

"Oh shoot, I forgot ... I need to use the restroom," said Duncan. "I'm going to run back into the restaurant since we have a bit of a drive ahead of us."

"Okay. Watch out for Pierre," Tommy joked.

As Duncan reentered the restaurant, Pierre headed him off, demanding an explanation for his return.

"I need to use the restroom."

"The restrooms are for patrons, sir."

"Uh, yes and we just ate here and gave you two hundred quid, which is much more than the tab plus tip would have been. So technically, I think we are patrons."

"I'm sorry sir. I cannot allow you to use the restroom. Now please leave."

Duncan looked around, and with no one else in sight he reached down, grabbed Pierre by the balls, and squeezed as hard as he could. Pierre grimaced in the torturous pain. He tried his best to gasp for air but found the attack so excruciating he had difficulty standing.

"Don't mistake me for my brother, okay? I will kick your little butt. Now, I'm going to use the restroom if I have to drag you in there with me. Got it?"

"Yes sir, yes sir," breathlessly replied Pierre, this time forgoing his French accent for that of a Scotsman.

"Wait, what happened to your accent?"

"Oh, that hurts. Please let go."

Duncan gripped even harder as he repeated his question. "What happened to your accent?"

"Oh, man. That smarts. You're killing me. Look, this is a French-themed restaurant, so we're supposed to act French. I made up the name and accent to go with the flow."

"I see. So Pierre isn't your real name?"

No, it's Charlie."

"Nice. And do you really have a no cell phone policy or were you trying to get my brother, who has a bit of a well-known reputation for easily losing his head, to go after you?"

"All right, all right ... yes! When I saw him, I thought I could get some easy cash if I jerked you blokes around a little and maybe he ended up punching me out. I heard he recently beat some circus clowns silly, and there's the well-known incident with the head of his record label, so I figured it wouldn't be too hard to get him to take a swing at me. My mate was back by the kitchen shooting the video on his cell phone. But apparently, Mr. Model's not as easily provoked as I heard he was."

"You're a real piece of work. I'm going to let go now, but my brother is standing outside, and I want you to go apologize to him. You got it? Don't say a word about us talking, or why you did it. Just apologize and walk away. Agreed?"

Charlie shook his head in acknowledgment signaling for Duncan to release his vice-like grip. Duncan proceeded to the restroom, after which he once again exited the restaurant as Charlie-Pierre passed him on his way in. The two men glared at each other but continued on their way as Duncan reunited with Tommy.

"Did you see old Pierre, there?" asked Tommy. "Darnedest thing. He came out and apologized to me for acting like such a jerk."

"You're kidding? That's amazing. You see, when you stay calm, good things happen."

"I guess so," affirmed Tommy as Duncan placed his arm over his brother's shoulder and they walked together back to the parking lot.

CHAPTER FORTY

READJUSTING HIS SCHEDULE after the false alarm surrounding his father's pneumonia scare, Tommy continued on his whirlwind promotional tour throughout Europe. It was then on to the U.S., where, unfortunately, he found the reception of his big comeback much cooler than expected.

City to city and state to state, each radio-station and television talk-show appearance featured an on-air interview with Tommy, and usually culminated with the playing of his new single, "Big Baby." It was a grueling, time-consuming effort to re-engage Tommy's loyal fans while hopefully also sparking interest in those newly discovering him. The interview-only format purposefully avoided the logistical nightmare and costs of performing live at the events as many artists often do when launching a new single or album.

Unfortunately, there was often extreme disappointment when producers and on-air personalities learned that Tommy would not be delivering at least one song in person, not even acoustically. Some even threatened not to book his appearance without a performance. As a result, Tommy often had to promise to return for an on-air acoustic show when he visited again during his next concert tour.

All, but two radio stations in the United States and one Swiss television talk show ultimately agreed to have him on.

After joining *Team Tommy*, Duncan had decided to accompany his brother through the remainder of the appearances in efforts to deliver a more organized and successful outcome. The television talk-show circuit in New York City went well, and Tommy was grateful for the few hours he shared with Bob Walker during their stopover. He knew it would likely be their last time together, and he treasured the moments.

Beyond New York City, Tommy found himself repeatedly walking away frustrated after interviews and personal appearances. He was definitely not feeling the level of love he had anticipated from the states. It was if everyone was just going through the motions out of courtesy for the past, even the fans. As a result, it was becoming painfully evident that they needed to kick-start some enthusiasm before the single died. Most radio stations only offered a short window of opportunity for a single's airplay to start climbing the charts. While "Big Baby" was struggling to gain traction on terrestrial radio, it was receiving much heavier rotation on satellite broadcasts. Some streaming platforms were also reporting growing interest, but overall Tommy was in the doldrums from a popularity standpoint, and it was painful to experience, especially considering how good the new single actually was.

In addition to Tommy's on-the-ground efforts, Galactic's radio promotions team was working "Big Baby" hard, making constant calls to radio station programmers begging for exposure. They had also engaged all of the top independent radio promotion companies to give it an extra push. While most at radio loved the single, many felt Tommy had been out of the game far too long to be viable, and seemed to be closing the door based on perception instead of possibilities.

Even with the underwhelming results, Peter Kirkinour remained committed to delivering upon his promise for a triumphant rebirth of Tommy's career. To bolster their attempts to gain airplay, Peter directed two of his top executives to join Tommy at each radio station visit. From station to station they put forth their best negotiation for spins but continued to meet with resistance and hesitation.

Unfortunately for Tommy, it ultimately boiled down to what programmers believed would hold listeners long enough for ads to air. With the almighty dollar being the driving force behind their decisions, swaying their opinions was a difficult task. From a business perspective, it was understandable, but it offered little deviation from the sure bets of young pop and rock artists. Their massive social followings could garner wide-scale publicity exposure with one controversial comment or revealing photograph. In many ways, Tommy was starting all over. This time, however, the game was played much differently, and it wasn't clear yet if he would be able to crack the code. He was also significantly older, and as a result, his cool factor and mass appeal were being held in question, often by decision-makers who were even older than he was.

Progressing east to west across the country while visiting the top ten major markets, it wasn't until they reached Denver that the vibe started to turn. Tommy, Duncan, Joel, and Dmitry sat together having lunch at a downtown restaurant. The table was silent in the depressed outlook of the days ahead. Instead of eating, Duncan was busy scrolling through his text messages and e-mail trying to figure out how to build some momentum.

"Hey, Tommy? Do you know someone named Pen?" asked Duncan.

Tommy thought for a second, staring blankly at his glass of water. When the light finally clicked on he replied, "Yeah, yeah.

Pen. She's that really cool girl I met at the record shop in London. Remember her, Joel?"

"Absolutely ... the one that took you into the secret back room with all of the rare vinyls."

"Yeah, that's her. Why, do you ask Duncan?

"Well I don't know how she got my e-mail address, but she just sent me a message saying, 'Tell Tommy I said hi, and you're welcome.'"

"That's odd," replied Tommy. "I wonder what she means by 'you're welcome.'"

"I wrote her back to see if I can get some more info."

"Don't bother. I doubt she ..."

"Excuse me," a young woman interrupted. "Can my sister and I take a picture with you? You're that famous rock star, Tommy Model. Right?"

"Uh ... yeah, sure," replied Tommy.

Dmitry positioned himself better for a possible intervention as the two twenty-somethings leaned in and snapped a photo with Tommy. They thanked him and walked back to their table where they sat, whispering and giddy with laughter, occasionally looking back at Tommy.

Duncan continued to scan his phone for details when three women, likely in their late thirties, walked by as they followed the hostess to their table. Having just passed Tommy, one stopped in her tracks. She leaned back even with Tommy's sight line.

"Oh my ... you're Tommy Model. Girls, it's Tommy Model!" she shrieked like a teenager. "You are so hot. Can we take a picture with you?"

"Sure, no problem," replied Tommy.

Two of the women kissed Tommy on the cheek, one from each side as Joel was instructed to take photos on each of the three women's cell phones. They thanked Tommy and progressed on to their table, staring at their prize images as they walked, and comparing each shot with the other.

"That's strange," Tommy remarked. "Two groups of women in less than a minute want pictures with me while we're sitting here wondering how we're going to turn things around. If only we could multiply them by a few million, we'd be set."

"Oh my ..." gasped, Duncan. "Here's why they're all after you. Look!"

Duncan turned his phone around to show Tommy a nude photo of himself. The butt end of an electric guitar rested on the floor at Tommy's feet with the neck extending upwards between his legs, the headstock of the guitar being the only thing covering his well-toned body from full exposure.

"Where did you get that?"

"It's on the internet."

"That's was a personal shot we took at the album photo-shoot a few weeks ago. I was between clothing changes and the photographer said, 'let's just go for it.' It was supposed to be for Amanda, and he promised no one would ever see it."

"Well he lied, brother, because there it is ... and on this one platform it's already had fifteen million views. I would say you're officially going viral now. There are even a couple of articles trending about how great you look at your age."

"Really? That's cool, I guess."

"It's going to blow up big time now! Reporters and bloggers are always competing for clicks, and they'll use your pic to drive their returns. I was so busy focusing on the radio audience numbers the Galactic guys sent me this morning, that I wasn't to the socials yet. I completely missed it until now. But this is great news, Tommy!"

"I don't understand. That photo is supposedly only with the photographer, maybe the label, and on my cell phone. Oh yeah, and on Amanda's cell phone too. So how did whoever got it, get it?"

"I received a reply from your buddy, Pen. She says, 'I hope you're enjoying the view. I figured you could use a little help getting the blood pumping. You're officially past the point of foreplay, so don't go limp on me now. Drive it home, Rock Star!' P.S. Bowie says hi."

"What's all that mean?" asked Dmitry.

"Her father is some big-time social media wizard," replied Tommy. "Do you think she had someone hack my phone and upload the picture? I'd be shocked if she did that."

"Well, however it got leaked, it's on fire. I did a little sleuthing, and if Pen is who I think she is, her father is a billionaire tech guy. Shoot. You hit the jackpot, Tommy! And you just met her the one time?"

"Yeah, in the record shop. I bought her this rare David Bowie vinyl 45 she had been wanting. You probably saw the video a few weeks ago. That's why she made the Bowie reference. I'm still perplexed though."

"Don't fight it, brother."

"I guess this is how it goes nowadays. We can kill ourselves making and promoting music, and then it all comes down to a naked picture to get people to listen. Whatever it takes, I guess. I better call Amanda. She is going to freak when she sees that if she hasn't already."

Within hours, Duncan was fielding calls, e-mails, and text messages from all over the world for requests to interview Tommy and help promote the new single. Other than the guitar accompaniment, the picture wasn't that unusual compared to other celebrities who had nude images leaked. The difference was, Tommy was now in his fifties, yet looked nearly as good as he did when he was in his twenties. That renewed sex appeal was what he needed to get the socials buzzing. With click-bait being the new online currency for many, anyone who could capitalize on the image for their own means was already doing so or soon would be. Every *view, like, share* or *mention* only further increased Tommy's trend ranking.

Duncan and the marketing team at Galactic went into promotional hyper-drive making the most of the unexpected opportunity. Even Peter Kirkinour called Tommy to congratulate him on how quickly he had become an internet sensation. He prepared him for the media onslaught that was surely on its way. Duncan was already finding it impossible to keep up and engaged his London publicity firm employees to help manage all of the communications and requests.

THE NEXT DAY, as the foursome boarded a private jet departing Denver and heading to Dallas, it had only been some twenty-four hours since the photo leaked. Tommy was already feeling the burn from being closer to the sun again. As he sat waiting for the flight to depart, he felt the urgency to express his concerns.

"Okay, look Duncan. I know we were praying for a miracle and here it is. But I told Peter when we started this thing, that I wanted to handle this promotional tour differently than I experienced in the past. For once, I would like to enjoy the process as much a possible. I don't want to get so overwhelmed that I don't even know what ends up anymore because that's when I fly off the rails. And I can't let that happen. As my brother, you cannot let me go there. That goes for you too, Dmitry. You've got to protect me from myself if it comes to that. It can go south very quickly for me. I can't do that again ... not for my sake, but mainly for Amanda, and Mum and Dad."

"Tommy, you're worrying too much. We've got this," replied Duncan.

"I know, but hear me out, so we're all on the same page. You can consider all of these offers that are coming in, but only bring them to me if the opportunity is so incredible that it would be idiotic for me to pass. Otherwise, let's stick to the plan. We have Seattle, San Fran, and L.A. to go after Dallas, then on to Sydney, Melbourne, Auckland, Nagoya, Osaka, and Tokyo. Let's make the most of those already planned events over the next week and a half. Then get me back home to start prepping for a tour. All right?"

"I understand your concern Tommy," replied Duncan, "But we've got to keep some forward motion going. It would be great if we could more frequently post comments, pictures, and Joel's video clips to the socials so we can ride this wave for a little while? Are you good with that?"

"Of course. That's easy to do. I just don't want to get pulled in a million different directions. Back in the 80's, the record labels threw a bunch of cash around and lined me up for every meet-and-greet, interview, and personal live performance they could. And all of that was done without any regard for how exhausted I became. They basically said the same thing ... 'Just do one more.' The problem was, the *one more's* never stopped. The only way to get through an experience like that, if you keep going at all, is drugs. You need something to get you high, then something to bring you back to earth, over and over again. It was a never-ending cycle."

"I understand, brother, but this is an extremely fast-paced world we're playing in now, and we've got to keep up, or we'll be left behind."

"I get it, Duncan. But just know that I will walk away from everything before I put myself through that torture again. Fortunately, I don't need the money at the moment. I'm really doing this because I love my music and I want to reconnect with the fans. I hope we can eventually do a tour as well, but if not ... I'll survive. As long as Amanda keeps loving me and I'm there for my family and friends when they need me, that's all that matters now. It took me a long time, but I've finally learned what's important."

As the pitch of the jet engines increased, Tommy cinched down on his seatbelt. He had been so intently looking at Duncan seated next to him that he didn't notice Joel filming the entire interaction. Unknowingly to Tommy, it had been streaming live to tens of thousands of Tommy's followers. Joel's job was to capture the intimate, unscripted moments whenever possible. While risky at times, so far it was having an endearing effect on viewers.

By the time the plane landed in Dallas two hours later, Tommy was one of the top trending celebrities, and his total social media presence had doubled. The newly dubbed *Tommy Nudie* had reached over sixty million impressions. What excited Tommy, even more, was another call from Peter Kirkinour during which he informed Tommy that in one day, the "Big Baby" lyric video had exploded from just shy of twenty thousand views to over three million. They were seeing similar massive audience growth on other major streaming platforms, and digital track downloads had surpassed 270,000 units. Peter remarked that they had never witnessed such an enormous increase in sales and streaming activity for an artist who had not recently delivered similar numbers. With a much younger generation suddenly becoming more aware of Tommy Model, his older videos, tracks, and albums were also seeing a vigorous resurgence.

AS TOMMY WALKED INTO THE DALLAS RADIO STATION, confetti cannons blasted into the air showering Tommy in seemingly endless strips of colored paper. The varying hues were only matched by the myriad of balloons lining the room. The employees all cheered for Tommy and warmly greeted him with hugs and handshakes as 'Big Baby' blasted through the sound system playing live over the Dallas airwaves. A young woman handed Tommy an electric guitar signed by the staff and begged him to reenact the now famous photo-shoot scene. Tommy laughed and hugged the woman as her knees buckled and two friends had to help her to a chair.

A few minutes later, as Tommy stood waiting for his introduction to enter the studio, he closed his eyes, thanking God for the opportunity to experience success again. With all that he had been through lately, the single act of kindness he had shown Pen, led to a phenomenon that suddenly turned everything around. Tommy was extremely grateful in the moment. He was on his way again, and the future seemed more hopeful than ever.

CHAPTER FORTY-ONE

THERE WAS NO DOUBT THAT "BIG BABY" WAS *BIG IN JAPAN*. Tommy Model had not been forgotten by the frenzy of Japanese fans that greeted him at his public appearance in the shadows of Tokyo Tower. The massive, red-painted, Eiffel Tower inspired structure served as a unique backdrop to the event, with the top spire looming some one thousand feet above Tommy and his interviewers.

The popular television talk-show male and female duo, Asahi and Himari peppered Tommy with questions and historical facts regarding his career. Watching in anxious anticipation, the crowd had consumed the parking lot next to the attraction. The throngs extended around the base and were packed in shoulder to shoulder in both directions along Tokyo Tower Street. Onlookers even peered down from the rooftops of office and residential buildings nearby. It was controlled chaos at its best, and Tommy loved the attention.

Tommy was barely able to get out half of a sentence in reply to a question before the roar and cheers from his adoring fans drowned him out. At first, he beckoned for the masses to allow him to speak. When it became obvious, they were more elated to merely be in his presence than to actually hear what he had to say, he embraced the interruptions and milked it for more.

To cap off the experience, the TV personalities challenged Tommy to an applause-voted karaoke competition. The hosts allowed Tommy to select his song from a printed list. Asahi revealed to the audience he had chosen Prince's, "Little Red Corvette," and Himari explained that she had picked Cyndi Lauper's, "True Colors." Tommy scanned the list until his eyes became fixated on the one song he knew he could make his own. For added effect, he refused to reveal it to Asahi and Himari, and instead whispered his choice into the DJ's ear.

Himari was up first and delivered a strong rendition of the Cyndi Lauper hit, receiving a powerful response from the crowd during and after her performance. To improve his chances, Asahi donned a wig and jacket reminiscent of 1980's *Purple Rain,* Prince. He launched into a scorching, heavily animated version of "Little Red Corvette," complete with air guitar solo. The masses went nuts, and Tommy suddenly realized, this contest would not be the cakewalk he thought it might be. Ever competitive and determined to win, Tommy stood in dramatic fashion and walked to the front of the stage.

From the first snare drum crash, the throngs before him pogo-hopped as Tommy erupted into Simple Minds', "Don't You Forget About Me." With more than ten thousand strong singing the classic intro in unison at a deafening level, it was clear as Tommy entered the first verse that he would win without question.

One of his favorite bands, Simple Minds also hailed from Scotland, and Tommy passionately sang through the first chorus while channeling his best Jim Kerr. Halfway through the second verse, a thought dawned on him as he heard the lyrics in an entirely new light. Tommy had always believed the song was about love-lost to the trappings and insecurities of youth. Now, he suddenly realized through the looking glass of his own recent experiences, that the message could equally translate to the fear of someone you love uncontrollably forgetting everything. Reflecting on his father's battle with Alzheimer's, Tommy found himself an emotional mess as he rocked through the last chorus. Forcing through the tears, he finished in a climax of "la, la la's" along with his zealous fans.

Conceding defeat, Asahi and Himari stood on both sides of Tommy raising his arms in the air and signaling victory. As his adoring fans continued to cheer, the two hosts bowed at Tommy, a gesture he returned in kind. He turned to the masses and with a wave farewell, jogged off the stage where Duncan, Joel, and Dmitry awaited. Security rushed them to a waiting car that exited the tower complex through a barricaded back service road. Tommy wiped the sweat and remaining tears from his eyes as Duncan hesitated but was too concerned not to ask.

"Joel, turn off the camera. What's wrong, Tommy? Why did you start getting all emotional out there?"

"We've got to do something to raise more awareness about Alzheimer's, Duncan. There's no reason Dad's going through this ... or why we're all having to watch it go down. There has got to be a cure."

"So singing that song brought this out?"

"Yeah, I got to thinking about the lyrics as they were coming out, and they reminded me of what we're going through with Dad right now. I don't want him to forget who we are, but I guess there's no stopping that now. I just want to do more ... for him and for others."

"Okay, well what are you thinking?"

"I know this sounds crazy, but what if we started an organization or a charity ... whatever it technically has to be to raise money and awareness for Alzheimer's. Through it, we'll help drive more research and ultimately find a solution. I know there are other organizations already out there, but if they were accomplishing all they could and putting money where it really needs to be, wouldn't there already be a cure? Doctors and scientists pretty much know what causes the memory loss, so I don't get what's so difficult about finding a way to prevent or even reverse it."

"It's probably a little more complicated than we realize, but I do share your passion and desire. I'll support you in the effort if you decide to take it on. Don't kid yourself though ... it will be a lot of work."

"I know, but when we start touring, we'll have a unique platform to reach a lot of people. What if we use "Don't You Forget About Me" as the theme song for the effort?"

"You want to use another band's song? Why don't you use or write one of your own?"

"No, I don't want this to be perceived as me promoting myself. Everyone knows that song, and it's very anthemic to begin with, so it's a perfect motivator. Maybe we could re-record it with a multitude of artists like they did "We Are the World" back in the 80's. And we'll get Galactic to donate the earnings from the record sales and streaming to the cause."

"I remember you were bummed they didn't ask you to perform on 'We Are the World."

"Yeah, well that's just one more reason to do this. And maybe some of the artists we record the cover with could even join me on stage during the tour when we perform the song live. That would be cool, wouldn't it? And every night before I introduce the special guests, I could explain to the audience what we're going through with Dad, a little about the disease, and encourage them to donate or just get involved. This could be huge."

"The more you say, the more I like the idea. If you're sure about it, I'll get started putting everything together. What do you want to call it?"

"Let's name it after Dad. How about, *Maddock's Memories*? That's straight from the hip though, so if that's not good, help me think of something else."

"Tommy, that's awesome! He'll love that. Well, at least for a moment he will. Mum will be super-excited about it though."

"Yes, she will? Hey, where the heck are we going? I thought we were on our way to the airport."

"Me too. Driver, we are going to the Narita, aren't we?" asked Duncan.

"Sorry sir, we have been asked to make a detour. We are almost there."

Sitting in the passenger seat, Dmitry turned to the driver with a defensive posture and demanded, "Pull the car over! Now!"

"I'm sorry Dmitry-san. I cannot do that. I have been asked to continue until we reach the Imperial Palace."

"The Imperial Palace?" questioned Tommy. "Why would we be going to the Imperial Palace? That wasn't on the schedule, was it Duncan?"

"No. Dmitry, do something!" instructed Duncan.

"Pull the car over, or I will do it for you," warned Dmitry.

"I'm sorry. Please be kind and patient. I want no issues. I am under direct orders from the Emperor."

The driver slowed as he reached the guardhouse at the entrance to the palace grounds. He spoke to the guard in Japanese and as the gate opened, continued on his way along the narrow, tree-shaded drive. Dmitry bristled at the situation that now seemed inescapable. He turned back to Tommy and did his best to console his boss.

"I think the smart move at this point is to see what they want. They probably are just looking to meet you in person, Tommy."

"Driver ... what's this about?" inquired Duncan. "This is no way to treat a famous guest in your country."

"I understand, sir. I don't believe this is in regards to Mr. Model though. We are there and here is Taichi now. He will explain."

A tall, muscular Japanese man approached the car. His spiked hair, goatee, and dark sunglasses only added to his sinister appearance.

"Taichi!" snapped Dmitry. "You've got to be kidding me."

"You know this guy, Dmitry?

"Yes. Unfortunately, I do. He was the man I beat out for gold and silver at the last Olympics I competed in. Let me see what this is all about."

Dmitry opened the car door. Rising from his seated position, he puffed out his chest appearing much larger than the massive hulking figure he normally was. He slowly approached Taichi and stopped just a few feet away as both men bowed in respect to one another.

"This is nuts. Let me out, Joel," instructed Tommy.

"I don't think that's a good idea right now."

"Joel. Move it or you're fired."

Joel tried to open the door, but it was locked. "It's locked."

"Driver, unlock the door," directed Tommy.

"I cannot do that, sir."

"Do it now, or I'm going to punch you in the back of your head so hard you'll ..."

Duncan interrupted, "Driver. Listen, I'm good friends with the Ambassador of Japan in London."

Tommy snapped his head towards his brother in surprise. Moving his mouth without uttering a sound, he asked, "Really?"

Duncan shook his head *no* but gestured for Tommy to play along as he continued. "This is not going to bode well, and the Prime Minister will hear about this. Let my brother out of the car, because he's only going to get more fired up, I assure you."

The driver looked in the rearview mirror, peering into Duncan's eyes and searching for truth. Falling for the bluff, he unlocked the door and Joel slid out allowing Tommy to follow. Duncan emerged from his side, and all three men made their way towards Dmitry and Taichi.

"Joel, start filming this in case it all goes bad," directed Duncan. "But keep it on the down-low if you can."

Activating his concealed belt cam, reserved for inconspicuous filming situations, Dmitry turned as they approached.

"It's okay, gentlemen. Taichi is still bitter about me brutalizing him in the Olympic javelin and shot-put competitions, so he's brought us here for a re-match it seems. He beat me in the hammer throw, but obviously, that wasn't good enough. And he just happens to be a good friend of the Emperor, so here we are. Apparently, there is a large gathering of royal family members, friends, and staff awaiting our arrival on the lawn."

"You have got to be kidding me?" remarked Tommy. "How long ago was this?"

"Twelve years."

"And you're still not over this, Taichi?" asked Tommy.

Taichi shook his head *no* without saying a word as Dmitry explained further.

"He's convinced I used steroids, and he was all-natural. Right ... look at this guy? Does he look all-natural?"

Tommy, Joel, and Duncan looked at each other considering the validity of the question, and all shook their heads in the negative.

"But he's convinced he can beat me, so I guess we'll do this and get it over with so we can get you back home, Tommy."

The group followed Taichi along a stone path that weaved in and around trees and gardens. They progressed over a small bridge traversing a tranquil koi pond. Finally, they emerged into a large open clearing as a group of approximately fifty or more people cheered and applauded their appearance.

Wasting no time, Dmitry and Taichi approached a row of javelins impaled into the ground. Taichi grabbed the first he touched, while Dmitry carefully inspected each spear. He pulled two from the line, testing their flexibility before making his final selection. Dmitry stretched and twisted his body, limbering up for his throw. Taichi opted to go first and with little preparation, rapidly ran several yards then launched his javelin high in the air with an energetic scream. It landed embedded in the field at a distance that was quickly measured to be 96 meters. The crowd roared with excitement as Dmitry looked on and smiled.

Readying himself, Dmitry immersed his mind into the seriousness of the moment and sprinted across the lawn. He sent his javelin arching equally as high up the field, but it landed a foot and a half short of Taichi's attempt. Neither were world record throws, but still respectable for two men who were now well-beyond their Olympic prime.

Conceding his defeat in front of Taichi's elated onlookers, Dmitry shook his opponent's hand, and they proceeded to the area marked out for the shot put throw.

Taichi insisted Dmitry go first this time. Eager to get on with it, Dmitry lifted the sixteen-pound metal ball. With his own personalized style, he leaned down, then up, then twirled with his free arm outstretched like an arrow as he let the orb fly with a monstrous roar. Landing at 19 meters, he seemed pleased and shrugged his shoulders towards Tommy, Duncan, and Joel, who was still secretively filming the entire competition.

Taichi was laser-focused as he approached the throw box and prepared for his effort. Pumping his lungs full of air, he coiled then unwound his body. With a ferocious grunt, he hurled his shot 19.3 meters, just beyond that of Dmitry's ball still lying where it had been buried deep in the lush grass. The audience was elated at Taichi's dual victories, and he re-solidified his dominance for Japan in the two events he had long ago been allegedly cheated out of. Once more, Dmitry graciously shook hands with Taichi who showed little emotion as the two men bowed and bid farewell.

As quickly as they arrived, Dmitry, Tommy, Duncan, and Joel were escorted back towards the car. Before re-entering the trees, Dmitry looked back to see Taichi intently watching his departure. He looked forward again, leaving his past and the failure of the moment behind as they progressed back along the stone path.

"Are you okay, Dmitry?" asked Tommy, concerned by his friend and bodyguard's unusually quiet and subdued demeanor. "I know it must be tough to lose something you rightfully won when it really mattered."

Hanging back slightly to avoid being heard by the others, Dmitry replied, "I didn't lose, Tommy. I let him win."

"What are you saying?"

"You see, he's been dealing with his defeat for twelve years. He could care less, but certain people here in Japan were highly embarrassed by the loss, and their pride won't allow them to let it go. He told me all this before you got out of the car. He's a multi-millionaire now and owns one of the largest fitness center corporations in Japan. I told him I would make it look good, but ultimately he would win and get everyone off his back. In return, I asked him to donate to your new charity, which you would send him the info for later when you're ready."

"Wow! You're always full of surprises, Dmitry. I can't believe that big ego of yours let him win. Seriously though ... thank you for asking him to donate. So how much are we talking, five hundred bucks ... maybe a grand?"

"Ha. Tommy, you should know me better than that by now. I go big or not at all, like your song "Big Baby" says. No ... you can expect that Taichi will be sending you a bank wire for a million dollars whenever you're ready. That will hopefully get *Maddock's Memories* off to a good start."

CHAPTER FORTY-TWO

A MONTH LATER, the report to Tommy and Duncan from Galactic Records indicated that "Big Baby" was performing well worldwide and exceeding everyone's expectations. Under the original strategy, the album launch should have been the next major hurdle. Not keen on interrupting the first single's delayed climb, the label execs had unilaterally decided to let it ride a while longer to squeeze as much life out of one song before moving on.

The revised plan called for "Big Baby" reaching its highest possible chart position in the U.S. Once that peak was achieved, Galactic would release and heavily promote another single, but ultimately would follow the same wait-and-see strategy they had employed with "Big Baby." Only after the second single had run its course, would the album then be released.

The problem was, depending on the longevity of the two singles, this new approach could involve a nine to twelve-month hold on a tour that needed to include new songs from the album as part of the setlist. The tour was also an effort to promote the entire album, not just a few tracks. Such a lengthy delay wasn't something Tommy was willing to consider. He was anxious to re-engage with fans and to start spreading the word about Alzheimer's and working towards a cure. He knew it was likely too late for his father, but the hopefulness surrounding his new mission outweighed reasoning, and he was determined to move as quickly as possible.

Letting his disappointment ring clear, Tommy paced throughout his Edinburgh home as he spoke on a conference call with Peter Kirkinour in New York, and Duncan at his London office.

"Peter, this is not what we discussed, mate. I told you I wanted to start touring as quickly as possible. You're treating me like a new and developing artist under a singles deal. I have an amazing album for you to work with and promote."

"No question about that, Tommy. We're trying to make sure you have the best chance for the album and the rest of the individual tracks to be successful when we do release them. This is a track-centric world we live in now, and fans don't much care about albums anymore. It's unfortunate, but that's the reality."

"I understand, but we've already put the band together and my new agent is lining up concert dates as we speak. And what if the next single flops? Will you release another, and then another until you find one that works? Is this shift in plans because your team is suddenly trying to better navigate a track-based reality? Or is this really about Galactic hedging its bets and trying to minimize costs? I know that the marketing campaign for the album launch is considerably expensive and the longer you can hold off and reap the rewards from releasing tracks, the higher your profit margin will be. I've been a student of this business for many, many years, Peter. I know all too well how this works."

"Tommy, of course cost factors into everything we do, but I promise you that's not the main concern here. You've been away for a long time. It's going to take more than one hit single and a semi-nude photo to get you to the level you were at back in the 80's. To be completely honest, you may never get there again because there isn't the same interest in artists and music as there was in those days.

Music used to be something that fans got excited about. They anxiously waited to hear and buy new records from their favorite artists and bands. Now, for the most part, music is just playing in the background of our lives. It's still important, but generally not with the same level of loyalty towards artists."

"Okay, but I can't tour if I don't have CD's and vinyls of the new album to sell with my other merchandise. Plus, there won't be any familiarity with my new music other than the singles, so I can't perform other new songs live. Maybe one or two at the most. I'm not going to have those awkward moments of disinterest during a show where I insist on playing songs no one has ever heard before."

"I understand, and I totally agree. There's also the consideration of not performing new music without having the availability to stream or buy that music. But I promised I'd deliver you a comeback to the level that's never been achieved before. I trust my team's opinion that this is the right path to take."

"Well, I don't mean to get all legal on you, Peter, but my contract does say that you can only sit on an album for twelve months after I deliver it. You're already three months into that time frame. The question is ... are you willing to go another nine months, because that's what we're talking about here if you release another single? And then after that, I can hear it now ... there will be a timing issue with another artist's album launch or some statistical theory as to why we have to wait even longer."

Tommy paused, then continued, "Hang on, Peter ... Amanda is looking at me like she needs something. What is it, angel? Can it wait a minute? Okay, thanks. It'll just be a few. Anyway, as I was saying, Peter ... I've heard it all before. And at that point, I'll start to feel like it's more about not re-upping my deal with that twenty million dollar signing bonus."

"Don't even go there. I gave you my word, and I stand by that. But you need to trust us to do our jobs. We're the experts on this side of things."

"I get that, but trust is a two-way street. You guys have already backed out on what we all originally decided would be the plan without discussing it with me first. You gave me your word about that too. Now here we are, and you're trying to put the blame on me, implying that I don't trust you. Help me here, Peter, because I've lived up to my promises. I mean, come on ... I just toured the world promoting a single."

"You know, Tommy ... you're absolutely right. So, here's what I propose. How about I go ahead and get your new recording agreement to you and your attorney, and Duncan of course. We'll also issue an addendum to your current contract. In that, we'll include language that if we don't deliver at least one million track equivalent albums by the end of the nine-month album release window, then you'll get half of the twenty million dollar signing bonus for your deal renewal, no strings attached. You can keep the money and walk away from Galactic if you want to. That should show you how serious I am about your success."

Tommy pondered the offer that seemed almost too good to be true. Sensing an opportunity, he responded, upping the ante a bit higher.

"Okay, but I also want you to allow me to go ahead and record "Don't You Forget About Me" with the artists of my choosing. I want a serious budget for the recording and the video. I also want you to agree to donate all of the income to a charity of my choosing, perhaps even the one we're working on creating. And I mean all of the income, not only my royalties and the producer's royalties."

Amanda had followed Tommy as he continued to roam the house selling his idea to Peter. She hovered behind him as he stood in front of the glass storm door overlooking the backyard and gardens. Turning back into the room, Tommy nearly ran into Amanda. In a startled reaction to her unexpected presence, he threw his free hand in the air as if asking again, what she wanted. Amanda shook her head and gave an expression beckoning Tommy to continue his thought. He walked out of the room and along the hall, as once again Amanda followed.

"I'm not sure what's going on here guys, but Amanda is tailing me all over the house, so I better wrap this up to see what she needs. To quickly finish my thought on the charitable income ... that would include Galactic's share of SoundExchange or any other direct licensing. I'll donate my artist share as well, and I'll only work with a producer who agrees to do the same. I think that the songwriters and publishers should be paid since they don't have much of a say in this. So if you have to deduct the mechanical royalties, that's fine, but other than that, I want all other costs waived including distribution fees. I'm sure you can figure out a way to take it as a write-off. This means a lot to me, and I want as much money as possible going to the effort to find a cure for Alzheimer's ... okay?"

"Agreed. Let's do it," responded Peter without hesitation. "My grandpa had Alzheimer's so let's make it happen and find a cure."

"Thank you, Peter. I've been burned so many times before, and it's difficult to let it go when a plan changes, but I'm trusting you on everything, mate. Please make a believer out of me."

"Oh, I will, Tommy. Now that we've got all that settled, what single do you think we should go with next?"

"Without a doubt, 'Relentless.'"

"Great! That's what we were thinking as well. At least that was easy. So, we'll get a promotional plan together and discuss it with you in a few days. We also have the "Big Baby" video shoot next week. The lyric video is doing great, but we need an official video that will visually get you in front of millions more fans. See, we're still spending lots of money on you, Tommy. Are you one hundred percent on board with the video treatment?"

"Yeah, I think it's very unique. I'm looking forward to seeing it all come together."

"Great. Well, we'll see you in L.A. for the shoot next Wednesday. Is there anything else you'd like to discuss?"

"No, I think that's it. I'm going to find out what my lovely wife is so anxious to speak with me about. Probably some new furniture, or a rug, or something else that beautiful, creative mind of hers has dreamed up."

The three men laughed and bid their farewells as Tommy started to search for Amanda who had suddenly disappeared. Calling throughout the house, Tommy finally heard her faint reply.

"What, honey? Where are you?" asked Tommy.

"Coming! I had to pee. Hang on."

Emerging from the hall bathroom, Amanda smiled from ear to ear as she approached Tommy.

"I'm sorry I couldn't get off the call sooner... but that was an important discussion, Love. I'll give the scoop on that in a bit, but I'm all ears for you now. So what are you so happy about? Are we remodeling another room, or is this about the swimming pool you want to put in?

"Nope."

"Well, what is it? Come on. Tell me. I'm game for whatever you want to do."

"It's not what I want to do, Tommy. It's what we're going to be doing for a while."

"Well after that call, I've got eight or nine months now before a tour starts if the plan doesn't change again. If it's a major construction project, we've got to figure out how to get it done before then, or you'll be on your own."

"Actually that's perfect timing, so that will work out fine."

"Great, so what is it?"

"Well my darling husband, I wanted to let you know that I ... am ... pregnant!"

"You're what?"

"You heard me. You're going to be a father!"

"Really?"

"Yes!"

Tommy and Amanda broke out in nervous laughter. Tommy leaned in and placed his hands on Amanda's cheeks, gently holding her face as they kissed. As he pulled away, he stared into her eyes which were shining with anxious tears of joy as Tommy wiped the same from his.

"I can't believe it! I'm gonna be a father! And you're gonna be a mother. How cool is that?"

"It's pretty darn cool," Amanda replied as Tommy returned his lips to hers.

CHAPTER FORTY-THREE

LIVINGSTON FRANCIS MADDOCK came into the world kicking and screaming like a rock star. Healthy, full of energy and very much his father's child, Tommy had spent the past few weeks mesmerized by his newborn son. But he was even more enamored with the grace and beauty of Amanda in full-on mom-mode. Although Livingston was also her first child, Amanda's consistently calm, confident manner made it seem like everything was exactly as it should be. By doing so, she minimized Tommy's naturally fearful and nervous tendencies throughout the pregnancy, birth, and now as the reality of raising a child was beginning to set in. And not just any child, but that of two famous parents.

As he held his son close to his chest staring out the front window of his Edinburgh home, it seemed like only yesterday that Tommy's life was completely upside down and hopeless. Now he was a father, a husband, carried a renewed dedication as a loyal son, sibling, and uncle, and had back-to-back number one singles propelling his career rebirth at a lightning-fast speed.

Eight months ago, he was desperately worried that his new album might fail under the ever-changing strategic decisions of his record label. Looking back, he was now grateful for the extra time the extended plan had afforded him. He had not only been able to be present for Amanda and now his son, but he had also been able to take a step back to properly plan a worldwide tour with his new talent agency. Together they had created a schedule that would be highly profitable yet enjoyable for Tommy, with plenty of downtime to return home and be with his family.

While he patiently waited for all of the pieces of the puzzle to magically fall into place, he had not only seen the first single, "Big Baby" reach number one in the United States, but also in the U.K., Canada, Australia, France, Sweden, and Germany. There were also several top ten results elsewhere throughout the world. The second single, "Relentless" had followed nearly the same trajectory with all, but Germany delivering a number one, and Mexico and Norway taking its place with the top spot honors. The next single, "Boomerang" was teed up and ready to be promoted alongside the continued marketing efforts behind the album.

Galactic had also beaten their deadline and released the full album in October, ahead of the holidays in an effort to maximize sales. Tommy decided to also title the album *Boomerang* since that one word seemed to perfectly exemplify his unprecedented career resurgence. In just over two months' time, the combination of album and track sales, plus digital streams had far surpassed Peter Kirkinour's goal of one million track-equivalent albums. In doing so, Tommy had lost out on the option to collect half of his twenty million dollar signing bonus early. But he knew the full payment would be coming soon, and the success of his comeback project was ultimately more important than any financial consideration.

The "Don't You Forget About Me" recording and video had been completed three months earlier. After much ado in meeting all of the legal requirements of a non-profit, Tommy's business management firm, Bolton & Hathaway had finalized the structuring of Maddock's Memories as an official Scottish charity. With Taichi's generous one million dollar donation and matching contributions by Tommy and his sister, Belle, the charity had the initial funding it needed to get off to a positive start. Tommy had even rented an office space in downtown Edinburgh where after the first of the year, a newly hired and highly-experienced team would head the charity's efforts.

With his band back together after the extended delay, rehearsals were going well, and final plans were being made for the tour. The first date was set to kick-off with a major blowout show in Edinburgh only three weeks away. Tommy was a busy man, but so far everything he had so clearly envisioned was right on target. He had developed a clarity for what he wanted to accomplish, realizing that he only truly struggled when he lost sight of his goals and the gratefulness for all of the wonderful people and things he already had in his life. It was the combination of determination and appreciation that he found to be the key to his continued success. One without the other was simply not enough.

That gratefulness was in full force as Tommy anxiously watched as a cavalcade of black SUV's pulled into the long drive leading to his home. A light dusting of snow covered the lawn and steam from the exhausts trailed behind each vehicle, hanging briefly in the frigid December air. He called out to Amanda who was in the kitchen organizing the feast she had prepared with the help of their personal chef.

"They're here!"

"Okay. I'll be right there," replied Amanda.

Tommy exited the living room and entered the hallway leading to the front door. He looked back and noticed a decoration had fallen from the large, well-lit Christmas tree beaming in the corner. With Livingston in arm, Tommy trotted over, carefully knelt and picked up the ornate, red and silver ball. He stood and placed it back on the tree. Pleased with the perfection of his arrangement, he hurried back to the hall and on to the front door where his guests were gathering outside.

Tommy opened the door and warmly greeted his family along with Amanda's parents who had all collectively agreed to spend Christmas at Tommy and Amanda's home this year. Though now favoring a walker, even Tommy's father was in good spirits as he entered the house.

"Hi, Dad," Tommy said as he leaned over to hug his father. "How are you doing?"

"Oh, I'm good, young man. I hear we're gonna eat soon and I can smell what must be roasted turkey and Cock-a-Leekie soup. I could use a brandy to warm my bones first. Can you help me with that, good man? What's your name again?"

Well-accustomed to his father's now constant state of confusion, Tommy smiled and rowed with the river's flow.

"My name is Thomas, Dad. Let's get you by the fire and everyone else settled in. Then I'll get you a nice glass of brandy."

Tommy led his father into the parlor room and sat him in a comfortable chair positioned in front of the warm fire. After gingerly handing Livingston off to Davina, he hurried to the kitchen to search for Cognac. Returning with spirits in hand, Tommy awaited his father's approval following his first sip. He then proceeded to embrace and chat with all of his other family members, most of whom were huddled around Davina heavily doting over Livingston. Tommy and Amanda's live-in assistant and part-time nanny, Nora entered the room serving a variety of hors-d'oeuvres created by the chef. Amanda reminded everyone to enjoy, but not to over-indulge since supper would be ready in less than an hour.

Tommy was fifteen years old the last time he, Belle, Duncan, and Fiona had all been together with their parents for Christmas. As he listened to Fiona telling a funny story about her children, Tommy found himself lost in the thought that this could be the last they would all spend together. His father had fully recovered from his bout of pneumonia, but with Alzheimer's steady progression, another year would likely lead to significant changes for Frank that no one wanted to think about, much less discuss.

Alone in front of the fire, Tommy returned to his father's side. Sitting beside him, he did his best to explain what his near future would hold.

"Dad, I wanted to tell you that I'll be heading out on a concert tour in a few weeks. I want you to come see me at our first big show here in Edinburgh. I have special seats reserved for you and Mum. Does that sound good?"

"Well, I have to check with my prison guard. She might not let me out that day. She's a real tough-cookie, that one over there. Look at her holding that baby, all innocent-like. You have no idea what she's all about when the cell doors are locked."

Disregarding the crazy-talk, Tommy never missed a beat. "You do realize that's your grandson she's holding? His name is Livingston Francis Maddock. Francis is your full name, you know? So we named him after you."

"I don't know about anyone named Francis. I've heard of Jonathan Livingston Seagull though. He was a bird. Do you think that's where that boy's name came from?"

"No," Tommy chuckled. "We just liked the name, Livingston. It sounds unique, smart, and powerful."

Frank nodded as he enjoyed his brandy and winced as it burned going down. "That's good stuff. It'll fix what ails ya ... that's for sure."

"So anyway, Dad ... you'll come to the show? I want you to see what we're doing to raise money for Alzheimer's research. After that, I'll be gone off and on for a while. I'm going to try to fly back home between dates as often as possible. When we get to the U.S.

shows that's going to be more challenging, but if you need me I'll drop everything and come home. You just say the word. Okay?"

"You got a cooking show you say? On the tele?"

"No, Dad. I'm a recording artist. I sing and perform songs I've written, usually in front of ten or twenty thousand people every night ... sometimes a lot more. I play indoor arenas and outdoor stadiums. You know ... like soccer stadiums."

"Oh, I see. Well, soccer is a good sport to take up. You look a little old to still be playing though. Hope you don't pull a hamstring or something. That could end your career quick."

"I'll be sure to stretch good beforehand, Dad. No worries."

"Good, good."

Tommy and Frank leaned back and watched the flames dance in the fireplace as the commotion across the room continued with Livingston momentarily the center of the universe. Catching Amanda's eye, she saw the subtle look of disappointment on Tommy's face. She smiled and mouthed the words, "Be strong. I love you," as he shook his head in agreement then turned back to the glow of the fire.

"Dad, I ..." Tommy stopped himself, knowing that his father would not understand and instead merely said, "Merry Christmas, Dad."

"Merry Christmas, Thomas," his father replied as he sipped another wisp of Cognac. It did not go unnoticed by Tommy, that his father had just delivered the rare gift of acknowledging his name.

CHAPTER FORTY-FOUR

THE EDINBURGH THEATER WAS ON FIRE as Tommy ripped through a set of his biggest hits and the three new singles. The intimate hometown crowd of two thousand strong sang along in chorus to every word. At times, they were so loud, that Tommy had difficulty distinguishing his own performance from that of his fans. He was having a blast and frequently glanced at his mother and father sitting in the VIP box to his left, high above the stage.

Although Frank likely had no idea who Tommy was, he occasionally clapped along with the rhythm. He even smiled every now and again, indirectly signaling to Tommy that he was having a good time. Ultimately, that's all that really mattered. For the first time in thirty years, his folks were finally able to see and experience their son in all of his rock star glory, and Tommy felt love and admiration beyond the limitations of conscious thought.

Halfway through the show Tommy introduced his father and explained the toll Alzheimer's had taken on his dad, as well as his mum and the rest of the family. He briefly explained what causes the memory loss and the eventual tragic ending that organ failure can lead to when the mind can no longer control the body. It was a purposefully downtrodden moment, but the audience was transfixed as Tommy explained the goal behind Maddock's Memories and encouraged everyone to donate to help find a cure.

He explained how he had selected "Don't You Forget About Me" as the theme song for the charity's efforts and that they would soon be hearing the new recording with a collection of the world's most famous artists contributing to the effort. In a surprise move even to her, Tommy invited Amanda on stage to perform the song alongside him. As she reluctantly appeared, the crowd erupted into applause and cheers even louder than Tommy had received during his entrance. As he greeted his wife with a hug and a kiss he looked at her and jokingly said over the mic for all to hear, "I think they like you just a little," sending the hall into another frenzy as the guitar player launched into the song's famous intro chord progression.

The rendition remained respectful to the original version, but with a few unique variations, the duo delivered a modern spin on the timeless classic. With a massive sounding finale, Tommy waved goodbye and ended with the traditional, "Goodnight, Edinburgh," a farewell he would repeat three more times during successive encores that lasted another forty-five minutes. The fans begged Tommy not to leave, and he gladly obliged their demands. It was only when the theater's management informed Duncan that Tommy could no longer continue due to a noise curfew, that he stopped returning to the stage for another round.

As he and Amanda entered the backstage green room, a long line of loyal *Model Maniacs* stood waiting for photo opportunities and handshakes. What Tommy didn't expect was the handfuls of cash that one person after another would give him for donations to the charity. He graciously thanked each fan and took time to engage with every person he met. Tommy would later learn that the collectively, the show attendees had contributed over forty thousand pounds, an amount far exceeding his expectations for one single night.

Two hours later, with Tommy's fingers and palm aching from the sheer numbers of hand-shakes he had returned, Dmitry escorted him and Amanda to an SUV waiting in the dark alley directly behind the theater. As Amanda entered the vehicle, a woman approached from the shadows and called out Tommy's name. Ever on guard, Dmitry approached her, cautiously holding out his hand in a show of force to stop her progression.

"Please, Mr. Model. Just a quick word," she begged.

Tommy was exhausted and just wanted to get home, shower, and sneak a peek at Livingston who was hopefully fast asleep under Nora's watchful eye. But ever the fan-pleaser, he stepped back from the SUV and walked towards the anxious woman. Amanda exited the vehicle and followed her husband. Dmitry continued to stand in between for safety purposes, but as the woman began to speak, it was obvious she was not a threat.

"I want to thank you for all you are doing to raise awareness for Alzheimer's. I've been going through it with my mother who was diagnosed about five years ago. It's been a long, difficult road ever since."

"I'm so sorry to hear that," Tommy replied. "What's your name?"

"It's Bonnie."

"Hi, Bonnie. This is my wife, Amanda."

"Hello, Amanda. It's nice to meet you. I won't take but a minute more of your time, I promise. I know you both completely understand how much of a life-altering experience it can be for those caring for someone with Alzheimer's. I think it's great that your charity is going to focus on helping to find a cure. But I wanted to encourage you to also try to find a way to help the caregivers, because that's where the real pain resides. We have to stand by and watch as our mothers, fathers, sisters, brothers, or friends transform into an almost unrecognizable character from the person we once knew. They can become extremely difficult to love when they continuously morph into a different personality every few minutes. And many of us give up our lives, our jobs, our savings, and sometimes even our marriages, as I did ... all to help take care of someone who usually has no idea you are even there, or who you are.

Bonnie visibly fought back the wave of emotion that was nearly upon her as she struggled to continue. "So please do what you can to find a cure, but also please try to find a way to help those caring for the victims of Alzheimer's. There is no hope in those homes, and the sheer will and determination it takes just to get out of bed every day and do it all over again is beyond belief."

Tommy and Amanda stood unmoving and speechless. Fortunately, with his mother, Amanda, and Belle, Tommy had a strong backup support team for his father. Together, they could ensure that the others all got a break when they needed it. They had focused so intently on finding a cure as the basis for the new charity that they had nearly overlooked the more immediate need. Bonnie was right. Maddock's Memories should also help those families who are currently struggling to keep going every day.

Tommy had personally experienced those hopeless feelings with his father on several occasions. But this woman, and likely millions more people just like her, were living and breathing the experience 24-7, often with no support system. Her words resonated in his heart as he reached out and pulled her into his embrace. She wept into his chest as he held her tightly and gently rubbed her back, making his best attempt to console her pain.

"Thank you for that reminder, Bonnie" Tommy replied. "We really needed to hear that. You have my word that we'll not only concentrate our efforts towards a cure but also towards helping caregivers such as yourself. I'd like to start by arranging for someone to come out and spend time with your mum."

"That's a great idea, Tommy," added Amanda as she compassionately looked into Bonnie's eyes and reached out to help steady her as she stood trembling, racked by the release of her pent-up frustration. "I'm a registered nurse, and I have other nurses who have helped me with Tommy's father at times. They're all experienced in dealing with Alzheimer's patients. I'll call one of my best friends in the morning and schedule a time when she can come over and give you an entire day for you to focus on you."

Bonnie gasped for air as she sobbed uncontrollably and hugged Amanda, relaying her gratefulness through her emotions. Her posture immediately transformed as if the weight of the world had been lifted. Stepping back from Amanda, she profusely thanked them both for the gift, but still, Tommy's mind beckoned him to take the offer one step further.

"What do you say that we find a way to give her more than one day?" added Tommy. "How about one day a week? You probably need at least that to do the things you need to do for you. You're obviously a brave, strong person, and your love and kindness are very inspiring. But if you don't take time for you, it's obvious that you physically won't be able to keep this up much longer. Give us your cell number, and we'll call you in the morning and arrange everything, okay?"

"Thank you, Mr. Model. I don't know what to say. I didn't want or expect anything when I approached you. Please know that I just wanted to help."

"And you have," stated Tommy. "As we provide support to more and more caregivers, you can look back on this moment and know you had a hand in making that happen."

Bonnie gave Amanda her phone number and they made plans to talk again in the morning. She hugged Tommy and Amanda again, then embraced Dmitry, who had also become slightly emotional. They exchanged farewells and Tommy and Amanda watched as she disappeared down the alley and back into the darkness of the night. Tommy placed his arm around Amanda's shoulder and leaned in to kiss her.

"Thank you for doing that. You're an amazing woman, and I'm so lucky to have you."

Amanda looked at Tommy, smiled and replied, "You are pretty lucky, aren't you? But so am I. This charity is going to be interesting to experience for sure. I hope we haven't bitten off more than we can chew."

"We'll find a way to make it work. Together we can do anything. But right now, let's get home and see that little rock star of ours."

Amanda shook her head in agreement, and together they hopped in the waiting SUV and departed for home.

THE NEXT MORNING as Tommy sat in the kitchen enjoying a cup of coffee and taming the lyric of a new song he was working on, Amanda entered the room with a perplexed look on her face. Tommy gazed up as she paced back and forth alongside the island.

"What's wrong, baby?" Tommy inquired.

"Well, I called Bonnie ... the woman we met last night after the show ... and the number she gave me rings to a church here in Edinburgh. I thought to myself... *well, maybe I heard the number wrong*. So I explained to the person who answered why I was calling and they were very puzzled. They asked me to describe the woman, which I did, and I told him her name was Bonnie."

"Right, so what did they say?"

"They have no idea who she is, but it turns out they have several members of their congregation and their outreach program who are struggling through the same challenges caring for parents and spouses living with Alzheimer's."

"Really? Did he say how many."

"Trust me ... you don't want to know."

"Amanda, how many?"

"Over twenty."

"Over twenty? In one church?"

"Well, they reach out into the community, so it's not just people who attend that one church ... but yes, over twenty. I know what you're going to say. And I do want to help, but we just had a baby, you have a new album out, you're getting ready to leave on tour, and you have your father to consider. We've got to take this slow, or we'll get overwhelmed very quickly."

"I understand your concern, but this is why we hired an experienced team to manage the charity. For you and me, our main role is going to be raising money and awareness so Maddock's Memories can do what it needs to do. Let's go sit with the team, explain the situation, and find a solution. As a couple, we are not going to have to save all of Edinburgh single-handedly."

"You're right. I'm sorry. I'm just a little upset that Bonnie tricked us like that."

"It sounds like she was being selfless. She obviously felt like us helping twenty people was more important than helping her. I've got an idea though."

FOUR HOURS LATER Tommy and Amanda arrived at a small, run-down house outside of Edinburgh. Although it was winter, the tall brown grass of the front lawn had obviously not been tended to in quite some time. Dead weeds choked the flowerbed, and the untrimmed shrubbery reached halfway up the faded brick facade. They knocked on the worn out, paint-chipped wooden door. A few seconds later, a woman's voice inside cried out, "Give me a minute, Mum! I'm really trying here," her volume growing louder as she approached.

Bonnie opened the door while wiping tears from her cheek in efforts of hiding her grief.

"Tommy! Amanda! I don't understand. How did you ..."

"How did we find you?" interrupted Amanda.

"Yes, I ..."

"You thought you gave us the slip, huh?" replied Tommy. "Well, our security guy is a bit of a detective, so you weren't as difficult to find as you probably thought."

"It was very kind of you to think of others before yourself," Amanda intervened. "But you need help, Bonnie. So you're gonna get it. This is my good friend, Kyla who is also a registered nurse. She's going to help you out with your mum for a few days and give you some much-needed rest."

"And if you give us your real phone number ..." noted Tommy, "our Maddock's Memories team will be in contact to arrange weekly support for you."

"Thank you both so much, but there are other people out there who need your help more than I do. I'd rather you concentrate on them."

"We can help them too," Tommy replied. "Please, Bonnie. Let us give you a piece of your life back."

Bonnie stared at the ground struggling with the thought of letting go. From within the small house, an older woman's voice called, "Hey! Where are you, you miserable wretch? I saw what you did with my money. You took it all! You better give it back, now!"

"I'm sorry," apologized Bonnie as she began to cry. "She was such a wonderful mother to me before this happened. She can't remember who I am, but she sure stays locked in on the thought that I've taken all of her money. I would never steal from her, but it's not a situation you can reason with."

Bonnie dropped her eyes downward again, further contemplating her situation. "All right ... I'll take the help. You don't know how much this means to me. Thank you, both, and you too, Kyla. I love my mum so much, but I've got to get a break, even for a few hours. Last night a friend watched her while I went to your show, but she told me afterward, it was too much to deal with, so I have no one left to help."

"Well, we're here to give you that," said Tommy as he put his arms around Bonnie. Amanda looked on with a giving and grateful attitude, but still very concerned as to where all of this was heading.

CHAPTER FORTY-FIVE

NEARLY A YEAR HAD PASSED while the *Boomerang World Tour* progressed throughout Europe, South America, Australia, New Zealand, Japan, Canada, and was now approaching the final dates of the North American leg. Tommy had frequently returned home to Scotland, sometimes only to spend a few hours with Amanda, Livingston, and his mother and father before heading back out again. The private jet costs were adding up, but Tommy had learned the true value of family, and he had no intentions of allowing himself to get caught in the illusion of fame again, especially at the expense of those he really cared about.

Throughout the tour, temptations circled Tommy like vultures, anxiously awaiting their turn at the kill. Beautiful women, who had been enamored by his persona most of their lives and cared little that he was now a married father, were determined to live out their fantasies of being with him. Many became quite creative in the effort, and some got very close.

In Berlin, a hotel front desk agent used her master passkey to sneak into Tommy's room where she stripped naked and crawled into bed with the sleeping rock star. She was quickly nabbed, and escorted to the hallway by Dmitry.

At a high-end restaurant in Tampa, Florida, a female Sommelier lured Tommy from his table into the establishment's expansive wine cellar under the guise of a tour and tasting. In the far back corner of the cool, dark room the woman removed her top and popped the cork on what she bragged to be a $2,000 bottle of champagne. She poured the bubbly down her chest while seductively encouraging Tommy to "sample the vintage" as it cascaded over her skin. He passed on the offer and quickly returned to his table.

In Boston, Massachusetts a well-known, female radio station personality who accompanied Tommy on a walking ghost tour, feigned fear inside the darkened second story bedroom of a historic, haunted mansion. Embracing Tommy for support, she surprised him with a kiss in the pitch-blackness as she fumbled to breach the waistline of his jeans, a move that Tommy abruptly stopped.

Many tried, but ultimately, everyone who did failed. Tommy was deeply committed to Amanda, and even though it was uncomfortable for both of them, he held true to his promise not to keep secrets, and faithfully told her about every incident.

In addition to a multitude of lovesick fans, there was a never-ending flow of drug dealers who were often masters of disguise working their magic to get into Tommy's head and ultimately his hands. There were also those who wanted to pitch fly-by-night business ideas in hopes of separating him from his money.

Ever on vigil, Dmitry held most culprits at bay long before they had a chance to get close. He also sensed when Tommy might be on the verge of compromise and did his best to remove him from those tempting situations. The awkward chance meeting between the two men over a year ago had turned out to be one of Tommy's greatest blessings. The focus and intensity Dmitry devoted to protecting his friend and boss from himself and others had become immeasurable.

Duncan had joined Tommy for some major-market appearances, but for the most part, had managed the helm from his

London offices. As both brothers and business partners their relationship had fortified, and together they were unstoppable. Duncan had helped propel Tommy to a level that surpassed everyone's expectations. Even though the extent of record sales his brother had achieved in the 1980's would never again be possible due to the impact of music streaming, from popular notoriety, chart success, and concert ticket sales perspectives, Tommy was without question in the top tier of the music industry once again.

WITH ONLY A MONTH LEFT ON THE TOUR, early on a rainy Monday morning in a Kansas City hotel room, Tommy received the news that Bob Walker had passed away. His old manager had been a mentor and father figure to Tommy for all of his adult life. While he had frequently contemplated that Bob should have probably tried much harder to guide him away from the career sabotage he had committed years ago, Tommy also clearly understood that all of the events in his life, good or bad, had now led to the moment he was in. If he had it all to do over again, he wouldn't trade a life with Amanda and Livingston for anything. It was a scenario that likely would not have come to fruition if he would have progressed along a different road. It had all worked out as it was meant to be, and owing a significant debt of gratitude to Bob, Tommy was devastated at the news of his passing.

A few days following the emotional call from Bob's son, Tommy was in New York City for the funeral where he delivered a moving memoriam of his friend and mentor. It was a somber event attended by hundreds of Bob's clients, friends, and family. It was obvious he was highly respected and loved by those who had known him. After being asked to attend the graveside ceremony with a small group of those closest to Bob, the finality of death hit Tommy hard, and he fought to hold back his anguish in the gray light of the cold October day.

Later that evening back in the safety of his hotel room, Tommy called Amanda and told her ahead of time that he was going to order room service and have a few too many drinks to help combat the mental pain he was fighting. He assured her that Dmitry was with him and would keep an eye to make sure he didn't do anything stupid. His plan fell a little short, and by the second whiskey and soda, he was fast asleep in the chair positioned next to the window overlooking the lights and energy of Times Square. Dmitry covered Tommy with the plush, white hotel robe and quietly closed the drapes, plunging the room into darkness. Dmitry situated his chair so Tommy would have to bump his legs if he tried to get up, and then sat, patiently keeping guard as his friend slept.

The next morning, still reeling from the emotional experience from the day before, Tommy was on a private jet heading to his show in Denver scheduled for later that night. It was only on the flight back that Dmitry finally dozed off to sleep following the utter exhaustion of keeping a concerned eye on Tommy all night. Free from Dmitry's gaze, sadness completely overwhelmed Tommy, and he wept. He had not only lost someone very dear to him, but the harsh reality of the previous day's events had beamed a bright spotlight on his own mortality, as well as that of his father whose health was diminishing rapidly.

AFTER LANDING AT DENVER INTERNATIONAL, while the plane approached the hangar, Tommy called Duncan unknowingly interrupting a dinner date with his fiancé in London.

"Hi, Duncan. It sounds like you're in a bar or a restaurant. I'm sorry to bother you, but I've been worried for the past twenty-four hours that I don't have a will. I want to make sure that Amanda and Livingston are taken care of and that you don't have a big headache on the business side if something happens to me. Will you please have one drawn up as soon as possible?"

"What's going on, Tommy?" Duncan replied shouting over the voluminous murmur of the busy restaurant. "Is this because of Bob?"

"Yeah, I guess so. But it's crazy I don't already have a will in place."

"You're right. I'll call an attorney and get the process started, but nothing is going to happen to you so get that out of your head. When you start excessively worrying, nutty things start to go down, so shake this off before it gets a hold of you."

"All right ... I need to go. We just landed in Denver, and they're giving me the eye to get off the plane. Let me know what questions I need to answer for the will. I'll talk to you later. And Duncan ... I know I don't say it, but I do love you, and I appreciate everything you do for me."

"I love you too, brother. I'm here to help you in any way I can. We'll talk soon. Stop worrying."

Tommy departed the airport and was chauffeured to a Maddock's Memories fundraising event in a nearby community park. As his SUV approached, thousands of attendees lined the drive applauding and pumping fists in the air showing their encouragement for his charitable efforts.

Word had traveled quickly that his father was failing fast, and although Tommy expected bad news from Edinburgh at any time, he pressed on raising money for the growing charity whenever he could. Internally, he was understandably concerned that when his father inevitably passed away, he would no longer have the passion and drive to continue. As a result, he had recently further intensified his push, now holding events in every city the tour visited.

With donations from fans, corporate executives, businesses, and celebrities flooding in, the charity had amassed nearly twenty-five million dollars over the course of the tour. The growth had required Maddock's Memories to expand its Edinburgh staff to handle the sheer volume of contributions, calls, e-mails, and mailed correspondence. The most significant challenge had shifted from raising money to determining the best areas to invest the funding. As promised, the charity had also focused on assisting caregivers across the globe, and with Amanda's guidance had developed a network of highly vetted medical professionals to donate their time and services to those in need.

Maddock's Memories had also partnered with several other smaller non-profit organizations. Most had been in operation for several years and had the existing connections and expertise to more quickly engage with doctors and scientists who were on the cutting edge of treatments and the never-ending pursuit of an Alzheimer's cure. There were several hopeful advances in testing and development because of the combined efforts. It humbled Tommy to see that what had started out as a simple idea, had grown into a potentially game-changing organization.

Dmitry opened the back door of the SUV. As Tommy exited, a deranged-looking man slid along the side of the vehicle approaching Tommy in a rage. The long, thick blade of a hunting knife extended from his hand as he raised it high, then quickly propelled his arm forward towards Tommy. With the speed of a superhero, Dmitry intercepted the assailant. He was too late to block the force of the blow with anything, but his own body. The knife plunged deep into Dmitry's upper chest just beneath his shoulder. He roared like a beast reeling from the agony of the strike. With a lightning-fast reaction, he slammed the man's head into the side of the SUV, knocking him out cold before Dmitry himself collapsed on the ground. Tommy dropped down next to his friend and immediately tried to pull the knife from Dmitry's chest.

"No, no, no, boss. Leave it in. It will help keep me from bleeding out."

"Okay, okay. Will someone please call 911?" screamed Tommy as those crowded around nervously chattered and looked on in shock, while a flood of other attendees raced towards the scene.

Fortunately, an ambulance was already on standby at the fundraiser, and within a few minutes the paramedics had Dmitry on a stretcher and were struggling to load him into the back of the wagon. A police officer arrived and forced his way through the mass of people that had surrounded the attacker who had come to and was attempting to stand to his feet. Finally reaching the assailant, the cop quickly cuffed the grungy, long-haired misfit and pushed him back through the crowd. Tommy had loyally stayed by Dmitry's side as the paramedics readied him for the trip to the hospital. But now as the cop made his way towards his car directing the staggering and reluctant rogue forward, Tommy's ire flared, and he charged to intercept the two men. Seeing the anger in Tommy's eyes as he approached, the police officer turned his prisoner away, placing his own body in between and halting Tommy in his tracks.

"Stop right there!" ordered the police officer. "Let me handle this."

"I just want to know why?" begged Tommy screaming at his attacker. "Tell me why?"

The man's head hung downward, his face shielded by his long, gray, greasy, and matted hair. He slowly raised his gaze then turned towards Tommy who looked on in horror.

"Eric? Eric Tucker? Are you kidding me? Is that you? What the ..."

The man remained silent, but the fire and intensity in Eric's eyes confirmed all Tommy needed to know. With a siren pronouncing its departure, Tommy looked back to see the ambulance wobble and sway across the uneven ground. It finally reached the pavement, leaving a trail of dust in its wake. Tommy was anxious to follow, but still trying to make sense of the attack, turned back to Eric.

"I can't believe you are still holding this much hate for me all these years later. You got yourself fired as my bass player because you were a mess then, and you're obviously still a mess now. My friend better not die or I will make sure you wish you never came into this world."

"Yeah, well give it your best shot because you've pretty much already done that. You ruined my life. Do you think anyone ever wanted to work with me again after the great Tommy Model fired me? And then you couldn't just let it go. No ... you had to talk trash about me all over L.A., and as a result, I've been struggling ever since. I've been homeless here in Denver for the past three years. Do you have any idea how humiliating that is, especially at my age? Now you're out here with all of these people, all holier than thou, raising money for some charity you started. If everyone only knew how evil you really are."

"Wow! How quickly you forget. You took a half million dollars from Jacques Morel to sabotage my career, you moron. Then after I fired you, you attacked me in a cocaine-fueled rage. And now you just tried again. Do you not see a problem with any of that?"

"You hit me with a cymbal?"

"Yeah, to keep you from kicking me! I think you're missing the point here, Eric. You just stabbed one of my best friends, and you were trying to kill me because of something you yourself caused thirty years ago. I have no sympathy for you, and I'm going to see to it that you rot in a prison cell."

"We'll see. You had better hope I don't get out! Because if I do, I'm gonna finish what I started."

"Keep running your mouth! Look around and you'll see a few thousand people who are recording all of this on their cell phones, so please keep talking."

Eric growled at Tommy as the officer jerked him forward and led him towards the waiting patrol car, while another officer began interviewing witnesses. Tommy watched in disbelief as Eric struggled against being placed in the back of the car. After a brief scuffle, the policeman prevailed, and with slight frustration showing through, he slammed the back door shut before heading back to rejoin his partner in the investigation process.

After giving the officer his version of events, Tommy addressed the fundraiser attendees with a bullhorn, thanking them for coming out and for all of their incredible support. He vowed to return for another event as soon as possible to make up for this one getting cut short. He then excused himself to head to the hospital to be with Dmitry.

AS HIS CHAUFFEURED SUV ARRIVED AT THE EMERGENCY ROOM ENTRANCE, Tommy was surprised to see Dmitry being wheeled out into the bright afternoon sunshine, his shoulder thickly bandaged, and his left arm in a sling. Tommy leapt from the vehicle and hurried to his friend.

"What are you doing? You need to stay in the hospital."

"No boss, I need to be with you. It's fine. The knife missed everything. It went clean through. They patched me up, gave me some antibiotics and painkillers, and I'm good as new."

Tommy looked up at the nurse standing behind Dmitry's wheelchair and asked, "Should he really be leaving this soon?"

"No, but he insisted he has a job to do and he signed a waiver going against the doctor's orders. He really should be admitted for observation."

"Well, that's what we're gonna to do then. Dmitry, let's go back in and do what they tell you to do."

"Tommy!" Dmitry firmly replied, grabbing his boss' wrist. "Please! I should have protected you better. That was too close. Trust me ... I'm all right. I need to be with you. The news is already out, and there could be copycats as a result. Let me do my job."

"How are you going to protect me with a bum arm? You need to make sure it's really okay. Let's go back inside, I'm begging you."

"You see this?" Dmitry raised his massive right fist, clenched so tightly it seemed to make a noise like old leather stretching. Tommy shook his head in affirmation as Dmitry continued.

"I only need one good arm to keep you safe. And if they take that, I'll use my legs. And if they take my legs I'll use my body again ... whatever is necessary. I promised Amanda I'd keep you safe, and I'm going to live up to my word. Now please get out of my way."

Tommy stepped back as Dmitry raised himself from the wheelchair with a repressed groan. Knowing it was a lost cause to resist him any further, Tommy leaned in and gently hugged Dmitry's good side then turned to open the door gesturing for his friend to enter first. Dmitry refused and instead instructed Tommy to climb in. Tommy smiled and shook his head in amazement while sliding into the back seat as Dmitry followed.

CHAPTER FORTY-SIX

ERIC SAT FACING TOMMY as the two men stared intently at each other through the glass partition. Tommy gestured for Eric to pick up the phone.

"What do you want?" barked Eric.

"Look, drop the attitude. I'm here to help you. Against my better judgment, considering you tried to kill me yesterday, my bodyguard Dmitry has decided not to press charges against you. Normally that by itself wouldn't be enough to get attempted murder charges dropped for someone who stabbed another human being. I also made a sizable donation to the police officers' fund, and my attorney pulled some strings, so now you're going to get released this afternoon."

"What? Are you nuts? After what I did and threatened to do when I get out?"

"You're not going to come after me, Eric, so let's drop the crap. And here's why. You need a chance to turn your life around, and if I don't help you accomplish that, this rage you have is never going to stop. Right?"

Eric's mood immediately shifted as anger left his eyes. He nodded his head, *yes,* as Tommy continued.

"We all deserve a second chance. I was fortunate enough to get one, and it changed everything for me. I want to extend you the same opportunity. But it's going to take some work, and I'm not sure you're up to that. Are you?"

"Yes, yes. Anything. I'm homeless, so what do I have to lose?"

"Okay. Well, I recall quite vividly that you had that fantastic hobby of making custom guitars back in the day."

"Yeah, I loved designing and creating those guitars. I made you one, remember?"

"And I still have it to this day. As mad as you made me for trying to destroy my career, I always respected your talent as a musician and craftsman, and it meant a lot that you took the time to make that guitar for me."

"Wow, I thought for sure you would have burned that thing in the fireplace."

"No. Actually, it was such a quality looking, feeling, and sounding instrument, that I was going to use it on the next album before you and I had our falling out and my career fell off the rails. What I'd like to propose is that we set you up to manufacture custom guitars. We'll start with some Tommy Model signature guitars that you and I will design together to get the company off to a good start. We'll be partners in the venture, but if all goes as I'm envisioning, you'll become the successful person you always wanted to be. But you've got to let go of this hatred. You made some mistakes, but let's put those in the past and look forward. Agreed?"

"I don't know what to say, Tommy. That sounds amazing. Yes, of course, I agree. Thank you. And I'm sorry for everything. I was an idiot for taking the money from Jacques Morel back then, and I should never have betrayed you like that. It'll never happen again."

"Good. Well, congrats, partner. I'm excited to see what we come up with. You probably don't have one, so I'm leaving a cell phone with my number in it that the guards will give you with your things when you check out. There's also some money and new clothes as well. I made a reservation for you at a nice hotel, and a driver will take you there when they release you later today. Call me tomorrow, and we'll start discussing next steps, including finding a permanent place for you to live."

"I'm speechless. You have no idea how much this means to me."

"Oh, yes I do. I nearly lost it all, mate. I understand what it is to get a reprieve from a downward spiral."

The guard interrupted, signaling it was time to end the visit.

"We'll talk tomorrow, Eric. Keep your focus on the long game and don't go crazy and blow the money on something stupid. It's not a lot, but it's enough to get you in trouble."

"I won't. Thank you again. I'll talk to you tomorrow."

Tommy left the county jail feeling at peace. With Dmitry's insistence that helping Eric was the best way to protect Tommy long-term, and Amanda's long-distance encouragement to allow goodness to prevail, Tommy had set his anger aside. Once again, by letting go, he had made another life-changing decision for himself, and someone else. It felt good, and as a bonus, he was very excited about having Eric's talent behind the making of his own Tommy Model guitars.

THREE WEEKS LATER TOMMY STOOD ON STAGE IN LOS ANGELES before a crowd of more than fifty thousand screaming fans. With a leap off the drum riser, he pounded the crescendo chord of his final encore song. Following a line-up bow with the band, he was officially done. After a year, the *Boomerang World Tour* was finally a wrap.

Following a few weeks and rest, he planned to start recording the next album under his new, highly lucrative record deal with Galactic Records. The twenty million dollar signing bonus was officially his, and he donated a significant portion to Maddock's Memories, paying his blessings forward.

Back home in Edinburgh, he found that fatherhood and rest were not synonymous. Amanda and Nora did their best to shield Tommy from Livingston's enthusiastic antics and powerful vocalizations when he was trying to rest or write new songs, but ultimately, it was hopeless with a one-year-old in the house. Tommy took it all in stride and loved every moment that he shared with his two favorite people.

Unfortunately, the bliss he felt at home did not extend to his mother and father's house. Frank had become completely despondent and spent his hours sleeping or blankly staring off into space. There were no more conversations, only occasional glances of acknowledgment, and not that something had been understood ... only that words had been heard. It was extremely difficult for Tommy, but after more than fifty years of marriage, Davina was lost and already alone. Tommy encouraged her to get out and visit with her old friends while he and others stayed with his father. She refused to leave the house, likely afraid that in her absence Frank would finally pass on.

As is the case with so many Alzheimer's victims, Frank had difficulty swallowing when he ate or drank since his brain was no longer properly communicating with his body. At some point, he had unknowingly aspirated food into his lungs. This had led to a second bout of pneumonia, a situation Frank had been able to fight off a year ago after the near-drowning incident. Now he was in such a weakened state, that even with antibiotics, his immune system was struggling to kick the infection. It was a bleak prognosis, and Tommy now visited every day, not knowing when the end might come.

IT WAS A 1:03 A.M. PHONE CALL FROM A HOSPICE NURSE that startled Tommy from a sound sleep and delivered the news he feared. His father was gone, having finally been defeated by the horrific disease. Tommy was calm at first as he shared the news with Amanda. He stood from the bed to put on the clothes he had kept neatly folded in his nightstand for an emergency situation such as this. Tommy didn't say a word as he dressed, and it was only when he began to walk that he collapsed in anguish and fell to the hardwood floor, weeping uncontrollably. Amanda did her best to console Tommy, but she too had grown extremely close to Frank. Tommy's breakdown only accelerated her own as together they held each other in a huddled mass on the floor. It was the thought of his mother that snapped Tommy out of his own sorrow as he stood and helped Amanda to her feet.

"We've got to get over there to be with Mum," Tommy stated, wiping the moisture from his tear-soaked cheeks.

"She's got to be a wreck," replied Amanda. "I'll wake Nora and let her know so she can watch Livingston."

WHEN TOMMY AND AMANDA ARRIVED AT HIS PARENT'S HOUSE, Belle was thankfully already there, and his mother was surprisingly at peace. Tommy knew she was likely somewhat relieved that Frank's struggle was over, but also in a state of shock, not yet accepting the reality that her husband was gone.

Determined to see his father one last time, Tommy cautiously peeked into the dim-lit bedroom. There Frank laid, propped up on three pillows in the final efforts to keep him more upright and help counter the fluid that had been consuming his lungs. Even in the low light, he could see the pale, unmistakable color of death cloaking his father's skin.

Tommy sat on the side of the bed next to his dad and reached for his hand, but pulled back quickly from the feel of his ice-cold fingers. He shook his head in frustration and disbelief that this was the way his dad would go out, and his heart ached that Frank never really truly knew that they had reconciled.

Tommy stood, leaned over and kissed his dad on the forehead, then left the room to rejoin Amanda, Belle, her husband, Richard, and Richard's mother in the living room. There, they all sat chatting about the weather mixed with idle, meaningless gossip. It was a surreal conversation, but if it kept Davina from momentarily accepting the fate of what had happened, it was worth the ignorance.

Shortly thereafter, the paramedics arrived. Once they had officially confirmed death for the technicality of the death certificate, the waiting mortuary transport team carefully and respectfully removed Frank's body from the house. Belle and Amanda had cornered Davina in the kitchen while the move took place. Once complete, they asked if she wanted to see her husband one last time before they took him away. She declined, stating that the image of his lifeless body was already burned into her brain. She didn't need any more confirmation or closure. He was gone, and that was that.

OVER THE NEXT FEW DAYS leading up to the viewing and funeral, Tommy received a flood of flowers, e-mails, and well over a million online postings from fans expressing their condolences. Hundreds of local well-wishers laid flowers and remembrances around the gated entrance to Tommy's home. It was touching, but overwhelming and Tommy struggled to keep it together. The reality of death he had begun to feel at Bob Walker's funeral three months earlier, had now found its way back to him again, and he was a mess.

The morning after his father's burial, it was an unexpected phone call from Bonnie that stopped his fall into utter despair.

"Tommy, I know you probably want to be left alone right now ..." said Amanda. She leaned against the doorframe leading into the den where Tommy sat in the dark, staring into oblivion. "But it's Bonnie, and I really think you should talk to her."

Tommy popped out of his daze and reached out for the phone.

"Hi, Bonnie ... how are you holding up?" he asked in a caring, concerned tone.

"I'm doing well, thanks to you and Amanda for getting me the help I need. My mum is hanging in there, and the experimental treatments you also helped us get are showing some positive signs. It won't reverse the course she's on, but if she could ultimately help others in the future, I know she would like that if she knew.

"That's good to hear, Bonnie."

"But hey ... enough about me. I really called to say that I'm very sorry to hear about your father's passing."

"Thank you. I appreciate that," replied Tommy in a somber tone.

"I also wanted to remind you that you truly are making a difference, and as long as you keep pressing forward with Maddock's Memories, your dad will live on forever through the good deeds the charity will bring to the world. In that sense, he'll be immortal, and that's an awesome thought. Right now, you may not feel like it, but I do hope you won't give up. You can possibly keep others from experiencing the heartache and pain we've had to endure of losing someone to Alzheimer's long before they ever pass away. We really need you."

Tommy was taken aback by her kind words of encouragement. Although he had all but officially announced that he would be stepping away from the charity, he now assured Bonnie that he would keep pushing forward. It was the kick in the pants that he needed, and he thanked her for the call.

He stood from his slouched position in the chair, walked out of the dark, dismal den and into the sunshine-bathed living room where he gently picked up Livingston who played at Amanda's feet. He kissed his son and looked down at Amanda.

"Let's go for a walk on the property. It's a beautiful day, my love. We need to make the most of it and live a little."

CHAPTER FORTY-SEVEN

TOMMY QUIETLY WATCHED THE TIP OF HIS FISHING ROD as it leaned against the rail of his small wooden rowboat. The stocked trout pond at the back of his property offered a tranquil escape from the renewed and frenzied interest in Tommy Model. For a brief moment, it felt good to do nothing except reflect on life, wet a line, and hope for a bite.

Songwriting and recording the next album was progressing well. Eric Tucker was finalizing the first prototypes for their new guitar venture, and Maddock's Memories was busy raising money and changing lives. Even before the tour had come to its conclusion, Tommy had been receiving a constant flow of film and television role offers, even though he had never acted in anything other than a school play. The paid personal appearance requests were proving to be never-ending, and Duncan had hired a team of accountants to keep up with the vetting of sponsorship deals and business opportunities. It would have been far easier to just focus on new music, but as Tommy often said, "The sun has finally re-emerged from behind a wall of dark clouds and now is the time to get a tan," so every legitimate pitch was considered.

For all of the positive things that were happening, it proved to be a daily emotional struggle for Tommy's mother to adjust to a life without Frank by her side. For a time, she had stopped eating and drinking properly, often slept until noon or later, and refused to leave the house or speak to her friends. To help ease the pain of her broken heart, Tommy and Amanda suggested she immerse herself into helping other spouses of Alzheimer's victims. It took some time to warm to the idea, but eventually she agreed to give it a go.

Within a few weeks, her spirits had lifted and she was living life once again. Even though providing guidance and support to others also struggling with the impact of Alzheimer's was an ongoing reminder to Davina of her own challenging experiences, the comfort she provided gave her a purpose and motivation to fight through her sorrow, and it was good.

With his mother now back on her feet, life was going better than Tommy had ever expected, but still, he was restless. He had no desire to tour again anytime soon, and he was thoroughly enjoying his home time with Amanda and Livingston. Yet, the experience of watching his father succumb to Alzheimer's had impacted him so profoundly that he too felt the need to do more ... much, much more. It wasn't acceptable to Tommy that a cure still seemed such a long way off. And while he had influenced hundreds of thousands of fans on tour to become active in the effort, he searched for a way to spread the message even further.

The boat pivoted on the anchor line as a gentle, spring breeze streamed across the glassy surface, creating faint riffles and blurring the reflection of the puffy white clouds floating above. Tommy looked down into the wavering image and noticed that one cloud pattern reminded him of a massive crowd of people looking towards the sun. The scene immediately triggered a thought. What if he organized a music festival that would raise Alzheimer's awareness and inspire volunteerism? It wouldn't be an event to raise money for any single charity but instead would present the facts about the disease in unique, interesting ways peppered in amongst performances by some of the most significant artists over the past several decades.

It was a crazy idea, but as his creativity began to flow, Tommy landed on *Remember This* as a possible name for the event. To make it somewhat different from other festivals, he would garner support from bands and artists whose careers began as far back as possible and up to the most current. As their performances occurred over the two-day extravaganza, the fans would advance through time from the 1970's, 1980's, 90's, 2000's, and so on. It would showcase the journey of music as the lineup progressed, and would give a nod to the gift of being able to remember ... an ability that most of us easily take for granted.

While searching for a catchy fan engagement idea, the phrase *put on my thinking cap* popped into Tommy's head. The visual concept of festival goers all creating and wearing hats that uniquely expressed their own personalities while showing solidarity to the cause, was born. It would be a massive undertaking, but excitement welled in Tommy, and he was anxious to get back to shore and start contacting those who could make the dream a reality.

As he began to reel in his line, a hard thump followed by a tap, tap singled Tommy to instinctively set the hook. After a short battle, he was eye to eye with a beautiful trout that he gently glided alongside the boat. He reached down and cradled the anxious fish in his hands. Tommy gently removed the hook and rested the helpless creature back in the water until he snapped to. With a flick of the tail, it disappeared from view.

Like the fish, Tommy knew the adventure he was concocting would leave him vulnerable and exposed, likely to much unfounded criticism. There would always be those who believed he had a personal agenda. But if he was able to reach an even broader audience and the effort started a movement that would build ongoing momentum for Alzheimer's research, it was likely worth the risk. He lifted the anchor, neatly rolling and stowing the line as his father had taught him as a young lad, then rowed back to shore.

FOUR MONTHS LATER, UNDER A CLEAR, MOONLIT SKY, Tommy stood in front of his mic at center stage and coaxed the massive audience into a frenzy. The sea of bodies seemed to stretch on endlessly, and the estimated one hundred thousand fans had anxiously awaited this very moment. One by one the artists who would perform the finale number of "Don't You (Forget About Me)" were introduced. As he had envisioned, nearly every fan had created a special *thinking cap* that showed their support for the fight against Alzheimer's. The massive video screens flanking the double stages had also occasionally featured live streams of participants who watched the two-day festival live across the globe. From the comforts of their homes or wherever else they might be, they too showed off their unique headgear, further inspiring others to do the same.

A somber dose of reality had preceded the elation of the final performance. A short-film reflecting the horrific impact of Alzheimer's had aired over the video screens and live broadcast feeds. Tommy had introduced the film by sharing his own experiences with his father, and he made it clear that he was no longer asking for fans to dig into their pockets for the cause. He just wanted them all to be aware that if a cure could not be found, it was a very real possibility that they too would experience a loved one, or even more tragically, they themselves might someday become affected by the devastating disease. He urged them to spread the word and invited everyone to continue to promote the *Remember This* message by challenging others to make their own thinking caps and share them with each other, both in person and via online platforms.

As the film concluded, the familiar guitar intro commenced. The powerful chord progression elicited a deafening response from the audience that seemed to stretch on for miles across the wide-open field. In unison, they all chanted the opening mantra of "Don't You (Forget About Me)." The powerful feedback was overwhelming, and Tommy fought his emotions. All of the dedication and hard work that had led to the day was finally a reality. His dream of engaging a massive number of people including those standing before him, as well as those watching live across the planet, had come to fruition, and now millions were connected to the moment.

Would it be enough? he wondered. *Would it ultimately make a difference in the fight for a cure? Would people stay involved and engaged? Would they volunteer to help others? Would they care beyond tonight? Do you care right now?*

Tommy paused his mental wrangling to sing his part of a verse as the magical, anthemic song, now with its renewed life and meaning, continued to reverberate into the warm night air. Only time and patience could answer Tommy's questions. Time, patience, passion, and humanity. But would it be enough?

CHAPTER FORTY-EIGHT

THE VERTICAL BLINDS hanging in the hospital room window swayed, slowly dancing in the steady flow of air streaming from the vent in the ceiling. The slats were partially closed causing the light from the mid-morning sun to enter the room in a subdued fashion, creating a somber, gray mood to the setting.

In the bed, a frail, elderly man, likely in his late eighties laid motionless, his eyes closed. The faint hiss of oxygen whispered from the clear plastic tube wrapped over the top of his ears and down his face, connecting the loop beneath his nose. Drip by drip, an I.V. port delivered fluids into his right arm, while a blood pressure cuff suddenly inflated around his bicep. The pressure briefly woke the man who grumbled incoherently, then dozed off back to sleep.

A nurse was busy tidying the room and re-stocking supplies when the doctor entered. A tall, lean man with jet-black hair and likely in his mid-forties carried a confident, commanding presence. His long white coat made his professional distinction clear. He carefully reviewed the most recent vitals then shook his head in disbelief.

"He's still holding on," the doctor remarked to the nurse. "He's a tough, old guy, but his family should prepare themselves for the inevitable. It's only hours at best."

A man and woman who appeared to be slightly older than the doctor entered the room, both carrying to-go coffee cups. Upon seeing the doctor, the man's sullen face lit up, and he quickly made his way to the foot of the bed where he nervously rambled off his thoughts and questions.

"Hi, Doc. How's he doing? Is our dad going to snap out of this? I want you to know that we've been trading off shifts day and night ever since they moved him here from the nursing home. We know he can't remember anything because of the Alzheimer's, but we've been talking to him a lot and telling him stories from the past, hopefully, to raise his spirits. We just don't know what else to do. It's been a tough road for several years now. He was the rock of our family before the memory started to go."

"I wish I had better news for you," replied the doctor. "The pneumonia has worsened, and his lungs are full of fluid. His oxygen level is fading fast, and his heart won't be able to keep up much longer. You should both ready your minds. I'm sorry, but he most likely won't survive the day."

"I just don't understand how this could have happened," stated the daughter fighting against her quivering voice. "We tried our best to take care of him at home, but it got to be too much. We found what we thought was the top local facility specializing in Alzheimer's patients. They watched him 'round the clock, performed physical therapy, made him sit up and get around, and gave regular baths. You name it ... they did it, supposedly to keep this very thing from happening. I feel like we failed him, Doctor. Can you please explain to me what went wrong?"

"You didn't fail him. As Alzheimer's advances in patients, they often can't swallow food normally because their brain is not properly communicating with the rest of the body. Additionally, when something goes into the windpipe and is aspirated into the lungs most of us have a gag reflex to attempt to expel the food or liquid. Unfortunately, the effects of advanced Alzheimer's can block that automatic response. So when substances become trapped in the lungs and cannot be naturally expelled, it's usually not long before an infection sets in."

"Is that what caused pneumonia?" asked the man.

"Yes. Pneumonia is essentially inflammation of the lungs that allows fluid or pus to fill the air sacs reducing oxygen output to the body. As the heart struggles to pump harder and harder, trying to compensate for the reduced oxygen levels, it simply can't keep that pace for very long. Even if the heart does power on for a while, reduced oxygen to the brain, kidneys, and other organs eventually cause the body to shut down. It's a bad situation all the way around, and I'm very, very sorry. But you shouldn't blame yourselves."

"Isn't there anything else you can do?" asked the son.

"We tried antibiotics, but it was so far along that reversing the course was a long-shot at best. I wish I had a better answer for you. I would spend as much time as possible with him today."

The man and woman nodded their heads in defeated agreement. The son visibly clenched his jaw while the woman wiped a tear from her cheek and began to reminisce.

"You know, he can't normally remember anything, but over the past few days, he's been seemingly reliving this dream about being a rock star. Something about a guy named Tommy Model. It's been quite a tall tale at times. He tends to get locked in on certain thoughts, even though it's not a real memory. So it's been somewhat entertaining, but sad. I think he really thinks he is this Tommy Model guy."

"Was he ever in a band or play any musical instruments?" inquired the doctor.

"Not that I know of. He was an electrician for most of his life, but I never heard anything about being a musician. Did you?" she asked turning to her brother."

"No. My favorite thing he said just yesterday was how he and several other artists recorded some song, then later performed it live in front of hundreds of thousands of people while it was being broadcast around the world to millions. He was quite descriptive and passionate about it all. It's been a little strange because he usually bounces from thought to thought, but this has been quite a drawn-out story."

"Well, we don't really know what Alzheimer's patients think about," explained the doctor. "I've seen them get focused in on certain subjects like that. It could be comment someone made, or something he saw on TV that triggered it"

The woman snapped her fingers then looked at her brother. "You know what ... I just remembered. All of this started one day when I couldn't find anything else to watch on TV, and I landed on a channel playing non-stop music videos from the 80's. For some reason I vividly recall that he opened his eyes and hummed along to that Simple Minds song, 'Don't You (Forget About Me).' I was shocked he could recite the melody. Then they aired a short interview with the lead singer and guitar player from back in the day. They were Scottish, and I could barely understand a word they said."

"You know what ..." replied her brother. "That was the song he said this Tommy Model and several other artists re-recorded and performed at some festival. And there was something about a charity. It was a bit much, and all mixed in with a lot of mumbling about someone named Amanda. I think he mentioned the name Livingston as well."

"I loved that song," stated the doctor. "Under the circumstances, it's an interesting title for him to key in on, isn't it? 'Don't You (Forget About Me)?' It sounds like he may have been trying to tell you something. I wouldn't so easily slough it off as just a fantasy. There may be more to it than you realize."

The doctor paused, forced a half-smile, and gently patted the old man's legs covered by a white blanket, then continued.

"I need to finish making my rounds, but please spend some time with him. Tell him you love him, and give him comfort. It won't be long now. If he wants to go out as a rock star, maybe just let him have that. It doesn't sound like such a bad dream after all."

The Beginning

www.ingramcontent.com/pod-product-compliance
Lightning Source LLC
Chambersburg PA
CBHW030346120726
47901CB00007B/1927